"You are one smoking widow," Dead Jimmy said. **"H-O-T."**

By the time the funeral rolled around, Dead Jimmy was as lively as ever, sitting next to Constance in the front pew of the funeral home, looking straight down her V-neck, black, sleeveless dress. It hit just above the knee, and she was wearing her nicest pair of shoes: black heels. This was her only nice black dress, and not exactly used often, since Jimmy's idea of a night out was to go to the Dairy Queen drive-through.

"I mean it, you look really hot," said Dead Jimmy, as he tried to get a look down her dress.

"Shhhhh," Constance said, and focused on the flower arrangements on either side of the coffin. There were lots of flowers. Constance didn't realize Jimmy was so well-liked in the county. Or maybe it was a sign of relief from people knowing that he wasn't around to break any more of their things.

First in her sizzling new series—praise for Cara Lockwood's

EVERY DEMON HAS HIS DAY

"Frightfully funny. . . . An expansive and quirky cast lends plenty of supernatural support."

—*Publishers Weekly*

Turn the page for more rave reviews!

"Sure to strike a chord with many readers. . . . Fun, entertaining, and enjoyable."

—Curled Up With a Good Book

PINK SLIP PARTY

"Readers will be delighted by the character-driven zaniness. . . . Snappy repartee and hot sex scenes keep the story moving along nicely."

—*Boston Herald*

"The perfect bath read."

—*Daily News* (New York)

"An amusing chick lit tale. . . . [A] comical contemporary caper."

—All Readers

"Hilarious. . . . I definitely recommend *Pink Slip Party* if you need a good laugh and you know you do if you've received one of those pink slips yourself."

—Mostly Fiction

"If you're looking for a perfect beach read, this adorable, romantic novel is it."

—*YM* magazine

DIXIELAND SUSHI

"A warm and friendly writing style."

—*Library Journal*

"A hilarious relationship novel. . . . Readers who enjoy chick lit will savor *Dixieland Sushi* because, like its main character, it offers a different take on the standard fare."

—Curled Up With a Good Book

ALSO BY CARA LOCKWOOD

I Do (But I Don't)
Pink Slip Party
Dixieland Sushi
I Did (But I Wouldn't Now)

—

Bard Academy
Wuthering High
The Scarlet Letterman
Moby Clique

Every Demon Has Day

CARA LOCKWOOD

POCKET STAR BOOKS

New York London Toronto Sydney

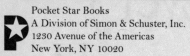

Pocket Star Books
A Division of Simon & Schuster, Inc.
1230 Avenue of the Americas
New York, NY 10020

This book is a work of fiction. Names, characters, places, and incidents either are products of the author's imagination or are used fictitiously. Any resemblance to actual events or locales or persons, living or dead, is entirely coincidental.

Copyright © 2009 by Cara Lockwood

This Pocket Star Books paperback edition February 2010

POCKET STAR and colophon are registered trademarks of Simon & Schuster, Inc.

For information about special discounts for bulk purchases, please contact Simon & Schuster Special Sales at 1-866-506-1949 or business@simonandschuster.com.

The Simon & Schuster Speakers Bureau can bring authors to your live event. For more information or to book an event, contact the Simon & Schuster Speakers Bureau at 1-866-248-3049 or visit our website at www.simonspeakers.com.

Cover art and design by Alan Dingman

Manufactured in the United States of America

10 9 8 7 6 5 4 3 2 1

ISBN 978-1-4391-7336-7
ISBN 978-1-4391-5935-4 (ebook)

Acknowledgments

I had much help in writing this book. Thanks to my darling daughters, who are angels in their own right—almost all of the time. Thank you to my husband, who did extra babysitting duty and sacrificed valuable fantasy football time. Thanks as always to Mom, who never laughs at an idea, even if it's really bad, and to Dad, who still thinks I might win a Pulitzer. Thanks to my brother, Matt, for helping me keep my sense of humor. As always gratitude goes to my multitalented agent, Deidre Knight, and my insanely insightful editor, Lauren McKenna. A special thanks to Shannon Whitehead for reading a demon of a first draft of this book. Many thanks to my Web guru, Christina Swartz, and a great big thank-you to my angelic marketing team: Elizabeth Kinsella, Kate Kinsella, Kate Miller, Jane Ricordati, Linda Newman, and Carroll Jordan. And a special thanks to Carol K. Mack and Dinah Mack, authors of *A Field Guide to Demons, Fairies, Fallen Angels and Other Subversive Spirits*, and to Rosemary Ellen Guiley, who wrote *The Encyclopedia of Angels*.

For Shannon, who could kick any demon's butt.

Every Demon Has His Day

One

The day Constance Plyd discovered her destiny, she was knee-deep in suds and bubbles, a mess of her soon-to-be-ex-husband Jimmy's making. Jimmy knew every last player who ever put on a Dallas Cowboy uniform, but seemed incapable of remembering routine household information, like the fact that you don't put Tide in the dishwasher, even if the Cascade is running low.

Constance couldn't believe on the day he was supposed to sign the divorce papers he'd made a mess. Jimmy, who'd never done a dish the whole time they were married, suddenly found the urge to run the dishwasher, mere minutes from the end of their marriage. And now her kitchen was covered in suds.

But she shouldn't be surprised. Jimmy was in an elite club of eejits. Just last year when he tried to change Constance's motor oil, he ended up draining out all her transmission fluid instead. In fact, there was no problem Jimmy couldn't make worse. He was the kind of man who broke most everything he touched, including but not limited to lawn mowers, generators, refrigerators, tractors, trailers, trucks, cars, and even, once, a spoon. Their neighbors scattered any time Jimmy came out on the porch, in case he was looking to borrow something, because if he remembered to bring it back at all, it would be in pieces.

The only thing Jimmy had ever managed to do right was inherit a modest income from his childless uncle, who accidentally struck oil when he was digging a well in his backyard in 1962. It wasn't Rockefeller money, or even Beverly Hillbillies money, but it was just enough to ensure Jimmy never had to work a day in his life.

Constance never thought she'd end up with Jimmy and his ever-dwindling fortune. But falling for him was a temporary lapse in judgment that Constance blamed squarely on Nathan Garrett.

Nathan Garrett, you see, was the youngest of the Garrett brothers, notorious throughout Dogwood County for their good looks and their fast hands. In high school, the brothers—a set of twins and the youngest, Nathan—pretty much were responsible for relieving the greater Dogwood County female population of their virginity between the years 1991 and 2000. After that, the Garretts moved on—the twins to Houston and Nathan to Dallas.

While on Christmas break from college nearly ten years ago, Nathan took Constance Hicks on a date, which, like nearly all of his dates, ended with her half naked in the backseat of his '88 red Mustang. Constance didn't mind at the time. It was only when he barreled out of town the very next day without bothering to call that she started to get resentful.

As time went on, that resentment grew and bubbled into something much more like hate when she heard through the grapevine from his former best friend that he kept a list of all the virgins he'd plucked, and she was known simply as Number Twenty-two. To add insult to injury, she ran into him at the Jiffy Lube on Route 9 three months later, and he didn't even give her a second glance or so much as a how-do-you-do.

It was after the Jiffy Lube incident that Jimmy Plyd happened to ask Constance out on a date, and she said yes out of spite, figuring that going out with the opposite of Nathan Garrett could only do her good. Jimmy had been so nice and kind then, and didn't manage to destroy anything on their subsequent first date, and Constance started to feel a little better about being left by Nathan. Jimmy, she could tell right away, was not the kind of man who left. He was the kind of man who stayed. He might burn down your garage, but he wouldn't up and disappear on you after.

He didn't blink an eye when she vented about Nathan Garrett. He just kept coming by every Friday night with flowers and a half-gallon tub of Rocky Road ice cream, wearing down her defenses until Constance got used to him being around. A year after that, he offered Constance her very own restaurant in the town square as an engagement gift, and while she wasn't sure she loved him, she definitely loved the restaurant, so she said yes.

She really believed she would grow to love Jimmy in time, but after nine years of flat tires, collapsing shelves, loose door hinges, cracked toilets, a shattered bathroom mirror, and one exploding washing machine, Constance had had enough.

Of course, her friends had been telling her for years she ought to divorce him, especially since most of them didn't know why she married him in the first place, but Constance didn't make that decision lightly. She'd carried around divorce papers in her Camry for nearly a year before finally giving them to Jimmy three months ago.

Now, as the suds piled even higher in the kitchen, nearly reaching the kitchen counter, and ruining any chance she had of making her state fair blue-ribbon-winning chicken-fried steak for the ladies of the First Protestant Church Bible Study class (who met every Thursday night), Constance felt, not for the first time, that if she ever ran into Nathan Garrett again, she would have some choice words to say to him. Because somehow, despite the fact that Jimmy was her own personal disaster, Constance still liked to blame Nathan. It just felt right.

She'd heard he was back in town, and she had a speech planned in her head, should she happen to bump into him. In fact, she had several speeches, all of which she'd honed after years of lying awake at night, wondering what he was up to, and specifically, whose life he might be ruining at that moment.

Constance grabbed a few tea towels from the counter to try to sop up the water, but it was no use. There was simply too much of it. She didn't have time for this. She was supposed to drop off the chicken-fried steaks on her way to the Magnolia Café—her pride and joy—

and the only gift Jimmy gave her that he didn't later break.

Cooking was the one thing Constance could do well. Romance and relationships, not so much, but get her within spitting distance of a saucepan and a stove, and she could whip up food good enough to make your mouth water for days. Jimmy had either ruined her kitchen out of spite or because he was hoping to put off signing those divorce papers—again. He'd been stalling for the better part of three months now, and Constance had had enough. She didn't really understand the procrastinating. Constance had signed a prenup (on his mother's insistence). Except for the Magnolia Café, which was deeded in her name, she'd get none of Jimmy's money. And frankly, she didn't want it. She just wanted Jimmy out of her life. At this point, she'd be willing to pay him to leave.

Besides, she was twenty-eight, and they didn't have children. Now was the time to go, when, as her mother said, her tires still had some tread left.

"Jimmy!" Constance shouted toward the back door. He was supposed to be in their attached garage, packing up the last of his "tools"—the ones he hadn't yet managed to break.

She listened, but heard nothing. Not that she actually wanted Jimmy to come help. His idea of helping would probably be to throw gasoline on the suds and then light them on fire.

As Constance tried to figure out whether she wanted to shout at Jimmy more than she wanted to try to save her new linoleum floor, she heard a loud whoosh of air, which slammed against the back door and rattled the windows. And then she was struck, suddenly, by the strong smell of something foul—a cross between burnt popcorn and Jimmy's gym socks. Her first thought was that Jimmy had started a fire in the garage—again—but there wasn't smoke, and this smell was worse than a fire. And there wasn't any cursing, either, which was a sure sign this wasn't a Jimmy-related calamity, since they all came with a chorus of cussing. In fact, the only sound coming from the garage was a thump, like a sack of potatoes being dropped to the ground.

And in that second, she knew it was something bad. Something really bad. Something worse than Jimmy.

She didn't want to open the back door because she somehow knew what she would find before she found it, but she steeled herself and did anyway. She stepped into the garage and the first thing she saw was a man in a black suit, with a double-breasted suit jacket along with a black baseball cap. He was standing over the body of her soon-to-be-ex husband, who was lying facedown next to his pickup truck, a screwdriver handle sticking out of his back. At first, Constance thought it must be some kind of joke. Then she saw the tiny trickle of blood that was running down from the screwdriver and pooling on the garage floor.

Jimmy was dead.

The man who had clearly just killed him turned and flashed her an unnaturally white smile. He tipped his black baseball cap in her direction, then, gingerly stepping over the blood puddle, handed her a business card with red letters. It read:

YAMAN
Demon at Large
Murder and mayhem since 550 BC

In her hands, the card disintegrated as she read it, burning from the edges until it was nothing but a pile of ash in her palm. When she looked up again, the man in black was gone.

Two

Business cards? Are you for real?" asked Shadow, facing Yaman, who now stood invisible on the corner of Constance Plyd's street, his voice floating somewhere above Constance's azalea bush at the end of the driveway.

"What? I'm trying to increase my market value," Yaman replied. "It's all about self-promotion. You have to get out there if you want to get credit. You ever read Jack Welch?"

Yaman waved a copy of *Winning* in front of Shadow's face. Shadow grimaced.

"You and your self-help books," he said, wrinkling his nose as if the book smelled bad. "You Pride demons are all the same," Shadow said, twisting and turning a little, his giant shadow body changing shape subtly, to make it impossible to tell just what sort of creature he was.

"Well, Glutton, you ought to take more time investing in yourself or you'll never get promoted. Like, take your name—Shadow. It's boring."

"It's what I *am*," Shadow pointed out.

"Right, but it has no pizzazz. Coke is sugar water, but you say Coca-Cola, and suddenly it sounds exotic. You should go with something snappy. Like Zazum, or Kilkore."

"I like my name just fine, thanks," Shadow grumbled. He stretched, throwing something that looked a bit like a wing across the ground. "So, are we really sure that she's the One?" he asked, nodding toward the house, where Constance was frantically calling 911.

"The general seems to think so. We had our orders."

"General Asmodeus has been wrong before. Besides, when was the last time he did anything really scary?"

"He seduced a bunch of nuns in France in 1647."

"Exactly my point. French nuns nearly four hundred years ago? I could do that blindfolded. What has he done lately? He's too busy hanging out in the Second Circle hitting on all the prostitutes."

"Well, he is a Lust demon. Those guys have a one-track mind," Yaman said.

"And when he isn't doing that, he's taking credit for the divorce rate. Big deal. Most couples split by themselves. They hardly need help."

"You have a point," Yaman said. "But have you *seen* him? He's ugly as hell. It's a miracle he managed to get the French nuns into bed."

"Anyway, my point is, if she's the One, why did she marry *that* guy? Isn't she supposed to have the Sight?"

"No accounting for human taste," Yaman sighed. "Why are you so worried, anyway?"

"It's been a long time since I've been on an assignment this important," Shadow admitted.

"Seriously? When was your last special ops?"

"Gomorrah," Shadow said.

"Are you *serious*? You were at Gomorrah?" Yaman asked, amazed. "That was a *total* fiasco."

"Tell me about it," Shadow said.

"You're lucky the general let you have a second chance."

"Which is why I don't want anything to go wrong this time."

"It won't—I'm here to make sure of it," Yaman said.

"You Prides are always way overconfident."

"Well, you Gluttons are always messy," Yaman said, nodding to a streak of something whitish on Shadow's chin—or at least the area where Shadow's chin ought to be. Shadow quickly wiped at his mouth.

"I just want to be sure we have the right woman. She *is* supposed to be the prophet, right?"

"Yes, for the hundredth time."

"So, if she's the prophet, why did you kill her husband? I thought we were supposed to be flying under the radar here."

"Glutton, you just don't know anything," Yaman said, shaking his head. "Trauma is supposed to help bring on the visions. I figure, we ax that annoying husband of hers, and—*bam!*—she'll start seeing the future faster, and then—voilà—we're promoted."

"It wasn't part of the plan," Shadow pointed out.

"Well, thinking outside the box is what helps you get promoted in Satan's army," Yaman said confidently.

"I thought thinking outside the box was what got you thrown into the lake of fire for a couple hundred years,"

Shadow said. "Following orders is supposed to get you promoted."

"Whatever," Yaman said. "Trust me, this will work. Jack Welch would approve."

"He never killed anyone."

"No, but he did lay off like two hundred thousand people from GE. Same difference."

"Hardly," Shadow said. "Well, your plan doesn't seem to be working so far. She still hasn't had a vision that I can tell."

"Yet," Yaman said. "Just wait. They're coming."

"Well, *I'm* not going to be the one to tell the general you murdered the prophet's husband."

"He was about to be her ex-husband, and anyway, the general will totally thank me. Oh, hell on a stick," Yaman added, glancing down at his feet and noticing blood splatters on his toes for the first time. "I think I ruined my shoes. Dammit. These are my favorite pair!"

"What do demons care of shoes?"

"Are you joking? They're Bruno Magli's," Yaman exclaimed. "I use them for all my best work."

Shadow snorted, clearly unimpressed. And before Yaman could properly respond, a squirrel ran up to them, stopping near the azalea bush. In one great lunge, Shadow pounced on the squirrel, eating it, tail and all. Shadow burped, and a bit of tail fuzz flittered in the air and onto the ground.

"You're disgusting," Yaman said, disapproving.

"What? I'm hungry," Shadow replied, burping again.

"You know those things are just rats with tails," Yaman declared, wrinkling his nose.

"And what's wrong with rats?"

Yaman let out a long, plaintive sigh. "I need a new partner," he mumbled to himself.

"I'm still hungry," Shadow said, eyeing a gray cat lurking near the row of hedges. The cat, however, sensing the demons' presence, hissed, raised its fur, and then ran straight off in the other direction. "When do we get to eat her?"

"Wait," Yaman said. "The general told us to wait."

Three

When Nathan Garrett got the call about the Plyd house, he was in the middle of trying to rescue Georgina Webber's cat from the roof of her house, again. He'd only been Dogwood County sheriff for a month, and already he'd been called out twice on Cat Patrol. In Dallas, where he used to work as a homicide detective, this was the sort of thing Animal Control would take care of, but in Dogwood County, more than a few miles east of the metroplex, this was apparently the kind of routine call fed into the sheriff's office.

If his old partner, Ron, were still alive, he'd laugh so hard his sides would hurt. But Nathan much preferred chasing tabbies to telling mothers their sons were dead. He'd been facing burnout a long time, but finally lost his taste for his work the morning he found Libby Bell, a five-year-old girl, raped and beaten and left to die in a Dumpster. In one of her hands, she'd still held a small teddy bear. From a certain angle, she'd looked just like his niece, Emma. And no matter how hard he tried, he'd never found the girl's murderer.

After that, Nathan just decided he'd had enough, and he quit. He never, as long as he lived, ever wanted to find another Libby Bell. When he closed his eyes, he could still see her tiny lifeless body, and as far as he was concerned, she was the last ghost he wanted chasing him. He'd had enough. He didn't need any more. He'd come home to Dogwood—his relatively crime-free hometown—with the intent of starting a new life, one without ghosts.

"Be careful, Sheriff," called Georgina from her porch. Nathan got the distinct impression that Georgina was staring at his butt. He was beginning to wonder if Georgina planted Puddles on the roof herself, just so she could see him climb up to get him.

He wasn't stupid. He knew what he looked like. And he knew he had a certain reputation, but honestly, he was leaving that life behind and turning over a new leaf. He hadn't even been out on a proper date in months. Sure, he'd had his share of girls in Dallas, but frankly, after you've dated three or four Dallas Cowboy Cheerleaders, they all start to look the same. Besides, he left Dallas in part because he wanted to put the flings behind him. He came back home looking for some peace and quiet and maybe a girl who could do long division. Sure, he expected a warm homecoming. He just didn't expect it to be *this* warm.

Georgina was one of a handful of Dogwood County divorcées. He put her age at around fifty, and she and her book club friends started calling the sheriff's office the second day he'd been on duty. They made up burglars, vandals, and one even managed to get a skunk into her garage. The book club ladies were beginning to be a nuisance.

"You *sure* are strong, Sheriff," Georgina called up to him, shading her eyes from the sun. "My, oh, *my.*"

Nathan sighed and rolled his eyes. Subtlety was not Georgina's strength. Neither were the pink hot pants she was wearing. She really should avoid spandex, he thought. Still, he was sure that Georgina and her friends were one of the main reasons he'd won the sheriff's election in a landslide. That, of course, and the fact that he was a hometown boy. Dogwood County never forgot a native son.

"It sure is *hot* out here," Georgina said, fanning herself and tugging at the collar of her shirt. "You want some ice tea?"

He was about to grab Puddles, who seemed to be just as unhappy as he was to be up on this roof, when the radio attached to his shoulder crackled to life, sending the cat scurrying away from him.

"Nathan, hold on to your tidy whities, we have a DB at the Plyd residence," came the voice of Ann, the spunky fifty-five-year-old dispatcher. "DB" stood for dead body. At first, his heart took a nosedive into his stomach, but then he remembered where he was—Dogwood County. It was probably a heart attack, or something benign and natural. There hadn't been a homicide here in twenty years.

"You're gonna want to hurry," Ann told him. "It's the Plyd place. Lord knows that Jimmy most likely finally killed somebody."

This was not funny, but even Nathan had to smile. Jimmy's clumsiness was legendary in the county. He had a rare talent for screwing things up.

"You'd better get going," Ann continued. "Check on Constance and make sure she's okay."

Nathan went stock-still with the radio in his hand.

There was only one Constance he knew living in Dogwood County. Cute as a button. The same freckle-faced, blue-eyed girl he'd rolled around in the backseat of his dad's Mustang the night before he left for the second half of his senior year at North Texas State. And he'd heard through the grapevine that she wasn't so happy with him after that. He guessed he should've called. But he had been going through an immature phase at the time. He called it his twenties.

"Constance Hicks?" Nathan asked, a sinking feeling in his stomach.

"Technically, Plyd. Jimmy's wife, or didn't you know?"

"She married *Jimmy Plyd?*" Nathan said, equally stumped, because somehow this news had escaped him. And he didn't like it. She was way out of Jimmy's league. Universe, even. He didn't care if Jimmy's family did have money. They certainly didn't have much of anything else.

"And you call yourself a Dallas detective," Ann sniffed through the radio.

"Formerly," Nathan quipped back. He felt uneasy, and he wasn't sure if it was because he was worried that Jimmy had killed Constance, or worried that he hadn't. Because he was sure if Constance was alive, she would have some hard words to say to him about his disappearing act, and he would deserve every one.

He scrambled quickly off the roof.

"You can't leave! I made some fresh ice tea!" Georgina whined. "And what about Puddles? You can't just leave him."

"I've got a call of the human variety, Ms. Webber, I'm sorry," Nathan said, putting on his sheriff's hat and sliding into his sheriff's truck.

The Plyd house sat on an acre of land along County Road 71, about five miles from the town square and a more than fifteen-minute drive from where he now was, even if he sped. The house was set next to about five other houses, mostly belonging to the weekenders—Dallasites who liked to play cowboy on the weekend. Unlike the Dogwood County lifers, who saw them as intrusive city slickers, Nathan didn't mind them so much. He couldn't blame them for wanting to get away. Just like he did.

Nathan sped down the two-lane winding county road with his lights on, and made the trip in just under fifteen minutes. He rolled his police truck up the drive to the house, noticing the well-trimmed azalea bushes at the end of the drive and thought Constance probably had everything to do with those. Just like the small herb garden by the side of the house, the potted plants of begonias on the wide wooden porch, and the cherry print curtains poking through the window of the kitchen.

It was a nice house, but nothing too fancy. It didn't scream money, like Jimmy's mother's place, which looked like a replica of Tara. This was a brick ranch, just your ordinary house, except for the fact that there were an ambulance and a deputy car sitting near the garage. Nathan, it seemed, was the last to arrive. He hoped his deputy hadn't already managed to muck up the crime scene. That is, if there was one. A flash of Libby Bell's broken body ran through his mind, and he quickly tried to blink it away. He took a deep breath before swinging open his door.

He saw a paramedic—Melissa Baker, a part-time volunteer for the county firefighters—leaning against the side of her ambulance, smoking a cigarette. Mel—her preferred name—was a short and fierce-looking woman who could probably drink Nathan and most of the men in the county under the table. He liked her, in part because she was one of the few single women in the county who didn't see the need to flirt with him.

"Those things will kill you, Mel," Nathan said in greeting, and as a way to calm the nerves in his stomach.

"I guess I missed that part of EMT training," Mel said, dumping what was left of her dwindling cigarette butt on the ground and grinding it under one thick-heeled boot. Her blond hair was pulled back in a messy ponytail and she was wearing no makeup as usual. She had a thick Boston accent, which right away set her apart from nearly everyone around here. She was that rare breed of Northerner who'd relocated to the South. She'd lived in Dogwood County nearly five years, but it didn't stop people from asking her where she was from. When she told them Boston, they'd just shake their heads and whistle like Boston was another country on the other side of the globe.

Nathan guessed there was a reason she'd moved so far away from home, but Mel didn't talk much about her personal life, and if you pressed her, she'd just shrug and say, "I hate those Boston winters," which seemed to be a good enough reason for most Dogwood lifers.

Mel did know a thing or two about saving lives. Last year, she'd saved a man and his wife after they flipped their SUV on a particularly curvy stretch of Route 9. An hour from the nearest trauma center, and Mel managed to stabilize the two all on her own. She had fast and agile hands, and was sharper than most, and Nathan appreciated this, especially since there seemed to be more Jimmys in the county than Mels.

"So, how's this for exciting, your first month on the job?" Mel asked him.

"I came here to get away from excitement," Nathan said.

"Well, looks like you came to the wrong place," Mel added. "This is sure going to throw a wrench in the movie." She was referring to *Devil's in the Details*, a movie being shot in Dogwood County starting in a couple of days, starring Dante London, reigning pop princess, and Corey Bennett, *People*'s Sexiest Man Alive.

"The movie is the last thing I'm worried about," Nathan said.

"County judge thinks differently on that score," Mel said. That much was true. The county judge was starstruck. He'd been talking about the celebrities coming to town for months. It was big news for Dogwood County, where the closest thing to a celebrity visit in the last twenty years had been the News Two weatherman from Tyler who rode in the Fourth of July parade five years ago.

Mel nodded to the body in the garage. It was facedown, and it was Jimmy, all right. He'd recognize that yellow jumpsuit anywhere. It was Jimmy's own version of a hazmat suit, which he wore while he fooled around in his garage. He didn't have a regular job, since his trust fund paid the bills, so he spent most of his time on projects of his own design that usually ended up with a call to 911. He wore the suit, Nathan guessed, to protect himself in case of a fire, something that seemed to happen more often than not when Jimmy was in the vicinity of gasoline. Of course, the suit didn't protect him from the screwdriver, which was buried handle-deep in the middle of his back.

Nathan couldn't help feeling relieved that it wasn't Constance lying there. Not that Nathan wished Jimmy dead, but it seemed to him that it wouldn't make sense if God claimed a pretty young woman like Constance and left a bumbling fool like Jimmy alive. Not that God's choices should surprise him by now. Not after he'd seen what happened to Libby Bell.

Nathan knelt down at a safe distance to examine the body.

"If you're like me," Mel said to Nathan, as she squatted down beside the sheriff, "you're asking yourself just how did Jimmy manage to get a screwdriver in his own back?"

"It wouldn't be beyond him," Nathan said, not wanting to make the logical leap to the obvious answer.

"Or his pretty little wife, either," Mel said, stating out loud what Nathan had already started to think. Nathan didn't respond, and the two stared at the body in silence for a few seconds. Nathan took in the scene. The angle of the screwdriver seemed to confirm that someone lodged that screwdriver in his back on purpose. Someone Jimmy didn't see coming, based on the look on his face. Still, something was wrong. It was too neat, Nathan thought. This wasn't a crime of passion. Everything about the scene was too orderly. Nothing in the garage was out of place except for the pool of blood Jimmy lay in, which had a tiny smear near the upper corner, with just the slightest indentation of a shoe print.

"By the way," Mel added, clapping Nathan on the shoulder. "You might want to tell Robbie to be careful where he steps."

And that's when Nathan realized the shoe print in the blood wasn't the killer's. It was the edge of a size-ten regulation sheriff's deputy lace-up boot. Robbie's.

Robbie was one of Nathan's three deputies. He was barely twenty-one and his idea of police work was hanging out at the local truck stop eating Cheetos and slurping down giant cups of blue slushies. He wasn't dumb so much as lazy, and he would've been fired ages ago except for the fact that he was the youngest son of the county judge, and you just didn't go around firing people related to the most powerful man in Dogwood County. Even if he had a habit of destroying evidence by sitting on it, or tripping over it, or dropping food on it. In fact, Nathan saw more evidence of Robbie's wake—a big blue slushie cup sitting an inch or two from the body in the garage.

Nathan sighed and picked himself up.

"Tell me he at least didn't spill blue slushie on the murder weapon," he said, and sighed.

"I'm sure he would've, if given five more minutes alone with the body," Mel said. "But I shooed him off to go interrogate the widow."

"Thanks, Mel. I owe you one."

"Just one?" Mel scoffed. "That's three already, and it's just your first month on the job. I'd say you're going to need a calculator to keep score."

Nathan gave Mel a rueful smile, and then stepped up to Constance's back door and peered in. He saw Robbie sitting at her kitchen table, obstructing his view. It had been nearly a decade since he'd seen Constance, and she had probably changed, he thought.

Just like half the girls he'd dated. In just the last week, he'd had more than his share of accidental meetings with exes that had scared the life out of him. Either his standards in high school were very, very low or some of the girls he knew had really let themselves go. So far, Mindy Conrad was the worst. She'd surprised him in the produce aisle at Kroger two days ago, and in ten years she had managed to gain double her weight while losing most of her teeth. Nathan didn't know how that worked, but guessed, by the contents of her cart, she ate her fair share of ice cream and pudding.

Nathan put his hand on the doorknob and prepared to turn it when Robbie dropped his notepad and bent down to get it. That left him with a perfect view of Constance. And for a second, he couldn't move.

She had the same stark, clear blue eyes and the same spattering of freckles on her small button nose. But somehow she looked different. She'd changed. Grown up. Her hair was a little longer and straighter, but still the color of wheat, and she had her slim arms crossed on the table. In ten years, she'd become more womanly, and less girlish, her roundness now slimmer. She'd always been in the moderately cute category. The kind of girl who was cuddly cute, but not beautiful. Now she was something much more than that. There was no way around it; she had just plain blossomed. She was take-your-breath-away gorgeous, the kind of girl who'd make you have trouble remembering your own name.

And in that instant, Nathan knew he'd made a terrible mistake.

Why, oh, why, didn't I call? he thought, as he took a deep breath and opened the door.

Four

Constance had her share of shocks that day, but seeing Nathan Garrett walk through her door nearly did her in.

She took one look at Nathan, his same darkly handsome self, those same sparkling brown eyes and crooked smile, and nearly lost it.

She had only just gotten herself together after falling apart when she called 911, and now this.

Of all the times and all the ways she'd imagined bumping into Nathan Garrett again, at the scene of her almost-ex husband's murder had never crossed her mind.

"You," she managed to sputter. It was the only word that would come out of her mouth, despite her having practiced three or four lengthy speeches in her head over the years. The only word she could think of was simply "You."

Nathan, at least, had the good sense to look sheepish. He knew he was in the wrong, and that only made her madder. And, oh boy, was she mad. She was so mad, she couldn't speak. So "You" was the only thing she said, and then she fell resolutely silent, her lips pressed in a thin white line, her eyes clouding with stars. Either she was going to pass out or she was going to kill him.

Nathan sent her an embarrassed smile, and it had the gall to be charming and disarming, with the telltale Garrett dimple in the right cheek. The same smile that had melted the hearts of dozens of Dogwood County girls back in the day, and at least twenty-one other virgins, and now here it was, working its same magic, which only made Constance want to spit. He could've at least gained weight, she thought, her eyes flicking to his flat stomach. He could've grown a double chin, or gone bald, or sprouted a unibrow. But he'd done none of those things. He was as damn fine-looking as he had been ten years ago, better even with age, and it just wasn't fair.

"Robbie," Nathan said. "Leave us a minute."

"Don't you move an inch, Robbie," Constance gritted out, eyes on fire. "Not unless you want another murder on your hands."

Robbie looked back and forth between the two, unsure of what to do. He had one of Constance's freshly baked blueberry muffins in one hand, and he was in midchew.

"Go on, Robbie. I think I can take care of myself," Nathan said. He gave Constance one of his dimpled smiles.

The smile made Constance so furious, words fled her head, so she just glared. If she was honest, she'd tell herself that part of her was glad Nathan showed up. Being angry at him gave her a nice distraction from what was really going on. Up until Nathan's appearance, she'd felt numb all over, and she was pretty sure this meant she was in shock, and that her body hadn't yet caught up to her mind, which already knew the truth: there was something really terribly strange happening here. Like something her tarot-obsessed mother would say was a bad stretch of cards. Really bad.

Not that Constance believed in tarot cards, or the boogeyman, or in anything that couldn't be explained straight and simple. Growing up with a supernatural-obsessed mother will do that to you. Constance was nothing if not skeptical of anything paranormal. But none of her straightforward thinking could explain the man with the self-destructing card. Was he a serial killer? A new breed who went around introducing himself to victims? But could it even be possible that someone like him existed in Dogwood County, which hadn't, as far as she could remember, had a murder in decades? And why give her his name? Yaman. It must be fake. First off, who has a name like that? And second, who kills a man and then *tells* you his real name and leaves you alive to talk about it?

Not to mention the man had just plumb disappeared, which Constance couldn't explain, unless he was a hell of a lot faster than he looked, or he'd managed to do some kind of magic trick. And why in the world did he kill Jimmy?

It just didn't make any damn sense. None of it.

Constance couldn't make heads or tails of it. And even stranger, she couldn't remember the man's face. She'd seen it. She was sure she'd seen it. But now she couldn't remember what he looked like. And until today,

Constance was never one to forget a face. Even those she wanted to forget—like Nathan Garrett's.

"Robbie, why don't you go call dispatch and tell them what we've found here," Nathan said. "I'll take my chances with Constance—I mean, Mrs. Plyd."

Constance couldn't help but notice he hung on to the words "Mrs. Plyd" a little too long, like he might be mocking her. He flashed her another smile, too, sealing the deal. He seemed to be finding this a little amusing. Her being married to Jimmy was something he found funny. Well, she thought, that was probably the last thing he'd ever find funny in what was left of his short life.

"Yes, sir, Sheriff," Robbie said, sounding a little disappointed. Constance couldn't tell if it was because he wanted to eat more muffins or because he just didn't want to get up out of his chair. Robbie—who was anything but slim—heaved himself out of Constance's kitchen chair with some effort. Blueberry muffin crumbs toppled from his uniform and onto Constance's kitchen floor.

"Mrs. Plyd," he said, nodding in her direction, "could I?" He was reaching for another muffin. Constance sighed and rolled her eyes. "Go ahead, Robbie," she said, offering up the last muffin in the basket. It's not like she planned to offer Nathan Garrett any, anyhow.

"Thank ya kindly," Robbie said, snatching up the baked goods and ignoring the disapproving frown that Nathan sent his way as he held the muffin in his thick fingers and turned to leave. He left a trail of bright red smudges on her kitchen floor, which was still slick from Tide bubbles. Constance realized with a start it was blood—Jimmy's blood.

And suddenly her anger at Nathan drained away, as did most of the blood from her head. She was starting to feel weak-kneed and woozy. Thank goodness she was already sitting down. She took a deep breath and tried to tell herself to be calm. Going to pieces wouldn't help anyone.

Nathan caught his hapless deputy on the way to the back door.

"Better watch your boots there," he warned, as both men cast their eyes down to Robbie's feet. Robbie, turning a little red, plucked off his bloody shoe and tucked it under his arm. "Right, sir. Thanks."

The sheriff let Robbie pass and then let out a small sigh. He looked at Constance with his big brown eyes, although she couldn't read his expression. Of course, he'd always been hard to read. Once you got past the dimpled smile and the swagger, you could never really tell what was going on in Nathan Garrett's head. I bet that's what made him a good cop, Constance thought. And then she shook the thought from her head. She wasn't going to allow herself to give him compliments. He was no good. Period. She didn't care if his return was the biggest news in Dogwood County since Margene Lawson, homecoming queen of 1991, posed naked as the day she was born for the June issue of *Playboy*.

He'd been gone ten years, but Dogwood County loved a good homecoming story. Especially when the prodigal son was a Garrett, whose return instantly made him the county's most eligible bachelor. He'd even been the talk of her book club last week, which was what made her decide then and there to stop going. She had joined the book club to discuss books, not to plot ways to get Nathan Garrett out of his shirt.

Of course, now that he was in her kitchen, with his shoulders so broad they seemed to take up the room, she realized why Georgina Webber had spent so long talking about the man's biceps. Too bad she knew what he was really like.

"I'm so sorry about Jimmy," he said first, fidgeting a little with the brim of his hat in his hands and cocking his head to one side. His brown hair curled around his ears.

Constance just stared at him, looking for any sign that he was making fun of her. He seemed sincere. But then Nathan was always good at acting sincere. Like when he told her he would call.

"And I'm sorry . . ." He paused. "About everything else."

Constance wondered for a minute if he even remembered what he was sorry for. Maybe that's why he said "everything else," which is a pretty good catchall when you're a Garrett, she thought. Those boys must've spent half their lives apologizing for one thing or another.

Constance just shrugged and looked away. Despite their history, she was finding herself distracted by his broad chest, which was connected to his very fit, very flat stomach. For years, she'd been hoping for a chance to give Nathan Garrett a piece of her mind, but now that he was standing here in her kitchen, she just wanted him to leave. He was dredging up feelings in her that she didn't like, and she just wanted some peace and quiet to try to figure out just what she'd seen in her garage, and whether or not she was going crazy.

"May I?" he asked her, grabbing the back of one of her kitchen chairs. He took a seat without waiting for her to answer. He either assumed the answer was yes or didn't care if it was no. Nathan, she noticed, was too big for her little dinette. She imagined that his knees were bunched up against the bottom of the small table. It seemed like he should be in the ads for Hungry-Man meals or Brawny paper towels. Normal-sized things were simply too small for him. Constance crossed her arms over her chest as if to protect herself from the Garrett charm that seemed to fill up her small kitchen.

"I know I'm the last person you want to see right now," Nathan said.

Constance just looked at him and sniffed. He had no idea.

"But I'd like to help you, if I can," he added.

Constance sent him a dubious look. She didn't trust him as far as she could throw him, and judging from the height and breadth of him, that wouldn't be very far.

"You want to *help* me, do you?" Constance couldn't keep the sarcasm out of her voice. "I don't think I need your kind of *help* just now."

She'd meant "help" as in disappearing on her with-out even so much as a good-bye, but Nathan just grinned at her, and Constance realized he thought she meant help out of her bra, which was what he'd been doing the last time she'd seen him. She blushed fiercely at the memory—he'd had her out of that bra in two seconds flat, no fumbling, naturally, like he'd been born knowing how to unhook a bra one-handed in the dark. She wanted to tell him to get his mind out of the gutter, but then he was a Garrett, so it wasn't just his mind that lived there but pretty much his whole self.

Nathan, realizing his dimpled grin wasn't working, changed tactics, becoming serious again. "Constance, I know I haven't been all that good to you," he said, sounding like he meant it. "But I am good at my job, and right now, I need you to tell me what happened, so I can find the person who killed Jimmy."

Constance jumped a little at the word "killed." She still couldn't believe Jimmy was really dead. This all seemed like something out of a bad dream. She still expected Jimmy to jump up and walk in the back door, saying it was all a practical joke. She simply couldn't wrap her mind around the fact he was gone.

"I'll tell you what I told Robbie," Constance said, after a moment. "But I don't think he believed me, and you probably won't, either." Constance remembered the startled look on Deputy Robbie's face when she'd told him what had happened. It looked like he was sizing her up for a straitjacket right then. She doubted Nathan would be more understanding.

"Try me," Nathan said, leaning in, eyes intent, just the hint of a smile at the corner of his lip.

"You'll think I'm crazy. Or lying."

"No, I won't."

"You will."

Nathan was becoming a little frustrated now. She could tell by the way he squinted his eyes. "Constance," he said in a warning tone. "Just spit it out already. While we're still young."

"While *I'm* young, you mean," she said evenly. He was two years older than she was, and she wasn't going to let him forget it.

"Are you going to tell me what happened or not?" Nathan sounded stern now. For a fleeting second, Constance wondered if he would arrest her if she didn't talk. She glanced down at the shiny silver cuffs hanging from his belt. They were just a few inches away from the gun he wore. He seemed much more intimidating than Robbie, who just looked like a giant teddy bear in a police uniform.

"Fine," Constance said. "Robbie will probably just fill you in, anyway."

So Constance told him everything. The noise she heard, and the smell, and the man in black, and the card he gave her. And she let it all tumble out like word vomit, because once she started, she couldn't stop, and besides, there was no use in holding anything back. Constance wasn't the kind of person who lied very often, and when she did she wasn't very good at it.

"It sounds crazy, I know, but the card just disappeared," she heard herself say in a rush. "It just burned up in my hand, but didn't burn me. Just turned to ash. Must've been some kind of trick card. I don't know. And when I looked up again, he was gone. Don't know how he did that. It was like some kind of magic trick. The whole thing."

Nathan looked at her a long time after she finished, and Constance thought he might burst out laughing at her, or call her crazy, or something like that, but his face was completely expressionless, and she couldn't tell at all what he was thinking. And then, after a long second, he just nodded slowly, as if he heard this sort of thing all the time: people pretending to be demons with business cards who disappeared into thin air.

"And you can't remember what this man looked like. Apart from he was wearing black jeans and a black jacket?" Nathan asked, completely serious, not a hint of a joke anywhere, and Constance realized with a shock that he seemed to believe her. Even with a crazy story like that. Despite her better judgment, she started to warm to him.

"That's right."

"So you didn't recognize him?"

"No."

"Did Jimmy have any enemies?" The way Nathan said this, as he leaned forward, made her think he was on her side. As if the two of them were on the same team.

"He had a lot of people annoyed with him. Including me," she said. "But none who would kill him that I know of."

"How about you and Jimmy? How were things between you?"

"We were getting a divorce, if that's what you mean," Constance said. "Didn't you know? I thought the whole county knew."

"You were?" Nathan asked, looking surprised for the first time, and was that a hint of something else—gladness?—Constance wondered. But then Nathan quickly put his poker face back on, so Constance wasn't sure she saw what she saw. "I've just been here a month. Didn't even know you were married until an hour ago. So, what was the trouble with you two?"

Nathan seemed to be enjoying this line of questioning a bit too much. The warm feelings Constance had for him started to cool.

"Oh, well, I'd been holding a candle for you for ten years and Jimmy finally got tired of it," Constance said, deadpan. "He said the life-size poster of you in the bedroom was just too much."

This stumped Nathan, who seemed to be buying it, proving that he was the narcissist Constance thought he was.

"Nathan Garrett, you are as vain as I remember," Constance said, shaking her head. It was her turn to smile at his expense. "I wouldn't hold a ten-carat diamond for you, much less a candle. Get over yourself." Nathan looked taken aback, but Constance continued before he could fight back. "We had the same marriage problems most people had, except, unlike most husbands, mine nearly burned down the house five or six times."

"And was there a problem with the . . ." Constance watched as Nathan struggled to figure out a nice way to say "money."

"I got a prenup," Constance snapped, used to people assuming she was a gold digger. "I wasn't getting anything except the restaurant," she clarified. Nathan looked stumped, so she added, "The Magnolia Café? On the county square? That's mine."

"I see," Nathan said, fully recovered now and back to business. "Was it final?"

"Not yet," Constance said. "I've been trying to get him to sign divorce papers for months. Of course, you know Jimmy. He doesn't do anything right. He divorces about as well as he fetched water for the Dogwood County varsity team."

Jimmy once spilled four separate coolers of Gatorade during a football play-off game back when Nathan was a wide receiver. The field was dyed orange for most of the game. He gave a low chuckle. "That well, huh?"

"Worse," Constance said, and couldn't help but smile. Jimmy might have been a nuisance, but he was always good for a story. She glanced over in the corner and saw that Jimmy had left his muddy work boots on her new welcome mat, the fifth one in as many weeks she'd bought at Mega-Mart because Jimmy had ruined each and every one with tar from his boots. If she'd told him once, she'd told him a thousand times to leave his boots on the porch. They didn't just stain, they also smelled.

The sheriff's eyes followed hers to Jimmy's boots, and then came back to her face, watching her expression carefully. But Constance didn't notice. She was too busy realizing at last there was no Jimmy to yell at anymore, and there would be no more muddy boots, and for a second, she felt a little bit of relief, and then she felt something else entirely. And the numbness she'd been feeling for the better part of an hour melted away a little bit, and a sob broke from her throat, and out of nowhere she had tears running down her face. Damn it. She was going to miss that useless almost-ex husband after all.

Swiftly, and as if he'd done it a hundred times before, Nathan pulled a pack of Kleenex from his pocket and offered her one. She blew her nose like an elephant, and inwardly cursed as her mascara ran down her face. The one thing she'd vowed to do was to never let a Garrett see her cry, and now here she was bawling like a baby in front of the one man she hated more than any other in the world.

She tried to order him out of her kitchen, but it all came out in a snotty blubber, and Nathan just put his hand on her shoulder and squeezed.

"It's okay to cry," he said, which just caused her to wail all the more.

Five

"So? Did the pretty widow do it?" Mel asked Nathan as the two of them sipped coffee back at the station and watched from a distance as Constance tried in vain to tell Maude Raines, the police sketch artist, what the man in black had looked like. Nathan had to agree with Mel. Constance was pretty—too pretty for Nathan's comfort. She tucked her long, wheat-colored hair back behind one ear and studied the sketch. A small crease of concentration appeared in her otherwise smooth forehead, and Nathan felt a strong urge to walk over and caress it away.

"Earth to Sheriff? Come in, Sheriff?" Mel said, looking at him strangely. Nathan dragged his gaze away from Constance and focused on Mel. He wondered if his feelings for Constance were obvious. It had been a long time since a woman had had this effect on him. In fact, despite all the rumors running around about him, he'd nearly sworn off girls. Not that he hadn't had offers, but he was tired of the shallow one-night flings that he'd perfected in his twenties. He wanted something more. He was looking for, like his brother Jake said all the time, "more than your daily special." To him, it meant a woman who actually had a brain and a personality, something that had been missing from the women he'd dated of late. Of course, part of that was his fault. You don't go through the Dallas Cowboy Cheerleader roster and expect to find your soul mate.

He made an effort to fix his face into a neutral expression.

"You know I can't comment on an ongoing investigation," Nathan said.

"That just means you don't know squat, and you know it," Mel said. "Office pool says the widow is guilty. It's two-to-one odds."

"There's already an office pool?"

"And you're surprised? These are the same deputies who bet who's going to eat the last donut."

"We don't have donuts, Mel," Nathan said, taking a sip of his coffee. "I think you're referring to our stereotypical morning pastries."

Mel barked a laugh. "Is that what you called them in Big D?"

"Something like that," Nathan said, watching as Constance frowned at the picture Maude held up before her. She wasn't sure that was the sketch, either, and this was Maude's third try.

"So, you gonna arrest her now? Or you gonna wait until after the funeral?" Mel asked, giving Nathan's arm a nudge.

He didn't want to arrest her at all, if he were honest about things. He knew Constance, or at least thought he did, and she didn't lie. She was the kind of person who told you if you had something in your teeth instead of waiting for someone else to do it. So that crazy story she spun was either the truth or she thought it was. The most logical explanation was that she'd gone plumb crazy and lost her mind, which also might explain why she married Jimmy in the first place.

Nathan realized he was making excuses for Constance, which was a bad sign. He couldn't quite tell if it was the fact that she was so darn pretty, or because he felt bad about how he'd treated her, or because she seemed so in need of rescuing. And he did have a weakness for damsels in distress. Like his brother Jake once told him. He knew how to rescue a girl, but he didn't know what to do with her after. Jake had gotten all holier-than-thou on him with the womanizing since finding his own soul mate six years ago. Of course, seeing Jake—who'd run through more girls than Nathan had—cry at the wedding five years ago made Nathan rethink things a bit. Jake, who'd sworn never to wear a wedding band, actually now wore his with pride. He and his wife, Katie, had a girl who would turn four this year, and far from being chained, Jake was the happiest he'd ever been. It made Nathan wonder, not for the first time, what his life might be missing.

"I take it this means you've got something riding on the office pool?" Nathan asked Mel, evading her question.

"Twenty bucks on the pretty girl," Mel said.

"Dare I ask why?"

"Sheriff, don't you ever watch movies? It's always the pretty girl who did it."

"She'd still need a motive," Nathan said. He was surprised by how defensive his voice sounded. Mel seemed surprised, too.

"You need a *motive* to kill Jimmy Plyd?" When Nathan didn't smile, she cleared her throat. "How about the trust fund, then? Or is that too obvious?"

Nathan just gave her a look.

"So, how about an insurance policy? You gonna check on that?"

"Already have," Nathan said. He had a call into Liberty Mutual, after seeing one of their envelopes on Constance's kitchen table.

"Are you fixing to interrogate her—or just sit and stare at her all day?" asked Ann, the dispatcher, who had come to join them at the coffeemaker. It was then that Nathan realized he'd spent the last few minutes just watching Constance. Maude had finished up her sketch and had already packed up her things. Constance was sitting there, managing to look irresistible despite the slight redness around her eyes—the only sign she'd been crying.

"Well, I might if everyone quit telling me how to do my job," Nathan grumbled. "And let me guess, you're in on the pool, too."

Ann, who hadn't bothered to take off her wireless headset, which acted as a headband for her salt-and-pepper bob, nodded. "Thirty bucks that you arrest her before the week is out," she said. "That is, *if* you ever get around to interrogating her." She paused. "You wouldn't be letting the fact you two used to date cloud your judgment, now?"

"You two dated?" Mel shook her head. She could see her money fly away from here if the office pool was rigged.

"And you're surprised, why?" Ann thumbed her hand at Nathan. "He pretty much dated every girl in the county. You know. Except me."

"That's only because you keep turning me down, Ann," Nathan said, and grinned.

"Oh, stop it," Ann said, giving Nathan a little shove. "I am way out of your league."

"Boy, don't I know it, too."

"So, when are you going to arrest her?"

Nathan glanced at Ann and shook his head. "Is anyone betting she *isn't* the one who did it?"

Ann and Mel both shrugged. "Robbie," Ann said.

"Robbie? That's it?"

"He's putting his money on it being a suicide," Ann clarified.

"You can't be serious. Even Robbie isn't that slow."

"I don't think he really thinks it's a suicide," Ann added. "I think he was just won over by the widow's muffins. Said a woman who bakes like that can't be a murderer."

"Now that sounds more like the Robbie I know," Nathan said, smiling despite himself. He cleared his throat then, and put down his cup of coffee.

"If you'll excuse me, ladies, I have a job to do," he said, leaving Ann and Mel to chat more about the office pool while he made his way across the room.

Constance had put her head in her hands, and slumped over slightly. She looked like an orphaned puppy, and the sight made Nathan's heart shrink just a little. He fought the urge to put his arm around her shoulders and tell her it would be okay.

"Constance?" he said softly.

She uncurled herself for him, lifting up her head at the sound of his voice, her eyes meeting his. He saw in the bright fluorescent light of the sheriff's office that her eyes were green. He'd always thought they were blue, but they were definitely green. And for a second, right before the distrust came in, he swore he saw a little bit of warmth there for him. If only for a second. But then she closed up, hardened herself, and put her entire posture on the defensive. She didn't trust him, and she clearly didn't like him, and he wondered how long she'd be like that with him. Of course, if she ever found out he was considering her a possible suspect, it might just be forever.

"Will you come with me?" he asked, and she nodded and got up, and he led her into his office. He could feel the eyes of Mel and Ann on him as he closed the door behind him.

Constance looked suspiciously around his office, as if rattlesnakes might jump out from the corners. He offered her a chair and she eyed it like it might be poisonous before deciding to sit down. She seemed pretty calm, considering. After her brief outburst at the house, she'd taken control of herself again and hadn't let go. Her eyes roamed the walls so that she could look anywhere but at him.

He took a quick look around and wondered what she'd glean about him from his office, and he guessed not much. He didn't have any cartoons up, or posters of cats hanging from tree trunks, or any pictures, save one: him and his old partner, in their raincoats, standing together in front of their unmarked squad car. It had been snapped two weeks before they found Libby Bell. One month before Ron had been shot in the line of duty, the two of them following a suspect in the Bell murder in an abandoned warehouse in downtown Dallas. It was one more unsolved murder, and it weighed heavily on Nathan's shoulders. He hadn't caught the man who'd killed Libby Bell, or the person who'd killed his partner, and he was pretty sure they were one and the same.

Constance was staring at the picture.

"That was my old partner," he explained.

"Oh, I see," she said. "Do you still keep in touch?"

"He's dead," Nathan said flatly. He regretted it the minute he said it because Constance blanched.

"Oh, I'm sorry. I didn't know."

No one around here did. Nathan had made a point of not telling that story. He didn't want the looks of pity. Or worse, the nagging looks of doubt. He'd blamed himself enough for his partner's death. It was a day that Nathan still couldn't fully explain. He'd been there, cradling his partner's head, the day he died. And Nathan still felt it was his fault. He didn't need other people second-guessing him, too. He preferred people to think he'd come home because he missed the country life, not because he was running away from the big city.

"It's okay," he said, waving his hand. Mentally, he shook himself. He had a job to do, and he wasn't doing it. It was time to get down to business. He met Constance's gaze and smiled. He always got more information by being nice. He had always been the "good" cop.

Of course, this time his smile had the opposite effect. As soon as he smiled, Constance stiffened and frowned. Boy, she really didn't trust him a bit.

"So, tell me more about this man you saw," Nathan began.

"I told you everything I know," she said, her guard up.

"But what was he wearing again? I just want to make sure I have it right." His question was part of a classic interrogation technique: go over and over the details to make sure your suspect is telling the truth. Eventually, even the smart ones will get something wrong because a lie is always harder to remember than the truth.

"Well, he was wearing all black and . . ." Constance trailed off.

"And anything else?"

Constance looked down at her lap, confusion crossing her face. "I-I don't remember."

"You don't remember if he was wearing anything else? Maybe a hat?" Nathan distinctly remembered her telling him the mystery man had a baseball cap on—a black one. But now Constance just blinked at him.

"I can't remember," Constance said, shaking her head. "I mean, I remember he was there, but that was it."

Nathan studied her closely, trying to tell if she was lying. Normally, when suspects tried to lie, they confidently stepped straight into one of the traps he laid for them. But Constance just seemed so . . . lost. Right now, she was biting her lower lip, her green eyes settling on her hands.

At this moment, Constance didn't look so flustered as much as genuinely baffled. She had either gotten much better at deception or she was telling the truth.

"Constance, I know this is hard," he said in his best you-can-trust-me voice. "But if you just try to concentrate, maybe you'll remember. No detail, no matter how small, is insignificant."

Constance nodded. "This is going to sound really stupid," she said. "But I can't remember anything."

"Can you remember his name?"

Constance's startled gaze quickly met his. "I-I-I know I knew it," she said. "He handed it to me on a business card, but I . . ." She paused and bit her lower lip again.

"Just take your time," Nathan said. "See if you can remember."

Constance closed her eyes, as if to concentrate. She looked, Nathan thought, like she was getting ready to kiss someone. He shook the thought from his head. He needed to focus now.

He let his eyes wander down, and found them latched onto her right thigh, which was crossed over her left. The slit in her skirt showed just the tiniest sliver of skin. He thought back to what she had felt like that night in the Mustang, but his memory was too foggy. He'd had too many dates in that car, and so many of them blurred together. This probably made him a bad guy, but then again, he had been just twenty. He'd matured since then. He took women on proper dates now, and usually there were at least sheets involved. Still, he felt a pang of guilt. He hadn't treated her right and he knew it. Forgetting what she looked like naked was probably the least punishment he deserved.

Constance's eyes opened. "I can't remember it," she said, the frown line in her forehead appearing again. "This is crazy, right? I should remember it. I just told you what it was, and now . . . Oh God. Am I going crazy? Am I losing my mind?"

"No, of course not," Nathan said calmly, although he wasn't quite sure. He'd never had a suspect forget her own account of the murder and then admit to forgetting it. This was a new one. But leave it to Constance to do things the wrong way around. "It's probably the stress—and the shock," he explained, and immediately she looked a little relieved.

She started to tear up again. She put her head in her hands.

"Jimmy didn't deserve . . ." She trailed off, tears choking her voice.

Nathan watched her carefully for signs of acting, but saw none. She seemed to be genuinely upset. Maybe she had really loved him.

She glanced out the window to their right, which gave an unobstructed view of the parking lot. Suddenly, she turned as white as a ghost.

"Did you see that?" she asked him, pointing out the window.

"See what?" he asked, suddenly concerned. He hadn't seen any movement from his peripheral vision, not even a bird.

Constance blinked fast several times, and then shook her head and laughed. "I think I'm hallucinating now."

"What did you think you saw?"

"Nothing—it was nothing," Constance said, shaking her head. "I mean, for a second, I thought I saw Jimmy—but that's not possible, right?"

Nathan didn't know what to think. First, his prime

suspect forgot what had happened, and now she was telling him she'd seen her victim wandering outside in the county parking lot? Nathan turned and looked out the window. He saw nothing but squad cars parked there. Was she trying to set herself up for some kind of insanity defense? Constance had always been a straight shooter before. This new, possibly crazy Constance was making him uncomfortable.

"I'm sorry, what were you asking me?" Constance said, focusing her green eyes on him. They looked big and lucid and decidedly *not* crazy. Just what was her game? She kept him off balance. He couldn't remember the last time a suspect made him this uneasy. He felt like she might be playing him. She was either innocent, which didn't look likely, or she was very, very good.

"You can't remember the assailant's name? The one you saw in your garage?"

"I know I should, and I remember *remembering* it, but anytime I try to think of it, I just blank," she said, the worry line appearing on her forehead again.

"Yaman was the name," Nathan said softly. He remembered it.

Her face lit up. "Yes, that's right. Yaman." Then her face fell a little. "Wait. If you knew it, why were you asking me?" Her eyes clouded. They were suspicious again. Her guard was back, and so was her dislike of him.

Nathan just looked at her. The two stared at each other for a beat.

"Were you *testing* me?" Constance asked, anger building in her voice. "You can't honestly think I'd . . ."

"That you what?"

"*Killed* Jimmy," Constance finished.

"Why don't you tell me?" Nathan said, leaning closer to her, so close he could smell her perfume. Gardenias, he thought.

"I think it's time for me to go home," Constance said, mouth tight, as she stood and clutched her purse with white knuckles. "Before I really do kill somebody." She glared at him as she said this.

"Go ahead," Nathan said, leaning back in his chair. It wasn't like he could arrest her. He didn't have enough evidence. Yet.

Flustered, she threw her purse strap over her shoulder and turned to leave.

"Constance," Nathan said, catching her just as she made it to the door. She turned, lips pursed and eyes still flashing. "I wouldn't leave town if I were you."

"Humph," she grumbled, visibly unimpressed by the veiled threat. "As if you could run me out of town that easy." She turned quickly, showing him a nice view of her backside as her heels clicked away from him on the tile floor.

He couldn't help himself. He smiled. This was going to be one hell of an interesting case.

Six

*C*onstance realized too late that Robbie had driven her to the police station, so she didn't have a car and couldn't very well drive herself home. She started walking blindly toward the town square, which she guessed was no more than a half mile away.

She was still shaking from her run-in with Nathan Garrett, and didn't know if it was because she hated his guts or because he clearly suspected her of murder. As if it weren't bad enough he didn't call, now he had to go add insult to injury by believing she was capable of breaking the worst of the Ten Commandments.

It would make sense, naturally, that the one man she couldn't stand might just be the one who would arrest her for a crime she didn't commit. That would be just great. Add it to the list of Things Gone Wrong in her life, and it would be near the top, right after Father Ran Off With Sonic Waitress in 1990 and Mother Reads Tarot Cards to Pay Bills and Becomes Laughingstock of Town.

But at the moment, Constance didn't have time to worry about her arrest or about Nathan Garrett.

She had a whole other problem. She could've sworn she'd seen her dead husband, Jimmy, wandering around the window outside the police station. She thought she saw him standing there, picking his nose. But then she blinked and he was gone. It was clearly an indication of her frayed mental state.

She sniffed back tears as she walked past the county courthouse. Jimmy might have been a screw-up, but he could be sweet, too, and nobody deserved to die like that. A few people on the street whispered as she went by, and she wondered if the news had already spread. But of course it had. This was Dogwood County, where gossip spread at the speed of light.

She soon found herself standing in front of the Magnolia Café. The hand-painted wooden sign out front made her heart just a little lighter. She pushed the door open and the bell dinged.

Inside, there were her tables, set with care. She'd insisted on white linens because she thought they looked best. The walls—exposed brick—were covered with oversized black-and-white photos of special Dogwood County moments, like the year the football team took state and last year's Fourth of July parade. She spent most of her time in this restaurant, and it was more home to her than her own kitchen. In the early days, she'd worked herself to the bone to get the restaurant up and started. Since then she'd had a few years of prosperity, but recently business had started to slow. She blamed it on the new rash of chain restaurants that had opened up near the highway. There was no way she could compete with a dollar menu. Recently, she'd had to pour even more of her energy into the restaurant to try to keep it afloat, but she didn't mind. To her, the restaurant was what she used to fill up the empty places inside herself. Anytime she felt lonely, or misunderstood, or just plain depressed, all that would change the minute she stepped into her café. As long as she could get to work and whip up a new special or spruce up the menu, she felt fine.

Usually, walking in through the doors lifted her spirits immediately. Normally, she liked the look of the café more than her own house. Except there was something missing today.

Customers.

The place was nearly empty. Constance glanced at her watch. It was at the later end of the lunch hour, but still. Normally, the place had at least a handful of customers. She wondered if this was the product of the competing Cracker Barrel at the interstate or something else.

"What in the world happened?" asked Jose, her short-order cook, general manager, and, since three months ago, full-fledged partner in the business. The squat, no-holds-barred fifty-something man with five children and twelve grandchildren put his hands on his white apron front and looked stern. "We heard on the radio about Jimmy! You okay?"

"On the radio?" echoed Constance. Her life had been on the radio? "What else did they say?"

"That there's a killer on the loose. That *you* are a suspect," Jose said, aiming a spatula at her.

"They already said I'm a suspect?" Constance asked,

amazed. She'd only just learned this fact herself about fifteen minutes ago.

"Well, not in those words," Jose said. "But they did say you were the one who found him, and you and he were alone in the house. But we don't believe it, do we?" Jose asked Martinez, the dishwasher, who simply shook his head.

"I can't believe it's already on the radio," Constance said.

"You know they don't have anything to report, especially now that Dogwood High is out of the play-offs."

"Still," Constance muttered.

"So, we *think* the customers are staying away today," Jose said. "I told Martinez they probably think if they come here, they'll get whacked or something. But in a few days, I'm sure they'll forget. At least, I *hope* they forget."

Jose was worried about his investment. With the café's financial woes lately, Constance had accepted a loan from him in exchange for making him partner. She would've asked Jimmy for more money, except, well, she was trying to get him to sign divorce papers, and she was done asking for things from him. Besides, she wanted to do this on her own.

"Great," Constance said. First, her almost-ex husband was murdered by a killer who thought he was a demon, and now she was going to go out of business. "Hey— where's Maria? And Janice?" These were her waitresses. They were supposed to be on shift.

"I sent them home," Jose said, and shrugged. "No customers today. Or probably tomorrow. Maybe Friday. Or when they arrest somebody."

"I still can't believe he's dead," Constance said, sniffing back sudden tears.

"Don't you dare cry for Jimmy!" exclaimed Jose. Jose wasn't a huge fan of Jimmy's. Not since Jimmy had the gall to suggest he put more salt in his spinach omelet. Jose had an impeccable palate, and wouldn't tolerate being second-guessed. And then Jimmy broke Jose's prized grill last year while trying to fix a broken knob. That had been the last straw.

"He didn't deserve to die," Constance said.

The front bell dinged, announcing the arrival of a customer, and Constance was half afraid she'd turn and see Nathan Garrett there, filling up the doorway and ready with her Miranda warning.

Instead, she saw Rachel Farnsworth, Constance's best friend since fifth grade, stride in carrying her baby boy, Cassidy, on one hip.

"Why didn't you *call* me?" she said, her long brown hair whipped up in a high ponytail, which bounced with every step. She managed to look annoyed and concerned all at the same time.

"Why call when news travels this fast? I think Dogwood County is the last place on earth we actually need cell phones," Constance said.

"True, but I'm your best friend, and I had to hear the news from Kendra Collins in the produce aisle at Kroger. I came over just as fast as I could. What on earth happened?"

Constance started to tell Rachel everything with Jose and Martinez looking on, and then pretty soon found herself welling up with tears again.

"Oh, Cassidy, Auntie Con needs a hug," Rachel said, and threw herself and her nearly one-year-old Cassidy onto Constance, who was folded into a four-armed hug that smelled like wet wipes and apple juice.

"Come on, honey, let me drive you home."

Constance's house was still taped off with police tape, the garage sealed, along with half of her kitchen. The officers, though, had gone, and apparently taken the evidence with them, including Jimmy's body. The bloodstain, however, was still there. Rachel took charge, ushering Constance quickly past the crime scene and through the front door.

Once in the kitchen, Rachel made a beeline for Constance's coffeemaker and filled the pot up with water from the tap. Constance liked the way Rachel took charge, acting like the mom she'd only just become less than a year ago.

"And brace yourself, I haven't told you everything," Constance said, sitting down at her kitchen table while the coffee brewed. "Nathan Garrett is back in town. He's the sheriff. He's investigating the case."

Rachel froze, midstep, and gaped. "They gave that man a *gun*?" She just shook her head and clicked her tongue. "Lord help us."

"I know," Constance said, agreeing.

Rachel knew all about the Garrett brothers. She'd dated Jake Garrett briefly when she was a sophomore in high school before she came to her senses. She'd also been the one to hold Constance up after Nathan left town and forgot to call. She'd also tried—in vain—to talk her out of marrying Jimmy.

"Tell me he at least got fat," Rachel said. "I heard one of the Garrett brothers got fat."

"Not this one," Constance said.

"Damn. That's too bad. I was hoping for instant karma."

"He looks the same, can you believe it? *And* he thinks I killed Jimmy."

Rachel's mouth gaped into an *O*. "Unbelievable!" she ranted on her friend's behalf. "The *nerve* of him." Then she paused. "You didn't, though, did you?"

"Rachel!"

"What? I'm just asking. Jimmy is downright annoying. No one would blame you for it."

"I didn't do it! I mean, obviously. I can't hurt anyone."

"Oh, sure, I mean, obviously. I just had to ask. I mean, you know. *I* might've done it. Remember when he ran his car into my magnolia tree?"

"Who could forget? He knocked it over. But still, I didn't kill him."

"Okay, I believe you," Rachel said. "Besides, when you lie, you do that hair thing." Rachel was referring to the fact that anytime Constance lied, she twirled a piece of hair around her finger. She'd had that nervous tic since grade school, and it was the reason she could never properly lie to the principal or teacher when the two of them got into trouble. Constance's inability to lie was legendary. She was like a walking George Washington with his cherry tree.

"I do not!" Constance lied, and played with a bit of her hair.

"You're doing it right now," Rachel pointed out.

Constance dropped her hair and crossed her arms. "Well, fine, then."

Rachel stayed with Constance far longer than she should have, making her drink coffee and eat the fresh-from-the-Kroger-bakery pie she'd bought for her husband, Kevin, who would be seriously ticked he wouldn't have dessert tonight.

"He'll get over it," Rachel said. "Besides, that man of mine could lose a few pounds. He looks like he's carrying our second child. And you know I wouldn't say anything except that stinker said *I* should think about going to the *gym*. Can you believe that man? I swear, ever since we got married it's like he's a different person."

"Da Da!" squealed Cassidy, and then giggled.

It was true that Kevin was at least twice as big as Rachel, and that Rachel wasn't in need of losing any weight. She was barely a size two in high school, and Constance guessed that even postpregnancy she might, on a bloated day, be a size four.

Back in high school, Rachel had been salutatorian and Kevin had been an all-state football receiver with a scholarship to Texas Tech. Kevin lost the scholarship after blowing out his knee at his senior homecoming game, and the two married after spending only a year in community college. They were now running Rachel's dad's hardware shop, doing daily battle with Mega-Mart, or as she called it, "That Evil Store."

Constance loved Rachel, in large part because Rachel wasn't afraid to share her opinions on anything and everything, and because she knew her better than just about anyone else.

"I just can't believe it—Jimmy's dead." Constance put both hands on her head.

"Not to be cruel, but maybe you should worry less about Jimmy and more about yourself," Rachel said. "Maybe you should get a lawyer."

"A lawyer! What for? I didn't do anything."

"But people are talking and you said Nathan was suspicious."

"Everyone thinks I did it, don't they?" Constance moaned and put her head in her hands.

"Listen, Constance, it'll be okay," Rachel said suddenly, patting her hand. "You're innocent, and even someone as thick as Nathan Garrett will have to see that."

"But even *you* had your doubts."

"Oh, come on, I didn't really," Rachel said, giving her friend an exaggerated eye roll. "And most other people around here aren't as eager to hang you as you think. You are the most law-abiding person I know. Don't you remember in tenth grade when you insisted we drive all the way back to that drugstore in Tarrant County because you forgot to pay for that tube of lipstick?"

"I guess so."

"And remember last year when you forgot to carry the one on your tax returns and spent the year trying to find someone at the IRS who would accept your check for five cents?"

"Yes."

"So, see? You couldn't kill somebody without being forced to come clean about it to someone. You, Constance Plyd, are completely incapable of doing wrong and not admitting it to someone. If you *had* killed Jimmy you would've been begging Nathan to lock those handcuffs on you and haul you away."

"I suppose you're right."

"By the way, you haven't been to That Evil Store lately, have you?" Rachel asked Constance, as she bounced Cassidy on her knee. Constance glanced guiltily at the mat with Jimmy's muddy boots on it. Jimmy destroyed enough mats that Constance simply couldn't afford to keep buying them at Rachel's store.

"Well, actually, now that you mention it . . ."

"Oh Lord. You *did*! I thought that welcome mat looked new," Rachel said. She gave a huff and sighed. "Oh, well, I suppose I can forgive you. But you should know that That Evil Store just got busted by the INS. Apparently, they had immigrants living in the Tupperware aisle."

"They did not!"

"They did," Rachel said, just as Cassidy broke free from her grasp and made a beeline straight for the closest electrical socket. Rachel grabbed him before he could stick his finger in it and then Cassidy proceeded to pitch a fit. Cassidy was a handful. Had been the moment he was born, and he didn't show any signs of calming down. "If there's anything that could kill this child, he wants to play with it," Rachel said, and rolled her eyes. "Cassidy! Quiet down, now. Or I *will* let you electrocute yourself."

Rachel's cell phone started ringing. She dug for it in her pocket, but Cassidy put his hands on it first, and the mother and son were soon in a tug of war while her flip phone blared the Dixie Chicks. Rachel didn't care what they said or didn't say, she liked their music, and didn't care who knew it. They summed up Rachel's personality nicely, Constance thought.

"Let Mommy have it, *please,*" Rachel said, plucking the phone from Cassidy's sticky hands. "Hello? Kevin! Hi. Well, what on earth do you *think* I'm doing? I'm raising your son, that's what I'm doing."

Constance couldn't help but smile. This was Rachel's answer any time Kevin called, even if Rachel was in the middle of a pedicure. Cassidy tried again to grab the phone, but when Rachel pulled away, the baby grabbed a handful of his mom's hair and tugged.

"Ow! Stop that!" Rachel commanded, but Cassidy just giggled. "No, not you. I'm talking to your sadistic son. And if you wanted a hot meal every night, you should've married that other Rachael. The one with the cooking show. I've got other things to do than to cook you food. Besides, what did I tell you about Constance? She needs us."

Out of the corner of her eye, Constance thought she saw a streak of yellow. The same color yellow as Jimmy's hazmat suit. She whipped her head around, but the corner of the kitchen was empty. No hazmat suit. No Jimmy. She blinked fast three times.

"Fine, fine, *fine,*" Rachel said, still huffing on the phone. "You're hopeless. Fine, *fine.* I don't want to argue. I'll be home soon." Rachel clicked her phone closed and sighed. "I need to find one of those self-sufficient husbands. You know, right along with pink unicorns."

This made Constance laugh and she instantly felt better. "You should go home," she said. "I'll be fine. Really. I'm tired, and should get some sleep."

"You sure you're going to be okay, honey?" Rachel asked, eyes full of concern. "I could drop Cassidy off and come back. You know, Kevin could watch his son for once in his life. It wouldn't kill him."

"I'll be all right. Really." Constance wasn't exactly sure this was the case, but if she said it out loud maybe it would be true.

"Okay, but I'm going to come back with more Kroger pies tomorrow. And maybe even a Kroger casserole," Rachel said. Rachel didn't cook. She came from a long line of women in her family who believed learning to cook or sew would only make men expect you to do it.

Rachel paused at the door and turned. "Now, you need anything at all, you call me, okay? This one"—she paused, nodding at Cassidy—"doesn't sleep, so call night or day."

"Thanks, Rachel," Constance said, feeling grateful.

After Constance saw Rachel and her baby boy off and waved at them from the porch as they left, she shut the front door and nearly tripped over a big pair of work boots. Jimmy's!

She crouched down to pick them up and then realized they shouldn't be there. Just a few minutes ago, she'd seen them lying on the mat in the kitchen. And now, somehow, they'd made it to the front door?

She got a tingling feeling at the back of her neck and tried not to panic. There had to be a reasonable explanation. Maybe when she wasn't looking Cassidy had moved them? It was possible, she guessed. Just not likely. They were heavy, and besides, she didn't remember the little boy leaving the room.

Constance shook her head and put the boots down by the door, thinking she'd deal with them later. She was too tired to think right now. She went straight upstairs and lay down, hoping that maybe in the morning things would make more sense.

After tossing and turning for hours, she finally fell asleep, only to wake with a start, convinced someone was walking around her living room. She sat up in bed, knowing she'd heard something, and her heart started thumping hard in her chest. What if it was the murderer? Come back to finish her off, too?

She fumbled for her cell phone, but it wasn't on the side of her bed as usual. She'd left it in her purse downstairs. Quietly, she sat up, then stood. She crept softly to the stairs, and listened.

Things seemed quiet. But then there came a creak and a squeak, like someone had just sat on her couch. She grabbed the nearest thing to her—an umbrella—and hoped she would be able to take the man's eye out. Quietly, she crept down the stairs, umbrella raised and ready to inflict what damage it could. She peered into the living room and found it empty.

But then she heard it—a snore.

Someone was definitely lying on the couch, but from this angle she couldn't see who. If it was the murderer, he wasn't planning to murder her at the moment, given the fact he was sawing logs loud enough to wake the neighbors.

She saw her purse on the table, and the cell phone sticking out of the side pocket. If she could get to that, she could call the police. She snuck over to it, peering over the back of the couch to get a look at her sleeping intruder, and saw a man lying there, mouth open and snoring. A very familiar-looking man.

She froze. Jimmy?

Couldn't be. Could it?

She shut her eyes tight and then opened them again. She took another look at the couch. Yep, she hadn't been imagining it. There, on her plaid cushions, was Jimmy, sprawled out, sound asleep and snoring, with his socked feet hanging over the edge of her sofa.

Now, because Constance didn't believe in ghosts, she knew she must be hallucinating—either that or she'd finally just gone completely bonkers. Looney tunes, just like her tarot-card-wielding mother, who had claimed to be able to see the ghosts of dead pets since Constance was five.

So Constance did what any sane person would do. She stepped slowly back out of her living room, closed her front door, and let out the breath she'd sucked into her lungs upon realizing her dead husband was snoozing on her couch. She just exhaled it out, nice and slow, and told herself that she was just imagining Jimmy there, with his stinky-socked feet up on her nice throw pillows, because it had been a long, stressful twenty-four hours. She was going to take a few deep, calming breaths and then open the door again. She told herself the couch would be empty.

She counted to three and then she opened the door again.

The couch was empty.

"Thank God," she breathed. She wasn't going crazy. She just had had a shock. And that's when she heard, out of nowhere, near her ear, the voice of her dead husband, Jimmy.

"We got any Bud? I'm thirsty," Dead Jimmy said, causing Constance to jump straight out of her skin, scream like the devil, and run straight across the living room and out her front door.

Seven

"I'm telling you, there's no way *she's* the prophet we're looking for," Shadow said, as he and Yaman watched Constance scramble over to her gold Camry and fumble with her keys. She dropped them several times before she got the right key into the ignition. "The general has to be wrong. Prophets aren't supposed to be scared of ghosts. And she's clearly scared out of her mind."

Yaman shrugged. "I guess prophets just aren't what they used to be."

"I should just eat her and be done with it."

"You can't. You know our orders," Yaman said. "We're supposed to wait until she has a vision that tells us who the mother of the Antichrist is supposed to be."

"Yeah, that's what I don't get. I mean, doesn't Satan just *choose* who he's going to boink? Why does he have to wait to see who the prophet sees him boinking? The Prince of Darkness can't just pick some random chick himself and be done with it?"

Yaman sighed and rolled his eyes. "You have no appreciation for finesse," Yaman said. "Sure, the devil could just go around having sex with just anybody, but then you end up with who knows what kind of Antichrist. Last time Satan tried that, he got a son who was half goat. He wasn't so much an evil powerhouse as a mutant who couldn't stop eating tin cans."

"Oh, right! I forgot about that."

"When Satan gets loose on earth, it's after a dry spell and he goes a little nuts, you know? It's like beer goggles, but a billion times worse."

"Beer goggles? I guess you'd call it that if you thought a goat was a supermodel."

"You know he's still embarrassed by that whole thing," Yaman said. "And he swears to this day that goat was Giselle. Or was it a gazelle? I forget."

"That's what they always say when they get caught," Shadow said. "No one wants to be stuck in public with a goat."

The two demons watched as Constance skidded out of her driveway and floored the gas, screeching off down the road, her eyes like saucers and her skin pale from shock.

"We should follow her," Yaman said.

"Okay," Shadow said, starting to float over the road. "Say, didn't the goat Antichrist get distracted from taking over the world because he was too busy eating most of a recycling plant?"

"Something like that."

"That's pretty funny."

"Satan doesn't think so. And you're a Glutton. You should be sympathetic about food issues."

"Humph," Shadow grunted. "I may be a Glutton, but I have standards. Empty aluminum cans? I'd have to be starving."

"You're always starving."

Shadow seemed to think about this a moment. "Good point."

Yaman wrinkled his nose. His partner's breath smelled like roadkill.

"Have you been eating squirrels again?"

"Possums," Shadow replied. "And one armadillo."

"You're really disgusting."

"You're the one who eats hot dogs. That's what I call disgusting. You have any idea what they put in those things? Anyway, you know I prefer to eat people. But you said to hold off a while. I don't know how much longer I can wait—I'm so bored. And when I get bored, I get hungry."

"You're hungry all the time—you don't need a reason." Yaman pulled out a copy of the latest *People* magazine. "Want to play a game of Guess Which Celebrity Sold Their Soul?"

"That's easy—it's *most* of them," Shadow said, as the two easily followed Constance's Camry as it swerved down the street and out to Route 9.

"Yeah, but bet you don't know which ones sold them to me, *personally.*"

"You don't know any celebrities." Shadow sounded doubtful.

"Do so. Pride demons always get the celebrities. You Glutton types just get CEOs and politicians. *Bor*-ing."

"Hey—I turned William Howard Taft. He was the twenty-seventh president of the United States."

"Yeah, which is why he weighed almost three hundred fifty pounds and is famous for getting stuck in bathtubs."

"And then there was Henry the Eighth," Shadow said. "He was totally mine."

"You turn anyone that *didn't* weigh more than three hundred pounds?"

Shadow thought about this a moment. "Nope," he said.

"Well, I can show you at least five people in this magazine who are my turns," Yaman said, sniffling a little as he tried to head off a sneeze. "And all of them are hot."

"Anorexic, you mean."

"To you, anyone who isn't morbidly obese is anorexic."

"Same difference." Shadow glanced down at Constance's car. Her driving was so erratic, she nearly blew through a stop sign. "She's going to have a wreck at this rate."

"Prophets are always terrible drivers," Yaman said. "You try driving and having a vision. It's like ten times worse than talking on your cell phone. And none of them can parallel park."

"Speaking of visions, when *is* she going to have one?"

"I don't know," Yaman snapped. "Do I look like a prophet to you?"

"You look like a demon with a dogwood allergy."

Yaman let out a loud sneeze. "All demons are allergic to dogwoods."

"I know," Shadow said, and sniffled. "And they're everywhere here, and I'm all out of Claritin."

"It's not easy to get any, either, since they make you pay for them one box at a time," Yaman said.

"Maybe we should just go eat someone who's taken some."

"That's your answer for everything."

Shadow paused, and then asked, thoughtful, "You think we'll get overtime pay?"

"I doubt it."

"Man, I need a new job."

"Oh yeah, I'm sure you can get one, too. 'Hi, I'm a shape-shifting Glutton demon who doesn't know Windows, but who can eat a small city.' Why don't you just post your resume on Monster?"

"Maybe I will."

"You know there are no actual monsters on Monster," Yaman pointed out.

"Well, there should be. Why do they call it that, then?"

"Hell if I know. But if you're really thinking of changing jobs, you should read this," Yaman added, handing Shadow a copy of *Who Moved My Cheese?*

Shadow gobbled it up in one bite and swallowed it whole.

"I said *read*, not *eat*," Yaman grumbled.

"What? It said it was about cheese."

"That's a metaphor. It's about business," Yaman said.

"Another self-help book?" Shadow made a face. "No wonder it tasted so bad."

"Hey, I think the prophet is making a stop," Yaman interrupted, as he glanced down below.

They watched as the gold Camry pulled into the driveway of a small house with a big sign out front reading PSYCHIC READINGS: DISCOVER YOUR FUTURE TODAY! It was purple and silver, adorned with sequined stars.

"Okay—our prophet is going to see a psychic? I *told* you she wasn't the real deal," Shadow said.

"That's not just some random psychic, that's her mother, stupid," Yaman snapped, annoyed.

"So our prophet caught one sight of a ghost and ran home to Mama?" Shadow let out a superior-sounding grunt. "This is going to be way easier than I thought."

"That is, if she ever has this blasted vision."

"Say, you done with that *People* magazine? Can I have it?" Shadow asked, hopeful.

"Not if you're going to eat it," Yaman said.

"Dammit," Shadow grumbled.

Eight

Constance found herself at her mother's house, her heart pounding a mile a minute in her chest, wondering if she was going to hyperventilate. She hadn't even meant to drive over to her mother's, but it made sense. Her mother was the only person she knew who actually believed in ghosts.

Constance looked up at the big sign in her mother's yard. Normally, she cringed with embarrassment at the sight of the big hand with the eye in the palm, but today it was kind of comforting. Constance was surprised her mother's neighbors put up with the sign, which looked like it ought to be at a carnival, not in a residential subdivision, but then again, Constance's neighbors proudly displayed an OU flag on their porch, which in this part of the country was sacrilege.

"I knew you were coming," Abigail said, the second she swung open her front door and saw her only daughter standing on the porch. Of course, this was what Abigail always said when Constance dropped by unannounced.

Not that it meant anything. Abigail was a good reader of people, but Constance didn't think she really had any psychic abilities. Unless you counted the ability to tell when the milk in the fridge had gone bad, or when you were wasting your time on a man.

As she stepped inside her mother's house, she was nearly strangled by the purple and silver glass beads hung in the archway. Being touchy already, Constance gave a little shriek and batted them away.

"They're for ambience," Abigail explained. Abigail was always adding something new and goofy to her house, where she gave tarot readings both in person and online at her website, FortunesByAbby.com. Her living room, and in fact her entire house, was a shrine to all things New Age. She had a statue of Buddha sitting in her living room on top of her television, and an entire library of books on four bookshelves, each one arranged by subject: the zodiac, tarot card reading, and the power of crystals.

Of course, this was all gravy to the main attraction: her reading room, which was covered from floor to ceiling in purple velvet with a table, chairs, and an actual crystal ball that she bought at a garage sale in Texarkana. Abigail charged clients $50 for a personalized reading, $100 for an extensive astrological forecast, and $150 for various spells and charms, usually about helping to keep your man faithful or punishing the men who weren't.

The reading room was one of many reasons Constance never invited friends over to her house when she was growing up. It was also the reason her house was always egged on Halloween.

"Mom, I . . ." Constance began.

"No—don't tell me," Abigail said, putting her long silver acrylic nails to her forehead and shutting her eyes, as if she were going to read Constance's mind. She pursed her overly glossed lips and looked as if she were concentrating. Her eyes were darkened with a deep purple eye shadow. Given the makeup and the nails, Constance guessed she had a client today.

"I'm getting a vision," she said, rubbing her temples like she was getting a migraine.

"Mom, would you stop?"

"I see you . . . and Jimmy . . ."

Constance paused a second, wondering if her mom really *was* psychic. Her mom cracked a heavily made-up eyelid to see if she was warm. Sensing she was on to something, she continued. "And that no-good Jimmy has finally signed the divorce papers! You're here because you need a notary."

In addition to being a (bad) psychic, Abigail was also one of the county's few official notaries. In a place as small as Dogwood County, people often held down two jobs.

"Not even close." Constance couldn't believe her mother hadn't heard the news yet.

"Jimmy didn't sign?" Abigail said, face falling. Abigail had never been a fan of Jimmy's. But apparently, the county's psychic was also the only living person in the area who hadn't heard he'd been murdered.

"You haven't heard?" Constance asked, amazed.

"Heard what?"

Realizing that her mother had no idea about the murder, her being a suspect in it, or Dead Jimmy making an appearance in her kitchen, Constance filled her in.

Her mother let out a low whistle, and shook her head slowly back and forth. "I never liked Jimmy, but I sure didn't wish him dead," Abigail said. "At the most I wished him a broken leg."

Constance sent her a look.

"What? You know that's what he deserved. Especially after he nearly burned down my house." Abigail was referring to the time when Jimmy tried to fix her air-conditioning and started a small fire in her attic, which he managed to put out by suffocating it with a box of Abigail's prized Halloween decorations. The decorations were ruined, and her house smelled like smoke and burnt papier-mâché for weeks.

"So you say it was a demon who killed Jimmy? That is worrisome."

"But what about me seeing his *ghost*?" Constance asked, trying to steer her to the bigger issue at hand.

"I'd say it's about time," Abigail said. "You've *finally* got the Sight."

Constance sighed. Abigail believed the women in her family all had the Sight, a gift that showed itself at different times for every woman. Typically, it meant being able to see the occasional ghost and be able to predict odd, completely useless happenings like when the house might need new siding. But Constance didn't believe in this at all, especially since Abigail couldn't predict much of anything except when her soaps would be on.

"Here we go again. Mama, you don't have the Sight.

If you did, you might've foreseen Daddy running off with the roller-skating waitress from Sonic."

"We're all blind when it comes to love," Abigail said.

"And presidential elections. And major weather catastrophes. And lotto numbers. And basically, anything at all that's worth a damn."

"Watch your language!" Abigail chided, causing Constance to let out a long, frustrated breath of air. She didn't normally cuss. But her mother's rantings about spirits and the Sight tended to bring out her worst side. "Besides, the Sight is what puts food on the table, lest you forget."

"How could I forget? Half the county thinks we're devil worshippers," Constance said, thinking about the first day of high school when Principal Thomas called her into his office and demanded to know whether or not she prayed to Satan. He made her promise she was a good Christian before he let her go to class.

"That's just the small-minded," Abigail said, waving her hand dismissively. "And now that you have your own vision, you'll see things differently. Maybe you'll even finally believe me when I say I see Digger."

Digger was Constance's pet terrier-pug mix who got flattened by a car when Constance was ten, shortly after Constance discovered she was allergic to dogs and they had to put him outside to stop her sneezing. She still felt a little responsible for his death, since it was her allergies that had evicted him from the safety of their living room couch.

"That dog is too dumb to know to go to the light," Abigail had said more than once. But Digger wasn't the only ghost Constance's mother saw. She also claimed to see other doomed pets, including two guinea pigs, three goldfish, five cats, and one ferret (all from various houses in the neighborhood).

"So you really do see Digger? That wasn't just something you made up?" Constance asked. Given the fact she'd seen her dead husband in her kitchen this morning, she wasn't sure now what to believe.

"He just dug up my begonias this morning," Abigail said, pointing out to her backyard where some of her flowers lay in disarray near her fence line. "Besides, I *see* that mangy mutt right this second. He's over by the magnolia tree, licking his boy parts at the moment."

"Ew," Constance said, wrinkling her nose.

"What? You would rather know he just tried to eat his own poop? That's what he was doing five minutes ago."

"*Mother.*"

Abigail shook her head and absently fluffed the bangs of her dyed blond hair, which were stiff with hair spray. "Well, you're one to talk," she said. "You've got your dead husband in your kitchen."

"Maybe I just imagined it," Constance said, trying to be reasonable.

"Oh, honey, you didn't imagine it," Abigail said, shaking her head. She gave Constance a brief look of pity. "I know it's hard for you, since you're the logical one in the family, but these things do happen."

Constance bit her lower lip. First her husband was murdered right in front of her by a man claiming to be a demon and then she saw his ghost? It was too much for one week.

"But what really worries me is that demon you mentioned," Abigail said. "Yaman, you said? I'm going to make a few calls to see if I can find out something about that demon."

"I'm sure he's not really a demon. He's probably a crazed serial killer or something."

"Don't be so sure," Abigail said, thoughtful. "Anyway, I know a woman in Pasadena who is an expert in demons. I met her at last year's psychic convention."

For once, Constance felt grateful that her mother's circle of friends tended toward the occult.

"You really think you could find out something?"

"Sure," Abigail said, patting Constance's hand reassuringly.

"I'm beginning to think maybe I imagined that part," Constance said. "I barely remember what the man looks like."

"Forgetting spells," Abigail said, nodding knowingly. "Evil spirits use them all the time. It's to fog their real intentions. And what did I tell you about Dogwood? It's like ground zero for their kind. And these dogwood trees aren't here by accident."

Constance had heard this a million times from her mother but never had reason to believe before now. Abigail had been trying to convince her since she was three that Dogwood County was some special mythical place. Apparently more than two hundred years ago, one of the first settlers of Dogwood, a Pastor Jeremiah Hicks—Constance's great-great-great-great-great-great-and-then-some uncle—claimed to have seen the devil at the edge of the town. The devil tried to entice him to give up his soul. Pastor Hicks had resisted the temptation, and to help protect the other residents of Dogwood, he planted dozens of dogwood trees in the county to help repel the devil. Most historians thought Pastor Hicks was a little crazy but agreed his intentions were good. Today, the county was full of dogwoods, and they had become the focal point of a festival every fall. They were the only known species to bloom twice a year, once in the fall and once in the spring.

"You know that Christ's cross was made out of wood from a dogwood tree?"

"Yes, Mama, you told me this story a million times. And the tree felt bad for it, and so Christ took pity on the tree and said it would never again grow big enough to make a cross. And then it became some kind of religious symbol."

"More than a symbol," Abigail said. "Dogwoods repel demons. Why do you think I have so many in my yard?" She motioned outside, where the five dogwood trees along the perimeter of her yard were in full bloom. "It's the only reason we've kept those buggers out of here. For some reason, demons hate dogwood. It's like garlic to vampires. Still, for one of them to kill in broad daylight . . . it just doesn't make sense. Normally, they just want to buy souls."

"How do you know so much about demons, anyhow?"

"Demon Convention in Utah five years ago, remember?"

"This is just so much to process," Constance said, putting her head in her hands. "I just don't know if I can believe it."

"There are plenty of things you don't see in this world. Evil spirits take many forms. Demons, spiritual vampires, and don't get me started on the incubi."

"Please don't start," Constance said. Abigail had been claiming Constance's father was an incubus—an evil spirit that sucked the life out of you—ever since he up and left. Constance never thought she meant it literally. She always figured it was something her mother said to help her drum up sales of her protection spells. Constance was a God-fearing woman, but she didn't put much faith in talk of the devil or of hell. At least, not in the literal sense. Now, of course, she wasn't so sure.

"You are so cynical and critical, such a Virgo," Abigail said. "Why don't you just take things on faith once in a while?"

"I'm low on faith right now," Constance said. She felt like she'd been low on faith nearly her whole life. Every time she dug up a little faith, she was always disappointed. "There has to be a rational explanation."

Abigail just sniffed, unconvinced. "And what about Jimmy's ghost? You think there's a rational explanation for that, too?"

"Maybe I didn't see Jimmy's ghost at all. Maybe I just imagined it." Constance was starting to feel a little more reasonable now that she was surrounded by her mother's healing crystals and New Age insanity. She couldn't really be buying into all this. "Anyway, I have bigger problems. The new sheriff thinks I'm a murderer."

"Oh, well, just have Jimmy's ghost tell him you're not."

"Oh, sure, that'll go over like a lead balloon." Constance started to tell her mom the new sheriff was also Nathan Garrett, her sworn enemy, but something stopped her. That something was most likely the fact that her mother happened to have a sweet spot for Nathan. Of course, she didn't know about the virgin list.

"I can sense a lack of focus in you. You need to get yourself cleared. What you need is a good home-cooked meal."

"No thanks," Constance said, putting up her hands. Abigail was a vegan, and was currently on some kind of macrobiotic diet that involved eating grains that Constance had never heard of along with lots of kale. Any time she ate at her mother's house, she spent the next two days in the bathroom. This was one of the many reasons she'd learned to cook at age twelve. She was tired of eating kidney beans and raw cabbage.

"You know you're going to have to go back home and face Jimmy sometime," Abigail said. "He's not going to go anywhere until he tells you what he came to say."

Constance sighed. "I just don't believe I really saw him. I don't believe in ghosts."

"Well, it doesn't matter because they believe in you," Abigail said. "I'd get home quick before Jimmy makes a mess of your kitchen. Ghosts are clumsy, and I'm guessing Jimmy's even worse than most."

Constance felt her stomach lurch. She wasn't crazy about the idea of going back to her haunted house alone.

"Want me to go with you?" Abigail offered. "I don't have another client until three."

Constance felt a pang of guilt. No matter how much

she back-talked or doubted, her mother still came through for her when she needed it. She told herself she ought to be nicer in the future.

Constance nodded. "Yeah, thanks, Mom."

"Well, come on, then. Let's see what the fuss is all about."

Standing outside Constance's front door, Abigail put her hand on her daughter's shoulder and told her to relax.

"Deep breaths. Deep breaths. Dead Jimmy isn't going to hurt you," Abigail said. "So, just open the door and ask him what he wants."

"You sure you couldn't just go in for me?" Constance asked, hopeful. She didn't relish the thought of coming face-to-face with Dead Jimmy again. As much as she tried to tell herself she wasn't scared, she knew that was just a lie.

"If I went in there, I'd scare him off, and then he'd just come back when you least expect him, like when you're in the shower."

Constance thought about this. Facing her dead almost-ex husband while naked didn't appeal.

"Besides, if he tries anything funny, I'm here," Abigail said, sounding resolute.

"What could he try?" Constance wondered aloud, but then decided she didn't want to know. "Never mind. Okay, here goes."

Constance pushed open her door and found the living room empty. She sighed, a little relieved. Maybe she had really just imagined the whole thing. She was beginning to think maybe being crazy might be preferable to living in a world where she could see dead people.

"Call his name," Abigail muttered, giving Constance a little shove, nearly knocking her into her kitchen door.

"Jimmy?" she half whispered,

"Louder," Abigail urged, pushing her fully inside the kitchen.

"Jimmy!" Constance shouted.

"What!" Dead Jimmy yelled back, appearing beside her. "You don't have to shout, for heaven's sake."

Constance nearly keeled over, but then she got ahold of herself and gave Dead Jimmy a good long look. There he was, plain as day. He looked like the last time she'd seen him alive, complete with hazmat suit and goofy grin, and didn't look at all like a ghost, except for the fact he'd appeared out of nowhere.

"You're dead," Constance said, managing to keep her voice steady despite the fact that everything she thought she knew about the world was being turned upside down.

"Well, no duh, Connie," he said, calling her by the nickname she had hated since grade school. "Getting a screwdriver in the back by a demon will do that to a guy."

Constance blinked hard twice. The man who killed Jimmy really was a demon?

"What did you say?"

"I was killed by a demon—remember? He gave you a business card," Dead Jimmy reiterated. "You know— the guys with red horns. Except they don't always have horns." Jimmy looked around the kitchen like he'd never seen it before. "Say, we got any beer?"

"Is he here?" asked Abigail, stepping into the kitchen right behind Constance and following her line of sight. She wheeled this way and that and managed to walk straight through Jimmy. She clearly didn't see him.

"He's here, Mama. You walked through him."

"Your *mother*? You called *your mother*?" Jimmy was not a fan of his mother-in-law.

"Well, what did you expect me to do, Jimmy? You scared me half to death." Constance put her hands on her hips, as Jimmy slouched down into a kitchen chair.

"You tell that lousy son-in-law of mine that he'd better be nice, or I'm going to have him exorcised."

Constance opened her mouth to tell Jimmy, but he held up his hand. "I can hear her—*unfortunately*."

"Tell him to get to the point and tell you what he's doing here and then to *get on into the light*, or wherever it is he's going." Abigail was talking to a kitchen chair, but Jimmy had actually moved and was now behind her, making a face.

"I'm dying of thirst, Connie. Got any Buds left? Gimme one and I'll talk." Dead Jimmy crossed his arms across his chest and gave Constance his stubborn look. Constance sighed, went to the fridge and pulled out a can of beer, and set it on the kitchen counter. Jimmy attacked it like he hadn't seen beer in weeks. Of course, being a ghost made things complicated, as his hand kept going straight through the can like smoke through air.

"Dammit," he cursed.

"You're a ghost, Jimmy," said Abigail, watching the can. "Ghosts have to relearn how to pick things up. You're gonna have to try a different tack."

"Tell your mother I can handle this just fine," Dead Jimmy said tersely, as he tried again to pop the top and failed.

"Would you tell me what you're doing here?" Constance said.

"The Big Guy sent me," Dead Jimmy said.

"God sent you to earth to torture me?"

"Who said anything about God? I'm talking about Peter. Saint Peter, as in the guardian of the Pearly Gates and all that. And he's tall. Really tall. Big guy."

"You saw the Pearly Gates of heaven." Constance couldn't keep the skepticism out of her voice.

"Why wouldn't I go to heaven? I went to church every Sunday."

"And you slept through every sermon," Constance pointed out. "You snored. Loudly. Once, you even fell out of the pew, Jimmy."

Abigail sniffed. "He fell out of a pew?" she echoed. "What does that have to do with . . ." She was only hearing Constance's side of the conversation.

"Mama—just wait." Constance held up her hand.

"Apparently, God saw through all that, and my heart is true," Jimmy said. "Besides, if you get killed by a demon who didn't buy your soul, you get special compensation. Kind of like a consolation prize."

"That explains it, then."

"And anyway, he sent me here to give you a message." Dead Jimmy managed to pick up the can with both hands, and it hovered over the counter about two centimeters. "Ha!" he cried, before it came crashing down on the counter again. "Damnation."

"Here, let me do it." Constance grabbed the can and popped the top. "There. Now talk."

"Okay, so, Connie, what do you know about prophets?"

"Prophets? What are you talking about?"

"I'm talking about *you*, Connie. You're one of them. A prophet. It's like that guy, you know, Charlton Heston was a prophet."

"You mean Moses? The character he played in *The Ten Commandments?*"

"Right—yeah, whatever. So that guy was a prophet. But he's a major prophet. You're just a minor prophet."

"What does that even mean?"

"Heck if I know," Dead Jimmy said, giving up on lifting the can. He simply pressed his face down to it and tried to sip. "But I think it means you see stuff. Visions."

"Jimmy, I've never had a vision in my life."

"More's the pity," Abigail said, shaking her head.

"Well, better get ready, because you're going to start having them. And soon. Oh, and something else, too."

Dead Jimmy managed to tilt the can a little to get a sip of beer, but it fell right through him, passing through his body like through air and splashing on the ground.

Constance shook her head. Even dead, Jimmy was making a mess of her kitchen.

"What else?" Constance prompted.

"What else what?"

Constance exhaled a frustrated sigh. "What *else* were you supposed to tell me?"

"Oh, right." Dead Jimmy glanced down at his hand. For the first time, Constance realized there was scribbled writing there. "Peter made me write it all down," he explained, holding up his hand.

"Smart guy, that Peter," Constance said.

"Anyway, Peter says, 'Seek the French bulldog in a pink sweater. Heed what he sayeth.' "

"Did you say French bulldog?"

"Yep," Dead Jimmy said, nodding.

"What's that about a bulldog?" Abigail echoed.

"Okay, hang on a second," Constance said, her head spinning. "You're telling me that I'm a prophet, chosen by God, and my mission is to *find a French bulldog in a pink sweater*?"

"Hey, I'm just the messenger, Connie," Dead Jimmy said, holding up his hands. "And apparently, he's a *talking* French bulldog in a pink sweater, since you're supposed to heed what he says."

"Oh, well, that makes all the difference, then. Since he talks." Constance felt like her head was about to explode. This was not the kind of spiritual awakening she'd imagined might happen to her one day. She sighed. "Where am I supposed to look for this dog?"

"I dunno," Dead Jimmy said. "But apparently, he's going to explain everything. Like what you're supposed to do here."

"I'm supposed to do something besides find a talking lapdog?"

"Yep," Dead Jimmy said. "And once you do it, then I get to go through the Pearly Gates."

"And the dog is the key to getting you back where you belong?"

"That's right."

Constance let out a long sigh. "Fine, then. Let's find this dog."

Nine

Nathan Garrett sat in his office, going over and over the file he'd started on the Plyd murder. He had piles of bank records and credit card receipts stacked on his desk along with a list of at least ten people Jimmy had talked to the week he died, and none of them seemed likely murderers. But he planned to ask around today about the Plyds' marriage, or, more technically, their pending divorce, to see if there was anything unusual.

He yawned and rubbed his eyes, having not slept well the night before, his dreams rife with memories of the Libby Bell case—nightmares he hadn't had for months. He hadn't dreamt of Libby Bell since moving back home to Dogwood, and thought he'd put those nightmares to rest, but they had come back, more vivid and haunting than ever. He kept seeing the day he and his partner were chasing down that Libby Bell suspect in the abandoned warehouse in south Dallas, the day his partner had been shot and killed. The suspect—a known pedophile—wasn't supposed to have a gun, much less a semiautomatic that he'd emptied into the dark. Six of those bullets hit Nathan's partner in the chest, and without a vest on that day, he hadn't stood much of a chance.

Nathan saw himself holding on to his partner as he bled to death, and had a flash of memory of the suspect dropping the gun and running the other way, shoes clattering on the concrete. Nathan glanced up in time to see that suspect literally fly three stories straight up and out an open window.

Of course, later, he'd told himself the man couldn't have flown. That was impossible. He must have had a rope or some kind of contraption Nathan hadn't seen in the shadows. Something that made him levitate straight up in the air and hop out the window. Nathan had spent months telling himself he'd imagined what he'd seen, that it had been the traumatic stress of holding his dying partner in his arms. That was what the police psychiatrist had told him. Blunt trauma can affect what you think you see. But with Constance talking about demons with business cards, Nathan couldn't help but wonder—was it an illusion? Or had he really seen a man fly?

It was hard to let his cynical policeman's mind open up long enough to entertain the thought of the paranormal. But if Constance was innocent, that meant she was telling the truth, as hard as the truth was to believe. And a nagging voice told him there was much more to this case than met the eye.

Still, he wanted to find a reasonable explanation. One that would stand up in court, and not just in a psychiatrist's office.

He took the coroner's initial report out of the folder

and studied it. It wasn't the final report by any stretch, just the coroner's initial findings, but so far it looked like Jimmy had died from his single stab wound. This was a methodical murder, not a crime of passion. And some spouses who ended up killing their exes in a rage could stab them twenty or more times before they even realized what they were doing.

Nathan picked up the printout of Jimmy's month of bank records, but didn't find anything out of the ordinary. No big withdrawals of cash, which might point to an affair. Everything seemed normal, except for the amount of money Jimmy paid at repair shops. Looked like he ended up spending at least five hundred dollars a month having one thing or another fixed.

A knock at Nathan's door made him look up. The county judge was standing there, a Styrofoam cup of coffee in his hand, a knowing look on his face.

"Thought I'd find you working early today," the judge said. The county judge's full name was John Marshall, but no one called him that. Everyone just called him "Judge." Nathan noticed he was wearing his usual uniform of a white button-down shirt, jeans, and black cowboy boots so polished they shined. His salt-and-pepper mustache was neatly trimmed, and his chin looked freshly shaven, like he'd just come from the barber's down the street. "Going to arrest that poor widow today?"

"How come everyone keeps asking me that?"

"You think someone else did it?"

"I don't know yet."

"Well, Driscott thinks Constance is the only suspect."

Nathan rolled his eyes. Paul Driscott was Dogwood County's young district attorney. He'd already called Nathan three times asking for his leads. Anyone who had spent five minutes with Driscott knew he had plans to run for state senator, and after that, maybe U.S. representative, and nothing sold voters in Texas like being hard on crime. He'd been cutting his teeth on misdemeanors and small-time burglaries, waiting for the perfect death-penalty case, and now he might finally have one. Only Nathan wasn't so sure. What he did know was that he didn't want to turn Constance over to Driscott. Not yet. He'd prosecute his own grandmother if it would lead to a successful election campaign.

"Well, I hope you're not letting the fact it's a pretty girl you used to date get in the way of your judgment," the judge continued.

The judge had been in charge of the county for the last twenty years, and had known Nathan since he was in diapers. It was sometimes hard for Nathan to convince him he was an adult who knew what he was doing. It was one of the pitfalls of coming back to the small county where he'd grown up. Everyone over the age of fifty just saw him as the reckless teenager who ran through girls. It probably didn't help matters that when Nathan was twelve, he'd accidentally toilet papered the judge's house, being under the mistaken impression it belonged to Julie Carter, Dogwood Middle School's head cheerleader.

Right now, the judge gave him an assessing look. "Is it true you took the widow around in your Mustang and then didn't call her after?"

"That's ancient history."

"Not the way I hear it." The judge was still studying Nathan. "You know it might help folks to stop talking if you settled down and finally got married."

The judge had been hinting around that Nathan should settle down ever since he came home to Dogwood.

"Might convince people you are serious about being sheriff," he added. "And that it's not something you are just playing at."

Nathan wondered if the judge counted himself among those people who needed convincing. Nathan was tempted to bring up his Dallas experience—again—but knew it would do little good. It was like anything that happened outside Dogwood was irrelevant.

"I'll see what I can do about that, Judge."

"See that you do," he said, and then paused. "You know we got them movie stars flying in today. Shooting that movie out there at the Higgins Ranch."

Nathan would have to be dead not to know. Not to mention the judge himself had only told him a hundred times. The judge was proud of Dogwood being a movie shoot. He thought it would boost tourism.

"You still going to have time to pick up Dante London from the airport this afternoon?"

Dante London—America's new pop princess—was high on the judge's priority list. He wanted to give her a police escort to the set, and make sure none of the locals bothered her.

"Yes, Judge," Nathan said.

"You know, if you need help with the murder case,

we could call in some state troopers. I want you to be focused on the movie, and not distracted."

"I can handle them both," Nathan said.

The judge gave him a doubtful look. "Don't bite off more than you can chew, boy," he warned.

Nathan was beginning to think he should've listened to both his older brothers. They had told him that returning to Dogwood was like coming back to the scene of the crime and expecting not to get caught.

"I can handle this case," Nathan said.

The judge took a long drag of his coffee. "Well, son, see that you do. We don't want it to affect the movie."

"Yes, sir."

The judge stood and turned to go. He paused at Nathan's door.

"And don't think that because you're elected I can't run a recall," the judge said. "Just something to keep in mind."

"Is that a nice way of saying you can fire me anytime you feel like it?"

"Something like that," he said, and sauntered out. One of these days, Nathan thought, he was going to have to get around to apologizing for toilet papering the judge's house. Not that it would do any good.

Nathan sighed.

Maybe if he knew what was good for him, he'd go to Constance's house this morning and arrest her and make the judge and everyone else happy, since they'd already tried and convicted her. But that wouldn't be doing his job. He had to investigate all options before settling on the obvious. He started making a list of the last people who'd seen Jimmy alive, based on the credit card records. He decided he'd start by talking to all of them. With any luck, one of them might be suspect material.

"Excuse me?" Nathan asked the thirtyish, heavyset clerk at the checkout stand at the county's only big supermarket, Kroger. He was there to ask about a big purchase Jimmy had made the day before he died. It was probably just beer, knowing Jimmy, but he was covering his bases, just to make sure. The clerk was sporting a dye job gone wrong—it looked like she'd fallen into a peroxide bottle and then spilled strawberry syrup on her hair. She was also wearing black penciled lips and silver gloss, and the combination was some kind of awful.

She glanced up at him, recognition in her eyes, and Nathan felt a quick stab of panic. Surely they hadn't . . . dated?

"Why, look what the cat drug in," purred the clerk. He glanced down at the name tag she wore on her blue and white uniform. It said JENNIFER. That didn't help him in the least. He'd dated dozens of Jennifers. None of them looked like a goth strawberry shortcake, either, that he remembered.

"Hi, Jennifer," Nathan said, smiling. But she flinched a little at the use of her name.

"My boss calls me Jennifer. You used to call me Jenny."

"Right! Jenny," Nathan corrected. That still didn't narrow it down much. Of most of the Jennifers, only a handful were Jens, one was a full Jennifer, and the rest were Jennys. "You look, uh, great."

Jenny's eyes narrowed, and she put her hands on her hips.

"You don't remember me, do you?" she asked him, and he felt a tad guilty. It was true that he didn't remember her.

"No—Jenny—of course I do," he lied.

"Where did I live?"

Nathan squinted. "In town?" he ventured. Most everyone did.

"Lucky guess," she said. "But you still don't remember. I can tell. I'm Jenny Johnson."

Sadly, this still didn't ring any bells. Nathan studied Jenny's face carefully. It looked familiar, but damned if he could place it. He glanced down at her fingernails and was shocked to find them about an inch too long and painted a sharp black and pink. She gave him a look of disbelief when she saw her name didn't register.

"Jenny Johnson! We dated for three months when you were a senior?"

Nathan was drawing a complete blank, and he was really starting to get embarrassed about it.

Jenny drew her mouth into a pout. "You said I was the best kisser you'd ever had!" she exclaimed, clearly holding on to the memory. Nathan, apparently, hadn't. He thought hard, and then suddenly remembered a vague date or two with a Jenny in high school. She'd been a straight redhead then.

"Jenny! You had red hair," he said.

"That's me!" She beamed. Then she frowned. "You know, you up and stopped calling me. I never knew why."

Nathan felt even more uncomfortable. That sounded

like him in his younger days. Why wasn't he nicer? He should've been nicer. To everybody—Constance and Jenny included. Then again, his brothers always told him that nice guys never got dates. And in his experience they were right.

"I'm sorry about that, Jenny," he said, wondering if he would have to apologize to half the female population of Dogwood before this investigation was over. "I was a bit immature back then."

"I'll say," Jenny added, but she was beginning to be appeased. Apparently, his smile still worked on her, even if it didn't work on Constance Plyd.

"So how are you, Jenny? What you been up to since high school?"

"Oh, nothing. Well, I did get married," she said, flashing him her ring. "You remember David Hayes?"

Nathan nodded. David was a tight end on the high school football team. He wasn't too smart, but he was nice.

"We got hitched a few years back. He's running a weed-and-feed business now, but work's slow. But I'm sure he wouldn't mind if we got together for a drink or something."

"Um . . ." Nathan said, stalling for time.

"I mean, we could have a little reunion. You know, for old times' sake. You remember what I used to do to you in the back of your Mustang?"

Nathan didn't remember, and didn't want to.

"Sorry, Jenny. I'm here strictly on business. I'm here to ask about Jimmy Plyd. Did you see him when he came in on Tuesday?"

"Maybe I did and maybe I didn't," Jenny said, crossing her arms, a little put out that her offer of drinks was rebuffed. "Besides, we all know that his wife killed him."

Nathan sighed. He'd interviewed at least five people that morning so far, and they'd all said the same thing. No matter how hard he tried to find another suspect, there just didn't seem to be one. Everyone in Dogwood had come to the same conclusion: Constance was guilty.

"How do you know that?"

"Well, wasn't anybody else in the house, was there? And I hear she said some guy in a black baseball cap did it, but that just sounds fishy to me. Everybody knows she just married Jimmy for the money, so it's not like she cared about him any. Besides, do you know her mother worships the devil? Maybe they gave him up in some kind of ritualized sacrifice."

"Jenny, Constance Plyd's mother does not worship the devil," Nathan said, annoyed. These were the same rumors that were going around before he left Dogwood. "She just reads tarot cards."

"Whatever you say," she said, doubtful. "And anyway, I heard Constance used to run around on Jimmy. And why wouldn't she? It's not like she loved him."

Nathan's eyes narrowed. He felt a tug at his stomach. Was it jealousy? "Constance was having an affair? You know who with?"

"No," Jenny said, smacking her gum. "It's just what people say."

"What people?"

Jenny squinted. "Just *people*."

"You remember what Jimmy bought on Tuesday?" he asked.

"Just some packs of Bud, some steaks, and some barbecue sauce, and a big bottle of lighter fluid," Jenny said, her annoyance with him overcome by her desire to gossip. "Oh, and four big fire extinguishers. Said he always needed them whenever he was going to grill, which he was going to do after he signed the divorce papers."

"Did he say anything else?"

"Said he was glad to be getting rid of the Magnolia Café," she said. "Said it was losing money faster than you could say boo."

"The café was in trouble?"

"Well, we had a couple of fast-food places open up near the interstate, not to mention that new Cracker Barrel that opened up last summer," Jenny said. "Doesn't look good for the café. But that's what happens when you worship the devil."

Nathan sighed. "Jenny, Constance does not worship the devil."

"Whatever you say," Jenny said, doubtful. "Say? Did you know Dante London is supposed to be in town today? Have you seen her?"

"Not yet."

"Oh my God, I am *such* a fan. And that Corey Bennett—he's so hot. He's in the movie, too, isn't he? You know he was Sexiest Man Alive last year."

"So I heard."

"I'm headed to the set the second I get off. I hear they're looking for extras on the movie."

"Good luck," Nathan said, thinking she'd need it. "And thanks for the information, Jenny."

"You leaving so soon?" she called as he made his way out the door. "You call on me if you want to get that drink sometime. I'm at Branson's on Thursdays!"

As Nathan was walking to the parking lot, his cell phone rang. He looked at the caller ID and saw it was the station.

"Sheriff?" Ann, the dispatcher, said after he flipped open his phone. "You sitting down?"

"What's going on, Ann?"

"We got that fax from Liberty Mutual you were waiting on—you know, the insurance policy for Jimmy Plyd?"

"Yeah," Nathan said, swinging into his police truck and shutting the door. "What's the amount?"

"You sitting down?"

"Yep."

"It's five million dollars."

Nathan froze. Surely he hadn't heard right.

"Did you say five *million*?"

"That's right, Nathan. Five million big ones," Ann said, and then paused for it to sink in. "So? Gonna arrest that widow today?"

"Ann," Nathan said in a tone that implied it wasn't her business to know.

"I'm just asking—the life insurance seems like evidence, and you know that the Magnolia Café is in trouble."

Was he the only one who didn't know that in Dogwood? "Where'd you hear that?"

"Jimmy told just about everyone last week," Ann said. "Short of putting up a billboard on Route Nine, he pretty much broadcast it to anyone who'd give a listen. He thought it made Constance look bad, and he was sore at her for getting a divorce."

"Sore? Why?"

"Well, 'cause obviously, she was way out of his league, and it only took her nearly a decade to figure it out."

That Nathan agreed with.

"So? Are you going to arrest her yet?"

"Not yet, Ann. Not yet."

"Well, you might want to head to the airport, then," she said. "Dante London's plane is headed in early. Judge says you keep her waiting a single minute, and you're fired, though I think he was kidding."

"I bet he wasn't," Nathan said, turning over his ignition and steering his truck to the road.

Ten

When Constance was a little girl, she would sit in the back of the church on Sunday and stare at the stained-glass window of the Virgin Mary, and ask her to give her a sign. Not a big one, just a little one, something to let her know that she wasn't all alone and that her praying meant something. A butterfly would do, flying over the chapel eaves, or a flicker of the lights above their heads, or a candle going out on the altar. Something. Anything to show that somebody up there was listening.

But no matter how hard Constance prayed, she never got her sign.

Constance decided after a while that maybe there was someone listening to her prayers and maybe there wasn't, but there was no way she'd ever know for sure.

And now, here was her almost-ex husband's ghost, sitting shotgun in her gold Camry, proof, at long last, that God existed.

She wondered if this was his idea of a joke.

"I don't see why you can't just open this beer for me,"

Dead Jimmy said for the hundredth time, pointing to the can in her drink holder.

"Because, Jimmy, you can't drink it. You're dead. And I'm not going to be driving down the highway with an open can of Bud." Constance sighed. This was supposed to be her spiritual awakening, what with being in the presence of an actual ghost. She never expected her glimpse into all things otherworldly would involve a conversation about Budweiser.

"I can *so* drink it. I know I can. I just need practice." Dead Jimmy looked at the beer longingly. "I never thought I'd have to do without Bud. It's kind of sad. Like giving up the love of my life or something."

"Maybe if you'd drunk less Bud, you wouldn't have broken so many things. You ever think of that?"

"Maybe, but my life would've been a lot emptier without it," said Dead Jimmy, focusing again on his beer can. "So where did you say we are going, anyway?"

Constance wasn't due back to the Magnolia Café until dinnertime, not that there'd be a big rush, anyway. Jose had told her on the phone that the customers were still staying away, so she'd spent the afternoon with Dead Jimmy. So far, they had dropped by the only pet store in Dogwood and the pound, and neither one had French bulldogs, much less talking ones in pink sweaters. Now they were headed to see Mae Kenneth, Dogwood County's most famous dog breeder, who happened to specialize in French bulldogs and Welsh terriers. One of her terriers actually placed in Westminster. She was the county's premiere dog expert. Her house sat on ten acres, and as Constance pulled into the drive, she noticed the backyard was a patchwork of dog obstacle courses, complete with small rings, little platforms, and poles for racing around. The porch was lined with ceramic casts of little bulldogs and terriers.

"Don't do anything to embarrass me," Constance told Dead Jimmy as the two made their way to the front door.

"Like what?" Dead Jimmy asked, giving himself a good scratch.

Just then, a Welsh terrier tore out of the backyard and came at them like a bat out of hell, barking and baring its little teeth. The thing was barely bigger than a roll of paper towels, but it looked ticked off for sure.

"What the hell?" Dead Jimmy exclaimed, and just when Constance thought she might have to kick the dog in self-defense, it collapsed on the ground by her feet and started wagging its tail and licking her shoes like it was her best friend.

The front door swung open then, and Mae Kenneth stepped on the porch. She was a tall and broad woman with shock red hair who was wearing a bright blue muumuu trimmed with little cut-out dogs on the collar and matching blue sandals. The bright red hair made her age hard to guess, but Constance put her somewhere between forty and fifty-five.

"That's Caitlin Elizabeth Victoria," she said, grabbing the black and tan terrier and tucking her under her arm. "Sorry about that—she's nearsighted and pretty much blind as a bat. She likes people, but only when she gets close enough to smell them."

Caitlin sniffed the air where Dead Jimmy was standing and gave a little growl.

"Yikes," Dead Jimmy said, taking a step back.

"Caitlin! Be nice," her owner scolded, giving her a little shake. "So? What can I do you for?"

"I called on the phone? It's Constance Plyd and I'm looking for a French bulldog."

"For show? Or for home?"

"Uh, home," Constance said.

"Well, you've come to the right place," Mae Kenneth said. "Come on in."

Inside, Mae's house was full to bursting with all things dog. Terriers and bulldogs were on every available surface, even on the throw pillows of the couch and the big wool rug in the living room. On the mantel stood rows of dog trophies, and above the fireplace, a painting of two French bulldogs dressed like Spanish conquistadors. Barking seemed to come from every room, and Constance's feet were suddenly tangled up by a rush of little French bulldog puppies, each one giving happy little yaps as they jumped at her ankles. Everywhere there was the hint of wet-dog smell, and every available surface seemed to sport a thin layer of dog fur. Being closed in with so much dander made Constance's eyes and nose itch. She tried to delicately peel the puppies from her leg without looking like she was doing so, and dug around in her purse for a Kleenex.

"Cute little buggers," Dead Jimmy said.

"Do you have any full-grown dogs I could adopt?" Constance asked, trying to suppress a sneeze as she swiped at her nose.

"Sure, sure," Mae said, leading her back to the kitchen. The teapot was covered with a giant cozy in the shape of a terrier, and all her pot holders were shaped like French bulldogs. "I only have a couple of adults who aren't for breeding, but you can take a look if you want. There's Lucy," she said, pointing to a French bulldog curled in the corner of the kitchen who didn't bother to raise her head when they came in the room, "and Napoléon." She pointed to another dog sitting near the front door. He looked to be at least ten pounds overweight, and gave a loud bark. He sat sloppily, with one foot sprawled out in one direction and the other collapsed under his potbelly. Constance studied each one carefully, hoping that one of them might give her a sign, like a wink, or a wave, or even an actual word—something to show they were the dog she was looking for. But she got nothing but blank dog stares.

"This might seem like an odd question, but do you have any dogs with pink sweaters?" Constance asked. She wasn't about to ask if any of them talked.

"Pink sweaters?" Mae echoed, confused. "Um, no, but you can buy that sort of thing online. There are designer dog clothes labels now, you know."

"Um, right, I was just wondering if you happened to have one with a pink sweater already."

"No, I'm sorry," Mae said, giving her a suspicious look.

"And are any of your dogs, uh . . . especially talented?" This was as close as Constance was going to get to asking her if any of her dogs spoke English.

"Oh, they're *all* talented," Mae gushed, and went on to list all the tricks of her brood, and how the shape of their legs and wide set of their eyes were markers of a pure breed. It was clearly a subject Mae was fond of, because she talked at length, down to the specifics of the breeding habits of Napoléon. "Of course, he developed testicular cancer last year," Mae said. "And we had to have him neutered."

"Ouch," Dead Jimmy said. "Tough blow."

Constance did her best to ignore him. She sniffled a little, trying to keep her runny nose under control, and rubbed at one eye.

"You have a cold?" Mae asked her, concerned, holding out a box of tissues in a ceramic tub shaped like a French bulldog.

"Just allergies," Constance said, taking a tissue and blowing her nose.

"I hope not to the dogs," Mae exclaimed.

"Er, uh, no, no," Constance said, twisting a strand of her hair. "So, uh, tell me more about the dogs. Are they, um, particularly . . . religious?"

"I don't know what you mean by religious, but French bulldogs are very smart," Mae continued. "They're also very easygoing with fantastic temperaments. Don't pay attention to the history of the name—you know, they became known as French bulldogs because they were once favored by French prostitutes."

"You don't say!" Dead Jimmy exclaimed.

"Why was that?"

"Well, they were easygoing and didn't mind taking short naps in hotel rooms," Mae Kenneth said.

"Well, I'll be damned," Dead Jimmy said, and let out a low whistle.

"But then the artistic types in France began to adopt

them, too, to show how daring they were," Mae continued. "And it looks like all these years later our celebrities are doing the same. You know, I hear the French bulldog is the new Chihuahua. Dante London has one. You know she's coming here to film that movie. I'm hoping to get a glimpse of her bulldog. I hear she's a fine specimen. Wait, I have a picture here somewhere."

Mae rummaged around the ceramic terrier-shaped magazine holder by her couch and pulled out a new copy of *People* magazine. Mae's hands barely covered the ample cleavage of Dante London, the barely legal pop-singing sensation who was threatening to take Britney Spears's place as America's pop princess with her smash single "Devil Made Me Do It." Dante was from a small town in West Virginia, and had more boobs than brains. The cover blared "I'm still a virgin!" which was amazing considering that in her last video she'd rolled around wearing nothing more than a red latex bikini and sequined devil horns in a giant tub of cherry Jell-O.

Mae held up the cover of the magazine, and Constance nearly froze on the spot. In the crook of Dante London's arm was a French bulldog—wearing a fuzzy pink sweater.

"Hey—*there* it is," Dead Jimmy said, pointing.

"Um, Mae, do you mind if I take a look at that?" Constance asked.

"Oh, sure, here you go," Mae said, putting the magazine down on the coffee table. "Now make yourself comfortable while I go get us some sweet tea."

Constance leaned forward as Mae retreated into the kitchen, and picked up the magazine.

And then something strange happened. The very second she touched the picture of Dante London, she felt like she'd been shocked by an electric current. Her eyes widened in surprise, and then they glazed over and rolled back in her head. She felt a surge of energy go through her, and she was frozen to the spot. And then the images came running past her eyes like TiVo on fast-forward.

She was having a Vision with a capital *V.*

And it was as vivid as it was sudden: Dante London, barely legal pop princess and queen of all things white trash, was destined to become the mother of the Antichrist.

Eleven

"Can we run the siren, y'all? Like, I've totally never heard a siren before," Dante London said to Nathan, who had picked her up in his squad car from the Dogwood County Municipal Airport after her personal jet had landed on the small runway. She had emerged from her plane wearing shiny aviator sunglasses, a fur bikini top, cutoffs, and UGG boots.

"No," Nathan said. He was more than a little annoyed to be on escort duty, but the judge had ordered him to do it, and he couldn't trust anyone else, especially Deputy Robbie, to make sure that Dante London got safely and without undue hassle from the airport to the set of her new movie, *Devil's in the Details*, at the Higgins Ranch.

Dante London stuck her considerable lower lip out in a pout.

"*Pretty* please?" she asked him, batting her eyelashes. Nathan thought she'd probably practiced this look in front of a mirror when she was eight and perfected it a decade later. He was sure this worked on most men, but he simply wasn't interested. He'd dated plenty of Dante London types in his past: pretty, spoiled, and without a single coherent thought in her head. He'd been down that road and he had no intention of going back.

Objectively, London *was* incredibly attractive, which was why she was voted by *Details* magazine as the Sexiest Jailbait in America three years in a row (pretty much until she turned legal last month). It didn't help that despite claiming to be a virgin, she liked to parade around in latex, leather, and in one case, nothing but red body paint on MTV's VMAs. But Nathan knew she was a headache just by looking at her, and he planned to stay a million miles away.

"The siren is for emergencies only," Nathan told Dante, who slumped back in her seat and crossed her arms across her chest. She looked like his niece—back when she was small enough to throw temper tantrums at Mega-Mart.

"That is, like, *so lame*, y'all," she said, wrapping her gum around her finger and then feeding it back into her mouth. Nathan wondered why she used the word "y'all" when there was only him in the car. He wondered if she knew it was supposed to be used when referring to more than one person. Then again, grammar was probably not her strong suit.

Out of the corner of his eye, Nathan saw a tan furry blur: Dante's pet of the month, a French bulldog named Pinky. It barked loudly from its seat, and started bouncing up and down and trying to scratch off its tiny pink sweater. Nathan wasn't an animal person.

"That dog had its shots?" he asked Dante.

"Are y'all policemen types always so much fun?" Dante asked. Nathan was surprised she actually grasped the concept of sarcasm. He said nothing, and she crossed her arms and stared out the window. The only sound for thirty seconds was her snapping gum.

Nathan didn't care if he was being rude. Having her quiet was a nice change of pace from her babbling on about Corey Bennett, like she had since the airport. Apparently, she was under the impression that he cared about how excited she was to meet him.

In *Devil's in the Details,* Corey Bennett played a washed-up bull rider who fell in love with a diner waitress played by Dante and then one—or both, Nathan couldn't remember—sold their soul to the devil to find love, or some such nonsense. He couldn't be bothered to keep up with the details. He did remember there was a rumor circulating that Dante initially took the script because she thought she'd be playing Flo from *Alice* and could get to say the line "Kiss my grits."

"Have you seen Corey Bennett, y'all?" she'd asked Nathan the minute she got into the car. "I mean, like, *oh my God*, he is, *like, such a freakin' fox*! I mean, if I *was* planning on losing my virginity soon, which I am, like, *totally not*, I would so give it up to him, you know? Of course, he has a girlfriend, that actress Jennifer what's-her-name, and I'm not a boyfriend stealer. I'm just saying that he is h-o-t, *hot*, you know?"

Nathan, who was almost at a loss for words, just stared at Dante London and told her to fasten her seat belt.

Now Nathan's radio crackled to life on his dashboard, and Robbie's unmistakable voice came through.

"Nathan? Do you copy? Ten-four."

No matter how often Nathan tried to tell Robbie not to call him directly on the radio (to instead go through Ann) or to use his name on the air, Robbie just didn't bother to do as he was told. It took an extra step on his part, and extra steps were not something Robbie was going to do. If you got one step out of him that was a miracle.

"Call dispatch. Ten-four," Nathan said into the CB. He couldn't keep the annoyance from his voice. He was pretty sure Robbie was just trying to find out what was happening with Dante London. He'd made it no great secret he was a fan. It was one of many reasons why Nathan had refused his request to escort the pop princess himself.

"Dispatch told me to stop bugging her and talk to you, uh, ten-four."

Great, now even Ann was working against him. "Go ahead, ten-four."

"You sure you don't need backup with Red Dress, over?" Robbie said. Red Dress was the code name for Dante London, as in Devil in a Red Dress.

"No," Nathan said for the millionth time. "And if that's all, I need to get back to work."

"No, that's not all," Robbie said. "I was calling to tell you that Mel is out at Mae Kenneth's place. Constance Plyd is there and she had some kind of seizure or something. Mae called nine-one-one."

Nathan felt his stomach tighten. "Is she okay?"

Next to him, Pinky the Dog barked fast three times.

"Mel says yes, but if you want me to check on her, I will."

"I'll do it. I'm nearly done here." And with that, Nathan hit the gas, sending Dante hard against her seat and Pinky the Bulldog soundly against her lap.

Twelve

F inally," Shadow said, as he and Yaman watched Mel come and revive Constance. They had watched the vision unfold in her head, a perk of being a demon. They could see visions, but only if they were watching the prophet at the time.

"Told you she was the real deal."

"Well, can't blame me for doubting," Shadow said. "Took her long enough to get around to one."

"So, Dante London? Not a bad choice," Yaman commented, tapping the *People* magazine in his own hand.

"Well, she's better than a goat, that's for sure."

"It's perfect, really, when you think about it. Slutty virgin—just up Satan's alley."

"I bet you're going to tell me she's one of your turns."

"No, actually," Yaman said. "You know the mother of the Antichrist can't be a turn. She's got to be pure—at least, in the beginning."

"Guess I forgot that part," Shadow said.

"Well, it's hard to remember details when you're busy eating everything in sight." A big gust of wind blew then and Yaman grabbed the brim of his black baseball cap to keep it from blowing off.

Shadow nodded to the cap. "What's with the cap? You losing your hair?"

Yaman's hands went reflexively up to his head. "Why do you say that?"

"You and the baseball cap. I thought only guys who were losing their hair wore those."

"Ever heard of Ashton Kutcher?"

"Even I know the trucker hat thing is way over."

"Well, whatever, I'm not losing my hair."

"Why don't you show me, then?"

"I will not."

"You are totally going bald!"

"Am not!"

"There's always Hair Club for Men," Shadow said, and burst out laughing. "A bald Pride demon—oh, that's ironic."

"Would you shut up? Plenty of sexy guys are bald. Like Bruce Willis." Yaman held up a copy of *People* magazine to show the tiny picture of Bruce Willis in the upper left corner.

"Right, that's why all the movie stars who sell their souls don't immediately ask for a full head of hair first off."

"Let's just go find the general and report what we saw," Yaman said. "Then we wait for more orders."

"Says the demon who doesn't like to follow them."

"Well, we have to at least get them first and then we'll see if we follow them or not."

"Whatever you say—Baldie," Shadow said.

"Watch it," Yaman said. "I could completely annihilate you."

"Oh, I'm sure."

"You doubt me?"

"Well, I'm not too scared of Pride demons. You guys are always too busy arranging your hair to fight properly. Or, in your case, hiding the fact you don't have any."

"Argh, I have *hair*—I told you! And I can kick serious butt," Yaman said. "I killed the prophet's husband, remember?"

"Yeah, like a total sissy. One stab wound with a screwdriver?"

"It was what was handy, and one stab wound was all I needed. I'm efficient."

"Or you're just squeamish."

"Hey, I let go a world of hurt on Joan."

"Of Arc? You killed her?"

"Yep," Yaman said. "Who do you think lit the stake she was burned at?"

"Bet you had a lot more hair then," Shadow said.

"Oh, that's it, I give up," Yaman growled. "Are you coming or not? We have to go see General Asmodeus."

"Right behind you."

Thirteen

Constance came to in Mae Kenneth's living room with Mel standing over her and Dead Jimmy right beside her, a worried look on his face. Constance tried to sit up, but a blinding headache hit her like a Mack truck and her eyes filled with stars as she fell back on the terrier-shaped pillow.

"What happened?" Constance croaked, still disoriented and dizzy, her head filled with images of Dante London and the devil.

"Damn, girl, I thought you had a stroke or something," Dead Jimmy said, relieved. "What happened was you went down faster than a porn star with the cameras rolling. I thought you died!"

"Feels like I did," Constance said, holding her head, woozy.

"Feels like you what?" Mel asked her, glancing over to where Dead Jimmy was standing and then back to Constance, a weird look on her face. Constance realized Mel thought she was hallucinating. Mel couldn't see

Dead Jimmy. It was the problem with having your dead husband following you around—everyone else thought you were crazy.

"Like I died," Constance said to Mel, focusing on her.

"Well, you didn't die. You just fainted."

"I just came back with the tea and found her on the floor," Mae said. "Is she going to be okay?"

Mel released the blood pressure cuff around Constance's arm and gave her a hard look. "You might want to get checked out," Mel told Constance. "I'd go see a doctor if I were you. Could be a seizure or something more serious." Mel snapped her paramedic bag closed. "Otherwise, I say take it easy this afternoon. Drink lots of fluids."

A knock came at the door and Caitlin Elizabeth Victoria the Welsh terrier barked loudly, announcing another visitor. Mae stood and opened the door, and in walked Nathan Garrett as if he owned the place.

"She okay?" Nathan asked Mel, who nodded.

"Your suspect is just fine, Sheriff," Constance snapped. "No need to check on me."

"Well, I'm wondering what you're doing here, since you're allergic to dogs," Nathan said. "I'm surprised you didn't have an asthma attack."

"Allergic to dogs?" echoed Mae, as if that was the worst thing she'd ever heard.

"You remember that?" Constance snapped, surprised. He hadn't even remembered her name at the Jiffy Lube all those years ago, and now he suddenly remembered she had allergies?

"I remember a lot of things about you," Nathan said, and the way he said it made Constance blush up to her ears.

"What are you doing here, anyway?" Constance asked, glancing down at her lap and trying to regain her composure. "Worried that your number one murder suspect is going to up and die on you?"

"Murder?" echoed Mae Kenneth.

"I never said you were a suspect," Nathan said.

"Oh no, you just implied I killed somebody."

"Maybe you two should get a room," Mel suggested.

Nathan and Constance said nothing, just growled at one another.

"You going to arrest me?"

"No."

"Then I'm going to go home." Constance stood, still dizzy, but managed to take the few steps to the door without tripping. Her head felt like it was coming apart in big, heavy pieces, but she managed to get outside. Dead Jimmy was by her side. He was doing his best to help her, but since he couldn't actually hold on to her, it was more of a nice thought than actual help.

"You want me to drive?" Dead Jimmy asked, trying to be thoughtful.

"If you drive the way you open beer cans, then no," Constance said, holding her head. She grabbed her sunglasses from her bag to shade her eyes from the glaring sunlight and tried to focus on getting her key into the ignition. "I'll be okay."

When Constance got home, she found—in addition to the fact that her garage was still taped up with yellow police tape—her mother's car in the driveway.

"Abigail is here," Dead Jimmy said, frowning. "Mind if I wait outside?"

"That's probably best," Constance said, swinging open the back door.

Constance found her mother kneeling on her kitchen floor drawing a pentagram in permanent marker.

"Mama! What on earth are you doing?"

"It's for protection," Abigail explained, as if vandalizing her new linoleum was as ordinary as bringing over a cherry pie. Constance also noticed her mother had brought over a basket full of dogwood blooms. She had put a few of them around the edges of the pentagram. It looked like a satanic ritual designed by Laura Ashley.

"But, Mom . . ."

"You said a demon killed Jimmy, didn't you? Well, this is supposed to keep them away."

"That looks like the sign of the devil, Mom."

"Well, the exorcist in Pasadena said it would work like a charm," Abigail said, drawing a circle in thick black marker on her floor. "Besides, I think of the two of us I *am* the one with the certified degree in white witchcraft."

This was true. Abigail had taken a correspondence course online. She had a certificate held to her refrigerator with a magnet that said PSYCHICS DO IT BETTER THAN ANYONE ELSE.

"So, did you find the dog in the pink sweater?" Abigail said, sitting up on her haunches. For a second, Constance thought her mother might really be psychic.

"Sort of," Constance said. "Dante London has one. I saw it on the cover of *People*."

"Oh, then it should be easy to talk to him. Just get

past her three bodyguards and all the security, and you'll be fine."

"I know," Constance said, groaning. She held her hand against her head. Her headache from the vision hadn't gotten any better.

"What's wrong?" Abigail asked.

"I've got the worst headache and the Sharpie fumes aren't helping." Constance slumped down into her kitchen chair and started rubbing her temples. This was a headache worse than any hangover she'd ever had. Abigail's head shot up, and she studied Constance closely.

"You had one, didn't you?"

"Had one what!"

"A vision," Abigail said, standing and recapping her Sharpie.

Constance groaned and held her head. "I guess. Maybe. I don't know."

"You did!" squealed Abigail, clapping her hands together. "My baby had her first vision!"

Constance just put her head on the table and sighed.

"Now you know why I am always getting those migraines," Abigail said. "*Now* you know! I was beginning to think the powers skipped a generation, but now look at you. What did you see? My first vision was of Elvis. Did I tell you that? I was twelve, and I picked up his record in a record store and—*bam!*—I saw his whole life. From birth until . . . well, death, which isn't until next year."

"Mom . . ." Constance suddenly felt a pang of guilt for never believing her mother all those years. Constance thought she was just making it all up, and the headaches were just her way of not doing things she didn't want to do, like take Constance to the playground or cook dinner. But it turned out they were very, very real. "You know I never believed you."

"Well, I bet you believe me now," Abigail said. "Here, drink some Dr Pepper. It helps with the headaches."

Constance took the plastic bottle her mother handed her and smiled. She felt closer to her than she had in years. "Thanks, Mom."

"So? What was it? Elvis? No. John Lennon maybe? Or, no, Jimmy Hoffa? Tell me!"

"None of those things. I touched *People* magazine and got a vision of Dante London becoming the mother of the Antichrist."

Abigail let out a low whistle.

"Seriously?"

"Seriously."

Abigail slowly sat down in her chair, letting the information sink in. "Well, this is a lot more serious than a dog in a pink sweater."

"Tell me about it," Constance said. "But, maybe it wasn't real? Maybe it was just a dream or something."

"No," Abigail said, shaking her head. "No, my dear, you had a vision. I'd stake my crystal ball on it. You have to trust what you see. Those visions are true."

"How do you know?"

"Five generations of women can't be wrong," Abigail said.

"But Dante London as mother of the Antichrist? It's so hard to believe."

"Harder to believe than Elvis is an antiques gun

dealer in Albuquerque?" Abigail asked, referring to her own first vision.

"I guess not," Constance said.

"Well, we have to do something about this Dante London girl," Abigail said. "Tell somebody."

"Who?"

"Maybe Pastor Allen?" Pastor Allen was the liberal Methodist preacher in town. He was open-minded, true, but he also didn't believe in literal translations of heaven and hell.

"I don't think he believes in the Antichrist."

"True. Maybe someone else." Abigail got a far-off look while she thought.

"So, Mama, how many of these visions am I going to have?" Constance asked, bringing her back to the present.

"I had one every month. But for you—who knows? Your grandmother had one every week, and her mother had one every day."

"Every *day?*" Constance had a flash of having the worst headache of her life every afternoon from here on out. It was enough to make her crazy just thinking about it. "How did she cope?"

"She drank—a lot," Abigail said.

"Great."

Abigail sent her daughter a sly look. "So, I bet that vision of yours didn't have lotto numbers in it, did it?"

Constance blushed. "No," she said.

"Or a weather report?"

Constance shook her head, embarrassed about all the years she'd spent teasing her mom about the randomness of her visions.

"See? You can't choose what you see," Abigail said. "Your visions choose you. And in your case, they have to do with the devil. Maybe that's what the minor prophet stuff is all about."

"But what do I do about it?"

"You still haven't talked to the pink sweater dog," Abigail suggested. "Maybe you should start there. But first, I'd lie down for a while, or that headache will never go away. And you've got Jimmy's funeral tomorrow, don't forget."

"The funeral! Oh Lord," Constance groaned, throwing her arm over her eyes. "I nearly forgot."

"Easy to do when the deceased is always with you. Oh! And I almost forgot. My friend in Pasadena emailed me some stuff about Yaman," Abigail said, grabbing her purse and digging around until she found some papers.

Constance took the pages, a chapter devoted to "Yaman: The Killer of the Tibetan God of Death," and despite her headache, she tried to focus. When she turned the page and saw a rough drawing of the demon, she nearly jumped out of her skin. It was a pretty scary-looking monster with multiple arms.

"He killed the Tibetan God of Death and is known for wearing a necklace of human heads?" Constance shuddered. "I don't remember him wearing any heads. Or having multiple arms."

"Sometimes people exaggerate a little," Abigail said. "Now, you better go lie down."

"I can't," Constance said. "I've got to get to the café."

"You can't take one day off? That restaurant is going

to be the death of you," Abigail said. "You spend your whole life there."

"That's because it is my life," Constance said as she walked out the door.

Constance took over her shift as manager and hostess at the Magnolia Café, but business was so slow it did little to take her mind off the whirlwind of events over the last two days. It didn't help that the few stragglers who came in for dinner came not for the food, but to get a glimpse of her and gather up some gossip about the would-be Dogwood County murderer. The gossips came, and spent more time eyeing her than their plates, and she felt more than a little like a bug under a microscope. Even when she retreated into the kitchen—normally her safe haven—she found herself distracted by the images she'd seen of Dante London and the devil. Even whipping up a batch of pecan pies didn't help take her mind off her vision, which seemed to replay endlessly in her head. It was so vivid, and yet she had her doubts it was an actual vision of the future. Maybe she'd just heard too much about Dante London over the last few weeks, given that she'd been the talk of the county since news of the movie shoot broke. She turned the vision over, again and again, in her mind, and it always came out the same way: Dante and the devil.

She was hoping not to think about it for a few hours, but the slow night at the café meant she had few distractions and could think of little else. For the first time in a long while, she watched the clock tick by, hoping for closing time. When it came, she hurried home.

She had an even harder time falling asleep, and once she did, she slept fitfully, her sleep marred by dark dreams, and she was startled awake early the next morning by the sound of howling. She sat up with a start, unsure of what it could be, but soon realized it was a dog. In fact, a small one, by the sound of it.

"What the Sam hell is making all that racket?" complained a sleepy Dead Jimmy, who sat up next to her and rubbed his eyes.

"Jimmy!" Constance cried, pulling up the sheets to cover her very thin nightgown. "You're not supposed to be sleeping in here."

"Sorry, Connie, old habits," Dead Jimmy said, trying to look innocent but failing.

"Get out," Constance said, pointing to the door. He might be dead, but it didn't mean Constance was going to let him see her nearly naked. They had been sleeping in separate bedrooms for the last six months, and she didn't want to backslide now that he happened to be a ghost.

"Fine," Dead Jimmy said, yawning. He stretched, and then disappeared.

Constance glanced around the room. "You *better* not still be here," she said. "And you *better* not watch me shower, either."

"Don't flatter yourself!" Dead Jimmy shot back. He was invisible, but there all the same.

Constance's face flushed red and her temper flared. "I knew you were still here! Jimmy—go downstairs—*now!*"

"Okay, okay, I'm going."

Constance waited, and then she heard the sound of the refrigerator door downstairs open and shut. She guessed he was in the kitchen. She'd never imagined her almost-ex husband could be more annoying dead, but there it was.

Constance fell back into her bed and sighed. She was still trying to make heads or tails of this whole mess, and she wasn't sure she understood any of it. The barking started up again—a high-pitched yipping—and she put a pillow over her head. None of her neighbors had small dogs. She figured it must be a stray. With a sigh, she threw off the covers, and grabbed her terry-cloth robe, slung it around herself, and stomped downstairs. The yipping got louder, and it sounded like the dog was sitting on her front porch. She swung open the front door, and there, sitting on her welcome mat, was a small tan French bulldog, wearing a fuzzy pink turtleneck and staring straight at Constance.

"Well, I thought you'd never open the door," the dog said in a crisp British accent, not unlike that of Anthony Hopkins. "I'm Frank. And I'm here to help you. Mind if I come in?"

Fourteen

I'm sorry, did you just *speak English?*" Constance blurted to the dog, dumbfounded.

"Well, I thought Chinese would probably be wrong for the occasion," the dog quipped. "But you probably don't want the neighbors hearing us, so would you mind letting me in?"

Constance sidestepped and the tiny lapdog trotted into her house and straight into the kitchen. He must have run into Dead Jimmy, because Constance heard her dead husband shout, "Jesus in a jumpsuit, what the hell is that? Looks like a squirrel in a sweater."

Constance was in the kitchen two beats later, and the dog, who was ignoring the stares of Dead Jimmy, turned to her and held out one little paw.

"Now, I don't think we've been properly introduced," said the dog. "My name is Frank."

"Um, Constance," she said, stooping low so she could clasp the tiny paw. She gave it a little shake and then let it go. She wanted to give herself a little pinch to see if she was dreaming, but thought that might be rude.

"If your name is *Frank*, how come you're wearing pink?" Dead Jimmy pointed to the dog's pink sweater.

"No accounting for human stupidity—especially with pop stars. Miss London, my owner, got my sex wrong," Frank said. "Anyway, I'm here to help you, Constance. I understand you had your first vision yesterday, and that it involved Dante London having the devil's child."

"You *know*?" Constance asked, amazed.

"Of course I know. I'm an angel-in-training," Frank said, hopping up on one of her dinette chairs. "I've been sent here undercover to keep an eye on Miss London, a duty I'm forsaking this morning to make contact with you."

"Since when are angels lapdogs?" scoffed Dead Jimmy.

"I'm not an angel yet. I'm *trying* to earn my wings," Frank clarified. "I'm only taking this form for this assignment."

"Oh," Constance and Dead Jimmy said together.

"Kind of like the Wonder Twins," Dead Jimmy said. "You know, one of them always took the form of an animal."

Frank rolled his eyes. "Right, that would make sense if I were wearing purple spandex and had a *twin*," Frank said, giving Dead Jimmy a look of annoyance. "Now, we don't have much time, Miss Prophet. I can't leave Dante alone for very long, but it's imperative that we start your training."

"Training?" echoed Constance, stumped, as she slumped into the chair opposite Frank.

"You don't think you just wake up one day and you're a full-fledged minor prophet."

"Well, up until two days ago, I'd never thought prophets—minor or otherwise—existed these days."

"Well, now you know they do, and you've got some work to do."

"If she's the chosen one, why does she have to do work?" Dead Jimmy asked, skeptical. But then, Jimmy was always skeptical of anything involving work.

"Because we don't have a lot of time. The mother of the Antichrist has to be a virgin, has to give her consent, and has to have sex during one particular week."

"Halloween?" Dead Jimmy asked.

"June sixth?" Constance guessed.

"October tenth," Frank corrected.

"That doesn't seem very satanic," Dead Jimmy said.

"Look, it's in the book of Daniel. Ten horns and ten kings," Frank said. "Look it up. But the horns and kings just mean the tenth day of the tenth month."

"But that's next week," Constance said.

"Bingo," Frank confirmed, nodding his small head. "Satan has a seven-day window, ending on the tenth. You see, he has seven days on earth before he has to go back to hell."

Constance held her head. This was all a little much to process. She still wasn't sure she believed it, despite the fact she had a dead husband and a talking dog in her kitchen. Call her stubborn, but to her mind this was all something that could be explained by something nice and simple like a brain tumor. Or her going plain crazy.

Frank put both his paws on her kitchen table and stood on his hind legs.

"Now, I understand you had a vision yesterday," he said. "Can you tell me any details?"

"I thought you already knew," she said.

"We only have rough outlines," Frank said. "We still need your help for the particulars."

"I just saw the devil and Dante London sitting next to each other in front of a big fireplace," Constance said. "They have sex there."

"You don't know where, though? Or when?"

"No," Constance said, shaking her head.

"Dammit," Frank muttered, shaking his head. "Okay, okay, we'll work with what we've got. Now, in the future, when you have another vision, you've got to concentrate, look for markers of place and time—landmarks or clocks on the wall—anything. You'll find that as time goes on, you'll be able to use your visions. And with practice you can even control when and how they happen, and you'll be able to zero in on details you need, like a newspaper on the countertop, for example."

"Wow—that's way cool," Dead Jimmy said. "You're like a superhero or something."

"Will I be able to see *anything* I want?" Constance asked, for the first time thinking that *if* this were all true, maybe it wasn't so bad.

"Not lotto numbers, if that's what you're thinking," Frank said. "Prophets can't use their visions for personal gain—monetary or otherwise. That includes seeing your own demise."

"Oh," Constance sighed, disappointed.

"And another thing—your visions can change depending on how people decide to act," Frank said. "So, while they're a guide, they don't *necessarily* come true. Free will makes seeing the future difficult."

"So you're saying I may or may not have visions that predict the future?"

"Most of the time, they'll be true," Frank said. "Every so often, someone may decide to do something different and change the future."

"But what about the headaches? Will I get those every time?"

"Until your body gets used to your new abilities," Frank said. "I hear that Excedrin works best. That or Dr Pepper."

Constance shook her head, feeling like she was still half in shock. "But why *me*? I don't understand. Why did God pick me?"

"No one ever knows the answer to that," Frank said. "He works in mysterious ways. We never know the whys. But you're not alone, if that helps. There are other prophets—and saints, too. None of them know why, either. You can ask him yourself when you see him. Might not be too long."

Constance went rigid, her focus suddenly sharp as she sat up straight in her chair. "What do you mean, not too long?"

"Oh, er, I mean nothing, nothing," Frank quickly backtracked, putting up one paw. "Forget I said anything."

Constance leaned forward and jabbed a finger in the dog's furry chest. "No," she said. "Tell me what you meant. Am I going to be meeting my maker soon? Is that what you're saying?"

"Well, prophets and saints—they don't usually live long lives," Frank said, not meeting her eyes. "It's just how things work out since there's the whole martyrdom thing and the fact that demons are usually after them."

Constance thought about Yaman standing in her garage and shivered. Dead Jimmy let out a low, solemn-sounding whistle.

"But don't worry, we'll do everything we can to make sure you survive this mission," Frank said. "I promise."

Constance pushed back her chair and started pacing her kitchen. "I didn't ask for this," she mumbled to herself. "I didn't ask for any of this. And now I'm taking advice from a lapdog!" She ruffled her hair and turned to face Frank. "What if I say no?"

"I'm sorry?" Frank asked.

"What if I don't want to do your training, or be a prophet, or whatever," she said. "Doesn't God allow us to have free will? What if I just say, 'Sorry, I can't help you'?"

"You could do that," Frank said, cocking his head to one side. "But it won't help you live longer. The demon that killed Jimmy has been following you. The devil needs your visions as much as we do, to plan his next move. The bad guys won't leave you alone, no matter how much you want them to. You'll be better off if you take my help. At least then you'll have a fighting chance."

Constance stopped pacing and slumped against her kitchen counter. She was just an ordinary person. The only thing she even knew how to do was cook, and she doubted whipping up a batch of fried okra would tip the scales in the war between good and evil. She wasn't a demon fighter. She wasn't even a true believer. Up until a couple of days ago, she wasn't even sure there was a God. She didn't see how any of this could possibly work.

"Constance, let me help you. It's your best bet."

"Okay, but I still don't like my odds," she said.

"That's what David said before he toppled Goliath," Frank said. "And look how that turned out."

Constance gave him a skeptical look. "Now I'm *David*? That doesn't make me feel any better."

"Would you rather be Goliath?" Frank asked her. And she had to admit, the answer was no. "Now, let's start your training."

An hour later, Constance wasn't any closer to controlling her so-called power than she had been when Frank walked in the door. She was, however, much closer to a total allergic meltdown, her eyes itchy and red and her nose running like a faucet. Frank had already shed quite a bit of fur in her kitchen, and the Zyrtec she'd taken hadn't kicked in yet.

"Ah-choo!" She sneezed loudly, causing Frank to jump a little.

"Sorry about the fur," Frank said again. He'd been apologizing since Constance told him she was allergic.

"Next time, do you think the Lord could send a calico cat as his messenger? The only things I'm more allergic to than dogs are cats."

"It's no picnic for me, either," Frank said, scratching behind his ear with his back paw. "More coffee, please?" he asked Constance, as he nodded at his empty cup.

She stood, grabbed the pot, and refilled his porcelain mug with decaf. Constance blew her nose again, and wondered what was stranger: the fact that she was supposed to be God's Chosen One or the fact that she was holding a conversation with a lapdog who happened to be drinking decaf coffee as he sat in her little dinette. It was all just a little strange.

"Okay, back to work. Time to concentrate," Frank told her again for the hundredth time. They'd been sitting at her kitchen table for the better part of an hour, and she'd yet to see any visions, despite the dog's furious coaching. "Concentrate *and* relax. Try to focus on Dante." Frank slid the copy of *People* magazine with Dante London on the cover closer to her. "Do what you did the last time you had a vision."

"But I told you, I just touched it and *bam!* Vision. I didn't do anything. It just happened." Constance picked up the magazine, but nothing had happened, just like nothing had happened for the last hour.

Frank took another lick of coffee. "Close your eyes. Focus."

Constance did what she was told. She focused. She concentrated. She really tried. But absolutely nothing happened.

"I can't do it," Constance sighed, throwing down the magazine in frustration.

"You *can*," Frank said, pushing his coffee mug aside. "You have to *believe* you can do it."

"Now you're saying it's about faith?"

"It's a big element," Frank said. "You have to believe in God, but more important, you have to believe in yourself."

Constance shook her head. "I'm not the kind of person who usually takes things on faith."

"Well, you need to become that kind of person and fast," Frank told her. "You need to stay one step ahead of the demons that are after you."

"You mean Yaman?"

"Yes, and his partner—a shape-shifting demon they just call Shadow," Frank said. "Yaman is a Pride demon and Shadow is a Glutton. Satan's army is divided into the brigades of the seven deadly sins, and having two from different brigades working together is unusual. It usually means a covert operation."

"Satan's army?"

"Satan has one and God has one, and we all have ranks," Frank explained. "Yaman and Shadow are the level of lieutenants, I think. They report directly to General Asmodeus, who's a pretty nasty fellow himself. Yaman and Shadow are very dangerous, and can do a lot of damage, especially to those people around you." He nodded to Dead Jimmy, who had fallen asleep on the couch in the living room. "So be careful. If I were you, I'd stock up on holy water and dogwood blossoms."

"Dogwood blossoms—they really work?"

"Not as well as holy water, but they do help."

"You know, two days ago I wasn't even sure there was a God," Constance said.

"Hmmmm," Frank said, looking thoughtful—or at least as thoughtful as a small lapdog in a pink sweater can look. "That may be your problem. Your doubts. They're eating at your faith. Let's try something else.

Maybe for you, seeing is believing. Get dressed. We're going to the DMV."

They pulled up in front of the only office of the Department of Motor Vehicles nearby, a twenty-minute drive to just inside the county line. Being the only DMV for a good forty-mile radius, its parking lot was, as usual, full, and there were two long lines that snaked out the door—one for driver's licenses and one for license plates. Proving that nothing at the DMV was ever easy, the AC was out, and all the windows were propped open, but it still didn't change the fact that the eighty-five-degree October afternoon was humid and stifling, and people in line were fanning themselves with their forms.

"What are we doing here? Do I need a license to be a prophet?" Constance asked Frank.

"No. The DMV happens to be crawling with demons. It's a demon training ground," Frank said. "These demons are observing human behavior, trying to find our weaknesses. When they've put in their time, they'll be promoted and go out and work as free agents."

"Are there demons in other places?" Constance asked.

"They're all around us. As are angels-in-training," Frank said. "Like me."

Constance took in this information and felt a little better. At least she wasn't alone. She glanced at the DMV office and got that weighty, depressed feeling that she always did whenever she had to deal with a government agency. Maybe Frank was right. Maybe demons ran the place. It would explain a lot.

"So what do I do?" Constance asked Frank.

"You have to look beyond the surface of things," Frank said as he trotted up to the door. "Train yourself to see *beyond* what's in front of you."

"But how?"

"Focus. Concentrate. It will come to you. Come on, let's go inside."

Constance picked him up and they went in, and they found the air even hotter inside than it was out. And it smelled like sweat and frustration. They stood to the side of the line, as a few people in it gave them assessing looks.

"Constance—time to focus," Frank whispered in her ear as Constance held him tightly under one arm. She looked up and saw the snaking line of people in front of them. She wasn't sure what she was supposed to focus on—the overweight man at the front of the line who was sweating so much he'd soaked through his shirt? Or the twenty-something girl with the hot-pink halter top who was cackling into her cell phone? None of them looked particularly evil. They just seemed like people.

"What am I looking for?" Constance asked, glancing from face to face. Each person looked ordinary. She recognized a couple of people in line as passing acquaintances, like the man who mowed her neighbor's lawn, and the county's agriculture agent, but no demons. Not that she'd know what a demon looked like. The man claiming to be Yaman in her garage looked as human as any of the people standing here.

"Anything unusual. Like, what about the DMV workers?" Frank asked.

Her eyes went up to the front of the line, where DMV workers sat behind a giant glass partition, looking bored. There was the woman with acrylic nails and an ultra hair-sprayed eighties perm, a man with a sweat-stained shirt and overgrown beard, a flat-nosed woman with hair pulled back so tightly her eyes seemed to be watering, and a man with bottle-thick glasses and a white button-up shirt buttoned to the very top.

"Focus on the one closest to us," Frank said. "The one with overly permed hair."

Constance shifted her gaze to the woman, who was busy arguing with a customer about his paperwork not being in order. Constance had always been taught it was impolite to stare, so it took a little willpower to focus in on the woman and not look away. She had neon pink finger-nails and a permanent scowl, and her bangs stood straight up from her forehead and curled up at the edges, like she'd gotten ready that morning in front of a wind machine.

"Now imagine you can see *below* what she's showing you," Frank said in her ear, his voice just a whisper. "See below the facade. Start small. Start with her hands."

Constance started with the woman's nails, and imagined she could see what they really looked like. At first, she saw the polish come off, and then the fake acrylic nails. Beneath them, she saw small, stubby, bitten nails, but then, the longer she concentrated, the more she saw something else. Slowly, the fingers were transforming themselves into something not quite fingerlike at all. Pretty soon, they weren't human fingers, they were green scaly talons. Startled, Constance glanced up at the woman's face, but instead of a human face, she saw a giant green lizard head, with a spiky yellow Mohawk of spines down its back and two giant fangs. The lizard scowled at her and whipped out a long pink tongue.

"Ack," Constance cried, startled. She looked down at her feet, and when she looked up again, she saw Lizard Lady had turned back into a woman. "What the . . . ?"

"What did you see?" Frank said.

"A big lizard," Constance said, glancing down at her feet. "Or I thought I did."

"You did it!" Frank cheered. "That's what she is. Her true form. Now, try again. Do you see any others?"

Constance wasn't sure she wanted to see any more. Lizard Lady wasn't the prettiest. Still, she forced herself to look at the other DMV workers. In short order, she saw a dog man, a cobra-headed bear, and a man with four heads, except all of them had a single eye.

Constance flinched and looked away. When she looked back, they were all normal-looking people again.

"Whoa, that is some trip," she said.

"I figured you wouldn't believe unless you saw with your own eyes. Now, are you starting to understand?"

"I think so," Constance said. She glanced up at Lizard Lady, who whipped her tongue out and licked her own eye. "Eww," Constance exclaimed, glancing away.

The DMV workers had taken notice of Constance and Frank by now. They were whispering among themselves and staring.

"Uh, Frank? They seem to have spotted us," Constance said, nervous. Even though she wasn't quite sure she believed what she saw, she didn't want to get any closer to Lizard Lady, just in case.

"That's fine. Let's go up and chat with Lizard Lady."

"What? Are you crazy? She's a lizard!"

"Don't worry," Frank said. "She won't hurt us. At least, not in daytime, and not with so many witnesses. Besides, demon trainees aren't allowed to actually murder anyone. They have to refrain from showing demon powers until they've completed their training program."

"Are you sure about that?" Constance asked, uneasiness in her chest as they walked to the head of the line closer and closer to the woman with the giant lizard head.

"Trust me."

"Hey!" cried the man at the front of the line. "Where do you think you're going?"

Constance paused. Frank barked three times and held up his paw. Instantly, the man calmed down.

"I mean, okay, go ahead."

"What was that?" Constance whispered.

"Angel-in-training trick," he said.

The lizard lady saw them and frowned. "What are *you* doing here, angel-wannabe?" she hissed.

"What? You not happy to see me, Delilah?" Frank said as Constance put him on the counter.

"Delilah? As in Samson?" Constance asked.

"No," hissed Lizard Lady. "Why are people always confusing me with that poser? I'm *way* worse than she could even dream of being."

"Delilah was technically a human, though she did make some mistakes," Frank said. "This Delilah is a full-fledged Envy demon, and demons don't like to be compared to humans."

"Humans," sniffed Delilah, like she smelled something bad, "are pathetic." She narrowed her lizard eyes to slits and glared at Frank. "You better get out of here before my boss sees you. He likes to eat angel-wannabes for breakfast."

"I'm not scared," Frank said.

"Well, you better be." Delilah stared hard at Constance. "So what are you? Saint or prophet?"

"You can't tell?" Constance asked Lizard Lady.

"You goody-goodies all look the same to me—all with the glowing halo," she said. "Let me guess—prophet? You look too dumb to be a saint, and prophets don't have to do anything but have visions. Not exactly brain surgery."

"Hey," Constance cried, insulted.

"So you *are* a prophet. Minor one, I'm guessing, by the looks of you."

"Delilah," Frank interrupted. "We need information. You don't give it to me, I'll exorcise you." Frank slipped his paw into his pink sweater and pulled out a small silver cross. Delilah visibly flinched.

"No way am I telling you anything," she said. "Why don't you take your little *prophet* and get the heck out of here? If my boss sees me even *talking* to you, I'm going straight back to hell—or worse."

"What's worse than hell?" Constance asked.

"Mega-Mart," Delilah replied quickly.

"It's one of the devil's outfits," Frank explained to Constance. "Another training ground for demons, but apparently the pay is worse."

"Barely even minimum wage," Lizard Lady said. "And hardly any benefits."

"Demons need benefits?" Constance asked. Lizard Lady just frowned at her.

"Delilah—we need to know anything you know about Yaman and Shadow," Frank said, brandishing the little cross with one paw.

"I don't know anything," she hissed. "They don't tell me anything. They tell the Gluttons and the Lust demons everything. We Envy demons always get the short stick around here."

"You always know more than you let on. We want to know what they plan next."

Before Delilah could move, Frank flipped the cross against her skin. It landed there with a hiss, and the air suddenly filled with the smell of burnt popcorn.

"Satan in a bathtub!" shouted Delilah, grabbing her hand. "You know that will leave a scar."

"Tell us what we want to know, or I go for the face next."

Delilah quickly glanced over her shoulder, making sure no one else was close by.

"I don't know where Yaman is, but I know they are into something big. My boss and a few others have been talking about a second coming."

"Jesus Christ?" Constance asked.

"She means second coming of the Antichrist," Frank said. "He came once before."

"Let me guess, Hitler?"

"Actually, no, he was half goat," Delilah said. "Big mess, that one."

"What else? What does the devil know?" Frank held the cross in a threatening way.

"No, that's it, I swear. You want more information, why don't you ask your *prophet*?" Delilah hissed, lashing her pink tongue in Constance's direction. "You shouldn't need informants. What gives? Is the Chosen One having trouble with her powers or something? Can't get her visions up?" Lizard Lady gave Constance a knowing look and smiled, like she found something funny.

"She can just fine," Frank said. "I'm just keeping you on your toes, Delilah."

"Well, you'd better watch it. As soon as I get out of here, I will *totally* be gunning for you, you mutt. Just wait until I unleash some serious envy on your ass."

"I can take it," Frank said. "That is, *if* you ever get out." Frank looked up at Constance. "Come on, Constance, let's go. You're going to be late for your husband's funeral."

In the car, Frank instructed Constance to drop him off near the movie set. Her mind was still a whirl of questions, but Frank was insistent that he had to go.

"But what am I supposed to do without you?" she asked, suddenly feeling like she'd been left alone to fly a spaceship, with no idea how to operate the controls.

"Just try and concentrate on controlling your visions," Frank told her as she stopped the car down the road from the movie set. "And you need to tell me whenever you get a vision about Dante. I'll be as close to her as I can most of the time, but I can't keep an eye on her at all times. So the minute you get a vision, call me on my cell phone. Here's the number."

Frank grabbed a scrap of paper from his sweater with one paw and handed it to her.

"You have a cell phone?" Constance asked, amazed. "But—where do you keep it?"

"An iPhone, actually," Frank said. "Dante is very generous that way. And another thing. You see any demons about, you *call me immediately.*"

"Okay," Constance said as Frank hopped out of her car. "But—wait—what about Jimmy? Since I've made contact with you, is he free to go to heaven now?"

"Jimmy's ghost will go back to heaven after we stop the devil."

"And if we don't stop the devil?" Constance asked.

"Then Dead Jimmy is the least of your problems," Frank said, starting off across the road. "If the devil gets his Antichrist, then it's the end of the world as we know it."

Fifteen

Jimmy's funeral was held an hour later at the Dogwood County Baptist Church. Constance noticed right away that the church was nearly empty, which was probably because the movie *Devil's in the Details* started shooting that very afternoon. Most anybody who was anybody had headed to the Higgins Ranch, on the opposite side of the county, to try to get a glimpse of the stars. Dead Jimmy, however, was taking it personally.

"Where *is* everybody?" Dead Jimmy whined, as the two sat in the front pew of the church. "Some movie is more important than *me*? Are you kidding?"

Constance tried hard not to look in Dead Jimmy's direction and not to respond. She'd already found herself carrying on full conversations with him in public, and she'd had enough of the odd stares. She knew she needed to cut it out, or she'd not only be arrested, she'd also be taken to a padded room. Still it was hard to ignore Dead Jimmy. He was loud, and he simply would not shut up.

"I'm going to go haunt some of the people who didn't show," Dead Jimmy vowed, his feelings clearly hurt.

"Would you be quiet?" Constance hissed. "I'm trying to concentrate."

Constance had been trying to re-create a vision since Frank had left her, but she'd had absolutely no success. She closed her eyes and tried again. Still nothing. She was beginning to wonder if she was really a prophet at all. Maybe the first vision had been a fluke. Of course, she had no idea if she was doing it right, either. It was a lot like trying to climb stairs without ever having seen any before.

Seeing the demons at the DMV had been a bit of a wake-up call. Clearly, she was stuck on this roller-coaster ride and had to see it through. She might not have a lot of faith, but she'd seen too many things she simply couldn't explain in the last couple of days, and she was tired of trying to put a reasonable explanation on it all. For once in her life, she decided, it might just pay to take things on faith.

Of course, now that she knew demons lurked all around her in the most obvious places, she began to wonder where else evil might be hiding. She felt like she'd been a zombie walking through a world filled with monsters and never even knew it. Part of her, deep down, thought that this made sense. It would explain why some people did really horrible things. Maybe they weren't really people after all. Maybe they were lizard ladies or three-headed monsters. It would explain a lot. But now she had to wonder if the woman sitting down the pew from her was a demon in disguise. She tried staring hard at the woman—one of Dead Jimmy's great-aunts who was probably in her eighties—but she got nothing. The older woman glanced at Constance strangely, which was because Constance was staring a hole through her trying to figure out if she had animal parts or not. Constance couldn't see any, but she didn't know if that was because Dead Jimmy's great-aunt was just a woman or because she, Constance, wasn't concentrating hard enough.

Constance looked the other way and tried focusing on her mother-in-law. If anyone was a demon in disguise, she thought, it might just be her. Doris Plyd had hated her on sight, and had been trying to convince Jimmy for years that Constance was a gold digger. There was no explaining to her that it had been Jimmy who'd spent months and months wearing down Constance's defenses. Constance never went after Jimmy for his money or anything else. It was Jimmy who did all the courting and he wouldn't take no for an answer. But Doris felt no woman was good enough for Jimmy. She didn't see his flaws like other people did. He was her only child, and if you told her Jimmy had a clumsy streak, she'd deny it until she was blue in the face.

She was a likely candidate for being demon possessed. After all, it was Doris who had uninvited Constance to family Christmas celebrations three years in a row because she hadn't yet produced a Plyd heir.

Constance stared, hard. Doris was wearing her Sunday best—a shell-pink Chanel suit and oversize pearl earrings. She had her salt-and-pepper hair up in a kind of French twist, her makeup, as usual, was flawless, and she was sporting a fresh manicure. She was weighed down in her usual set of bling: her oversize emerald ring she bought in Europe a few years back; her diamond tennis bracelet; the three-carat engagement ring and matching five-diamond wedding band and her diamond-encrusted platinum Rolex. At her feet was a Louis Vuitton bag that was big enough to hold three bowling balls.

Doris liked people to think the Plyd Family trust fund was endless, but Constance knew the truth. The Plyds weren't wealthy beyond limits. In private, Doris re-used paper plates and tinfoil and often turned off the air-conditioning—even in the middle of July—to cut down on costs. She counted every penny, and wanted to make sure that Constance never saw any of them. The fact that she'd lived off Plyd money for the time she and Jimmy were married and hadn't even had the decency to pro-vide her an heir was something her mother-in-law could never forgive.

Constance stared hard at Doris, half expecting to see a vampire or werewolf beneath the Chanel suit. After all, it was her only son's funeral and her eyes were dry and her expression distant. Doris had never cried that Constance had ever seen, or shown much emotion ever. Constance concentrated and stared hard at her mother-in-law but she saw nothing out of the ordinary. Doris was simply Doris. Constance felt a little disappointed. Doris frowned at Constance, and she looked away.

"What are you staring at Mom for? She got some-thing in her teeth?" Dead Jimmy asked. When Constance didn't answer, he added, "Say, if I forgot to mention it before, you look mighty fine."

Constance was wearing a black, V-neck, sleeveless dress, which hit just above the knee, and she had on her nicest pair of shoes: black heels. This was Constance's only nice black dress, and not exactly used very often, since Jimmy's idea of a night out was a spin around the Dairy Queen drive-through. Still, the dress wasn't Chanel or anything close, and Constance could feel Doris's judgment. Doris always put Constance in a catch-22: her run-of-the-mill mall clothes weren't good enough for the Plyds, but if she ever bought anything designer, Doris would say it was too expensive. Constance could never win.

"Thanks," Constance said. Dead Jimmy might not have been the best husband, but he was never stingy with the compliments. Unfortunately, he just never knew when to stop.

"I mean it, you totally look hot," said Dead Jimmy, giving her a wink. "You are one smoking widow. H-o-t."

"Shush now," she muttered, pretending to pick a piece of lint off her skirt. She looked away from him and focused on the flower arrangements on either side of the coffin. There were lots of flowers. Constance hadn't realized Jimmy was so well liked in the county. Or maybe it was just a sign of guilt since nobody showed. Everyone sent flowers and then headed off to try to get Dante London's autograph.

"Like whoo-wee, hot," Dead Jimmy went on.

Constance sighed. It was a sad commentary on her life that the only man who thought she was attractive at the moment was her dead husband. Her dead *almost-ex* husband, she mentally corrected. It was just sad.

"Shush," Constance said, causing a couple of other

people in the pew to turn to look at her, including Doris
Plyd, who gave her a look that could cut glass.

Constance ignored her, just as she'd ignored Doris
when she'd accidentally overheard her telling her neighbor, Maureen Davis, that she suspected Constance had
something to do with Jimmy's death. Rachel had told Constance before the funeral that her mother-in-law had been
spreading the same story pretty much through town.

Still, Constance knew, Doris wasn't alone in her
suspicions. Nathan already thought she was Public Enemy
Number One.

Constance didn't know what was worse, the fact that
she was a suspect or that even Constance had a hard
time believing her own alibi and she'd *been* there. Constance glanced around the church and saw Rachel, who
was trying to stop Cassidy from tugging on the hair of
an old woman in the pew ahead of theirs. Rachel didn't
look up.

Constance continued her sweep of the church, looking for another friendly face, but instead found herself
eye to eye with Nathan Garrett, as he slid into a seat in
the back of the church. Constance whipped back around
in her seat without thinking, and knew for certain that
he was there for her. Was he planning to arrest her? she
couldn't help but wonder.

"Boy, Nathan has his eye on you," Dead Jimmy said,
echoing her own thoughts. "And not in a *good* way."

"I wish you came with a mute button," Constance
whispered through clenched teeth to Dead Jimmy, who
only shrugged.

Constance thought she could feel Nathan's eyes burning into the back of her head. Casually, she turned, as if to look for someone she knew, and found herself again locking eyes with Nathan Garrett. She sent him an evil eye, and he just shook his head and grinned, as if getting evil stares was twice as amusing as reading the Sunday funnies. This just made Constance angrier, and she glared all the harder.

If anyone around here was a demon, she thought, it would be a Garrett. But the more she stared, the more he just looked like his usual charming self. No extra heads appeared on his shoulders, and he didn't morph into a snake or bat or anything demonlike. Nathan was just Nathan, nothing ugly about him. Another disappointment. She whipped her head around and exhaled a frustrated sigh.

"Smooth move," said Dead Jimmy.

"If you really want to help me, why don't you march back there and tell him *I* didn't kill you?" Constance whispered, trying not to look at Dead Jimmy. "In fact, why don't you just tell everyone?"

"I wish I could, Connie. But no one can see or hear me but you and Frank." Dead Jimmy's eyes dropped down to her neckline. "Say, did I mention you are *hot*? You wearing a new bra under there?"

"Argh. Just shut *up*," Constance hissed at him. Next to her, her mother-in-law gasped.

"Excuse me?" Her penciled brows furrowed and her overly lined lips drew into a thin line.

"N-n-nothing," Constance stammered quickly. "I . . ." But by then the funeral's music started, drowning her out.

* * *

After laying Jimmy's body in the ground, Constance did her best to avoid Nathan Garrett. He'd been watching her like she was a piece of fried chicken ever since the start of the funeral. Dead Jimmy was buzzing in her ear, and she was having a hard time pretending to be normal and not a person who saw dead people and demons. She just didn't feel like she could deal with Nathan Garrett now. But as a condolence line started to form in the vestibule and Nathan lined up front and center, the fourth person in line, she realized there would be no avoiding him. Not unless she bolted. Now.

"Excuse me," she said to Doris, who stood next to her, as she covered her face with her hand and half walked, half ran toward the nearest exit, not caring who was staring at her. She just couldn't take Nathan Garrett. Not with his big shoulders and Hungry-Man dinner arms and decidedly *not* demonic smile.

She slammed open the door and breathed in the warmer-than-usual October air.

"What the hell are you doing? My funeral is still going on," Dead Jimmy said, drifting after her, bringing with him a cool breeze of air.

"No, it's not. It's over," Constance said, fumbling in her purse for her keys, heading straight to her gold Camry. "I'm going home."

"But, Connie. Mom sprung for Bud in *bottles*. It's a serious affair," Dead Jimmy wailed. "And I want a longneck."

"Don't you ever get tired of beer? Good Lord, the last thing in the world you need is to add to your beer belly."

"Are you saying I'm fat?" came a voice that definitely *wasn't* Dead Jimmy's. Constance whipped her head up in time to see she was two steps away from colliding with Nathan Garrett. He was leaning against the side of her car, all six feet two inches of him, looking relaxed and comfortable, like he was in his living room. But then, Nathan always looked comfortable. He was flashing those Garrett dimples at her, and she had to admit they worked on her more than she liked.

"I didn't see you there," Constance said, thinking that if she had, she would've run in the other direction. And just how did he beat her out to the parking lot, anyway? Could he fly, too? Maybe it was a new Garrett brothers power—in addition to making her life miserable, they could now defy the laws of physics.

"Constance, I'm beginning to get the impression that you're avoiding me," he said, crossing his arms across his broad chest and giving her a smile that didn't quite reach his eyes.

"But we had such a nice, long talk the other day when you called me a murderer," Constance said, finding her voice and her resolve after being temporarily shaken by his presence. She had enough to worry about what with being haunted by her dead almost-ex husband and potentially being the target of some serious evil forces. She wasn't going to let a local sheriff push her around, even if he was a Garrett, with a smile that ought to be in a Crest Whitestrips commercial. "You going to insult me again?"

"Well, I was going to ask you what you planned to do with the money," he said. "Pay off the debt on the Magnolia Café? Or were you just going to run off and open up a new restaurant in Mexico?"

"How did you know the Magnolia Café was in debt?" Constance snapped, wondering just who he'd been talking to.

"Everybody knows," he said. "Jimmy didn't make it a secret."

Constance gave Dead Jimmy a look that could melt most people. He, however, just gave her a weak shrug.

"See," he started, "I was going to tell you . . ."

"And what are you talking about? What money?" Constance asked Nathan. "I don't get any money from Jimmy. Just the Magnolia Café, which as you pointed out, is in debt. It's not a net gain."

Nathan slowly uncrossed his arms and pushed himself away from the car, so he and Constance were toe to toe.

"So, just so I understand," he said, looming over her. "Your official position is that you don't know about the five-million-dollar life insurance policy Jimmy had? The one where he named you the sole beneficiary?"

Constance felt like her ears were stuffed full of cotton. Surely she didn't hear right. "Five million *dollars*? You're sure?"

Out of the corner of her eye, she saw Dead Jimmy backing up, moving away from her and talking at the same time. "I was going to tell you, I just forgot! Remember my cousin was selling life insurance back a few years ago? I sort of upped our policies to help him out, and I meant to tell you, but it was only an extra fifty dollars a month and I . . ."

Dead Jimmy saw the look on her face and broke out into a run across the cemetery grounds. *You'd better run, you little weasel*, Constance thought. This made her look guilty as hell. Jimmy could've bothered to mention it. She saw that he was headed for the graveyard, where one or two visitors were still milling about, and then, as if remembering belatedly that he was a ghost who could come and go as he pleased, he disappeared with a little pop.

I'm going to get you, Jimmy—you can run, but you can't hide.

"Constance?" Nathan asked, a puzzled expression on his face. Constance wondered if she'd said that out loud. "I just asked you if you'd come down to the station with me. Maybe you can tell me a little bit more about this insurance policy you know nothing about."

"I suppose if I say no, then you'll just arrest me anyhow," Constance said, folding her arms across her chest.

"Something like that," Nathan said, a little gleam in his eye. He was enjoying the prospect of her in handcuffs a bit too much, she thought.

"Fine," she said, and followed him back to his police truck, feeling the eyes of about a dozen onlookers burn into her from the parking lot, including her mother-in-law, who was nodding her head like she'd seen this coming a mile away as Nathan helped Constance into his police truck.

Out the window of Nathan's truck, Constance locked eyes with Rachel, who was balancing Cassidy on her hip and giving her a worried look. At least there was one person on her side.

Sixteen

"T his is police brutality," Dead Jimmy told Constance, as he sat beside her in the little interrogation room where Nathan had placed her without water or coffee. Dead Jimmy had mustered up the courage to reappear next to Constance about thirty minutes prior, once he realized he could just disappear any time her temper got up. Nathan hadn't actually arrested her, as in fingerprints and Miranda warnings, so Constance didn't know what he planned. She glanced at the big mirror on the wall and wondered who was on the other side.

Dead Jimmy gave Constance a glance. "I sure could use a Bud," he said.

Constance didn't answer. None of the cameras in the room would pick him up, she knew, and talking to thin air wouldn't help her case any.

"You still mad about that insurance policy?"

Constance gave a subtle nod.

"I thought it was a *good* thing, Connie. You know how accident-prone I am. I thought I'd have you set up for life."

For a split second, Constance felt bad for being mad at her dead almost-ex husband. Sometimes the little bugger could be sweet.

"I didn't count on getting myself murdered," Dead Jimmy added practically. "Hello out there!" Dead Jimmy shouted, waving his arms in front of the mirrored glass. "What does a ghost have to do around here to get a Bud?"

As if he'd been heard, the door to the interrogation room swung open, and Nathan came strolling in, tape recorder and notepad in hand. The look of his smug smile made Constance's blood boil.

"Ready to confess yet?" Nathan asked her, sliding into his seat, giving her a dimpled grin.

"And make your job easy for you? Never."

"It might make things easy on yourself if you just tell me what really happened." Nathan flipped on the tape recorder and opened his notepad, ready to take notes.

Well, she was going to give him something to write down, but it wasn't going to be a confession.

"I already told you. I didn't kill Jimmy. I don't have proof I didn't right now, but I will get some. You just need to give me a little time." Constance folded her arms across her chest. Maybe she could drag Frank in here and have *him* explain it all to Nathan, she thought.

"Look, Con," Nathan said, putting down his pen and looking her straight in the eye. "You need to be honest with me. I may be the only one who can help you."

Constance met his stare, wary. She seriously doubted that.

Nathan reached out and clicked off his tape recorder.

"I mean it," Nathan said, tapping his pen on his notepad. "The county judge wants you locked up already. I haven't put the handcuffs on yet, but I might have to, if you don't give me something I can use."

"Like what?"

"Like did Jimmy beat you? Was it self-defense?"

"No," Constance and Dead Jimmy said at once.

"I resent the implication," Dead Jimmy continued, pounding a ghost fist on the table, but it went straight through without leaving a mark.

"Maybe when he was drunk, he got a little rough?"

"When he got drunk, he just passed out," Constance said, and shrugged.

"Yeah—I never hit nobody," Dead Jimmy agreed. "Unless you count the floor, which I did hit a couple of times pretty hard." He gave Constance a sheepish grin.

Nathan dropped his pen and let out an exasperated-sounding sigh as he ran his hands through his thick brown hair. He seemed to be getting frustrated. Constance couldn't quite figure out why.

"Maybe it was just a bizarre accident? It happened and you panicked, and told the story about the man in the black suit as a cover? It's okay if you panicked. I can help smooth things over."

Constance shook her head. "Nope."

Dead Jimmy, for his part, had taken to dancing around Nathan and putting devil horns on the back of his head. It took all of Constance's concentration *not* to watch him do it. He'd even started poking his hands entirely through Nathan's forehead to make the horns look more authentic. The way Dead Jimmy was dancing and jumping around

Nathan was kind of funny, but Constance couldn't afford even the slimmest of smiles. She refocused her attention on Nathan and studied him. She put her palms flat on the table that separated them and tried not to look at Dead Jimmy, who'd started doing a little jig.

"Are you really trying to help me?" she asked him, leaning forward. "Or are you just trying to get me to admit to something I didn't do?"

Nathan met her eyes, not blinking, oblivious to Dead Jimmy. "Con, you're in a whole heap of serious trouble here. I may be the only friend you have. The whole county has pretty much decided that you did it, and the county judge and DA can't wait to get you in a courtroom. The DA wants to go for the death penalty and run for state office."

"Whoa," Dead Jimmy said, and gave a low whistle as he dropped the devil horns. "That ain't good."

"They all think I'm *guilty?*" she cried, amazed. She knew the judge and the DA, and hadn't thought they'd just assume she was capable of murder.

Nathan nodded, folding his arms across his chest.

"Well, I guess you just really don't know some people," she said, shaking her head and tapping the table with one finger. "I'm the most honest person *in this county.*"

"You have to admit, though, it's pretty suspicious. And you being the kind of girl who married Jimmy and all."

Constance's eyes rose sharply to meet his. "What 'kind of girl' do you mean?"

"Well, a girl who married Jimmy for his money," Nathan said, not backing down as he grabbed the edge of the table. "And probably spent most of the marriage running around on him."

"Running around on me!" Dead Jimmy exclaimed, shocked, as he turned to stare at Constance. "Connie? Is it true?"

Constance went completely white, and then she flushed a dark red. Her eyes spit fire, and she was so angry, her hands shook.

"*That's* what people are saying about me?" she hissed, outrage written on every inch of her. She was spitting mad. "I'll have you know that I may not have loved Jimmy like he loved me, but I *never*, repeat, *never* cheated on him," Constance gritted out.

"You tell him, girl!" Dead Jimmy cheered.

"And I didn't just marry him for his money, for your information."

"You didn't?" asked Dead Jimmy, a little puzzled. "I thought for sure . . ." Constance ignored him.

"I married him because he was very nice to me at a time when I needed it."

"Aw, I was? Connie, that's sweet." Dead Jimmy beamed a smile.

"It was right after you left, in fact," Constance continued. "You could say it's *your* fault I married him in the first place."

"Me?" Nathan asked, honestly baffled. "What did I have to do with it?"

"Does the number twenty-two mean anything to you?"

"No."

"Well, your ex–best friend, Tony Kendall, said you

kept a list of all the virgins you ever had, and I was simply *Number Twenty-two*."

"Tony Kendall is a liar," Nathan said, flushing red. "Which is why we're not friends anymore. You can't believe a word he says. I don't know how many virgins I've dated, or otherwise, for your information. I don't keep score."

"And you didn't recognize me at the Jiffy Lube." Now that Constance was actually voicing all her grudges out loud, she realized how childish they sounded. They were the resentments of a teenager. She'd held on to them all these years, but they were really, actually, kind of silly.

"At Jiffy Lube? When?"

"Three months after we . . ." Constance trailed off, blushing fiercely. "Never mind. You didn't remember me. You didn't even say hello. Acted like I wasn't even there."

"Well, I'm sorry if I didn't remember you," Nathan said. "But if it was three months after, that's when my dad died, and I was a little distracted at the time. I wasn't noticing much of anybody or anything then. I was pretty much a zombie all the time."

"Oh," Constance said, suddenly feeling incredibly guilty. She'd had no idea.

"You couldn't have known," he said, as if reading her thoughts. "My dad lived in California. Had a heart attack and just died. And anyway, I'm sorry that I didn't call. I really do regret not keeping in touch."

Constance found herself being sucked in by the sincere look in his big brown eyes. Then she remembered he had her trapped at the police station and was trying to pin a murder on her. She wouldn't be sidetracked by his Garrett charm. Not this time.

"Yes, well, Jimmy was nice to me when you weren't," Constance repeated as she looked away from him. She had to try to stick to her guns. "And that's how we ended up married. Not because I wanted his money. Because he was nice to me."

A knock came at the door and Ann popped her head in.

"Sheriff, you'd better get out to the Higgins Ranch. Dante London's been calling for more police protection. Apparently, she wants to go to Mega-Mart."

Nathan frowned, and Constance couldn't tell if it was because of Ann's abrupt interruption or the fact that he had to go running after Dante London.

"Buzz next time, okay, Ann?"

"You using the interrogation room for something untoward?" Ann asked, her eyes flicking to Constance suspiciously.

"No, but, well, it's just protocol."

"Fine," she said, shrugging. "You'd better get to the Higgins Ranch soon, because you know Miss Pop Princess has the county judge on speed dial."

"Thanks, Ann," Nathan said, and stood. Ann ducked back out of the room, and Nathan turned to Constance. "I'll have Deputy Robbie come in and take you to your cell."

"Cell? You're keeping me here?"

"Just till I get back. I have some more questions for you." Nathan stood and gathered up his tape recorder and notepad.

"That could be hours!" Constance stood and threw

back her chair, and its metal legs made a loud scraping sound on the concrete floor. She couldn't believe he planned to keep her there all day and possibly night. It was inconsiderate even by Garrett standards.

"Trust me," Nathan said, face solemn, as he turned to go. "It's for your own good."

"For mine, or yours?" Constance asked him. "Seems like maybe you're bowing to pressure. Like from the judge?"

Nathan paused at the door and turned, his mouth set in a thin line.

"I make my own decisions," he told her.

"You sure about that?" Constance challenged.

Nathan paused, as if he were going to answer, but then he thought better of it, and put his back to her as he turned and left the room without another word. She'd hit a nerve, apparently, and she was glad of it. It was about time she ruffled that Garrett cool.

"That went well," Dead Jimmy said, slumping into the chair where Nathan had been sitting. "If I were you, I'd get a lawyer."

Constance just glared at Dead Jimmy, her heart pounding and her temper still flaring from her run-in with Nathan. She couldn't believe she was really stuck here. She glanced up at the ceiling. If she was really supposed to be the Chosen One, then surely God wouldn't let her sit in jail? Of course, then she remembered there were a lot of famous Biblical characters who were jailed unfairly. She thought about Daniel and the lions for a second, and shivered. At least the Dogwood County Jail didn't have lions.

Deputy Robbie came in then, and Constance exhaled a sigh as she held out her wrists.

"You might as well just put the cuffs on," Constance said. "I know everybody thinks I did it."

"Aw, put your hands down, Mrs. Plyd," Deputy Robbie said, blushing a little. "I'm not going to arrest you. That would be a crime, what with you baking the best blueberry muffins in the county. You want some coffee?"

"Sure, Robbie, that'd be swell." Constance was beginning to warm to Robbie as she followed him out the door. Once in the hall, they both heard some commotion out in front. Robbie paused to listen.

"Now, Ann, you better let me back there!" came a familiar voice. It was Rachel, and she wasn't taking no for an answer. "And if that no-good sheriff of yours is here, I want to talk to him, too. Arresting a widow during a funeral is just about the tackiest thing I've ever seen."

Deputy Robbie looked sheepish. "Kind of agree with her there," he said, meeting Constance's eyes.

"Technically, she wasn't arrested," Ann said.

"Well, if she's not under arrest, then I'm taking her home," Rachel declared. "Even I know you can't hold her here without charges, and I only ever had one law correspondence course. Constance! Come out here!"

Constance glanced at Robbie. "Go on," he said after a beat. "I'll tell Nathan you got a lawyer—so you might want to go call one."

"Will do, Robbie," Constance said. "And you get free blueberry muffins for life. Anytime at the Magnolia Café."

Robbie's face lit up. "You mean it?"

"And anything else on the menu," she said.

The deputy clapped his hands together like a little boy who'd just seen his loot under the Christmas tree.

"Aw, thanks, Mrs. Plyd."

When Constance walked out, Rachel breathed a sigh of relief. She shifted Cassidy onto her other hip. "I was worried *sick* about you," she said. "When I saw Nathan take off with you, I didn't know what to think."

"He just took me in for questioning," Constance said.

"Still, in bad taste," Rachel said. "Course, I wouldn't expect much better from a Garrett. Come on, let's go."

"Gladly." Constance followed Rachel out to her mini-van. Constance took the front seat, while Rachel buckled Cassidy into his car seat in the back.

"Thanks for coming to get me," Constance said. Absently, she noticed a yellow flyer stuck under Rachel's windshield wiper. It was a notice asking for extras on the set of *Devil's in the Details.* She reached out the window to yank it free and get a better look, but as soon as she touched it, a surge of energy went through her, and she knew she had another vision coming on. This one came on fast and furious, just like the first. She tried to slow down the pictures, like Frank had said, but they sped by on fast-forward, everything a blur of images and motion. This time she saw Corey Bennett, and she saw him talking to Yaman. He was working for the devil, having sold his soul ages ago, and now he would be the person to lure Dante to the devil.

Frantically, Constance searched for markers of place or time, but didn't see any except for her own restaurant, which came up in a sudden swoop in front of her. She saw Corey Bennett and Dante London dining there. But she had no idea when this would be, and didn't have any way of finding out that she could see. The vision ended far too abruptly, without warning and without giving her much of anything to go on.

When she came to, Rachel was staring at her with a worried look on her face. "You okay, hon?" she asked. "Maybe we better call Mel. You don't look so good."

Seventeen

"That went great," Shadow grumbled, as he and Yaman returned to Dogwood after consulting with General Asmodeus, their commanding officer. They'd just told him about the prophet's first vision, and he hadn't been happy that said vision didn't have a time or place. He and Shadow were gliding over Dogwood, invisible to most.

"I don't know what he expects from us," Yaman complained. "We're not prophets. We just told him what we saw. Not our fault her vision was incomplete."

"Man, I need a new job," Shadow complained. "I'm tired of temperamental demon bosses. I mean, why'd he have to go and *bite* me?" Shadow lifted up one wing, exposing a half-moon-shaped bite.

"Totally uncalled for," Yaman agreed. "He's pretty violent for a Lust demon, I have to admit. Usually, they're total pansies."

"Thing is, he should've been biting *you*. You were the one who killed the prophet's husband."

"I *thought* I was doing us all a favor."

"Well, the general says you just made her stressed and the visions are now all scattered to pieces," Shadow said, bending and unbending his wing as if to work out the soreness.

"How was I supposed to know? I thought it was a good idea at the time. And, besides, I couldn't wait around all millennium for her to get around to her visions. I have an appearance to keep up. I mean, I'm way overdue for my weekly waxing and facial."

"And your Hair Club for Men meeting?"

Yaman sent him an evil look. "They don't have meetings," he snapped. "It's not like Alcoholics Anonymous."

"There's not a twelve-step plan for balding?"

"I'm not even going to dignify that with an answer."

Shadow chuckled to himself. "Anyway, I still say Asmodeus should've bitten you. You didn't even take off your baseball cap in a show of respect."

"I *don't* take off the cap. I told you."

"Why? Got hair plugs under there you're ashamed of?"

"I have a *full* head of hair, thank you."

"Which is why you aren't showing it."

"I just like the cap, okay?" Yaman pulled it down more over his eyes. "Besides, Asmodeus bit you because you kept going on about being hungry. He was tired of it and so am I."

"Whatever. The guy is a first-rate jerk. Even for a demon."

"I hear you. He makes Gordon Ramsay look like an anger management therapist. I don't know how he managed to get promoted, anyway."

"I heard his uncle or someone called in a favor."

"Isn't that always the case? It's all who you know. I swear, that's why I'll never become a general, because I don't have any good connections." Yaman sighed and stuffed his hands in his pockets. Beneath them, the Higgins Ranch came into view. It was a sprawling ranch of a hundred acres that was currently being used as the main set for the filming of *Devil's in the Details*.

"I thought you knew all the celebrities."

"Yeah, sure, but they only carry so much weight," Yaman said. "You never heard of Sean Penn actually swinging an election, did you?"

"True enough." Shadow sighed. "Maybe I'll defect to God's army."

Yaman did a double take. "And become *goody-goody*? Ugh, no thanks. Besides, you'd have to wear white all the time. Even your shoes. Even *after* Labor Day."

"You have to wear clothes?"

"All the time," Yaman said. "Unless you're the Holy Spirit. But that job's already taken."

"Dammit," Shadow said. "Guess I'm stuck then. So tell me again—who are we seeing?"

"Corey Bennett. The actor."

"Can I eat him?" Shadow asked, hopeful.

"Definitely not. He plays for our side."

"He does?"

"How else do you think a zit-prone overweight kid from New Jersey became America's Sexiest Man Alive?"

Eighteen

Corey Bennett sat inside his trailer on the movie set, peering closely into a mirror and trying to figure out if the small red spot above his eyebrow was the beginning of a zit or something less formidable. He never broke out before the first day of shooting. In fact, he never broke out at all. Not once since he was eighteen. He was famous for his smooth, flawless complexion. The camera loved his skin, and now his skin seemed to be failing him. This didn't seem possible. He had *blemish-proof* skin.

"Corey?" called a voice from his bed. "What are you doing?"

"Yeah," said her twin. "We're ready for Round Two."

Corey glanced at the twins in his mirror, two perfectly identical blond Playmates of the Year, and they were both naked, showing off their perfectly man-made bodies. He suspected that together they were half made of silicone, not that he cared. Their names were Kitty and Candy or maybe it was Cindy and Katy—he couldn't remember, not that it mattered. They knew *his* name, which was the important thing.

They were ex-girlfriends of Hugh Hefner, on set to shoot a cameo scene for the movie. Normally, he was above taking Hef's castoffs, but he had a weakness for twins, and besides, he hadn't had sex at all for two whole days, not counting the blow job given by the passably cute flight attendant at twenty thousand feet yesterday.

It had taken him exactly two seconds to convince the twins to come to his trailer, and less than ten minutes before they both had their clothes off. Really, it was becoming embarrassing how easy it was to get women to take their clothes off for him. All he had to do was smile.

But then, that's what he'd been promised, all those many years ago, when he'd been eighteen and two hundred fifty pounds, running his Black Sabbath records backward on his turnstile for hours at a time, begging the devil to come to him. And come he did. He appeared wearing a black double-breasted blazer, and he had the hint of a widow's peak, and he'd told the young, ugly Corey Bennett that women, fame, and money could be his in exchange for his soul.

Corey didn't even think about it before signing over his immortal soul. Two months later, he dropped a hundred pounds and lost his virginity to the hottest girl in school. A week after that, he got his first TV commercial, and a month later, a recurring part on a TV detective show. Before he knew it, he was boinking supermodels and Playmates on a regular basis—a trend that didn't stop just because he happened to have a serious girlfriend.

And he hadn't had a single breakout since he was

eighteen. But now *this*. A red spot. *On his forehead*. Could it be that his pact with the devil was wearing out? Sexiest Men Alive didn't have breakouts. Next, he'd balloon back to his pre-soul-selling size. He glanced down at his now-flat stomach, a flicker of worry on his face. He lit up a cigarette to calm himself and took a big drag.

"*Corey*," whined Candy or Kitty, he couldn't tell which.

"Come back to bed!" sang the other.

Corey exhaled smoke and glanced up again, seeing his reflection and theirs in the mirrors that surrounded his trailer bed. There were mirrors on the walls and ceiling, all the better to see himself at all angles when screwing. It was a clause in his contract. All his trailers had to have these mirrors. Otherwise, how could he ever enjoy sex? The best part of doing a new girl was *watching himself do it*.

He spent a lot of time looking at his own body. The perfectly sculpted six-pack abs that took him next to nothing to maintain, and the chiseled muscles in his chest and arms that he kept simply by doing a handful of push-ups a day.

"In a minute," Corey said, still distracted by the red dot. He'd not had so much as a whitehead for twenty years. And now this. It was a tragedy. Worse than that. A calamity. Of the worst proportions. If it was a breakout, he'd have to call his agent. Have them reschedule his scenes today. He couldn't go before the cameras like this. He looked like a monster.

Behind him, the twin Playmates were giggling and smacking each other's bare bottoms, hoping to get his attention as they bounced on his bed. But he was still fixated on his blemish.

A hard knock came on his trailer door.

Annoyed at being disturbed, when his contract *clearly* stated that he was not to be interrupted except by his personal assistant, who knew not to knock when he had women in his trailer, he smashed his cigarette into a nearby ashtray and shouted, "Who is it?"

"Someone you need to talk to," came a familiar and yet not-so-familiar voice.

Whoever that was is going to be fired in about two seconds, Corey thought as he put on a robe and left his bouncing Playmates. He opened the trailer door an inch and saw . . . the devil. In his black blazer. The one who'd taken his soul. Except this time he was wearing a baseball cap, too.

"We need to talk," the devil said.

"Do we ever," Corey replied, opening the door wide enough to let him in.

The Playmates squealed in embarrassment and hurriedly tried to cover themselves when they saw Yaman in his black blazer and baseball cap march into Corey Bennett's trailer. Yaman found this false show of modesty funny, considering they'd bared all and more in a few dozen issues of *Playboy* and three *Playboy* videos.

"Girls," Corey said, since he couldn't remember their names. "This is an important producer. Mind if we have a second or two alone?"

Recovering quickly from showing a stranger their breasts, the twins giggled, threw on robes, and headed for the door.

"Don't be too long," one of them cooed at Corey at the trailer door.

"Sure thing, sweetheart," he said, blowing her a kiss. She pretended to catch it.

"I see you've been enjoying our deal," Yaman said, as the two twins bounced out of Bennett's trailer on their plastic platform stiletto heels.

"What's *this?*" Corey demanded, ignoring the comment as he pointed angrily to the tiny red spot on his forehead. "*This* wasn't part of the deal."

"About that . . ."

"I mean, if you're Satan, and I give you my soul, *the least you can do* is make sure I don't have any *zits.*"

"I never said I was Satan."

"You're not Satan?" Corey whipped around from the mirror and stared, openmouthed, at the man in black.

"Nope."

"Then who the hell did I sell my soul to?"

"Yaman, demon at large," Yaman said, bowing a little and producing a business card. He handed it to Corey who watched it turn to ash in his hand, shock still on his face.

"I work for a guy who works for a guy who works for Satan," Yaman clarified.

"You can't be serious," Corey said, slumping down, putting his forehead on the vanity. "I sold my soul to a *middle manager?*"

"You didn't seem to care at the time. Besides, bigger demons in the hierarchy don't have time to listen to eighteen-year-olds with Black Sabbath records. That falls to us little guys. We get enough souls and then we're promoted."

"You sound like you work for Mary Kay."

"Also one of our outfits," Yaman said, giving Corey his too-white smile.

"Great," Corey said, sitting down and running his hands through his hair. "So what happens now? Do I become fat and ugly again? Is your power wearing off?"

"Yes and no," Yaman said. "The thing is, Corey, you're dying."

"I'm *what*?"

"You've got cancer," Yaman said. "The zit is caused by the cancer, which is right now in your lungs, your liver, and part of your brain. I told you to be careful about the after-sex cigarette, but you didn't listen."

"You never told me that!" Corey exclaimed.

"Oh? I didn't. Darn. My bad." Yaman flashed him a particularly evil grin.

"I can't have cancer," Corey said, even though in his gut he knew this would explain a lot. Like waking up in the middle of the night coughing. Like his nagging chest cold that didn't seem to want to go away.

"You've got three months, tops," Yaman said. "Then I collect your soul."

"But I've got a movie to film," Corey protested. "And I'm only thirty-two!"

"You're thirty-nine," Yaman corrected. "And anyway, there is a way you might be able to extend your time on earth. My boss's boss wants a favor, and if you help him, then you'll get more time on earth."

"How much more time?"

"Till the end of the world," Yaman said, grinning again.

"What do you want from me?"

"The favor should be easy for you," Yaman said. "All you have to do is get Dante London into bed."

Corey Bennett just stared at the demon for a full second. Then he threw back his head and laughed.

"I was already planning on it," Corey said. "I sleep with *all* my costars. At least all the ones who are under the age of twenty-five. Besides, I've only had about a dozen virgins. They never know what they're doing, of course, but being first with Dante—it would be worth it."

"But here's the catch," Yaman said. "You can't actually have sex with her."

Corey's face fell a little. "I'm sorry. I don't follow. You said . . ."

"I said get her into bed. Then you have to let me take care of the rest," Yaman said, rubbing his hands together in a way that Corey Bennett didn't altogether like. But, he decided, he wasn't going to press the issue. He didn't really have a choice, did he?

"And then you take away the cancer?"

"And then I take away the cancer," Yaman said, showing Corey his best salesman's smile.

Nineteen

"You sure you're going to be okay?" Rachel asked Constance as they sat in her driveway. "I still think I should call Mel and get you checked out."

"No, I'm fine, really," Constance said, holding her head to keep it from falling apart. The postvision headache made it hard to concentrate on anything, even Rachel's thread of conversation. "I just have a headache is all. I just need to rest. It's been a stressful few days."

Rachel gave her a dubious look as Constance pulled herself out of the car and put her purse under one arm. "Okay, but if you need anything you call me, okay?"

"Okay," Constance agreed, waving as her friend backed out of the drive. Constance pushed open the front door and kicked off her black heels. She went straight for the fridge and grabbed the last Dr Pepper there on the bottom shelf. She drank half of it, and then put the cold can against her head and moaned as she slumped into a chair at her dinette. Lord, but her head hurt. She wasn't sure these visions were worth the hassle. Sure, she now knew that Corey Bennett was evil's puppet and planned to use her restaurant, but she didn't know much else. She knew they would eat chicken-fried steak, but that wasn't exactly a bit of useful information.

She was beginning to know what her mother had felt like all those years with completely irrelevant visions of Elvis. Constance sighed again, the Dr Pepper starting to take effect as the headache receded just enough she could actually lift up her head without seeing stars. She needed to call Frank. Maybe he could glean something more useful from what she'd seen. Or maybe he'd just be disappointed in her—again. She'd tried to get more details. She had. But the vision had simply come on too strong and too fast.

She picked up her cell phone and dialed Frank's phone. She got a busy signal. She tried again, then went straight to voicemail. She tried a third and fourth time and got a message saying the cell phone user was out of range.

Then she called Jose at the Magnolia Café.

"*Dios mío!* Are you okay? I heard Nathan Garrett took you in. You better not be using your only phone call to call me," he said.

"How did you know about that already?"

"Everybody's been talking about it. We got nearly a full house today, everyone here is buzzing about it. You being arrested was pretty good for business. Not to mention we've got all the movie people about. You'd be surprised how much lighting people eat!"

"Great," Constance said, grabbing her head. "But, Jose, we have to close the restaurant."

"What? Why?" Jose sounded suspicious.

"It's just—we have to. Just for a couple of days,"

Constance said. She didn't want to try to explain how the devil was going to use her little café to seduce the would-be mother of the Antichrist.

"But business is just getting good!" Jose cried. "I don't get it."

"Please," Constance said. "In memory of Jimmy, okay?"

"You know I could fill in for you for the next few days. You wouldn't have to come in on shift, and we'd still get business."

"I know this sounds crazy. But please, for me?"

Jose sighed. "I'm not going to talk you out of this?"

"I'll pay you back what we'll lose for being closed. I promise. Just for a day or two, okay? I'll call you when we can open again."

"Okay," Jose said reluctantly. "But as your partner, I think it's a bad idea."

"I know. But I appreciate it," Constance said.

"Can we finish out lunch, at least?"

"Yes, finish out lunch, but no dinner," Constance said, thinking that would probably be safe. She tried hard to remember the time of day in the vision, but it seemed to her like it was nighttime. At least, there were lit candles on the table, and those never came out until after six.

"Okay, boss." Jose clicked off and Constance knew she'd be explaining that decision to him for a long while.

"What's *that* all about?" Dead Jimmy asked Constance, appearing at her left side. Constance jumped a little. She hadn't gotten used to her dead almost-ex appearing and reappearing every now and again. And he didn't help her headache one little bit.

"Do you have to do that?"

"Do what?"

"Scare the dickens out of me. Why don't you just walk into a room like a normal person?"

"Because I'm a ghost, that's why. We don't walk. We float."

"Then can you go float somewhere else?" Constance dropped her cell phone and put her head in both hands and groaned.

"I'm here to help, remember? Until we foil the devil's plans."

"Well, if you want to help, can you scrounge up some Excedrin? I've got to go find Frank."

Devil's in the Details was being filmed about ten miles west of the town square. The Higgins Ranch was a hundred acres of ranchland once used for raising cattle, but it had recently become famous as a backdrop for a couple of B movies. The white farmhouse up front and the sprawling back country were the perfect setting for your typical Western, modern cowboy romance, or anything involving lots of horses, some trees, and good sunsets.

It was also protected as a historical landmark and run by the Texas Women's Heritage Foundation, a group that Constance had catered for just last year at their annual banquet at the ranch. Today she brought her state-fair-award-winning chicken-fried steaks with her, hoping they'd help her get inside. They were for Henry Murphy, the full-time property manager, who would no doubt be around somewhere. He loved Constance's steaks, and would probably give her a tour of the movie set after one glance at the Magnolia Café take-out bag.

Even though it was nearly dinnertime, there were still loads of cars parked on Route 9, and clusters of gawkers along the fence leading up to the house. The front gate, Constance saw, was closed, and a guard was on duty.

"How are we going to get in?" Dead Jimmy asked.

"Back way," Constance said, steering her Camry down an unmarked dirt road a quarter mile from the front gate.

"So, you going to tell Dante London she's been picked by the devil to be the mother of the Antichrist?" Dead Jimmy asked.

"No, I'm just going to find Frank and tell him what I saw, and hopefully he'll handle it."

"Oh yeah, leave saving the world up to a dog in a pink sweater. Real smart."

"I can't save the world, Jimmy. I'm not a superhero. I'm not an angel. I'm just *me*. I can't even get these visions right. The only thing I know how to do is cook, and unless the devil can be slain by baking pecan pie, I'm best sitting on the sidelines."

"But God picked you," Dead Jimmy said. "You're supposed to be the Chosen One."

"Well, God made a mistake," Constance said, driving down the twisting dirt road that led to the barn.

"Someone sure got up on the wrong side of their Chosen Bed this morning," Dead Jimmy said.

"Jimmy!" Constance growled. "Not helping."

"Hey, hey, no need to get snappy. I'll go," Dead Jimmy said, and disappeared with a tiny poof.

Constance parked her Camry behind a white trailer, one of many leading up to the back of the white ranch house. From the back, Constance was amazed at how easily she simply walked onto the set. There was a little guarded gate, but it was open, and the guard on duty wasn't anywhere to be found. She walked through and saw that there were dozens of people busy moving things about, like lights and cameras and big cases of equipment. In fact, there were so many people at work that one more didn't seem to bother anyone. Most of the set workers were concentrated out near the barn, where she saw bright lights, a few cameras, and a tent with director's chairs in it.

While she glanced around for a sign of Frank, she laid eyes on Nathan Garrett, who was standing near a white trailer, conversing with a woman wearing a headset and carrying a clipboard. All the air went straight out of Constance's lungs, and she flattened herself against the side of a nearby trailer, hoping against hope that Nathan hadn't seen her. The last thing she needed was to get arrested for trespassing on top of murder, which she was positive Nathan would do eventually. He'd made it crystal clear he thought she was capable of killing. Killing *and* being the kind of woman who slept around. Anger pricked again at her stomach.

While she was flattening herself against the side of what smelled like the catering trailer, she heard a loud screech and saw a man half stumble, half fall out of another trailer. He seemed to be in a life-or-death struggle with what Constance thought was Frank. The little French bulldog had grabbed onto his shoulders, and was snarling viciously. Upon closer inspection, Constance saw that the man trying to get the dog off his back was, in fact, the famous Corey Bennett. "No one touches my hair!" he yelped, as Frank scratched and clawed at Corey's sideburns.

It looked like Frank had already figured out Corey was evil. Guess her vision was even more useless than she'd thought.

As Corey struggled with the dog, Dante London poured out of her trailer right after him, crying, "Pinky! Bad dog! Bad, bad dog!"

"What the . . ." Corey shouted, his face turning red as he struggled with the dog, coming ever closer to Constance, who could only watch in amazement as Frank pawed at Corey's hair and growled, and then let out a small river of yellow pee down the side of Corey's head and shoulder. "Get the hell off me!" Corey shouted, grabbing Frank by his front paws and flinging him hard.

"Pinky!" shouted Dante London in concern as Frank soared through the air, legs and tail flailing, just a streak of pink fuzzy sweater. He was headed straight for the side of the catering trailer and would've hit the tin wall at high impact, but was saved at the last second by Constance, who reached out her arms and caught the fur ball.

Frank glanced up and mouthed a grateful *Thank you*.

"Oh, thank *God*," breathed Dante, rushing away from her pee-soaked costar and toward Constance, where she cooed at Frank like he was a baby. "You saved her!"

"Unfortunately," Corey mumbled under his breath as dog pee dripped down his sideburns. "I've got to go get cleaned up," he said sulkily, stomping back toward his own trailer.

"Um, bye, Corey!" yelled Dante after him. "I'll see you later, yeah?"

Corey grumbled something Constance couldn't hear and then threw up a hand in a reluctant wave.

"I can't thank you enough," Dante said, now turning to Constance as she scooped the little bulldog into her arms. "Oh my *God*, when I think about what could've happened when she slipped out of Corey's arms."

"Slipped?" Constance echoed. More like was hurled. But she let it slide.

"My poor little Pinky," Dante cooed.

"Pinky?" Constance couldn't help but smile a little. She looked down at Frank, who gave her a little shrug. "Actually, Miss London, I was hoping to borrow Fr-, er, I mean Pinky, if I could," Constance said, even as Frank whined.

"Is this about my dog's shots? 'Cause she's had 'em, I think."

"No, I'm, uh, the dog groomer," Constance said.

"Oh my *God*. I'm such a goofus," Dante squealed, giving Constance an exaggerated eye roll. "But she was just groomed yesterday. Are you sure you're with Doggie-licious?"

Constance blinked fast. "Um, that's right. Doggie-licious," she said. "And, uh, we missed a spot yesterday. I have to apologize. Normally, we're very thorough." Constance felt her eyes start to itch. Frank's fur was already starting to disagree with her. She knocked a bit of his fur off her shirt and hoped she didn't sneeze.

"Really?" Dante asked, unsure.

Out of the corner of her eye, Constance saw Nathan

turn the corner. He hadn't spotted her yet, but it would only be a matter of time.

"Yes, that's right. And I need to do this *now*," Constance said, holding up her bag of chicken-fried steaks as if it were her dog-cleaning supplies. "It's extremely important."

"Okay, then," Dante said. "Let's go back to my trailer. Dog grooming waits for no one!" she singsonged, leading Constance and Pinky into her trailer. Once inside, her cell phone sprang to life with her latest single, "Burn Me, Baby."

"Oops, that'll be my agent. Let me take this call. One sec," she said, picking up the phone and then slipping into another room in the trailer and shutting the door.

"Did you have another vision?" Frank asked as soon as Dante was out of earshot.

"Sure did, and I tried to call you, but you don't get service out here," she said.

"It was probably demon interference," Frank said. "They're crawling all over the set. So? The vision?"

"Looks like you already know it," Constance said. "Corey Bennett is working for the dark side, and he's going to help get Dante London to the devil."

"I thought so," Frank said. "He smelled like one of theirs." Frank wrinkled his stout little nose. "You get a time or a place?"

"Corey is going to take her to my restaurant, the Magnolia Café."

"What a stroke of luck," Frank declared. "Just close the restaurant down."

"I did already."

"Good work."

Just then, Dante emerged from the next room with her cell phone still in her hand.

"Sorry, y'all," she drawled to Constance. "But we're going to have to do the dog grooming later. My agent just called, and *Hollywood Today* has a camera crew on set, but they're only here for an hour, and I don't do interviews without Pinky."

"No problem, Miss London," Constance said.

Frank hopped up into Dante's arms just as she was heading out of the trailer. Frank turned to Constance before he left and said, "Go home. I'll call you," while mimicking making a telephone call with his paw. He looked like a little brown furry secret agent.

Constance wondered for a minute if Dante had heard him actually speak, but the pop star didn't seem fazed. She just gave his head a little pat and walked on. Looked like Constance was the only one who understood him.

Standing on the little stairs of the trailer, Constance looked quickly both ways, but saw Nathan had gone. Thank goodness. She breathed a little sigh of relief. At least she wouldn't be arrested. That was, if she could avoid him long enough to get to her car. As she walked, she realized, a beat too late, that she'd left behind her chicken-fried steaks, but decided not to loop back for them. She'd done her duty, delivering the message to Frank, and that was all she could do.

The crowds of people she'd seen before milling and working on the set had disappeared, and she guessed it was dinnertime, or they had wrapped for the night. The set was a little eerie so empty, and Constance picked up

her pace, remembering what Frank had said about demons being about.

She didn't take another step before two strong
hands came at her from behind, one of them wrapping
around her mouth, and pulling her in between two
white trailers.

Her first thought was, *Demon!* Should she struggle?
Scream? And why wasn't she at least wearing a cross?
Damn her lack of planning.

Before she could decide her next step, she was whirled
around and came face-to-face with Nathan Garrett.

"Now, before I arrest you," he drawled, his face close
and his dark eyes on hers, "would you like to tell me just
what on earth you're doing here?"

Constance felt her heart speed up, and she wasn't
entirely sure it was just because she was still mad as
hell at him. Nathan's hands were strong and big around
her arms, and she couldn't help but remember the last
time they were this close and he'd unhooked her bra
with one hand.

"None of your business," she said crossly.

"I think it is my business," he said, tightening his
grip slightly. "Since you're supposed to be at the police
station."

"Ow, fine, stop the police brutality," she said, trying
to wiggle free. "I'm trying to get an autograph."

The lie sat awkwardly on her tongue. She hated to lie.
Every inch of her being rebelled against it, and yet she
couldn't very well tell Nathan the truth. He'd lock her up
in a second. The space between the trailers Nathan had
pulled her into was snug, and she was inches from him.

Even as he loosened his grip on her arms, she felt like he sucked the oxygen right out of the air. She couldn't breathe.

Nathan was looking at her skeptically, his dark eyes penetrating and sharp. She couldn't fool him.

"You're a Dante London fan?" Nathan said, a small smile playing at the corners of his mouth. He found this funny, apparently. Constance had to admit she wasn't likely to be following teen pop.

"Oh, um, well, not exactly."

"So do you want to tell me what in Sam hell you were doing in her trailer just now?"

"Yes, I know, I, uh, well . . ." Constance struggled to think. It didn't help that his nose was inches from hers, or that he smelled like cinnamon gum. And she'd forgotten how broad he was. She felt tiny by comparison.

Focus, Constance, she told herself. This was a heck of a time to be distracted by a Garrett, especially one in a sheriff's uniform sporting sharp brown eyes that seemed to know everything she was going to say before she said it. Not to mention she was mad at him. *Mad.*

"Just trying to drum up business for the Magnolia Café," Constance said, thinking fast. "I brought samples."

Nathan studied her, a skeptical look on his face. "Where are they?"

"I gave them to Dante London, of course. She's a Southern girl. She loves chicken-fried steak." Constance surprised herself—that lie actually sounded good. It would be ironic if working for the Lord made her a better liar.

Nathan slouched back against a trailer, crossing his

arms across his broad chest. "I believe you're lying to me, Constance Plyd."

"Am not."

"Are too." Nathan tapped her left hand. Constance realized too late it was absently twirling a strand of her hair. "You always do that when you lie."

Constance turned an even deeper shade of red and dropped her hair.

"So you going to tell me what you're really doing here?"

"You wouldn't believe me if I told you," she managed, meeting his gaze with more bravery than she felt at the moment. After all, if she was doing God's work, she couldn't exactly feel guilty about it. She didn't ask to be a minor prophet, did she?

"Try me," Nathan said, leaning closer. She had to crane her neck to meet his eyes, which were so close to hers now that she could see his pupils. They were round and big and dark. He was moving in, and she reflexively put up a hand, which met his chest. It was strong and solid, and she could swear she felt his heart beating beneath the uniform.

"I . . ." Constance began, faltering. She felt like he had her in some kind of magnetic lock, a Garrett tractor beam, and she couldn't help but move closer to him. She found herself arching on tiptoe.

And then she did something she'd never imagined she'd ever do again in her whole life.

She up and kissed Nathan Garrett straight on the lips.

It was a tentative kiss at first. She hardly knew what

she was doing. She was on autopilot, as if something about him—the way he looked, the way he smelled—made this moment inevitable since the morning he'd strolled straight into her kitchen and back into her life.

His lips stayed closed, but he didn't push her away. She realized what she was doing a little too late. She pulled back a bit, eyes wide in surprise, searching out his. His dark eyes locked on hers, and even as she tried to find the words to apologize, he gathered her closer, pushed her against the opposite trailer, and covered her mouth with his.

And the way he kissed her wasn't like the innocent peck Constance had laid on him. This was an open-mouthed, ravenous kiss, with his body pressed hard against hers. She could feel his hunger for her, a desire that went much deeper than she'd ever thought possible. And her body responded, completely and totally, as if he'd remembered all the right buttons to press. If she came equipped with slot machine lights, the lights would be flashing and bells dinging, ring-a-ding-ding.

It was Nathan who finally pulled away, leaving them both weak and panting, and not sure what to do next.

Constance saw it on Nathan's face. He looked guilty, and a little embarrassed, as if he weren't sure what he'd done. He clearly thought he'd made a mistake. Maybe he hadn't felt what Constance felt. And then Constance just felt mortally embarrassed. Not only had she just kissed her sworn enemy, but apparently she'd done so badly.

"I-I-I have to go," Constance managed to sputter, and by some miracle, she managed to get her jellied legs to move. Nathan didn't stop her, as she slid away. Constance put one foot in front of the other, trying to get as much distance between them as she could. It was only after she'd made several long strides that she realized she was walking in the opposite direction from where she needed to go. Her face tomato-red, she turned and walked back the other way, feeling Nathan's gaze on her as she passed him. In fact, she felt his eyes on her all the way to her car.

Twenty

Constance was so flustered by Nathan, she didn't notice the two demons floating nearby.

"Oh dear Satan, but that was gross," said Yaman, wobbling a little as he and Shadow turned to follow Constance from the movie set. They rose up, floating high above her, as she shakily got into her Camry and turned over the ignition.

"Ugh. Kissing—disgusting," Shadow agreed, then groaned. "I think I might be sick."

"Wait until we land, for hell's sake," Yaman chided. "I don't want squirrel guts all over me, thanks. Besides, this jacket is Armani."

"Ar-*what*?"

"Ar . . . Never mind," Yaman sighed. "It's not like you'd know anything about fashion since you don't wear clothes."

"Nice of you to notice," Shadow said sarcastically. "Was it the fact I'm a *shadow* clue you into that one?"

"Whatever. I think that prophet did it to us on purpose."

"I doubt she knows that Pride and Glutton demons hate PDAs," Shadow said.

"Still," Yaman said, wrinkling his nose, "I'm going to have to go kill something just to get the bad taste out of my mouth."

"If you get to kill someone, then I get to eat someone," Shadow said. "Fair's fair."

"Ugh. Fine. I'll restrain myself." Yaman sighed. "But I'm going to need therapy after this."

"Therapists are pretty tasty," Shadow said. "Nice and tender."

"You have a one-track mind." Yaman looked down and saw Constance back out of her parking space, nearly hitting another car that she didn't see. That car honked at her.

"What? I'm just saying, you should really just let me eat that prophet. If she's going to go around kissing everybody and having visions with holes in them, then you have to let me eat her."

"No. You heard what the general said."

"I know. I know. We have to take her alive."

"She's the key to all this. Satan doesn't know what the Big Guy's next move will be until she has another vision. Satan isn't going to come to earth until the coast is clear."

"Coast is clear of what? Goats?"

"Ha. Funny. No, God's troops. Last time, God sent his Archangel Special Forces. And those guys are seriously badass."

"Tell me about it!" Shadow said, and shuddered, remembering his own run-in with the wrath angels. "I saw enough of them at Gomorrah. I hope they don't come this time."

"Me, too," Yaman admitted. "Any sign of them and I am totally out of here."

"Coward," sniffed Shadow, whose stomach gave a loud grumble. "So why don't we just kidnap the prophet? Then we wouldn't have to follow her around all day—and as a bonus, she wouldn't kiss anyone, either."

"Hey—that's not a bad idea, Glutton." Yaman considered this a moment. "Of course, if she's a prophet, she might see us coming."

"Her? Are you serious? She can't even control her visions yet. She couldn't predict a sneeze, much less us. Besides, she ran right by us and didn't even notice."

"That's true."

Yaman watched as Constance gunned her car down the small dirt road, whipping it onto Route 9 and nearly colliding with an oncoming car. The other car slammed on its brakes and honked at her.

"Told you prophets were terrible drivers. That's her second near accident in five minutes," Yaman said, nodding down at the driver Constance had just cut off in her haste to get away from the Higgins Ranch. "It's amazing she's still in one piece, driving like that."

"All the more reason we should kidnap her," Shadow said. "For her own protection." Shadow sniffed and then sneezed. "As an added bonus, we could take her and hold her someplace *away* from all these damn dogwood trees. They are totally giving me a sinus headache."

"Me, too," Yaman agreed. "Okay, let's do it. When?""

"Tonight," Shadow said. "I can't materialize fully

in the day. And in the meantime, I should probably eat something to keep my strength up. How about that mini-van down there?" Shadow pointed to the car behind Constance's.

"No." Yaman shook his head for emphasis.

"The billboard, then?"

"Nope. Too conspicuous."

"Arrrgh," Shadow growled, holding his head. "I'm starting to get a hunger headache."

"Okay, okay, *fine*. Take the garbage truck, but wait until it goes beneath that underpass and there aren't any other cars around."

"You got it."

Shadow flew off almost before the words were out of Yaman's mouth.

"But don't take too long," Yaman shouted after the floating apparition. "We've got a prophet to kidnap."

Twenty-one

Constance sat at her kitchen table on top of her mother's pentagram and for once wasn't thinking about her mission, the demons that might be after her, or whether or not she would ever be free of her dead husband's ghost. All she could think about was Nathan Garrett. It had been the same since the evening before, when she'd driven home from Higgins Ranch, barely remembering to stop at stoplights on the way home, she was so rattled.

She just kept replaying that kiss in her mind over and over, and kept asking herself what it meant, even as a part of her said the very fact that she couldn't keep her mind on her heavenly mission was probably proof enough Garrett worked for the devil. As if she needed any after that toes-on-fire kiss. Something that good just had to be a sin.

Constance, dressed in her pink cotton pj's and terry-cloth robe, crossed her legs, sliding one pink bunny slipper over the other, and sighed. Her right bunny slipper was missing its left eye, and patches around her heel were coming undone. She'd have to get new ones sometime, but these were so comfortable, she hated to think of parting with them. Even if they did look a little worse for wear.

It was early, and the sun wasn't quite up yet. It was just shy of five. Constance had fallen into a fitful sleep, and then come awake with a start in the middle of the night. She'd had another dream about Dante London and the devil, and it was so vivid that it took her a good long while to realize she was in her bed and not in between them as they shared their first kiss.

She'd tossed and turned for a bit after that, but there was no getting back to sleep, so she'd pulled herself from bed and put on the coffeepot. The kitchen was quiet. She couldn't hear Dead Jimmy snoring, but she guessed that didn't mean much. He came and went like a stray cat.

As soon as she poured herself a cup of coffee and sat down, her thoughts immediately turned to Nathan Garrett. Why had he kissed her like that? And what was the meaning of the expression on his face after? She couldn't make sense of it, but her face burned in embarrassment just thinking about it. It was her fault for kissing him in the first place. She didn't know why she'd done it. Or why she couldn't stop thinking about it, either. Hadn't she spent the last ten years fuming because she'd let herself go too far in the backseat of Nathan's car? And now here she was allowing herself to daydream about him because she'd succumbed to the Garrett charm in a moment of weakness. She knew better than to fall for a Garrett a second time. The whole family was bad news, and the last thing she needed now was more trouble.

Besides, what if he was just trying to mess with her head? Last time she checked, he thought she was the prime suspect in Jimmy's murder. Not that she blamed him, exactly. It was a lot to process on faith. Was coming on to her some kind of ploy? Maybe he was trying to make her confess.

A loud thump from the living room made Constance start. She froze to the spot, coffee mug in the air, listening. There was another thump, followed by some rustling sounds, like someone or something going through paper.

Instantly, she thought, *Yaman the demon is back. He's back and he's going to murder me, now that he's killed Jimmy.*

She realized too late that she had been a sitting duck all this time, and that instead of daydreaming about Nathan Garrett, she ought to have planned for this very thing. Shouldn't she have expected the demons to come back? Frank had said they wouldn't hurt her, or at least not kill her, since they needed her visions. But what if he was wrong?

She set her coffee mug down on the table and put her hand to her throat, but she wasn't wearing the tiny gold cross she saved for Sundays. She scanned the kitchen and saw a few dogwood blossoms on the edge of her mother's pentagram. She grabbed them, held them out, and slowly walked into the living room.

She glanced from corner to corner, but the living room was empty.

A movement out of the corner of her eye made her spin around, and she saw it was just the edge of her curtain blowing in the breeze: a breeze that was blowing in through an open window.

She felt a shiver down her spine. Had whoever—or whatever—killed Jimmy climbed in through the window? Was the demon wandering around her house now, waiting to pounce on her?

She felt a cold hand on her shoulder then, and nearly jumped four feet in the air.

She screamed, and so did Dead Jimmy, who'd snuck up behind her.

"What the hell are you trying to do? Scare me to death?" Constance sputtered at Dead Jimmy, waving the wilted flowers at him. "I thought you were a demon."

"And you were going to exorcise me with some dead flowers?" Dead Jimmy looked at the dogwood blooms doubtfully.

"Something like that," Constance said. "What were you doing here, anyway?"

"I *live* here," Dead Jimmy said. "And I was just going to ask you the same thing. I was upstairs sleeping when I heard some racket down here."

"You mean you didn't open that window?" Constance said, pointing to her curtains, still fluttering.

"Nope," Dead Jimmy said, shaking his head.

Constance felt a chill again. If it wasn't Dead Jimmy, then who? As she was pondering this, she got a whiff of something familiar and foul. The same smell she'd smelled the morning Jimmy had been killed—a cross between burnt popcorn and Jimmy's gym socks.

"Move," Constance cried to Dead Jimmy. "Move *now."*

Constance suddenly remembered the kitchen—and her mother's pentagram. It was as good a thing to try as any, she thought, and stumbled through the swinging door. Constance stood in the middle of it, with Dead Jimmy by her side.

They both stared at the kitchen door, which slowly swung back and forth until it came to a stop. For several long seconds, nobody moved, and there was no sound. Then suddenly, behind them, a sharp wind blasted through the back door from the garage, sending the screen door slapping hard against the kitchen wall.

"Aaaah!" Dead Jimmy screamed, clutching at Constance's sleeve with cold ghost hands.

Constance barely had time to register Dead Jimmy when she saw something dark and shadowy slink in through the open back door. It took on various shapes as it went, looking sometimes like a wolf with more than one head and sometimes like a giant snake. It clung to the ceiling and the wall like some kind of slow-moving tar. She remembered the Lizard Lady at the DMV, but this demon was much, *much* scarier. Any lingering doubts she might have had that demons existed flew from her mind. She knew now they were real. Too real. Constance watched the shape as it made its way across the kitchen ceiling and floor, stopping just short of the barrier of the pentagram and the wilted dogwood blooms as if there were some kind of invisible force field.

"I'll be damned," she said out loud. "Mom and Frank

were *right*." She tossed one of the flowers at the shadow creature, and it wiggled and then sneezed as it backed slowly away.

"I'm getting the hell out of here!" Dead Jimmy shouted.

"Don't leave the pentagram!" Constance called, but too late, as Dead Jimmy ran back toward the living room. His forward momentum, however, was stopped as he ran smack dab into the man in black.

"Yaman," Constance whispered. He was wearing the same black baseball cap with his black suit. And as he met Constance's eyes he gave her a slow, evil smile. She felt a sinking feeling in her stomach. This was not good.

Yaman grabbed Dead Jimmy by the throat, and lifted the ghost high above his head. Dead Jimmy fought to get free, kicking his feet and tugging at the demon's viselike grip.

"Prophet," Yaman said, meeting her eyes. Constance felt suddenly very cold. She could feel the shadowlike creature moving behind her. She gave it a quick glance, but saw it had still not managed to break the barrier of the pentagram. She sent up a silent thank-you to her mother. She vowed she would never call her crazy again.

"It's time for you to come with us," Yaman said, his words dripping venom. Behind her, she could hear the tarlike creature hiss. Dead Jimmy continued his struggle against the demon's grip. Oddly, his face was turning red, even though he was a ghost who shouldn't, technically, be breathing.

"Why should I?" Constance asked with more bravery

than she felt at the moment. Frank had said they needed her for her visions. Surely they wouldn't kill her. They needed her alive.

Behind her, the tar creature took the form of three dogs' heads and snapped their jaws. She flinched, even as their tongues hit the edge of the pentagram and made a sizzling sound, as if colliding with a bug zapper. The creature hissed loudly and dropped back into its bloblike form. Constance glanced around the kitchen looking for her cell phone. She needed to call Frank. He could help, she was sure, but she didn't see her phone. She might have left it upstairs.

"We've got your husband," Yaman said, shaking Dead Jimmy. He was still kicking and making alarming wheezing sounds.

"He's my almost-ex husband and he's already dead," Constance pointed out.

"There are worse things than being dead," Yaman said, and while Constance couldn't think what those things might be, she suddenly believed him.

"Still not convincing me to come with you," Constance said, her eyes darting around the kitchen looking for something within her reach that she might be able to use as a weapon. Of course, she didn't have the first clue about fighting. Her only training was watching reruns of *Buffy the Vampire Slayer* on TV. She hardly thought that counted for much. Besides, Buffy fought fake demons and vampires. Constance hardly knew what to do with real ones. She glanced up and saw Dead Jimmy still struggling. "Why don't you just disappear, Jimmy?" she asked him.

"Don't you think I'm trying?" Dead Jimmy coughed out.

"He can't," Yaman said. "Not while I'm here." Yaman shook Dead Jimmy by the neck. "Maybe this will change your mind," he added, and suddenly let go of Dead Jimmy, who gasped and grabbed his neck. But instead of falling to the ground, Dead Jimmy suddenly levitated in the air.

"Hey, what the hell . . . ?" he muttered even as Yaman guided him with his hand straight up toward the ceiling, slamming him flat on his back next to the kitchen light. Next, Yaman began levitating other objects in her neatly arranged kitchen: the bread box, a few dirty plates from the sink, all of the sharpest knives out of her butcher's block, and all the vintage kitschy additions she'd added to her kitchen since falling in love with the retro look on Rachael Ray's *30 Minute Meals*. The knives and dishes began swirling around her kitchen in a fast-moving circle, like a tornado in Crate & Barrel. The knives whizzed past her in a whirlwind of metal, and while the blades didn't slice the plane of the pentagram, they still came dangerously close to her ears. Constance ducked, and put her arms above her head, even as her butcher knife whipped by.

"Come with us now," Yaman said. "Or die here."

The tar creature behind her hissed in agreement.

Constance felt her heart pounding. She was scared, no doubt, but she also knew that if she moved from the spot where she was standing even worse things might happen. She had to fight the urge to go running as fast as her legs would take her in any direction away from here. She had to stand where she was, even as Yaman hurled her dishes to the ground about a foot from her, shattering them and sending shards dancing across her kitchen floor. She tried not to cry as some of her best Fiesta ware broke into tiny pieces.

"You need me," Constance said, hoping they didn't call her bluff. "You need my visions."

"Some visions," sniffed the shadow behind her.

"It's true we need you alive," Yaman said. "But doesn't mean we can't have fun with you first. You don't need all your fingers or toes, for instance, to have visions."

"Or your arms," Shadow added.

Constance shuddered.

"Help!" Dead Jimmy shouted, as Yaman pinned him to the ceiling and began using him for target practice with her steak knives. He sent several whizzing straight through him and into her ceiling. Dead Jimmy flinched, even though he was a ghost who wasn't supposed to be able to feel anything. "Connie! Do what he wants!" Dead Jimmy said, covering his eyes.

"That can't hurt," Constance said to Dead Jimmy.

"No, but it's not all that comfortable, either!" Dead Jimmy shouted back even as Yaman sent a knife through his head. "Feels like I have a brain freeze!"

"We're waiting, *Prophet*," Yaman hissed at Constance, and threw up his hands. Her refrigerator started to shake, as well as the rest of her major appliances. They were all handpicked with care—and she nearly cried out when her prized convection oven toppled forward. She loved that oven. The dishwasher door flew open with a clang, and her gas burners all came on in a whoosh. Yaman glanced over at the burners and a sly smile crossed his face. In an instant, he levitated two dishtowels over to the burners and set them on fire, and then sent them swirling around her head. They came close enough that Constance could feel the heat from the flames, and small sparks landed on her robe. Frantically, she beat them with her hands.

"I asked once *nicely*," Yaman said. "And you should have listened." With a flick of his wrist the towels went sailing toward her cherry print curtains. They went up like a Christmas tree in July. The flames sailed up to the ceiling, setting the paint on fire and sending smoke toward Dead Jimmy, who was now trying to wiggle away, even as Yaman kept him pinned. The tops of the cabinets caught next, and the air filled with smoke. Constance's eyes and throat started to burn, and fear made her chest constrict. She wouldn't be able to stay put now. She couldn't just stand there and burn to death. Yaman saw the fear in her eyes and his smile got wider.

"If you come with us now, I promise I'll let my friend eat you quickly after we get what we need," Yaman said, nodding to the tar creature who lunged forward again at her, hissing. "And we won't even torture you, *much*, if you give us what we need quickly."

Constance pulled her robe over her face and knelt down in the pentagram, trying to get below the smoke even as it grew thicker. She had no idea what to do next, and she felt the panic start to rise. The smoke was so thick now, even near the floor where she was crouching, that she could barely see Yaman anymore or the black tar creature or Dead Jimmy. She felt like she couldn't breathe.

Through the smoke, she saw the flash of headlights shine through her window and the telltale burst of red and blue police lights. And she heard the brief wail of a siren.

Nathan, she thought. Had he come to save her? *Thank God*, she prayed, and then she passed out on her kitchen floor.

Twenty-two

Nathan saw the smoke before he'd even pulled up in Constance's driveway. He radioed in for EMS and the volunteer fire guys, but it might take them a half hour or more to get to the Plyd house. This was the country, after all, and things did move a little slower out here. Nathan guessed by the smoke and the flicker of flames coming from Constance's kitchen that she didn't have thirty minutes. He prayed she wasn't inside.

He hadn't been expecting this. He'd come with the intent to arrest her. He should've brought her in at the Higgins Ranch, but he'd been distracted by the kiss. More distracted than he should have been. He could've sworn she hated him, but she'd been the one to kiss him first. You could've knocked him over with a Post-it note. He hadn't seen that coming. But once he did, he sure liked it. She tasted like strawberries and cream.

But once he regained his senses, he realized he couldn't let the mounting evidence go anymore, and he had spent the entire twenty minutes it took to drive over to Constance's place steeling himself for the task ahead. He kept telling himself that he had a job to do and it wasn't personal, but the words sounded weak in his head, no matter how often he thought them.

But now, seeing the smoke rise from her house, he didn't care about anything but knowing she was safe.

A flicker of doubt passed through his mind. What if she was trying to destroy evidence? The fire licked the roof above the kitchen and traveled to the garage. Pretty soon there wouldn't be much of a crime scene left. He decided he didn't care. He wanted Constance to be okay. Period.

He kicked open his car door and hopped out, just as he saw a figure emerge from the garage. At first he thought it might be Constance, but then he realized it was too big to be her. He whipped up his flashlight and gun, and pointed both in the direction of the shadow.

"Freeze! Police," he shouted on instinct.

The beam of his flashlight hit the shoulder of a man. Nathan couldn't see his face because he was turned slightly and running away from him. But he could tell one thing—he was wearing all black, and on his head he had a black baseball cap.

"Yaman!" he shouted, on a hunch, and the man slowed slightly and turned his head.

I'll be damned, he thought. *It is the same guy.* The guy Constance swore was at the scene of Jimmy's murder.

"Stop right now or I'll shoot."

Yaman just grinned a little, and then turned away from him, running toward the line of trees next to the house.

Nathan planted his feet and squeezed the trigger twice, aiming for the man's torso. Unlike in the movies, most cops didn't aim for the legs or arms. They were too hard a target to hit. He went for the midsection, and he knew he'd hit his target. He was barely twenty-five feet away, and Nathan was a very good shot. And yet Yaman didn't even pause as he trotted easily into the trees. Could he have missed? At this range?

Nathan shook off his disbelief and started running, but Yaman had already disappeared into the trees. Nathan had barely taken three steps when he thought he heard something from Constance's house. A cry for help.

He paused for a second, the urge to run for Yaman strong in his blood. He didn't like letting his man go. But then the cry seemed to get louder. Someone was in the burning house, and that someone was Constance.

He holstered his gun and turned and went straight for the house, where the fire was starting to eat away the roof. Pretty soon, the whole house would come down. Nathan whipped off his jacket and covered his face with it. He ducked inside the back door, the smoke thick as he trailed his hand along one flame-free wall to keep his bearings.

The cry grew stronger as he stepped into the kitchen, but the smoke was so thick he couldn't see his hand in front of his face. He stumbled into a chair, and then his left shoe hit something thick and solid on the ground: a leg.

"Constance!" he shouted, bending down and feeling her sprawled out on the floor, limp. She didn't respond to him at all, and he was beginning to wonder how he'd heard her cry at all. She was passed out. He prayed she was okay.

Above his head, the kitchen ceiling cracked and popped, and a big chunk of it fell on the floor not five feet from them. He had to get moving and fast. Nathan picked her up, slinging her over his shoulder, and then made a run in the direction of the back door. The flames were hot in his face, and the smoke was so thick it was choking him, but he made it outside through the garage. Coughing himself, he gently laid Constance down on the grass a safe distance from the house, which was now a big ball of flame and smoke.

"Constance? Can you hear me?" he shouted at her. She didn't move, or even groan. Frantically, he checked her vitals and came up empty. "Don't do this to me!" he said, and he started CPR immediately, pumping her chest and covering her mouth with his. He didn't have time to think about anything but getting her breathing again. After a few seconds that seemed like hours, Constance started coughing.

Thank God, he thought.

"Constance? Can you hear me? Are you okay?"

Her eyes fluttered, and then met his.

"Yaman . . ." she croaked, her voice sounding hoarse.

"I know," Nathan said, nodding. "I saw him running from the house. I didn't catch him, but I will, Constance. I promise."

She shook her head.

"He really is a . . ." she began, but her voice seemed to fail. Nathan heard the EMS and fire truck sirens in the distance. Help was on the way.

". . . a demon," she managed before her eyes fluttered closed.

Confused, Nathan furrowed his brow. "Demon?" he asked her, shaking her awake again.

"Frank," she moaned. "I need to call Frank."

"Who's Frank?" Nathan asked urgently, but she'd already slipped back into unconsciousness. She was still breathing and she had a strong pulse, but there was no rousing her this time.

The ambulance pulled up seconds later, and Mel had her on a stretcher within minutes. He gave Mel the short version of what happened, and told her to be careful. There was a man on the loose who'd tried to kill Constance once. He might try again.

Mel gave him a doubtful look, but eventually agreed to a police escort to the hospital. Nathan then radioed Robbie, who promised to meet the ambulance on Route 9.

"You're the boss," Mel had said. "Does this mean I'm going to lose my twenty bucks in the office pool?"

"It might," Nathan said.

The firefighters arrived minutes after the ambulance, and had the blaze under control within the hour, but much of the house was a loss. They told Nathan he'd be lucky to salvage any evidence from the garage, given that it was pretty much just a charred mess. Lucky for him, he'd taken pretty meticulous pictures of the crime scene, and had collected all samples of evidence he needed. They were all away at a crime lab in Dallas being analyzed.

Nathan sent Robbie to the hospital to guard Constance's room, and had Mel give him periodic updates on her condition. It seemed that she was stable for now, having been given oxygen and an IV. Nathan wanted to go to the hospital, but first he had a crime scene to investigate. The sun was up, and he wasn't about to let anything get by him. Not this time.

He sent the rest of his deputies who weren't working on babysitting movie stars out around the woods to look for the suspect. He'd fled on foot, and Nathan thought he couldn't have gotten far. As the firefighters packed up their gear, Nathan went around the rubble that was once the garage, looking for Yaman's shoe prints. He found the ones he was looking for.

There, in the mud near Constance's garage, were the shoe prints, clear as day. With a jolt, Nathan realized he recognized the prints, with their distinctive zigzag pattern. They were Bruno Magli's. Size ten.

He'd know those shoe prints anywhere. They were the same as those by the Dumpster where he'd found Libby Bell. It was the only clue they'd had in her disappearance. He'd lived with that partial shoe print for months.

And now, here were those same prints, outside Constance's house, taking the same path Yaman had used to go into the tree line.

Nathan didn't believe in coincidences. Still, why would a murdering pedophile want to kill Jimmy and set Constance's house on fire? It didn't make any sense.

Neither did the fact that Yaman seemed to be bulletproof.

Nathan didn't believe he'd missed. Not at that range. And even if Yaman had been wearing a vest, he would've stumbled a little or flinched. The impact of those bullets hurt, even if you were protected. There hadn't been a hitch in his step at all. It was all a little too strange.

So was the fact that Yaman's footprints simply stopped after four or five steps, as if he'd disappeared into thin air.

Nathan's radio crackled to life on his shoulder.

"Sheriff," came Robbie's voice over the radio. "Constance Plyd is awake. Thought you'd want to know."

Nathan straightened, still staring at the footprints in the mud. It was time, he thought, to get some answers.

Twenty-three

Constance came to in the county hospital feeling like her throat was on fire. It was like when she'd had her tonsils out when she was eleven, only about a million times worse. Her head was pounding, too, and it took her a minute to remember what happened.

Yaman. Her house. Dead Jimmy!

She glanced around the hospital room, but she didn't see her dead husband's ghost. She wondered if Yaman had somehow taken him. She sure hoped not. She might not like Dead Jimmy, but she didn't want him being tortured by a demon with a sadistic streak, either. She hoped he was just hiding out somewhere.

"You all right, Mrs. Plyd?" asked Robbie, who was standing by her bedside. Constance couldn't help but feel a little disappointed that it wasn't Nathan standing there. She could've sworn it was Nathan who'd taken her out of the house. But maybe she'd been hallucinating. Or dreaming. Her memory of what happened after Yaman set the curtains on fire was foggy at best.

"She's fine," said Constance's mother, Abigail, who bustled into the room carrying a Styrofoam cup of ice water. She was wearing a pink tie-dyed tunic and a matching turban on her head, along with some really large silver topaz jewelry. "Now, you let her be."

"Yes, ma'am," Robbie said, a little taken aback by Abigail's entrance. She had that effect on people. "I'll be outside if y'all need anything."

"Wha . . ." Constance croaked, but then her voice gave out.

"Don't try to talk," her mother ordered. "They had a tube down your throat for a few hours, said it was to help you breathe." Abigail waited until she was sure Robbie was out of earshot. "Now, tell me the truth. It was that demon again, wasn't it?"

Constance nodded.

"My pentagram work?"

Constance nodded again.

"See? I told you I knew what I was doing," Abigail said, sounding superior and flattening the side of her turban with one hand. "And you never have any faith in your mama. Here, take a sip."

Constance took a drink of the ice water. Swallowing was hard. It felt like her throat was swollen.

"What time is it?"

"Nearly eight. Sun's setting," Abigail said, nodding toward the first-floor window, which was facing the parking lot. "You were out nearly all day. But you don't have to worry about demons," Abigail said, nodding knowingly. "I've got the place covered."

Constance looked around and saw her entire room was filled with dogwood blooms.

"Thanks, Mama," Constance croaked, feeling a gush of gratitude.

"And I brought you this," Abigail said, handing her a pink water gun. "It's filled with holy water—well, technically, water from the River Jordan. But my friend in Pasadena said it would work. I swiped some from the big tub at the First Baptist Church."

Constance squeezed the trigger and a tiny bit of water shot out. "Thanks, Mama."

"As an added bonus, your room is right across from the hospital chapel," Abigail said. "I requested that. Figured it couldn't hurt."

"Have you heard news about my house? What about my kitchen?"

"I'm afraid it looks like they couldn't save your house—or your kitchen," Abigail said, looking sad. "I'm sorry."

Constance felt a hard pang in her chest. Her beloved kitchen, in the house she'd spent so much time decorating and keeping with care, was gone.

"We'll build you a new one, don't you worry about a thing," Abigail said. "Meantime, you can live with me. I've got your room all ready."

"Is it outfitted with crosses and holy relics?"

"Am I a psychic? Of course it is!" Abigail sing-songed.

Constance suddenly felt very glad. Things weren't quite hopeless after all. "But wait, Mama, I can't live with you. The demons could hurt you. They could . . ."

"Oh, pish posh. I'm not afraid," Abigail said. "We can handle them. We Hicks women are tough." She gave

Constance a smile. "We're not scared of demons or anything else."

Constance realized, suddenly, that she had to get ahold of Frank. He'd told her to call if she saw any demons, and she most certainly had. Constance sat up and tried to shuffle to the edge of her bed.

"I need to call Frank," she told Abigail.

"Here, let me get you a phone."

With a start, Constance realized she didn't have Frank's number. It was in her purse, which had probably burned down with the rest of her house. "I don't have his number. But I need to talk to Frank."

"Who's Frank?" It was Nathan Garrett, who'd managed to sneak up on Constance, again. He was leaning in the doorway of her hospital room, arms crossed over his broad chest. He had a look of determination in those brown eyes, and something more.

"Why, Nathan Garrett," said Abigail, "I remember when you got in trouble for kissing all those girls on the playground in elementary school. You reformed yourself any?"

"No, he hasn't," Constance answered for him.

Abigail glanced at her daughter, a curious look on her face. Abigail didn't know about Constance being Nathan's twenty-second virgin, and Constance wanted to keep it that way.

"Nice to see you, too, Mrs. Hicks," he said, tipping his hat. "Do you mind if I talk to your daughter alone?"

Abigail took one look at Constance's face, which was begging her not to go, and smiled.

"Not at all," she said. She bent down and gave Constance a kiss. "I've got to head home anyway to run my eight o'clock tarot chat room tonight. I'll be back tomorrow morning, okay, sweetie?"

"But, Mama . . ."

"Got to run," she said, and skipped out the door.

Nathan pushed himself away from the doorframe to let Abigail pass, and Constance found herself, once again, alone with Nathan Garrett. Only this time, she suspected, he wouldn't try to kiss her. After all, she still had an IV in her arm and she looked like hell. She wished she'd put on some lipstick the second she woke up. She probably looked paler than a ghost.

Nathan took a seat next to her bed and leaned forward, his brown eyes studying her carefully. Constance was painfully aware that she was wearing only a hospital gown, and it was as thin as paper.

"So? Who's Frank?"

"Nobody you know," Constance said. Technically, this was true.

Nathan gave her a skeptical look. "Fine. So you want to tell me what happened?" He was all serious, as serious as when he'd pulled her behind the trailer and kissed the life out of her. She tried to banish this thought before the blush started creeping up on her neck, but she was too late. Already, she was thinking about his fingers in her hair. Her face felt like it was on fire. Not a good start.

"You wouldn't believe me if I told you," she said, glancing down at her hands so she didn't have to meet his eyes. As it was, they seemed to be boring right through her.

"Try me," he said, as he leaned closer to her. He wasn't

going to stop until she told him everything. Of this she was certain. Her best hope was to stall him. Maybe she could fake fainting.

"He's my insurance agent," she lied.

"You're lying," Nathan said, flashing her a knowing smile and nodding at her head. "The hair thing again."

"Oh, hell," Constance swore, dropping the ends of her hair and grasping her hands tightly in front of her.

"How about you start from the beginning," Nathan said.

"Yaman came back," she said. "He tried to kill me and set fire to my kitchen."

Constance decided to leave out the fact that he was definitely a demon with the power to levitate objects and terrorize her dead husband's ghost. Leaving out information wasn't the same as lying. Not exactly. She also decided not to mention she was pretty sure this all had something to do with the devil trying to get into Dante London's pants. Even in her own head, the story sounded ridiculous.

"You said he really was a demon," he pressed. "After I pulled you out of the house. What did you mean?"

So Nathan *did* rescue her. She hadn't been dreaming. The blush on her cheeks grew even hotter. He'd carried her out of her burning kitchen like her hero, and she'd been wearing her anything-but-sexy cotton pj's and threadbare bunny slippers. Not that she should care. But she did. She really did.

"I just meant that he's a bad man," Constance said, tightening her fingers together in her lap and fighting the urge to play with her hair. This wasn't a lie. Exactly.

He might not be a man, per se, but he was definitely bad. She thought about the look in his eyes when he'd hurled steak knives at her head. She shuddered. Definitely bad.

She sighed and then looked up at Nathan again. He had a critical look in his eye.

"I know you don't believe me," she said, and glanced out the window.

Suddenly, everything felt hopeless. How was she ever going to defeat a demon or the devil? She wasn't brave. She didn't know Kung Fu. The only allies she had were Dead Jimmy—if he hadn't been kidnapped—and a talking dog. The odds just weren't in her favor. "I mean, I wouldn't believe me, either. It sounds ridiculous. I know you think I'm making Yaman up. I'm sure you think I'm crazy, and that's fine. Just lock me up somewhere."

The tears welled up in her eyes before she could stop them. She told herself it was probably the morphine drip, or whatever they had in her IV. Normally, she wasn't so emotional. Then again, normally she wasn't supposed to save the world from the Antichrist and fight the powers of darkness, either. It had been a bad week.

Without even a pause, Nathan reached over to her bedside table and grabbed the box of Kleenex. He offered her one calmly. Of course, as a Garrett, he probably had more than his share of experience dealing with hysterical women. He waited until she'd finished blowing her nose and wiping at her cheeks before speaking.

"I saw him, too, remember?" he said softly.

"You did?" Constance suddenly felt hope again. If Nathan actually believed her, then maybe he could help. "Did you catch him?"

"No," Nathan said, a sharp look of disappointment crossing his face. "It was saving you or catching him."

"I guess I'm lucky you picked me," she said, blowing her nose. She tried to make it a dainty sound, but there just wasn't a nice way of clearing out the passages.

"Not so lucky," Nathan said, glancing down. "I came to your house to arrest you. For Jimmy's murder."

Constance felt like she'd been kicked in the stomach. "Oh," she said, glancing down at the wad of tissue in her hand. She shouldn't be surprised, she guessed. He was a Garrett. They always disappointed in the end. "And what about now? Still going to arrest me?"

Nathan was silent a long time, studying her face. "Not today," he said, and smiled. His smile was contagious, because Constance felt her lips curve up, too. "Got to wait until we get the all clear from the doctor."

"That's a relief," she said. "I'd hate to go to jail wearing this," she added, tugging at her blue hospital gown. "It's a little drafty."

Nathan laughed a little. "Not the most practical thing to wear to jail, I agree," he said. He leaned forward a little, and then met her eyes. Both of them fell silent, and Constance felt her stomach flip. Was he going to kiss her again?

The heart monitor she was hooked up to started beeping softly. Her heart was racing. Nathan looked at it, then at her, and chuckled again.

"Do I make you nervous?" he asked, a slow smile playing on his lips.

"No." Of course he did.

Nathan laughed.

"What's so funny?" she asked him.

"You're playing with your hair again," he said, pointing. Constance blushed fiercely and dropped her hand. It hit the side of her bed rail and accidentally knocked against the button that turned on the TV perched in the corner of the room. It was set to an entertainment news show, and the volume was set to the highest setting. As Constance fumbled to turn it down, the woman on the television started talking about Dante London and her new movie shoot.

Dante's face appeared on the television, snapping gum and talking to a reporter, and Constance felt a surge go through her hand where she was touching the remote controls for the television. The room started to spin, and she knew what was coming next.

Another vision.

It hit her hard and fast, and she was only able to see Dante London and Corey Bennett together at dinner at the Magnolia Café. The same vision she had had last time, only there was more detail this time. They were drinking wine, lots of wine, and Constance saw Corey put something—a white powder—into Dante's drink when she wasn't looking. Then they were suddenly somewhere else, a bedroom, or a hotel room, where Corey Bennett turned the lights low and Dante London, seemingly woozy from whatever he'd spiked her drink with, stumbled to the bed, where she planted, face-first.

Constance tried hard to slow down the vision, to figure out where they were, but she simply couldn't control the visions yet.

She did see Corey Bennett open the door to wherever they were, and Yaman strode in, a smile on his face. The floor suddenly opened beneath his feet, and a great dark hole appeared in the carpet, where something even more sinister than Yaman rose up from the ground. Constance couldn't see the creature's face, but she knew without knowing how that that was the devil.

The last thing Constance saw, before the vision ended, was the shadow of the devil moving toward the limp body of Dante London.

Twenty-four

N ice plan with the kidnapping," Yaman said, sarcasm in his voice, as he and Shadow hovered outside Constance's hospital window.

"What? I didn't expect her to have dogwood blooms. Or that damn pentagram."

"She couldn't predict a sneeze, you said," Yaman complained. "She *clearly* knew we were coming."

"How was I supposed to know? She seemed pretty clueless for a prophet. I thought it was a good bet. Besides, you're the one who ran out of there when the fire started. We could've just waited her out and grabbed her once the pentagram had burned enough."

"I didn't want my new sport coat smelling like smoke," Yaman said. "Takes forever to get out that smell."

"You can't be serious," Shadow said. "You're a *demon*. Smoke is supposed to be your friend."

"Yeah, well, it ruins good fabrics."

"You Pride demons are such sissies," Shadow said.

"What did you say?"

"You heard me!"

"I'm going to pretend I didn't hear that," Yaman said. "Because we have a job to finish."

"I'm getting tired of this job," Shadow said. "I say I should just eat her."

Near Yaman's feet came a muffled cry. Dead Jimmy was tied up and bound, like a pig, with his hands and feet together.

"Shut up, *you*," Yaman said, and gave Dead Jimmy a kick. "We've got plans for you yet, *ghost*."

"Um, *hello*, I'm still *hungry*," Shadow growled. "Why can't I at least eat the doctor?"

"What happened to the garbage truck?"

"I digested that hours ago," Shadow said. "Now, let me have the doctor. I love people with advanced degrees."

"You just can't," Yaman said. "We don't want too much attention. This whole thing is supposed to be a covert operation."

"Oh yeah, covert as in 'stab the prophet's husband with a screwdriver' covert."

"I *told* you we weren't talking about that anymore."

"And what about the vision she just had? We now know how Bennett's going to do it and where. Shouldn't we tell the general?"

"I don't think we should tell him yet," Yaman said.

"But he told us to report any new visions . . ."

"Maybe we could figure this out ourselves, and cut out the general, and go straight to Satan himself," Yaman proposed. "Then maybe I'll get promoted."

"You mean, '*we*.'"

Yaman did a double take. "Right, yes, of course. I meant *we* would get promoted."

"I've always wanted to be a general."

"The stars would look nice on your non-clothes."

"Is that sarcasm?"

"What do you think? Anyway, if I were a general, then I could do whatever I want," Yaman said. "I wouldn't have to go on these stupid prophet-sitting missions."

"You mean if *we* were generals."

"That's what I said."

"You said if *you* were a general."

"Well, I meant it like the royal 'I.' "

"There *is* no royal 'I.' "

"Are you going to sit there and argue with me all day? Or are we going to agree to try to cut the general out of this?"

"You know my feelings about the general," Shadow said. "He *bit* me."

"Okay, then *we* are in agreement."

"Yes, *we* are," Shadow reiterated.

"Good."

"Good."

"Fine."

"Fine." Shadow paused. "So? What now?"

"Let's try the kidnapping plan again. But *this* time you're going to do it on your own."

"Why do I have to do all the work?"

"Because it was your idea. And the first time, you blew it."

"I didn't blow anything, Pride demon. We had her right where we wanted her."

"In a protective seal neither of us could break."

"I could've figured out a way in, but *nooooo*. You had to set her house on fire."

"Thought I could scare her out."

"Instead you scared yourself out."

"Shut up," growled Yaman. "Anyway, you've got work to do. Get going."

"You're not coming with me?"

"Well, you seem to think you can handle it fine by yourself. So go on. Handle it." Yaman glanced down at Dead Jimmy. "Besides, someone has to babysit the ghost."

"What are we going to do with him, anyway?"

"I don't know, but I figured he might come in handy. Now, you'd better get moving."

Shadow narrowed his eyes and spat. "Fine. But I'm going to eat the sheriff. I'm starved."

"Whatever," Yaman said, sounding exasperated. "Just get the prophet. Eat whomever you want. But hurry up, will you? This ghost smells like skunky beer."

Twenty-five

Oone minute Nathan was talking to Constance and the next her eyes had rolled back in her head and the machines attached to her arms went haywire. Nurses rushed in, and a doctor, too, and then they were asking him if she had epilepsy, and he didn't know. He was pushed to a corner as all the medical personnel rushed around her bedside, and he felt his stomach tighten. It was the same feeling he'd had when he saw her house in flames. He was worried about her, a bone-deep worry that he usually only felt for blood relations like his niece or older brothers.

Constance came to again quickly, and one of the nurses plucked her IV out of her arm while the doctor pulled him aside and told him they'd need to put her under observation overnight and send her to a bigger hospital to get a CAT scan if the seizures continued. No one could tell him if the seizures were serious, or what they meant.

Left alone with Nathan again, Constance looked sheepish, almost embarrassed.

"You been having those episodes long?" he asked her finally.

"No," she said. "Just since Jimmy . . . uh, well, since Jimmy . . ." She seemed to have a hard time saying "died." "But they're nothing to worry about, really. My mother gets them, too, and, well, trust me, they won't kill me."

Nathan looked at her with skepticism. The seizures didn't look like nothing. Not from where he was standing. He saw her wince and put her hand to her forehead like she had a raging headache. And he had the distinct feeling she wasn't telling him everything. She wasn't lying, but she wasn't being completely honest, either.

"Can I get you anything?" he asked.

"A Dr Pepper would be great," she said. "Or a Coke. Anything with caffeine. Helps with the headache."

Nathan nodded. He remembered a vending machine in the hall not too far from Constance's room. He could be there and back in a minute or two. He hesitated, not sure if he should leave her, in case she had another attack or Yaman came back to finish what he started. Still, it would only be a minute or two. He supposed it was safe.

"Be right back," he said, and slipped into the hall.

The minute he was there, he regretted going. Would he be fetching a drink if it were Jimmy in that bed instead of Constance? He hardly thought so. He needed to stop thinking about Constance as someone he wanted to do favors for and start thinking about her as a suspect. He might have seen Yaman, but there was no telling whether he was really the guilty one, or whether he and Constance might have had some kind of deal to get rid of Jimmy together. A deal that clearly went bad.

Of course, it was a lot easier to be tough-minded when he wasn't staring at her pretty heart-shaped face. When he didn't have to look into those green, green eyes. He popped quarters into the vending machine and pressed the button, and a plastic bottle rolled into the bottom tray. He bent down to pick it up, and that's when the lights above his head went out.

He straightened and waited a half second, expecting the backup generator lights to come on. This was a hospital. Lights just didn't go out. The backup generator didn't kick on. The only lights were those from outside in the parking lot and around the hospital, which shone in through the big windows. He glanced down the hall toward the nurse's station, but he didn't see a nurse. In fact, he didn't see anybody. No doctors. No orderlies. No one.

Something was wrong. Dead wrong.

The hairs on the back of his neck stood up.

He glanced back down the hall. At the end, in the shadows, he saw someone moving. He flattened himself against the wall by the vending machine and unlatched the holster at his hip, resting his hand on the handle of his gun. It was probably just a nurse or a patient, but it could also be Yaman. Maybe he'd come back to finish the job he'd started.

Nathan narrowed his eyes and focused hard on the shadow, which was moving methodically toward him. Nathan had excellent night vision. At least, he'd always thought he did. His old partner used to tease him about being able to see in the dark with his eyes closed.

But no matter how hard Nathan concentrated on seeing the figure behind the shadows, he couldn't. Even when whoever it was passed a lighted window, no more detail became apparent. Strange. It seemed that no matter how much light fell, it was still entirely shadow. He couldn't see the man's face, no matter how hard he tried.

And even more odd, the shadow wasn't moving like a man. It seemed more like a dog. A really big dog.

He's a demon, Constance had said.

The words made Nathan feel something prickly in his stomach. He shook the irrational fear from his head. Nathan was a practical man. He didn't believe in ghosts. Or demons. It was probably a man. It had to be.

Whoever it was, the shadow seemed to be going methodically from room to room, as if looking for something. Nathan decided he wasn't taking any chances. He slipped back into Constance's room. She looked at him wide-eyed, and he put his hand to his lips, to show her to be quiet. She nodded.

"Can you walk?" he whispered.

Gingerly, she slid out of bed, her bare feet on the floor. Her hospital gown gaped a little, and she grabbed its edges. She seemed so vulnerable and delicate. She needed someone to protect her. Nathan vowed to be the one to do it as he took her free hand and led her to the door. A quick scan of the hall revealed the shadow had moved up to a hospital room five doors down. Nathan glanced back the other way. The exit was too far to sprint to if they wanted to go unseen. Their best option was the door across the hall—the hospital's chapel. He tightened his grip on Constance and then pulled her across the hall.

Inside, the chapel was small, and on the wall hung a stained-glass panel featuring a cross and a dove. At one end, there was a very simple altar made up of a wooden table and a cross, and around it were three rows of folding chairs.

He pulled the door nearly shut behind them, leaving it open just enough that he could see the hallway. Constance squeezed Nathan's hand, and he could feel her fear. He wanted to tell her that everything would be okay, but he didn't know that for sure. He heard the figure coming closer. Nathan dropped Constance's hand and drew his weapon, aiming it at the floor. She pressed herself against his back, and he could feel her breathing, sharp and rapid. He put his arm out to reassure her, and that's when he saw she had a water gun in her hands. Where did she get that? And how would it help them? It was plastic, see-through, neon pink. No one would ever think it was a real gun. Did she think it would protect them? Then again, maybe she wasn't thinking straight after her seizure.

He put both hands on the handle of his gun and leaned a bit farther away from her, keeping his eyes focused on the doorway and Constance's room.

The shadow moved across his field of vision, just like he'd thought it would, and headed straight for Constance's room. Now was Nathan's chance to get a good look at the man, to see if it was Yaman. But what he saw made no sense. It wasn't a man at all. And it wasn't a dog, either. It was something else. Something Nathan had never seen before.

Big, black, and furry, it was the size of a small pony. It had four legs, Nathan could clearly see, but where its head should have been, instead of one, there were three. Nathan blinked and looked again, because surely he was hallucinating. But no, it was a three-headed dog. A massive, giant, three-headed dog, with three sets of sharp fangs and red eyes that seemed to glow in the darkness. One of the heads sniffed the air and turned, as if able to smell Nathan's fear. It swiveled toward him and met his eyes, even as Nathan, temporarily frozen with shock, willed himself to do something. The head growled and Nathan, acting on instinct, shut the chapel door quickly and locked it, ushering Constance against the back wall. He raised his gun so it was aimed at the door. Whatever he'd just seen, if it came in here, he would blow it back to hell.

"What the hell was that?" she whispered.

"Hell if I know," Nathan said, pointing the gun at the door, his finger on the trigger, nervous sweat rolling down the middle of his back. Of all the things he'd ever seen as a police officer, this was definitely the strangest, and it scared the hell out of him. He flashed back to Yaman taking two bullets without flinching and wondered just what he was dealing with here.

Outside the door came an unearthly-sounding howl, and behind him Constance gasped and squeezed his arm. After a long pause, the dog—if that's what it was—hit the door hard, and it shook with the impact but didn't come open. Constance stiffened behind him, but Nathan kept his gun steady. He only hoped whatever that thing was, it wasn't bulletproof.

The door rattled twice more, and then there was silence.

"Is it gone?" Constance asked, her voice shaky.

"I don't know," Nathan said. He wasn't sure he wanted to find out, but he couldn't very well just stand around and hope for the best, either. He glanced behind them and saw there were two small windows to the left of the altar and they looked out onto the parking lot. He could see his sheriff's truck sitting there, just ten feet away. The chapel windows were already open. All he had to do was push the screens through and climb out.

The dog rattled the door again, causing Constance to yelp. This time, the dog cracked the wood in the door. It wouldn't be long before the door came off the hinges entirely.

"We've got to get out of here," Nathan said. He holstered his gun and pushed the wooden table that served as the altar closer to the wall. He grabbed the gold cross sitting on it and used it to punch out the screens. Then he lifted Constance up on the table and motioned for her to climb out. She crawled out the window just as the door came apart, wood splinters flying everywhere. Nathan whipped around in time to see all three heads of that dog bare their fangs at him. He whipped out his gun and fired twice at the dog, but the bullets didn't seem to make a difference. The dog just stood its ground, not flinching.

Of course it did. As if a three-headed dog would be fazed by physics and lead.

Nathan didn't wait to see whether or not it came after him. He turned and scrambled through the window.

In the parking lot, he grabbed Constance by the hand and ran toward his truck. She was holding on to the gold cross from the chapel, and he wondered why, but didn't have time to ask. They didn't make it four steps before the giant dog leaped in front of them, from seemingly nowhere. How did it get there so fast? And without Nathan seeing or hearing it approach?

Nathan pulled Constance behind him and fired until his gun clicked empty. The bullets zipped right through the dog like he was a ghost, and landed in the cars behind him. Nathan felt the fear in his stomach rise. He had no way of stopping this creature, whatever it was. In seconds, they would be torn limb from limb. The dog's three heads seemed to grin at them, their big, long fangs dripping with drool. It hunched back, as if preparing to leap. Nathan squared his shoulders and prepared for impact. He'd fight this thing with his bare hands as long as he could to try to keep Constance safe.

The dog leaped, and that's when Constance moved from behind him. She threw the cross at the dog, and it landed on one of its paws with a sizzle, causing the dog to yelp and fall to the ground, limping. Next, she aimed her pink water gun straight at the dog and fired five rapid squirts. The gun looked like it held water, but it hit the creature like acid, burning one of the dog's sets of ears and eyes, hurting it so badly that it yelped again in pain and dropped to the ground in a roll, desperately rooting its injured head against the ground as if trying to rub off the liquid.

Nathan took back his earlier thoughts about the uselessness of squirt guns. Clearly, Constance knew what she was doing.

"Come on, let's go," Nathan grunted, grabbing Constance's hand and running for his truck. In seconds, they were inside, and he had turned over the engine and thrown the truck in reverse. He whipped it around, tires screeching, and headed for the road. In his rearview mirror, he saw the dog still rolling on the ground. He looked forward and suddenly, in his headlights, Yaman appeared, standing there in the middle of the highway, calmly, wearing his signature black and giving them a half smile. For a second, Nathan considered hitting the brakes, but then he stomped his foot down hard on the gas. He braced for the inevitable thud, but just as his truck got to Yaman, the man leaped up, jumped on his hood, denting it, and kicked a foot out to the windshield, causing a big crack to run up the middle. And then, just like that, he flew straight up into the sky.

Just like Superman.

Twenty-six

Constance clasped her hands in her lap over her pink water gun—*Thank you, Mama*, she thought—and said the Lord's Prayer, again. She glanced over at Nathan, who was silent, his eyes on road, strong hands gripping the steering wheel, and wondered what he was thinking. She hardly knew what to think herself, and at least she'd been warned to expect the worst. She hadn't thought the worst would be a three-headed dog, but then again, she didn't think like the devil.

Thank God for her mother's quick thinking with the holy water or River Jordan water or whatever it was. She needed to get more of that. And fast.

"What *in the hell* was that back there?" Nathan sputtered suddenly. "What is going on?"

Constance glanced over at Nathan. How could she explain?

"I don't know," Constance said.

Nathan put both feet on the brake pedal and skidded to a stop in the middle of the highway, tires screeching.

"If you don't tell me what you know and right now," he said, eyes flashing with heat, "I am going to leave you by the side of the road."

Constance could tell he was serious.

"It was a demon," she said.

"A demon?" Nathan echoed, unbelieving.

"That's right. As in devil's minion. A demon. An evil guy. A monster."

Nathan stared at Constance, and Constance stared right back.

Nathan put his foot back on the accelerator. "Demon, of course it is. Because we usually have so many of those in Dogwood County this time of year."

"It's true, I'm not lying." Constance held up her hands to show she wasn't twirling her hair.

"And what's in your squirt gun? Acid?"

"Holy water. Technically, River Jordan water from the Baptist dunk tank—you know, the baptism tub."

Nathan threw back his head and laughed. "Holy water! Sure. Next thing you're going to tell me I ought to drive a stake through its heart."

"Maybe," Constance said. "I don't know how you kill it."

"Unbelievable," Nathan mumbled. "And why you? Why do they want you? Wait—don't tell me. They are after your chicken-fried steak recipe?"

Nathan sounded like he was going to lose it. Not that Constance blamed him. Plus, her explanation wasn't going to help.

"I'm a prophet," she said, cringing at how ridiculous it sounded. This caused Nathan to laugh some more. "A minor one," she added, but this didn't make it sound any better and Nathan just laughed harder.

Eventually, Nathan's laughter died down, and he wiped at his eyes. "Demons!" he exclaimed. "Prophets! In Dogwood County! Next you're going to tell me that Deputy Robbie is the Second Coming."

"Well, if you're just going to laugh, then I won't tell you any more." Constance crossed her arms and looked out the window. It wasn't her fault this whole thing had fallen into her lap. Last week she'd been a nonpracticing Baptist, and now she had no choice but to believe. She wasn't going to waste her time trying to convince an arrogant Garrett that what had happened right in front of his nose was real.

Nathan chuckled, then sighed. He glanced over at Constance, who had her head turned away from him.

"I'm sorry, but it's just so hard to believe," he said.

"You have a better explanation for a three-headed dog who doesn't like crosses or holy water?"

Nathan's expression grew more serious. He glanced in his rearview mirror and then at her. "Nope," he said, and shook his head.

Nathan picked up the radio on his dash, but it didn't seem to be working. Nothing came through but static. Nathan wondered if it had anything to do with the dent in his hood and his cracked windshield. Or the flying man or demon or whatever he was that had nearly killed them.

"Damn," he said. "Those demons of yours know how to jam a radio?"

"I don't know. I'm no expert."

He reached into his pocket and pulled out his cell

phone, but it was inexplicably dead, like the battery had been drained, and he dropped it on the dash in frustration.

"I'd be better off back in Dallas," Nathan said. After a minute, he leaned over, brushing Constance's knees, and popped open the glove compartment. He dug around in the corner until he came out with a small gold necklace with a tiny gold cross.

"Just in case," Nathan said, as he put the cross in his pocket.

"You keep those there just for this kind of emergency?" Constance asked him.

Nathan gave her a sidelong glance. "Not exactly. It belonged to . . ." He stopped short, as if not wanting to say the name out loud. Constance got the impression it was someone close to him. ". . . a little girl I knew. Her name was Libby Bell. It's a long story."

Constance waited for him to say more, but when he didn't, they fell into a short silence. Constance wondered where they were going, but wasn't sure she wanted to know, in case Nathan planned to drive her to jail.

Eventually, Nathan pulled his truck down Main Street, the opposite way from the jail, and parked in the driveway of a yellow Victorian house with a big, wide porch, complete with white wooden porch swing. And Constance saw with relief, there were giant dogwood trees pretty much surrounding the house like sentinels. She felt immensely safer just looking at them.

"Where are we?" Constance asked, the first to break the silence.

"My house," Nathan said in a voice that sounded sur-

prisingly normal, given that they had just had a brush
with hell spawns. "It used to belong to Reverend Hicks,
back in the day."

"The founder of Dogwood?"

"So they say," Nathan said.

She stepped over the threshold and noticed for the
first time pentagramlike carvings in the stone tiles at her
feet. They looked like the one her mother had drawn on
her kitchen floor. She wondered how many of those were
hidden around the house. She felt decidedly safer, but she
still wasn't planning on letting the water gun out of her
sight. It was still half full.

The next thing Constance noticed about Nathan's
house was that it was surprisingly neat. Jimmy was the
messiest man on earth, and given that he was the only
one she'd ever lived with, Constance had assumed all
men were like that. But Nathan was different. His place
was spotless and tidy, the furniture neatly arranged. His
living room furniture was leather and the color of dark
chocolate. As in most bachelor places, the walls were
completely bare, and there weren't any knickknacks anywhere. It was a little cold-seeming and could've used a
woman's touch. But he had nice furniture, and Constance
had to give him points for that.

If Jimmy had been left to his own devices to decorate
a house, he would have used only furniture he found on
the curb or at the dump. He hadn't believed in paying for
furniture, even though the La-Z-Boy he'd carted home
from the dump had been infested with fleas and smelled
like malt liquor.

Georgina and the book club ladies would be spitting

mad that they'd missed this, that was for sure. They'd kill to be where she was standing right at this moment. As far as she knew, no one had ever seen the inside of Nathan Garrett's new house. There was great speculation among the ladies of Dogwood County about what it looked like. Since he'd lived some years in Dallas, people assumed it could be anything. They had a healthy suspicion of all things from the city, where people ate raw fish on rice and spent most of their lives stuck in traffic.

Constance stood on gleaming maple floors, and couldn't help but sneak a look in the kitchen, which, she saw, was equally pristine. No dishes in the sink or stacked on the counter. Either he was extremely neat or he spent very little time here, she thought.

Constance stood awkwardly in his foyer, trying to squeeze together the ends of her hospital gown that seemed always in peril of slipping off and completely exposing her backside. Seeing her discomfort, he tossed her a folded T-shirt from the couch. It said "Dogwood County Sheriff's Department" on the sleeve. He gave her a pair of mesh shorts, too.

"The bathroom's over there," he said, pointing to a door over her shoulder. He turned and punched some numbers into a keypad near the front door—an alarm system, she assumed.

Constance went into the bathroom and shrugged out of the hospital gown. The T-shirt was way too big, and the shorts swam on her. Constance had no doubt she looked ridiculous, but anything was better than the hospital gown, which was only a small step above naked.

When she emerged, Nathan was in the kitchen

spooning ice cream into a bowl. "Ice cream or beer?" he asked her. When she gave him a quizzical look, he added, "That's all I've got in my fridge."

"Ice cream," she said, thinking this was all a bit too surreal. Ten minutes ago she'd nearly been eaten by a three-headed dog, and now she was sitting in Nathan Garrett's kitchen eating ice cream.

Nathan studied her intently. She felt a little uncomfortable under his gaze. She was all too aware of the fact that she was wearing his too-big clothes—as if they'd just had a sleepover.

"Now that we've got the important things out of the way," he drawled, "you want to explain how all this started?"

Constance stabbed her ice cream with her spoon. "You won't believe me."

"Why do you keep saying that?"

"Because I'm not sure *I* believe it."

Nathan crossed his arms and leaned back against the counter to show he wasn't going anywhere. "You can go slow. We have all night, because neither one of us is leaving this kitchen until you tell me everything."

Constance swallowed hard, and started the story from the beginning. She told him everything, starting with Dead Jimmy's ghost and ending with her visions of Dante London becoming the mother of the Antichrist.

Nathan took it all in slowly, only whipping up his head when she talked about Frank, the talking French bulldog in the pink sweater. And when she finished, he let out a long, tired-sounding sigh.

"I told you you wouldn't believe me."

"I didn't say that," Nathan said, even though his body language screamed his doubts. "I saw what I saw tonight, and I have no better explanation for it—yet."

He was remarkably calm, considering. He leaned back against the kitchen counter and curled one finger through his front belt loop.

"So why you?" he asked. "Why are you a prophet?"

"I don't know," she said.

"And why would the demons kill Jimmy?"

"I don't know," Constance said. "Jimmy doesn't know, either, exactly. Maybe the demons thought it would help them get to *me*. I don't know."

Nathan shook his head slowly. "I'm beginning to regret not paying attention in Sunday school," he said.

"You and me both," she said.

"So, do you think you can stop him? The devil, I mean," Nathan said.

"I don't know," Constance said, looking down at her bare knees. A bit of hair fell in her face and she tucked it back behind her ear. She realized that somewhere between her burning kitchen and the hospital, she'd lost the clip she usually wore to keep her hair out of her face. She normally wore it in a ponytail, especially since she spent most of her time in the kitchen. Now it was loose and in her face, and she wasn't quite sure what to do with it.

"I like your hair that way," Nathan said, fixing her with a look that seemed to be telling her something more. "You should wear it down more often."

Constance didn't know what to say to this. In fact, she never knew what to say to compliments. "Thank you" just seemed conceited somehow, and denying them felt worse. And what was Nathan doing, anyway, staring at her like that? She started to feel the blush creep up on her neck before she could stop it. She desperately tried to think of something to say to change the subject, but as usual when Nathan Garrett was in the vicinity, she felt tongue-tied.

Outside the kitchen window, the floodlights, triggered by some motion in the yard, came on, causing her to gasp and drop her spoon on Nathan's otherwise clean floor. It landed with a *plink*. She grabbed the water gun on the kitchen counter and held it in shaking hands. Nathan peered out the window, and she held her breath, fearing that the demons had come back. He pulled himself away from the counter and stood in front of Constance, as if to protect her from the window. Just when she was about to throw herself into full-on panic mode, a raccoon the size of a dog jumped up against the window and caused them both to flinch. It had a Mr. Goodbar wrapper in its paws and was happily licking it.

Both of them sagged with relief, and let out a little nervous laugh.

"Just a raccoon," Nathan said. "And it has one head, so I don't think we need to worry."

"Close one," Constance said, smiling.

But their relief was soon replaced by something else. They were so close now that Constance had to crane her neck up to meet his eyes. There was an electricity between them, surely he could feel it? She glanced at his broad, thick chest and felt a powerful urge to put her hand there, and before she knew it, she had. He looked down at her hand and then back to her eyes, and the next second, he was dipping down to kiss her. It was a soft kiss at first, gentle, almost comforting, and then it became deeper, more insistent, and Constance felt him put his hands around her waist and lift her up to the kitchen counter. From then on, everything became a blur of hands and lips and tongues, and Constance felt like the room was spinning, but in a good way. She wrapped her legs around his back and pulled him closer to her, not stopping to think how insane this was. His hands were under her shirt, roaming up her back, when he stopped to take a breath.

"We shouldn't," he said, a little out of breath, his dark eyes cloudy.

Nathan was right, Constance thought. There were a million reasons to stop. For one, they were being chased by demons who could make an appearance at any time. Getting distracted and especially getting naked would probably not be the best way to prepare for climactic battle with ultimate evil. Then there was the whole tricky thing about him being the officer who was supposed to arrest her, and the fact that now he was in the middle of this whole mess as deeply as Constance was. And finally, there was the distinct possibility that all this sexual energy just boiled down to the fact that the two of them had had a near-death experience, and having hasty sex might or might not lead to one of the worst relationship mistakes yet in Constance's sad and sordid romantic history. Because he was, without a shadow of a doubt, a no-good Garrett. Because only a Garrett could make her feel this much like throwing away what was left of her common sense.

But despite all the very good, very practical reasons they ought to knock it off, every nerve ending in Constance's body told her to keep going.

"You want to stop?" Constance asked, disappointment pulling at her stomach. Nathan searched her eyes.

"No," he said, his voice a little hoarse. "Do you?"

Constance shook her head.

"Good," Nathan said, and then scooped Constance up in his arms as if she weighed nothing and carried her straight upstairs to his bedroom.

Twenty-seven

I feel violated. I think I need to take a shower," Yaman said to Shadow as they hovered over Nathan Garrett's front lawn.

"Well, you could join the lovebirds, because it looks like that's what they're doing," Shadow replied. "Along with other things."

"Oh, no—no, no, no," Yaman said, shaking his head and covering his eyes. "What is he trying to prove, anyway? This isn't a Cialis commercial."

"I feel sick," Shadow said.

"Well, you should. This is all *your* fault, Glutton. All you had to do was get them, and you couldn't manage it."

"I got sprayed in the face with River Jordan water, Pride," Shadow reminded him. "It still stings."

"Serves you right for getting lost in the hospital. Who gets lost in a hospital? The rooms are all *numbered.*"

"I don't remember you giving me a room number."

"I totally gave it to you—right before you went in. But you're the one who decided to do the dog form. You're always dumbest when you're the dog."

Shadow snarled at Yaman. "You'd better watch what you say."

"What? Or you'll try to eat me, but get lost on the floor of a hospital wing instead? Please. I'm not scared. Besides, if Satan finds out you screwed this up . . ."

"Me? You were too lazy to come with me. Told you I needed backup."

"Yeah, well, you're always messy when you eat," Yaman pointed out. "And these are new pants."

"And you call yourself a hell spawn. Prides are so prissy."

Shadow was distracted by the raccoon near Nathan's kitchen window. In one big lunge, he swallowed the thing whole, including the Mr. Goodbar wrapper.

"I thought you were nauseous," Yaman said. "How can you eat at a time like this?"

"I can always eat."

Yaman suddenly sneezed loudly. "Damn these dogwoods!"

"You're telling me," sniffed Shadow, rubbing the spot where his nose should be.

"I'm not going to be able to take this much longer," Yaman said.

"You talking about the dogwoods or the naked dance?" Shadow asked, nodding at the window.

"Both. I mean, he's a *sheriff,* for hell's sake. And I'm pretty sure what he's doing to her is illegal in at least seven states."

Both demons looked back through Nathan's window. Both made faces and turned away.

"Oh, hell in a handbasket, that's disgusting," Yaman said.

"Ugh. I might have actually just lost my appetite," Shadow said. "What do we do now?"

"Maybe we can go get the Magnolia Café opened, since that's where Corey Bennett is supposed to take Dante London," Yaman said, and sneezed again. "I've got to get away from these dogwoods."

"First good idea you've had all day."

"Well, at least I *have* ideas. Other than eating people."

"Grrrrr."

"I'm scared, really."

"One of these days, Pride . . ."

"You'll try to eat me, I know. So uncreative."

"Or maybe I'll just eat your baseball hat," Shadow said. "And take some video of your bald head and post it on YouTube."

"You'd better not, or I will tell people you order non-fat lattes."

"That's the best you can come up with?"

"Just shut up and let's go—this ghost is getting heavy," Yaman said, nodding to the giant bag he'd put Dead Jimmy in, which he was carrying over one shoulder. "We can call the restaurant manager—what's his name, Jose? He'll open up the restaurant if we tell him Corey Bennett needs it. Then we tell Corey to take Dante there."

"Fine, Pride. But if this plan doesn't work, I swear, I'm just going to start eating people."

"Deal," Yaman said.

Twenty-eight

Nathan watched Constance sleeping and wondered why he wasn't more worried about what kind of mess he'd just made. It was probably because none of this seemed real. Like maybe it was all a dream. Yaman disappearing. The three-headed dog roaming the halls of the hospital. The idea that the woman lying next to him was on a mission from God.

Because he was pretty sure what they'd done for the last hour was anything but holy.

Nathan wasn't a superstitious man by nature, so he looked for something that might reasonably explain all of this.

Just like the Libby Bell suspect who flew straight up twenty feet, an inner voice told him. Could the boogeyman really exist? He just didn't know. It was all so far-fetched. He'd really rather believe he'd been hallucinating. But he knew what he'd seen with his own eyes at the hospital. And whatever that was, he'd never seen anything like it.

He glanced up at the clock, and with a start he realized it would be light soon. They had a long day ahead of them, most likely, and he would have a lot of explaining to do at the Sheriff's Department about the damage at the hospital.

He thought about pulling himself from the bed and getting dressed, but he just didn't want to leave. It was that simple. He didn't even care that his arm was falling asleep.

Constance turned her head into his chest and sighed, snuggling closer to him. He could hold her forever, he decided.

That was when his doorbell rang. Constance shifted and sighed as Nathan pulled away from her and grabbed a pair of jeans on his dresser. He shrugged into them and walked quickly to his front door. He swung it open and saw no one.

Then a little dog barked, down near his ankles. He looked down and saw Dante London's dog, the little brown bulldog in the pink sweater. It barked again and walked straight past him and into his house.

"Hey—wait a second!" Nathan cried, trying to grab the squirrelly little thing, but it was too fast.

A minute later, he saw a groggy-looking Constance sitting up in bed, the dog in her lap, whining and barking and pawing at her leg.

"I know I was supposed to call you, but I just didn't have time, and then the demons came," Constance told the dog. The dog barked and yipped. "I understand that, Frank, but there just wasn't time. And then, I didn't have your number or any other way of getting hold of you, and . . ."

Nathan looked on in disbelief. Constance was talking to a dog. She hadn't been lying about the dog in the pink sweater, apparently, but as far as he could tell, it wasn't speaking English. It was speaking dog. It yipped and barked again.

"This is Frank?" he sputtered. "The Frank you were talking about?"

Constance looked up. "Yes, I told you."

"You said he spoke English."

"He does," Constance said. "Don't you hear him?"

Frank barked three times fast.

Nathan felt cold all over. She was batty. This much was clear. She'd gone off the deep end.

"All I hear is barking," Nathan said, dumbfounded. "He's just a dog."

The dog growled at him.

"I know, Frank, but he doesn't mean anything by it," Constance said, giving the dog a reassuring little pat.

Maybe the seizures were a symptom of something else—like a brain tumor. Didn't those make you think you heard voices sometimes? At any rate, Constance had the insanity defense locked up. He'd be happy to be star defense witness in her case.

"Are you sure you're feeling okay?" he asked her, worry wrinkling his face.

"You don't hear him *talking*?"

"Nope," Nathan said, shaking his head.

The little dog barked again. "Frank says you're a cynic, and cynics will never be able to see the true nature of things unless they open their minds to the supernatural."

"That's a convenient explanation," Nathan said. "We should tell that one to your psychiatrist."

"Nathan, I'm not making this up. Frank *does* talk."

"Oh, I'm sure he does."

"You can't believe I'm making this up. You saw that three-headed demon last night. How do you explain that?"

"Loss of sleep," Nathan said. "I haven't gotten a good night's sleep since Jimmy's murder. Probably just a stress-related hallucination."

Frank barked several more times.

"So, why do we need to go to St. Mary's Church?" Constance asked the little dog, who barked again. Constance turned to Nathan. "Well, Frank says we need to go meet Father Daniels. Says he has some weapons for us."

"Weapons? What kind of weapons?" Nathan echoed.

"Big ones, Frank says."

Nathan shook his head.

"I don't think he believes us," Constance told the little dog.

Frank barked and then howled.

"Frank also says, 'Remember what your old partner told you the day he died and we'll all be all righty-o end of day.' That's a direct quote."

Nathan felt his whole body go cold. What his partner said? No one knew that but Nathan. He'd been lying in Nathan's arms, bleeding to death. His partner—the most staunchly atheist and nonreligious man Nathan had ever met—had raised up his head and said, "Well, I'll be damned. I was wrong. There is a white light," and then he'd died. Nathan had never told a living soul that story. Was that what Frank meant?

"Now, are we going to stand around and jabber some more or are we going to get moving to St. Mary's Church?" Constance asked Nathan.

St. Mary's was the only Catholic church in Dogwood County because Catholics were as rare as spotted owls in this part of the world. St. Mary's was well off the beaten path, far down an old country road, back near a creek that flooded every spring. The church itself was tiny, and it only had a handful of parishioners, as far as Nathan knew. It could be because the church was one of the few not air-conditioned—Father Daniels didn't believe in making his parishioners feel comfortable. He had made more than one joke about how the heat would help them be reminded of where they were headed if they didn't come to mass every Sunday.

"So why didn't we come here sooner?" Constance asked Frank, who gave a few yips as they pulled up in front of the old church.

"What did he say?" Nathan asked, wondering what she'd come up with this time.

"Said that Father Daniels went renegade a few years back. Said he's really militant and prone to using excess force against demons, so you don't usually ask for his help unless you're intending to firebomb someone."

"Great," Nathan said, hopping out of the driver's side of his truck.

Nathan glanced up at the old church, which looked like one of those old chapels you saw in movies based on Jane Austen books, only about five times smaller. Inside, there was barely room for the middle aisle, and five benches were crammed in on either side. The air was hot and steamy, like a toaster oven set on high. Above the altar, there was a large crucifix, complete with crown of thorns and lots and lots of blood. Jesus was also wearing nothing but a very tiny loincloth, which—in addition to the lack of air-conditioning—might explain the church's unpopularity in the region. Dogwood County folks didn't take kindly to nudity, even on the Lord and Savior.

" 'Bout time you showed up," Father Daniels said, walking purposefully up the middle aisle as if he'd expected them. He happened to be chomping on an unlit cigar, and looked a little like George Peppard from *The A-Team*, as if he were an ex–government agent just working undercover as a priest. The cigar stump gave him the air of a military general. "I've been waiting for days. You know the devil could be on earth already."

"Wait a second—you know about all this stuff?" Nathan asked, amazed. Somehow, Constance and Father Daniels were in on this little devil conspiracy.

Frank yipped twice.

"Prophet training not going so well, huh?" Father Daniels said, taking out his stump of a cigar and peering at Constance.

"Hey," Constance protested. "How do you know that?"

"Just a hunch," Father Daniels said, chomping down again on the cigar. "Frank, you should've come to me earlier. I could help."

Frank barked several times.

Father Daniels grimaced. "Oh, come on. That's ancient history. Are they still complaining about Belfast? I exorcised the demon, didn't I? I mean, I did take down a couple of buildings, but in the end, the demon was gone. I'd say it was worth it."

"You destroyed a city block?" Constance asked. "Seriously?"

"Demon fighting can be messy," Father Daniels said with a shrug.

Frank yipped some more.

"You can understand this dog?" Nathan asked Father Daniels, not quite believing what he was saying.

"Well, he's speaking English, son. You'd better pay attention," Father Daniels said.

Frank barked again.

"And, Frank, the diocese didn't demote me, for your information," Father Daniels said. "I happened to *ask* for the Dogwood assignment. And it's not the smallest church in the country, either. There are two more that are, technically, smaller."

Nathan glanced back and forth between Father Daniels and Constance, and wondered whether they had practiced the act with the dog and why they were partners in all this. Why were they trying so hard to convince him this was all really happening?

"Who's the devil's target?" Father Daniels asked Constance.

"Dante London," Constance said.

Father Daniels nodded. "Figures—that little tart. You can't go dancing around in a devil costume and expect the devil not to notice."

"Can you help us?" Constance asked.

Father Daniels peered at her, and then looked back at

Frank. "You didn't even tell her how to exorcise a demon, did you?"

Frank barked.

"Haven't *gotten* to that part?" cried Father Daniels, amazed. "That's what I would've taught first." Father Daniels dug around in his pocket and pulled out a few holy wafers. "Here," he said, handing Constance a couple. "You can use these on low-ranking demons. On higher ones, you need holy water or blessed weapons."

"I don't understand," Constance said, picking up the wafer. "What's the difference?"

"All demons have a concentration of evil about here," Father Daniels said, pointing to his head and to the center of his chest. "It enables them to keep a physical presence in this plane. The holy water and wafers help loosen that concentration, and if it's loosened enough, then the demon loses its grip on this world and is sent back to hell."

"Sounds pretty straightforward," Constance said.

"Well, it's not," Father Daniels said. "The higher ranking the demon, the harder it is to exorcise, and you try putting a wafer on the forehead of even an enlisted demon when he's mad. It's not easy. You get, say, a lieutenant and you might as well just eat these wafers, 'cause they won't do squat. You need something much stronger. Here, let me show you."

He led them all to the altar, where he pulled at the big golden cross at the table. The tabletop flipped down, revealing a hidden cache of weapons, large and small. Nathan did a double take. There were guns, knives, a crossbow, and even a giant samurai sword.

"What the—" Nathan cried, taken aback. The last place he thought he'd find a stockpile of weapons was a church.

Nathan's cell phone buzzed in his pocket. It had come back to life after a night sitting on the charger. He dug it out of his pocket. It was the station. He didn't feel he could ignore it.

"Hello?"

"You mind telling me just what happened at the hospital last night?" asked Ann. "Looks like a twister hit it. And we've been calling you on your radio all morning."

"It's broken," Nathan said.

"How did it . . . ?"

"Long story," he said, not wanting to get into it at the moment. "Everyone okay at the hospital?"

"Fine as far as I know," Ann said. "There weren't any critical care patients at the hospital. But the black widow is missing and the DA is having a fit. He thought you were wrapping up the case with her."

"Is that what you're calling Constance now?" Nathan asked, a little peeved. "Black widow" seemed unduly harsh. "Whatever happened to 'innocent until proven guilty'?"

"Oh, please."

"Anyway, she's not missing. She's with me."

"You taking her in?" Ann sounded excited.

"Possibly," Nathan said.

"If you could do it by three, that would help my odds in the pool quite a bit," Ann said. "I'll split the pot with you, if you want."

Before he could say another word, an arrow whizzed

by his head. He craned his neck and saw Constance poised with a crossbow in her hands, a look of total surprise on her face.

"Oops," she said, giving him a sheepish look. "Sorry."

"Ann, I've got to go," Nathan said, frowning. He flipped his phone closed. "What the hell is going on here, Father? Do you have a permit for that crossbow?"

"I don't need a permit," Father Daniels said, bristling. "I'm working for a higher authority."

"We're not going to be using unauthorized weapons," Nathan said, taking the crossbow out of Constance's hands. Constance just frowned and dug deeper into the stash, coming out with what looked like a battle-ax. She tried a practice swing, but it was so heavy, she nearly lost her balance.

"Give me that before you kill somebody," Nathan snapped, grabbing it easily out of her hands.

"What do you propose we use when Yaman and his buddy come calling again?" Father Daniels said. "These weapons were all blessed by the pope."

"Pope Benedict?" Constance asked.

"Yes, as it happens, but Benedict the Eighth in 1020 AD," Father Daniels said. "The guns were blessed by Pope John Paul II."

"He blessed *guns*? I don't believe it."

"The bullets are filled with holy water, and besides, it's a holy war we're talking about," Father Daniels said. "Take no prisoners."

"Okay, let's just stop here for a minute," Nathan said. "So far, I've put up with *all* of this craziness, but I have to draw the line at playing GI Joe."

"My son," Father Daniels said in a soothing voice, as he put a hand on Nathan's shoulder and pulled him away from Constance and Frank. "Let's talk, shall we?" When they were far enough out of earshot, Father Daniels turned to Nathan and spat out his cigar stub on the floor.

"Okay, now it's time to cut the bullshit," Father Daniels said, giving his shoulder a hard little shake. Nathan started at the sound of a priest swearing.

"I don't know what you mean."

"Come on, Nate. We both know this isn't your first dance at the supernatural rodeo," Father Daniels said.

"Supernatural rodeo? Is that a real term?"

"You of all people know there are bad things out there. Things that aren't human."

"If you're talking about the three-headed dog . . ."

"Now I'm talking about what you saw long before Jimmy Plyd was murdered. You and I both know that you've seen stuff in your line of work that you can't explain."

Nathan's head shot up, and for a second he saw the Libby Bell suspect levitate and wondered how on earth Father Daniels knew about that.

"How did you know?" Nathan asked softly.

"I didn't, actually, it was just a guess," Father Daniels admitted. "Demons usually are on the wrong side of the law."

"So, you tricked me."

"You've got to get your head in the game," Father Daniels said, tapping Nathan's temple. "It's game time. And Constance needs all the help she can get. She doesn't believe half of this, either, which is why she can't do what she needs to do. If she has your doubts in her ear all the time, then earth is pretty well doomed."

"But . . ."

"Look, son, I'd love to give you a few months to process this whole spectacular thing called your spiritual awakening, but we just don't have the freakin' time," Father Daniels said, tapping his watch. "So do us all a favor and skip the whole doubting, self-questioning stage and just jump feetfirst into the I'm-a-true-believer-now stage, okay? And if you can't do that, why don't you just get the hell out of the way so we can do our jobs?"

"Huh," Nathan said, still a little bowled over by Father Daniels's bluntness. "You know, I was expecting more of a pep talk."

"That *was* a pep talk," Father Daniels said. "Now, what's it going to be? You on board or are you leaving?"

Nathan, still a little taken aback, walked back to Constance and Frank, who were busy filling a duffel bag with weapons.

"Okay, folks, I think I've had enough," Nathan said, his patience spent. "You do what you have to do. I'm leaving."

"You're *leaving*?" Constance asked him, amazed.

"I've had enough of talking dogs and flying men and crazy priests—sorry, no offense, Father."

"None taken," Father Daniels said.

"I'm sorry, but you're just *going*?" Constance asked, her face flushing red. She wasn't taking this news well.

"You don't need me," Nathan said. "You need the exorcist. Or some kind of miracle. I'm *not* that miracle. Father Daniels can help you much better than I can. I don't even think I believe in all this." Nathan waved his hands to show the church and the world at large. "And you're lucky I don't just drag you to a padded room right here and now. I should arrest you, but I'm not going to."

"Thanks for the favor," Constance snapped, sarcasm in her voice, as she angrily shoved a knife into the duffel bag.

"It *is* a favor."

"But you *saw* the demons last night," Constance said, dropping the duffel bag and standing. "How can you turn your back on what you saw with your own two eyes?"

"I don't know what it was I saw last night," Nathan said. "I just don't know. I'm sorry. It's just too much."

"Nathan Garrett, you are *not* leaving me. Not again."

"I'm sorry, I just can't stay," he said, shaking his head and turning to leave.

"Let him go," Father Daniels said, putting a hand on Constance's shoulder even as she stared daggers at him. "Just let him go."

Twenty-nine

Constance shouldn't have been surprised when Nathan abandoned her—again. He was a Garrett, and they were about as dependable as the weather. Yet, watching him walk out of that church hurt more than she liked to admit. She realized that she was already half falling in love with him, if she wasn't in love with him already, and that could lead to nothing but trouble. And if he couldn't manage to spend an afternoon with her when the world just might end, then she doubted the prospects were good for a long-term relationship.

Well, she didn't have the luxury of walking away from this, she thought. She was supposedly the Chosen One, and she had to stick it out. She wasn't a Garrett. She saw things through.

"No-good Garretts," Constance ground out when she could speak again.

"It's probably better this way," Frank said gently. "Besides, he could have done worse. He could've arrested you again."

"Humph," Constance grunted, not at all convinced that Nathan had just done them a favor. "So, now what?" Constance asked aloud, but as soon as she voiced the question, her eyes filled with stars and another vision came upon her like a lightning bolt.

She saw Corey Bennett and Dante London at her restaurant. She saw them as if looking in through an outside window, and she saw the *Dogwood Weekly News* dispenser outside the restaurant's front door. Quickly, she zeroed in on the paper. It was today's date. They were going to have dinner at her restaurant *tonight.*

Constance blinked several times and the image went away. She came to half sitting, half slouching in front of the altar.

"Whoa, you okay?" Father Daniels asked her. "You slipped there."

"I had a vision," Constance said, turning to Frank and then to Father Daniels. "Corey Bennett is going to drug Dante London at my restaurant tonight. And then afterward, that's when the devil is going to, well, you know. Have his way."

"Well, what are we waiting for? Let's go," Father Daniels said.

"Wait, we can't just go barging in there and tell Dante London that the world's most bankable movie star is working for the devil. She wouldn't believe us," Constance said. "We need a plan."

"We could firebomb the café," Father Daniels proposed. "I have grenades." He held up a couple.

"But Dante London could be killed!" Constance exclaimed.

"Yeah, but if she's dead, she can't give birth to the Antichrist."

"John, *this* is why we didn't come to you in the first place," Frank chided. "You've got to tone it down by about ten notches. You're always trying to kill flies with Buicks."

Father Daniels shrugged. "Okay, fine, so you want her alive. Why don't we just take her by force? We can tie her up and keep her in the basement until the week is up."

Frank and Constance both looked at Father Daniels. "You can't just kidnap one of the world's most famous pop stars," Constance said.

"I have to agree there," Frank said.

"But we've got a crossbow—and the Lord—on our side," Father Daniels said, holding up the ancient weapon.

"That won't matter if we're all in jail," Constance pointed out.

"Let's try something else first," Frank said. "Constance—how do you feel about working as a waitress tonight?"

"You look perfect," Frank said a half hour later.

Constance glanced down at her outfit, which she had borrowed from Father Daniels's clothes-drive closet. She wore a simple black skirt and white blouse, only the blouse was a little on the small side and she felt like if she took in too deep a breath, the buttons might become little plastic missiles with enough velocity to take out someone's eye. This would be fine if it were a demon eye she happened to be pointing toward, but the likelihood of that was probably slim at best.

The plan they had come up with was basically the kind of plan you could manage to cobble together in ten minutes in an un–air-conditioned church vestibule with a priest prone to violence and a French bulldog in a pink sweater. Constance thought it seemed like a good plan at the time, but maybe anything would seem sensible in that kind of environment.

The plan was this: Constance would be Dante London's waitress, and keep a close eye on the table, especially for any sudden moves on Corey Bennett's part. She would try to prevent Dante London from being drugged, if possible. If not, Father Daniels would intervene, somehow trying to keep violence to a minimum, and together they would all prevent Dante from going anywhere alone with Corey Bennett.

Constance knew it wasn't a great plan, but it was just now dawning on her that Dante London might recognize her as the would-be dog groomer, and then her cover would be blown, and then they'd have to go with Plan B, which involved kidnapping Dante London and holding her in the basement of Father Daniels's church for the next twenty-four hours.

"Come on, kids, let's blow this pop stand," said Father Daniels, who was still wearing his collar, but now also had on combat boots and jeans. He also sported an ammunition belt crossed across his chest, and at least three gun holsters, all loaded with weapons. He looked like he had enough ammo to start a small war. "What? Never seen a priest packing heat before?" he asked Constance, when she just kept staring.

"Don't you think that's a bit overkill?" Frank asked him.

"When you're dealing with the devil, *nothing* is over-kill," Father Daniels said.

Father Daniels offered to drive, and in the back of the church, under a giant tarp, he walked them to a big green Hummer.

"Army issue," Father Daniels said, sounding proud. "And blessed by the pope."

Constance looked at it dubiously, but she and Frank got in. It only took a few minutes to get to the café. Constance rode white-knuckled nearly the whole way, since the Hummer seemed too big to stay between the dotted lines, and Father Daniels kept pushing cars out of their lanes.

"Shove it, you asshole!" he screamed at a Buick that honked at them. "We're on a mission from God!"

"Just get us there in one piece, John," Frank said, as Father Daniels swerved off the highway and lay on his horn.

Father Daniels steered the Hummer toward a space down the block from the restaurant. The space was too small for the Hummer, and eventually Father Daniels gave up, driving the thing half on, half off the sidewalk.

"Subtle," Frank said.

"It's demon-proof," Father Daniels explained. "It's not meant for city driving."

Constance eyed Father Daniels's bullet belts, which he wore criss-crossed across his chest like Rambo.

"Can you cover that up?" Frank asked, nodding toward the belts. "It's a little conspicuous."

"But if I cover up, then how do I put evil on notice?" Father Daniels grumbled, as he readjusted his ammo belts. "The whole point is I look intimidating."

"You look crazy, you mean," Frank said. "I think maybe you should wait in the car. Be the lookout."

"Lookout? That's for pansies," Father Daniels spat, frowning.

"Just be the lookout, okay?"

"Fine." Father Daniels crossed his arms to show he wasn't happy about the decision. "But if I see something, I'm using this."

He held up what looked like a bazooka.

"Just not to incinerate any innocent bystanders," Frank said. "Ready to go?" Frank added to Constance, holding up one paw.

"I suppose so," Constance said, scooping him up in one arm.

At the café, there were a few onlookers already camped outside. Apparently, word had gotten out about Dante London and Corey Bennett. She waded through the small crowd outside, pushing past a couple of photographers with bags of gear, and unlocked the front door with her key.

Once inside, she saw Jose first. His face lit up with recognition. "Hey—you're okay!" He bustled over and gave her a big bear hug. Martinez, who was behind the lunch counter drying off glasses, put them down and hustled over, too, joining in for a group hug. Frank was jostled and manhandled a little, and gave a little bark.

"Long story," Constance said.

"We heard about your house. We're sorry," Jose said. Both he and Martinez nodded their heads with solemn expressions. "We tried to call you, but no answer."

"My cell was in the house," Constance said.

"Very sad," Jose said, nodding. "They know what caused it?"

"Gas leak," Constance lied.

"Your mother came by. She was worried about you. You should call her," Jose said. "Said she went by the hospital this morning, and it looked like something crazy happened there."

"Yeah, we had some kind of storm," Constance lied. "Tornado. Can you believe it?"

"Damn twisters," Jose said. "A nuisance. By the way, you going to introduce us to your new friend the health code violation?" he pointed to Frank.

"This is Frank," Constance said. "I'm dogsitting for a friend. And he'll be fine here for one night. He's very clean."

"Whatever you say, boss," Jose said. "So, I assume you heard about Dante London? I figured you'd definitely want to open the restaurant up for her. She could be the key to bringing the customers back. I know you said to keep the restaurant closed, but we did close it for a day. And technically, this is just opening it for two people. Besides, you can't pay for this publicity." Jose nodded to the crowd standing outside. "And we might even be mentioned in *People* magazine."

Martinez nodded to one of the photographers waiting around outside to get a picture of Dante and Corey.

Constance couldn't blame Jose for doing what he thought was best. She watched as he bustled around the restaurant, fixing napkins and place settings. He'd even put out fresh flowers on every table, a detail he normally would've skipped. Constance noticed the entire restaurant was set, despite the fact that just one couple was coming to dine tonight. She admired Jose's hard work. He was a good partner, even if opening the restaurant was a bad idea. One of the worst, in fact, given that it could just mean the end of the world.

Constance opened her mouth to tell Jose this, but then shut it again. He was a religious man—always wearing a cross—but she doubted even he'd believe her. She remembered Nathan's look of pure skepticism that very morning. He'd thought she'd completely lost her mind and he'd actually seen a three-headed dog with his own eyes.

"Can they salvage anything from your house?" Jose asked.

Constance thought about the flames licking the ceiling of her kitchen. "I don't think so," she said. Visions of her perfectly retro kitschy kitchen completely destroyed made her sigh.

"You okay?" Jose asked her, meaning more than just her physical self.

"I'll live—I think," Constance said. She gingerly put Frank down on a chair near a table and sat to help Jose fold napkins. Sitting inside her restaurant, she was starting to feel a little more like her old self. She might not be a great Chosen One, but *this* was something she knew how to do. At the café, she didn't have to think about how she didn't have a home to return to anymore, because the restaurant always felt more like home than her house.

"Okay, let's get ready," Constance said, shaking off her sadness. "And by the way, I'll wait on Dante tonight."

"But I promised Martinez!"

Martinez, who was drying off some glasses, gave Constance a shy smile.

"He can refill their water glasses, that's a promise," Constance said, and smiled back at him. "But I'm going to wait the table tonight."

"You pulling rank on us, chief?" Jose asked.

" 'Fraid so, Jose."

"Well, I guess it's only fair. They're only coming here because somehow Dante got hold of one of your chicken-fried steaks," Jose said. "You been giving them out like business cards or something?"

"Something like that," Constance said, thinking back to when she'd accidentally left the bag of steaks in Dante's trailer. The take-out box had the restaurant's name and phone number on it. She must have thought they were sent especially for her.

"Well, good work," Jose said, giving her an approving nod.

"What have you done for prep so far?"

"Only everything," Jose said. "But you can peel some potatoes if you want."

"I'm on it," Constance said, and grinned.

It was another couple of hours before Dante London and Corey Bennett arrived, a full hour and a half past the scheduled reservation time, but then when you've bought out a whole restaurant for the night, Constance supposed, it didn't matter what time you bothered to show up. By then the crowd outside the restaurant had grown threefold, and a few dozen people had set up lawn chairs, like they were going to watch the Fourth of July parade. She supposed the publicity could only be good for the café, and having extra people around might keep Corey Bennett in check. Especially the three or four paparazzi standing near the front of the restaurant.

The stars pulled up in a silver Mercedes, with Corey behind the wheel, and they didn't bother to come in the back entrance or ask for a discreet arrival. Neither seemed to care if they were photographed together having a romantic dinner for two. They were already holding hands, which seemed out of line to Constance. Corey Bennett was easily twice Dante's age, and if the tabloids were right, he already had a girlfriend. They waded through the flashbulbs. Dante paused to sign autographs, but Constance noticed that Corey didn't bother to sign any, just pressed forward, a look of slight annoyance on his face. He kept ushering Dante forward, not wanting to stop to talk to fans.

Dante London bounced into the Magnolia Café wearing what looked like dental floss with sequins, which put most of her girl equipment on display, and Corey Bennett was wearing a black suit with a gray shirt, and a diamond-encrusted TAG watch that probably cost more than Constance's house. They sat themselves down at the table in the back, away from the windows, just as Constance had foreseen. They looked exactly as they had in her vision, and she experienced a powerful sensation of déjà vu.

So, it hadn't just been a dream, then. She had had a vision of the future. *A real vision.* A small part of her had doubted all along that the visions she'd been having actually meant anything. But now here it was: hard proof.

She could see the future. She already knew in advance what each of them planned to order. Just like she already knew that Corey Bennett was going to clean his plate, and Dante was going to barely touch her food.

"This is weird," she whispered to Frank, who was hiding in the kitchen, out of view of Dante, lest she recognize him. "It's just how I pictured it."

"You *are* a prophet," he reminded her. "That's how these things are supposed to work."

"I know, but it's still weird." Constance paused. "You know, I didn't see myself in this vision."

"Well, plans change, and now you're in it," Frank said. "You decided to come here. Before, you hadn't made the choice to come. It's free will at work."

"But what if Dante recognizes me from the set?"

"She won't," Frank said. "She's terrible with faces and even worse with names."

As it turned out, Frank was right. Neither Dante London nor Corey Bennett bothered to look her in the eye. Waitresses were beneath the two of them, it seemed, despite the fact that one was born in a trailer park and the other had sold his soul to Satan.

She took their orders quickly, keeping a close eye on Corey, but she knew he wouldn't make his move until after he'd eaten. That much she'd seen in her vision. At least, unless he decided to change his mind. Constance wondered just how much she could count on her visions if they kept changing based on what people decided to do or not do. She supposed this would be another reason to learn how to conjure them up at will. If they were always changing, she needed updates, like a cable news ticker, or the information would quickly become outdated and use-less. Constance closed her eyes and tried to concentrate again, just like Frank had told her to, but nothing came. Even when she was staring right at Dante London, no new visions popped into her head. She drew a complete blank.

"Order up!" Jose called, dinging the bell in the kitchen. Constance jumped a little. Jose had whipped up their food in double time. She picked up the plates and headed to the table, eyeing Corey as he finished off the last roll in the bread basket.

"About time!" Corey whined as Constance put the plate in front of him.

Dante, for her part, leaned back a little so Constance could slide her plate in, but didn't stop talking about her hair—the subject she'd been fixated on since they had their appetizers.

"And *then*, like, oh my God, you won't believe it, but my hair extensions, like they started coming off," Dante said, picking up her fork and then waving it around for emphasis. "You know they're, like, not supposed to do that, right? And I swear, it was *the worst* day of my entire life. My hair! It's my signature. It's what *I'm known for.*"

Hair was most certainly *not* what Dante was known for, Constance thought, considering she was nearly spill-ing out of her dental floss halter top.

"Need anything else?" Constance asked them, hover-ing a little at the table as Corey started to dig into his food like a man who hadn't eaten for days.

"We're fine," Corey mumbled, mouth full. He would definitely wait until *after* he'd eaten to spike her drink,

Constance thought. This was a man who wasn't going to be deterred from his meal. She wondered how he managed to put food away like that and not show it. But then, it was probably part of the devil's bargain.

Constance walked away from the table and Dante's voice carried easily across the restaurant, following Constance to the other side. Dante talked about hair extensions for the next thirty minutes solid. Even Jose and Martinez were starting to look bored. Constance thought hard about how this was supposed to be all for a higher good, and that it was probably no surprise God would be asking her to make sacrifices. She just hadn't expected them to take the form of conversation from a vapid, self-centered pop princess. If she had to listen to Dante talk about her hair for five more minutes, she might just poison Dante herself. She wondered how Corey was able to stand it, but then she realized it was because he had his head down in his plate like a hog rooting for truffles and probably hadn't heard a single word since the plate of food was put before him.

Just as Constance had envisioned, Dante took only three bites. She'd been talking far too much to eat. Maybe that's why she was so skinny, Constance thought. She glanced over at Jose and Martinez, who were both manning the lunch counter and barely bothering to conceal the fact they were watching the two stars eat. When they saw Constance looking in their direction, both of them pretended to be cleaning. Constance shook her head and then ducked inside the kitchen, where Frank was keeping watch for demons.

"Anything yet?" he asked.

"No, but I know a lot more than I ever wanted to about hair extensions," Constance said. "Any demons yet?"

"Nope," Frank said. "And I just talked to Father Daniels about five minutes ago. He hasn't seen anything, either."

"Good," Constance said.

"Hold on—what's Corey doing?" Frank asked, peering through the crack between the two swinging doors.

"Wait! That's it, he's doing it," Constance said, suddenly realizing that the view she had was the exact same one she'd had in her vision. Dante had bent over to grab something from her purse, and Corey was tapping a vial of powder into her wineglass. "That's it—that's the drug," she said with a shock.

Once again, her vision had proved true.

"Surprised?" Frank asked, as if reading her mind.

"I guess it still takes some getting used to," Constance said. "So what do I do now? I didn't see myself in the vision. In the version I saw, Dante drinks the wine and Corey lugs her off to the devil."

"Get the wine," Frank said. "Make some excuse. Do what you have to, just don't let her drink it."

Dante was still rooting around in her purse. Constance hurried over to the table, trying to figure out a plan. When she got close enough, she heard that the conversation had turned to topics a little more interesting.

"So you're *really* a virgin?" Corey was asking now.

"Technically," Dante said, abandoning her purse and sitting up. She had a tube of lipstick in her hand, which she applied while holding up a knife for her own reflection.

"I mean, I've *totally* messed around. You know, with *other* holes."

Constance couldn't help herself—she coughed, surprised, trying to suppress the laugh that was about to bubble out of her throat. Dante might be a millionaire, but she definitely didn't have class.

The cough caused Corey to snap his head up and look at her, probably for the first time since he'd sat at the table. He narrowed his eyes at her, giving her a not-so-nice look. Uh-oh. That wasn't good. Constance quickly looked down.

"All finished?" Constance asked, taking Corey's licked-clean plate.

"No," Corey said in a voice laced with annoyance. "Leave the plate, would you?"

Constance glanced at it, noticing that the only thing on it was a tiny sprig of parsley. Did he plan to eat that, too?

"Um, Miss London?" she asked Dante. "All done?"

"No, she's not done, *either*. Now beat it," Corey grumbled.

Think, Constance. You've got to do something, she thought. *And fast.* Corey was staring a hole through her, and she was starting to look like one of those gawking fans. Just then, Dante, unperturbed by Corey's rudeness or Constance's hovering, reached for her wineglass.

"Um, wait, l-let me g-get you more wine . . ." Constance stuttered, shooting her arm out in the direction of the wine bottle, but hitting Dante's wineglass instead. The ruse worked, because Dante's wineglass plunked over, the drugged wine spilling onto the tablecloth and straight down the front of Dante's microdress.

Oops. Constance had meant to dump the wine, just not in Dante's lap. Now it was Dante's turn to frown.

"This is couture!" she exclaimed, jumping up and patting at the front of her dress, which barely had room for five or so sequins.

"*Dios mío,*" Jose said, smacking his forehead, no doubt seeing hundreds of thousands of dollars in revenue go down the drain as he and a stunned Martinez looked on.

"We could sue you for that," Corey threatened Constance.

"Oh, Corey," Dante said. "You're so sweet."

Constance rolled her eyes.

"Y'all have a bathroom or what?" Dante asked.

"In the back, to your left," Constance said, as Dante shimmied past her. She was barely out of earshot when Corey spoke.

"Now, listen, you little tart," Corey growled. "I'm serious about suing. I could buy you and this little shithole a hundred times over."

He paused to let the seriousness of his threat sink in. Corey glanced down at Constance's too-tight blouse. His eyes wandered down and then up again.

"Of course, if you want to *do* something for me, maybe we could work something out," he added with a leer. His meaning was clear, and while Constance was sure his fame and good looks worked on most women, they certainly weren't working on her. He had all the markings of a Garrett-in-training, and while she ought to have been swayed, given her history, she wasn't the least bit interested. Maybe this meant she'd grown.

"I don't think so," Constance said.

"What do you mean *you don't think so*?" Corey asked, shocked. Apparently, he wasn't used to being told no. His face morphed from surprise to worry. "You don't want to sleep with me?" He grabbed her wrist now, because she was backing away.

"No thanks," she said, trying to free her arm, but he only gripped it tighter.

"But *why*? Why don't you?" He was shaking her arm now, and it was beginning to hurt. He tightened his grip.

"Let go," Constance demanded, trying to free herself. Out of the corner of her eye, Constance saw movement by the lunch counter. It looked like Jose and Martinez were either coming over to help or moving to get a better look at the unfolding drama.

"But *why*? Tell me why!" He was beginning to sound like a fourth grader. "Is it because of this?" He pointed to a tiny red dot on his face. "It is, isn't it?"

Constance had had enough. She wasn't about to be intimidated by this guy. He wasn't a demon with special powers. He was human, just like her, except he'd chosen to play for the bad guys. She was the one in the right. Not him.

"I don't date people who've sold their souls," Constance said quietly.

Instantly, Corey went stock-still and a little pale. His grip loosened, and she whipped her arm free.

"How did you know that?" he hissed at her, voice half fearful, half menacing.

"Just stay away from Dante London," Constance said, feeling a little braver now that she had him off balance. "I know what you plan to do, and don't think I won't stop you."

"Who are you?" Corey asked, fear suddenly flickering in his eyes. "Just who *are* you?"

Before Constance had time to answer, Father Daniels—in his full Rambo mode—burst through the front door of the restaurant, brandishing a sword in one hand and a semiautomatic in the other. "Demons are coming!" he shouted, and then ran straight for the women's bathroom.

A second later, Dante London screamed.

Constance watched the whole fiasco unfold as if it were in slow motion. Father Daniels, in an attempted kidnapping of Dante London, burst into the women's restroom stall, dropped his weapons, and grabbed her like a sack of potatoes, flinging her over one shoulder and trying to make a run for the back door. Corey, Jose, and Martinez were after the priest instantly, as he tried to waddle out the door. Dante, it appeared, was not as light as she looked, and it was even harder to carry her as she was pounding and scratching at him. Then came the fatal blow: she somehow managed to land a well-placed stiletto heel into his groin.

While his Hummer might have been demon-proof, Father Daniels's pants were no match for Jimmy Choo, and he went down in a crumpled ball, clutching his groin and screaming that he'd been permanently injured. Dante toppled down next, her skirt rising up and showing him, as well as all the paparazzi lurking in the alley behind the restaurant, that she was going commando. She'd learned nothing from Britney, apparently.

Corey started to kick Father Daniels while he was down, but thought better of it in front of the cameras, and stepped back while sirens wailed in the distance. Jose and Martinez restrained Father Daniels between them, holding him fast by the arms. Constance searched the alley, but saw no sign of Yaman, or any three-headed dogs, or anything that might remotely approach a demon, except for Dante London herself, who had managed to get to her feet and recover enough dignity to land another swift kick to Father Daniels, which caused him to curse and sag again. Constance could just see the cover of next week's *Us Weekly*: "Dante Goes on Rampage and Attacks Priest." This would not be a good night for any of them.

"Someone call the police!" Corey demanded.

But someone already had, because the sirens were close now, and Constance saw Nathan's police truck speed through a stop sign at the corner and skid into the alley. Nathan had changed into his uniform since Constance had last seen him, and he was now carrying a gun and looking very official. He also looked very mad.

"Finally! The police," Corey said, sounding exasperated. "You there," he added, pointing to Nathan. "You need to arrest *everyone*."

In short order, Corey explained what had happened. Nathan soon cuffed Father Daniels, after patting him down for weapons, which took a considerable amount of time considering he was packing a lot of heat. He got the cuffs on Father Daniels and ducked him into the truck, and then he turned to Constance.

"Come on, you too, Con," he said, a no-nonsense expression on his face.

"Me? What did I do?"

"Yeah, what did she do?" echoed Jose.

"You know damn well," Nathan said, grabbing her not so nicely by the arm and spinning her around so her belly was against the hood of the car. She felt cold metal handcuffs slide on her wrists and then fasten with a click.

"These aren't necessary," she sputtered, but Nathan was having none of it. He pushed her into the truck's backseat, alongside Father Daniels.

"Who took a whiz in that guy's Cheerios this morning?" Father Daniels grumbled, sitting on his cuffed hands.

Frank came out of the restaurant then, barking furiously, and Dante scooped him up in her arms. "Dognapping!" Dante cried. "I've been looking for Pinky since yesterday!"

"I'll just add it to the charges," Nathan said.

Constance frowned at him from the backseat of his police truck. "I liked you better when you just up and quit on me."

"Me, too," Nathan grumbled, slamming the door.

Thirty

It was a quiet ride to the station. Any time anyone tried to talk, Nathan cut them off. He wasn't interested in hearing excuses or explanations. He'd played along with these wild stories about the Apocalypse long enough, and now things were such a mess that he'd most certainly lose his badge over it, if not be prosecuted for gross incompetence. Sure, he'd seen some weird things that he couldn't explain, but he wasn't sure Constance or her so-called talking dog had the answers, either. He'd not seen any sign of demons, or whatever they were, since the night at the hospital, and maybe he wouldn't see them again. In the meantime, he had real problems to worry about. Like just what was he going to tell the county judge when he asked why a priest had accosted Dante London.

"You're making a big mistake, bucko," said Father Daniels from the backseat.

"He's right. We have to go back," Constance cried, leaning forward in her seat and pulling against her handcuffs. "We can't let Corey take Dante. The devil is coming and . . ."

"Shut up!" Nathan growled. "There will be no talk of demons or Satan or the Antichrist or so much as a Lord's Name In Vain in this truck. Understood?"

"But Nathan . . ." Constance tried again.

"*Enough*," Nathan shouted.

"Frank's with them, you know," Father Daniels said quietly, looking at Constance. "That's one good thing."

"Yeah, but he needs our help."

"If you two don't stop talking right now, I'm going to shoot at least one of you," Nathan threatened, glancing in the rearview mirror.

Constance and Father Daniels fell silent.

Nathan's cell phone kept buzzing, and at least three of those calls were from the county judge himself, but he didn't pick up the phone. First, he was going to do his job, like he should've done days ago. He was going to take Father Daniels and Constance into the station and figure everything else out later.

"I never should have left," Nathan muttered, regretting his decision to leave them all at St. Mary's earlier that afternoon.

"That's right—you shouldn't have," Constance said.

"I mean, leaving you at the church. I should've just arrested you all then, and saved myself a giant headache."

"Humph," Constance grumbled.

"I can't believe I ever even let myself believe a little bit in all of this," he said. "You are all certifiable."

Constance got really quiet then, her mouth in a thin

white line and the anger seeping out of her like steam.

She was so angry, in fact, that when Nathan handed her over to Robbie to be processed for the murder charge, she just huffed, "Oh, sure, fine. That, too, why not?" and gave him a look that would've withered a lesser man.

"And, Robbie," Nathan said sternly. "When you're done here, go pick up Dante London. We'll need her statement, and we might need to watch her for her own protection."

Robbie's face lit up. "Yes, sir. Right away, sir."

Nathan resolutely didn't look at Constance as Robbie put her hands out to be fingerprinted. He could feel her eyes on him, burning a hole through his head, but he couldn't help that now. Still, it took every ounce of self-control to keep walking away from her and to his office. He wanted to shake some sense into her. He wanted none of this to be true.

"You're in a world of trouble," Ann, the dispatcher, said to Nathan, catching him just before he went inside his office door. "The judge *and* the district attorney are waiting for you in your office, and they aren't very happy."

Nathan steeled himself and then swung open the door.

The county judge, wearing his white button-down, jeans, and shiny black cowboy boots, stretched out his legs and gave Nathan a long, hard look. The district attorney was wearing a suit, and looked overdressed as usual. He gave Nathan a smug smile, but it was the judge who spoke first.

"Well, boy," he said in his deep East Texas twang. "You *trying* to get fired or you just having a bad day?"

Thirty-one

"This," Yaman said, floating invisibly over the mob of paparazzi outside the Magnolia Café, "is *definitely* your fault."

"Mine?" the Glutton demon sputtered, indignant. "*This* is not my fault."

"I told you to stop eating roadkill. It makes you smell even worse than usual. Plus that trash truck just put you over the top. That priest could probably smell you coming from a mile away."

"I ate a vending machine, too, *for your information*," the Glutton said. "It had plenty of Tic Tacs."

"Not enough to cover up dead raccoon and dirty diapers."

"Besides, *you* were the one who insisted we come and make sure everything went smoothly so we could go to Satan and take credit. We could've just waited down the street like *I* suggested. But no. *You* had to see firsthand what was going on. And you Pride demons say we Gluttons are impatient."

"If you took a little pride in your personal hygiene, we wouldn't be in this mess."

"And if you hadn't been so full of yourself, we wouldn't be in this mess, either," Shadow said evenly.

"Hey, wait a second," Yaman said, looking around him and patting his pockets as if he'd lost his car keys. "Where's Dead Jimmy?"

"I thought you were watching him," Shadow said.

Yaman sighed and rolled his eyes. "I told *you* to watch him, Glutton. What? Were you too busy eating flattened possum to take care of business?"

"Hey—there's nothing wrong with possum."

The two demons were about to come to blows when there was a flash of lightning and crack of thunder above their heads.

"Is that . . ." Shadow started.

"Who I think it is?" Yaman finished for him, looking up.

"Asmodeus," said a figure that dwarfed both demons. He was huge, and looked like a hodgepodge of animals. He had three heads: one a rooster, one a ram, and one that looked like a really ugly man. His feet were a tangle of hooves and rooster talons.

"General," sputtered Shadow quickly, bowing in submission. "We didn't see you. . . ."

"Yeah, sorry, Red," Yaman said, not bothering to bow. "I should've figured you were around when the lovebirds started arguing."

"Silence!" said General Asmodeus's middle face as he waved a hoof. "The demon in chief is *not* happy with either of you. And neither am I. And *don't* call me Red. I am one of Satan's Joint Chiefs, and you'll treat me with the respect I deserve, or you both will be stocking footballs in the sports equipment aisle of Mega-Mart. Understand?"

"Yes, sir." Shadow gave him a salute.

"That goes for you, too, Yaman."

"Yes, sir!" Yaman said with mock enthusiasm.

"You here to save us?" Yaman said. "Or do you have some nuns to see?"

At this, both Shadow and Yaman snickered.

"Enough!" Asmodeus bellowed, stamping one of his claws and grabbing Yaman by the throat. His laugh was choked off midcough. "No more nun jokes or I'm skipping Mega-Mart and I'll just tear you limb from limb right here."

"Sorry, sir," Yaman wheezed.

"Yes, sorry, General, sir," Shadow seconded.

"This was supposed to be a covert operation, but now you've got at least three mortals who know about you," Asmodeus said. "Maybe more. We've got to fix this mess you made and fix it now or the demon in chief will have all our heads."

"Right, sir!"

"We're with you, General!"

"And so you know, the nuns were an accomplishment in 1647," Asmodeus said defensively. "I got promoted for that."

"I'm sure they were—and French ones, too—notoriously difficult to seduce," Yaman said, straight-faced.

Asmodeus narrowed his eyes, as if trying to figure out whether Yaman was being facetious or not.

"That better not be sarcasm, soldier," he said.

"Never, sir," Yaman said, deadpan.

"And another thing," Asmodeus said. "Just when were you going to mention the prophet had another vision? You weren't *holding out information*, were you?"

Yaman went silent, sending a guilty look to Shadow.

"No, sir, we weren't," Shadow said quickly.

"Right, we were just, uh, delayed."

"Right. Delayed," Asmodeus said, skeptical. "Had nothing to do with you thinking you'd try to be heroes and go straight to the devil?"

"No, no, no," Yaman said. "We would never do that!"

"Never," Shadow agreed.

"Sure," Asmodeus said. "Well, now I'm here to clean up your mess, so you can kiss that promotion you were hoping for good-bye."

"We weren't hoping for any promotion."

"A Glutton satisfied with the status quo," sniffed Asmodeus. "Now you're going to tell me you're not hungry."

"Well, no, of course not, but . . ." Shadow started.

"You guys just try not to screw anything else up, okay? I'm going to fix this mess," Asmodeus said. "First, I'm going to get the prophet, since you two can't seem to keep up with her. I'll make her tell us where the devil is supposed to meet Dante."

"Is the demon in chief already on earth?" Yaman asked.

"Soon," Asmodeus said. "Very soon. He's waiting to find out just *where* he's supposed to make an appearance. And he really doesn't like to be kept waiting."

"Of course not."

"I don't blame him."

"Now, if you two knuckleheads will excuse me, I've got some work to do," Asmodeus said.

"Can we help?" Yaman asked.

"You've done enough already. Just stay put," Asmodeus said as he pushed past the two demons. Lightning flashed behind his head and he dove toward the police station.

Thirty-two

Constance sat on the cold metal bunk bed in the county jail cell and sighed. Her anger had dissipated some, and she was calmer now that she was staring at a cell door. Here it was, her future, staring out at her for probably thirty to life. Nathan had given up on her and there was probably more than enough evidence to convict her of Jimmy's murder. That was, if the world didn't end first. Or she didn't get eaten by a demon in the meantime.

She slumped and put her head in her hands. She was supposed to be the Chosen One, and yet she couldn't even muster a single vision when she needed it. Any way she looked at it, she'd failed. She'd never asked for any of this, and yet here she was. She'd screwed up big-time, and the entire planet was about to suffer. Millions of people would probably lose their lives, and it was all her fault.

She didn't think that anyone had ever messed up this badly, ever.

Constance sighed. Of course, the irony was that

now, at long last, she really believed. She'd had her doubts before, but seeing Dante London and Corey Bennett in the restaurant had pretty much silenced any doubts she'd had left. They had done everything she'd seen in her vision. She could no longer deny that her visions were real; that they were predictors of the future, and that she was perhaps the only person who could stop the devil. Sure, her newfound faith was a little late, now that she was locked up in jail with no hope of escape and Dante was wandering around somewhere out there protected only by a small French bulldog and about to become seduced by Satan.

"I guess I'm just a little slow," Constance said, looking up at the ceiling of the jail. "But then, surely you knew that when you chose me in the first place."

She didn't get an answer from the Lord Almighty. Not that she expected one. She didn't want to doubt God's plan, but having her as the person to save the world was a little iffy in her mind. She couldn't even save her marriage, and she was supposed to save the planet? It was a stretch.

Constance grabbed the cold metal bars and pressed her head against them. She closed her eyes and focused on the jail and the single question: What now?

And then, just as if she'd asked for it, she got a surge of light through her whole self, and a vision came upon her. A vision of the jail, with the lights out, and a big, monstrous demon she'd not encountered before lurking in the shadows as it snuck through the halls looking for her. It wasn't an ordinary demon, either, it had three heads—those of a rooster, a ram, and a man, one of the ugliest animal combinations she'd ever seen. And he was big—and scary.

Constance blinked hard, and then she was back in her cell, the lights on, no demon about. And it wasn't like the other visions, when she'd been struck as if by lightning. This one ran through her mind without her feeling like she was being electrocuted. And, she noticed, her head wasn't throbbing, either.

She sat down slowly. Wait a minute, she thought. The last time she'd had a vision and this time, she'd asked the same question: *What now?* It was as if the question were the trigger to bring about her second sight.

She had to try that again. Make sure it wasn't some fluke.

She closed her eyes and concentrated again on the ugly demon, asking once more the question *What now?* In an instant, the jail cell transformed again into the darkened one, the demon huffing and puffing as it came down the hall. And then, in her vision, she saw herself flat against the back wall of her jail cell, and Dead Jimmy popping his head through. A minute or so later, Dead Jimmy had managed to pull her straight through the wall and to safety. By the time the demon got to her cell, she wasn't there.

She opened her eyes again, and she was back in her lighted cell, back to the present.

"I really *did* it," she exclaimed, amazed, her heart pounding as she jumped up from her seat and pumped her fist in the air. "I had a vision! And I escape!" Two very good pieces of news, she thought. Maybe it wasn't too late to save Dante after all.

She felt a little flicker of hope in her heart. Maybe she hadn't doomed the entire world.

She did a little victory dance, but before she could finish her celebration, the garish fluorescent lights above her flickered, then popped. She pressed her head between the cold metal bars of her cell and tried to peer out into the hall. All she could see was the tiny hallway leading to the big metal door. The lights behind the door went out. Then the hallway light went. And then, finally, her cell light.

In the dark, goose bumps rose on her arms and she felt a chill in the air. *It was really happening. Her vision!* And then her stomach sank when she remembered the massive three-headed demon headed her way. She flattened herself against the back wall of her cell and tried to breathe. *Dead Jimmy saves me*, she reminded herself. *I am not going to die here today.*

She heard a rattling against the big door at the end of the hall, and she swallowed hard. Despite knowing that Dead Jimmy was going to save her, she still felt her heart pound a mile a minute in her chest. Knowing you were going to be saved and waiting for it to happen really didn't help much with the fear. She wondered if this was what Daniel had felt with the lions. Sure, history said he was all calm and such, but maybe at the time, he felt like she did. Just a little beyond anxious.

Another loud boom sounded at the end of the hall. The door was opening. *Where is Dead Jimmy?* He was taking his sweet time!

That's when a cold hand settled on her shoulder, and Constance, in a fright, felt like she jumped straight out of her skin. She whirled, and came face-to-face with Dead

Jimmy, who was grinning like an idiot, embedded in the concrete wall, half in and half out of her jail cell.

"Jimmy! What the hell took you so long?" Constance hissed.

"Well, jeez, Connie, good to see you, too," Dead Jimmy said. "I've only been held hostage by a couple of crazy demons for I don't know how long, and I only *just* escaped because I was trying to rescue you, but maybe you want to just rescue yourself?"

Coming down from her fright, Constance felt the anger quickly seep away.

"Sorry, Jimmy. I'd like the help, please," she added, contrite. "It's just there's a . . ."

A loud crashing sound at the end of the hall caused them both to jump.

"Demon?" whimpered Dead Jimmy.

"Yes, a . . ."

But Dead Jimmy had disappeared back through the wall.

"Jimmy!" hissed Constance. "Jimmy, you come back here!"

Reluctantly, Dead Jimmy put his head through again. "Sorry. I panicked."

"Well, stop it. You're supposed to pull me through this wall."

"How am I supposed to do that?" Dead Jimmy looked perplexed. "You're not a ghost."

"I don't know, but I had a vision you did it, so somehow you do it."

"Well, *how'd* you see me do it?"

Constance thought about it. "You just took both hands and pulled me on through."

"Like this?" Dead Jimmy asked, trying to take her wrists in his hands but his fingers went right through them.

"No, not like that. You really *grabbed on*. You had a good grip."

A loud bang sounded at the end of the hall, causing Dead Jimmy to jump.

"Hurry," Constance implored Dead Jimmy. "Concentrate."

"You sure you saw me do this?"

"I'm sure. You can do it. It's already going to happen, all you have to do is try a little harder."

"Hey! Wait a second, I just remembered something St. Peter said," Dead Jimmy said. "You know what? I think I *can* do this."

"Told you," Constance said.

"Yeah, yeah, I think I can remember what he told me to do. Okay, yep, I got it. All right, give me your hands."

A cell door banged open. Someone or something was coming. It was now or never.

"Here goes nothing," Dead Jimmy said, and that's when he grabbed her hands, and Constance felt his cold touch seep under her skin. But it didn't stop in her hands, it crawled through her arms and up her chest and into her head. It felt like an all-over-the-body brain freeze, and then her body went numb. So numb, she couldn't move her arms or legs. But Dead Jimmy could, and did. She felt him moving *for* her, and before she knew it, he walked straight into the wall. She tried to shut her eyes and brace for impact, but instead of slamming into the concrete, she suddenly found herself out on the other side, blinking back the bright light of day.

You did it! Constance exclaimed, except that Dead Jimmy still had control of her body, and so she only thought the words. They didn't come through her mouth.

"Hey, I *did* do it. Connie, you were right!" Dead Jimmy said, and made her do a little jig.

Stop it, Jimmy! she chided, but it only egged him on. He started making her smack herself in the head.

"Why you hitting yourself, huh? Why you hitting yourself?"

Jimmy!

"What? I'm just having a bit of fun. I could make you pick your nose next. Or make you strip nekkid and run around the town square."

You do, and I'll exorcise you, swear to God.

"Fine," Dead Jimmy sighed, sounding put out. He released her body and she felt the cold rush out of her, and suddenly she was herself again, and Dead Jimmy was, well, Dead Jimmy. He was standing in the parking lot, scratching his man parts through his hazmat suit.

"Thanks," Constance said, her voice and body under her control again.

"You're welcome," Dead Jimmy said, and grinned. "Although the streaking would've been fun. You need to loosen up."

Constance felt something damp, and looked down to discover that her too-tight white shirt was now completely wet.

"What's this?" she cried, trying to pick her shirt away from her skin. It was damp, all right. It felt like it had been dipped in a giant vat of hair gel.

"You ever see *Ghostbusters?*" Dead Jimmy said. "You've been slimed."

"Jimmy! I'm going to . . ." But before Constance could finish her threat, behind them, in Constance's former cell, they heard a whoosh of air, and a loud groaning sound as the bars seemed to bend under some great weight.

"How about we not stick around to find out what the heck that is?" Dead Jimmy interrupted.

"Good idea," Constance said, swallowing her anger for the time being.

"Come on. I'll get us a car." He floated through the windshield of one of the police cruisers in the parking lot. Within seconds, he'd hot-wired the car from inside. "Where to?"

"We've got to try to find Dante London," Constance said. "There might still be a chance to save her."

The minute the lights went out in the jail, Nathan knew what was happening. He was in the middle of being told, in no uncertain terms, that he was under indefinite probation, and should anything else out of the ordinary happen under his watch, he'd be summarily fired. The county judge didn't care that sheriff was an elected post. He'd damn well fire him, anyway.

He'd also had to listen to Paul Driscott, the district attorney, prattle on at length about how he'd jeopardized his case, how he'd have to work even harder to amass the evidence against Constance (Jimmy's assumed killer), and that if she went free it would be his fault.

And they didn't even know he'd slept with her, so Nathan should've counted himself lucky. But he didn't feel lucky.

Nathan didn't like being lectured to, and he especially didn't like being lectured to by two people who didn't know the first thing about police work, and spent their days hiding behind their law degrees and their big desks. Neither one of them had been chased by a three-headed dog, for instance. Or had their partner die in their arms.

"What on earth?" the county judge bellowed, as the lights flicked off and a thunderous sound like a train roared past their windows. "Is that a twister?"

"I heard one hit the hospital yesterday," Driscott said.

Nathan was already on his feet and heading to the holding cell where Constance was, knowing in his bones that he was already too late. It was just like at the hospital last night. The power went out, and then the three-headed dog showed up. He knew something was after her, the demon or whatever it was, and it was faster and stronger than he was. And he didn't even have any holy water. He ran past the booking desk and saw Constance's water gun. Robbie hadn't filed it yet. Figured. He was always lazy about police paperwork. Instinctively, Nathan grabbed it, and broke into a run to get to the holding cell.

The lights were already off, and the booming sound was even louder here, and everything was dark—even darker here than in the front because here there were no windows. He felt more than a little silly pointing the water gun at the darkness, but he reminded himself that whatever he was dealing with didn't play by the usual rules.

A strong wind blew hard from *inside* the cell. It seemed like there was a tornado inside for a second, whipping Nathan's hair into his eyes, pulling at his clothes. He blinked a few times and his eyes adjusted to the blackness.

Constance was in the second cell to the right. Nathan knew this because he'd asked Robbie to put her there. It was the solitary cell, the one where she wouldn't be bothered by anyone else, in case there were more arrests today. He got to the cell, but the bars were bent and warped, as if something strong had pulled them apart, and inside, the bunk bed, normally screwed to the wall, was ripped off its hinges and lying upside down on the ground. The single toilet was also ripped up and dented so badly it was almost unrecognizable. No sign of Constance.

Instead, standing in the middle of the rubble was a giant shadowy figure that looked a lot like a rooster. Wait, check that, a ram. Nope, a rooster . . . or was it a man? Whatever it was, it had three heads. Well, of course it did, Nathan thought. That's how these things came. The thing was distracted, tossing up pieces of the cell as if it had lost something. Its back was turned to Nathan, who braced himself, aimed his water gun at the middle head, and fired. The water hit the ram-rooster-man straight at the back of his middle head, and the water sizzled and burned, and a smell like burning cheese went up in the air. The creature shrieked, grabbed the backs of its heads, and then turned into a whirling cyclone of black dust, disappearing straight down the drain in the middle of the floor.

He blinked, and wondered if he'd killed it. He hoped so.

Nathan breathed hard, panting, and knew he could

no longer say none of this was real. It was *very* real. He hadn't imagined that three-headed dog, or Yaman flying, or now this creature, whatever it was, that had just made a quick exit down a drain. He'd spent too long denying what was right in front of his face. In the last sixty seconds, he'd become a true believer.

He glanced around the debris littering Constance's cell and wondered what had happened to her. Worry knotted his stomach. Was she alive? Had she been devoured by the monster? Or had she, against all odds, escaped?

He'd been too slow to protect her. He should've had her inside a church, surrounded by priests, not all alone, without even so much as a cross in a tiny jail cell. She'd tried to warn him, tried to tell him, and he'd refused to listen, despite the fact that he knew something was at work here that he couldn't explain. And he'd left her alone, to face that *whatever it was*. He'd failed her in every possible way.

He sank to his knees. She had to be dead. The cell was destroyed, and there wasn't a way out that he could see. He noticed there wasn't any blood anywhere and took a little comfort in that. Maybe her end had been quick.

"Hello? Anyone there?" shouted a familiar voice from the back of the jail. It was Father Daniels. Nathan raised his head, then got to his feet slowly.

He wiped his face and took in a deep breath as he walked back to Father Daniels's cell. He felt an anger bubbling in him, an anger that he quickly turned from himself to the creatures responsible for all this. He wanted to get back at them in the worst way possible. He owed Constance at least that. He could finish her mission for her, for one, and send every last demon in Dogwood back to hell. He had no idea how to do this, but he suspected Father Daniels did.

"Oh, it's you," Father Daniels said, looking disappointed.

"Can you help me hunt some demons?"

Father Daniels raised his eyebrows. "Crisis of faith over, eh?"

"Can you help me or not?"

"I can if you get me out of here."

Nathan grabbed the keys from his belt and unlocked Father Daniels's cell.

Thirty-three

W here the hell did he come from?" Asmodeus barked. Both Yaman and Shadow were trying to hide snickers. The three of them were hiding out in the main sewer line below the jail. It was high enough for Yaman and Shadow to stand, but Asmodeus had to duck so his heads wouldn't hit the ceiling.

"Harder than it looks, isn't it?" Yaman said.

"Silence!" Asmodeus thundered, striking out at Yaman with one of his claw feet while he held a hoof gingerly against his burnt head. "You two were supposed to be on the lookout. You didn't warn me he was coming."

"We were trying to figure out where the prophet went," Shadow protested.

"Yeah, and it didn't help that you turned out the lights on us."

Both Yaman and Shadow neglected to mention they had been in a heated discussion about what was more disgusting to eat—rotten eggs or saints—when Constance and Dead Jimmy had made their escape.

"Well, do either one of you screw-ups have any ideas?"

Shadow looked blankly at Yaman, who shrugged.

"You guys are a joke," Asmodeus said. "A complete joke."

"You're the one who got sidetracked by a pink squirt gun," Yaman said. "Besides, we offered to go in with you. But no, you wanted to do it yourself."

"Silence!" commanded Asmodeus. "I've had enough of your insolence. I'm going to see that the two of you are demoted. You'll be cleaning out the lavatories in hell for the next millennium." Asmodeus glanced over at Shadow, who was busy munching on something soggy. "Tell me you didn't just *eat* something you found down here."

"What? I'm nervous, and when I get nervous, I get hungry," Shadow said, belching loudly.

"You're always hungry. Nerves don't have anything to do with it, Glutton," Yaman said.

Asmodeus waved a hoof in front of two of his three noses. "Not the smartest, is he?"

"Nope," Yaman said.

"Sorry," Shadow said, hiccupping.

"Anyway, we've got to think. The devil only has a few hours left, and he's going to be royally pissed if we don't have more details about where he should meet Dante and when."

"How about we just pick a place?" Yaman said. "I mean, we don't have to rely on the prophet for everything. We're past any part where the demon in chief might do a goat. I'd say we could just pick a location and tell him the prophet saw it in a vision. How would he know the difference?"

Asmodeus considered this a moment. "You might be on to something."

"Like a promotion?"

"Don't push your luck." Asmodeus held his head a second and sighed. "But the devil will want to know the prophet saw him succeeding at this location. He'll want details."

"Just make them up," Shadow said.

"I don't know. It sounds risky."

"Are you, like, the only demon in the world who has a problem with lying or something?" Yaman asked, raising an eyebrow.

"I don't have a problem lying," Asmodeus said, frowning.

"Wait—I get it—you're bad at it, aren't you?" Shadow asked him. "Worried Satan is going to see right through you?"

"No," Asmodeus said, but he sounded a little doubtful.

"A demon who can't lie, well, now I've seen everything," Yaman said, rolling his eyes. "You're a general for hell's sake. Pull it together, man. You can *lie*. It's not hard."

"The devil is hard to lie to," Asmodeus said. "He's a little intimidating."

"I hear he's short," Shadow said.

"That makes it worse. He's got short-man's complex, and it makes him *more* intimidating."

"Okay, look, we'll coach you," Yaman said. "You'll get through it, no problem. And if you do, then we get promoted."

"Fine. If you can help me pull together a story that saves all of our butts, then you'll get promoted."

"Excellent. Now, here's what you do. Tell the devil to come to the Higgins Ranch."

"Why there?" Shadow asked.

"Why *not* there?" Yaman snapped. "Now, don't interrupt. I'm on a roll. So he meets us all there, and we bring Dante to him. I hear there's a nice comfy master bedroom on the second floor there. It has a fireplace *and* a Jacuzzi. He gives her a drink, talks her into the deed, and they have the bed right there. *Bam!* Instant Antichrist."

"That doesn't sound half bad," Asmodeus admitted.

"Course it doesn't. It's *my* idea. So go tell the devil. We'll wait," Yaman said.

"Hey, you're not supposed to be ordering me around," Asmodeus growled.

"Yes, sir. Sorry, sir. I mean, if you're *ready* to go, now would be a good time," Yaman amended.

"That's better," Asmodeus said. "Okay, I'm going. You two clowns stay right here until I get back. If Satan doesn't buy the story, then I'm telling him it's all your fault."

"Our fault!"

"Yes, yours. Now wait here."

"Right *here*?" Yaman asked, looking around the smelly, dark sewer.

"Right *here*," Asmodeus said, and then clapped his hands and disappeared in a clap of thunder that reverberated through the small enclosed space.

"Ow, that hurt my ears," Shadow said, putting his wings over his head.

"Mine, too. The general needs to work on his exits."

Another clap of thunder cracked through the sewer line, causing Shadow and Yaman to cover their ears. Asmodeus appeared before them.

"Back already?" Shadow asked.

"I took the express train," Asmodeus said. "And Satan bought it. He's coming to the Higgins Ranch. You two go there and make sure nothing screws this up for us. I'm going to go get Dante."

"What about our promotions?"

"If we get through this, I'll make you both captains."

" 'Colonel' has a nicer ring to it," Yaman said.

Asmodeus grumbled and sighed. "Fine, colonels it is."

"Sweet!" Shadow exclaimed.

"Now you two get moving," Asmodeus said. "The demon in chief will be at the ranch within the hour."

Thirty-four

Constance dialed Frank's number again from the pay phone outside the Snack 'n' Shack on Route 9, but got no answer, just a fast busy signal. She knew it was a long shot to reach him, since she hadn't been able to get him on his cell before, but she didn't know what else to do.

"Any luck?" Dead Jimmy asked, appearing beside her.

"No," Constance said, slamming the receiver down. A trucker walked by and eyed Constance's wet button-down with some interest. She quickly crossed her hands over her chest. The borrowed shirt had been too small to begin with, and now that it was wet with Dead Jimmy slime, it certainly didn't fit any better and the coverage was worse. "I need to get some fresh clothes."

"Do we really have time to worry about fashion? I thought we were supposed to save the world."

"I'm practically indecent," Constance said, motioning to her shirt.

"I like you that way," Dead Jimmy replied, wiggling his eyebrows.

"Oh, stop it." Constance sighed. She would have to do this herself. First, she was going to figure out where Dante London was and how long they had until the devil did his business. She wasn't going to let him get away with ruining her world. Not when she had something to say about it.

Constance didn't know where to find Dante London, so she closed her eyes and summoned a vision of the pop princess. She saw her and the devil sharing champagne in the bedroom she'd seen before. She focused her mind and told herself to widen the picture so she could see where they were. In an instant, the picture grew larger, as if she were using a telescopic lens, and she saw they were on the second floor of the big white house at the Higgins Ranch.

So *that's* where they'll be, she thought. She looked for signs of the time and saw that the sky was completely dark, which meant it was far after sundown. They had several hours yet to save her. The devil didn't have her yet, and even if he did, they hadn't done the deed. She could tell by the snippets of conversations she heard in the vision that the devil was doing his best to convince her to be his. She hadn't decided yet.

Her eyes opened. "We still have time to save Dante," she told Dead Jimmy, a little breathless. "They're going to be at the Higgins Ranch tonight, after sundown."

"Whoa—really? Did you see that in a vision? 'Cause you didn't even look like you normally do. You didn't even faint!"

"I didn't?"

"Nope," Dead Jimmy said. "Your eyes didn't even roll back in your head. You just closed your eyes like maybe you were trying to remember something. Normally, now's the time you keel over."

Constance realized he was right. She didn't feel even the slightest headache. She supposed it was another bonus of learning to control her powers. Apparently, when she was in control, she didn't faint or get a seizure.

"Good to know," Constance said.

"So now what?" Dead Jimmy asked.

"Let me see," Constance said, shutting her eyes and concentrating. She asked the question, "What now?" In response, she got a stark picture of her at her mother's house, getting a change of clothes and stocking up on dogwood blooms.

"First, we have to stop at Mama's house," Constance said, opening her eyes.

"Your mother?" Dead Jimmy whined. "Why not just feed me to the demon back there?"

"Don't tempt me."

Fifteen minutes later, Constance and Dead Jimmy were standing on Abigail's porch. She swung open the door, and upon seeing Constance, clutched at her heart.

"I thought you were dead or worse," she cried, pulling her daughter inside and hugging her so tightly she couldn't breathe. "I saw what happened to the hospital, and I just knew they'd gotten you. And then I heard you'd been arrested again, and then . . . well, don't *ever* scare me like that again!"

Abigail sounded as angry as she had when Constance was twelve and had stayed out past dark and hadn't bothered to come home until well past dinner.

"Dead Jimmy is with me," Constance said. "He saved me from a demon, and got me out of jail."

"Well, then, he's most certainly welcome in my house," Abigail said, beaming. "Help yourself to the good stuff, Jimmy. It's in the liquor cabinet in the living room."

"Woo-hoo!" Dead Jimmy cried, and pumped his fist.

Constance gave Abigail the quick version of events. Only Constance's mother would accept a quick rundown involving demons, Dante London, and the devil without blinking an eye. She took in all the information, and then told Constance to go get changed while she scrounged up some dogwood blooms.

Constance stood in her mother's bedroom trying to find something decent to wear that wasn't covered in Dead Jimmy slime, but she was having a hard time finding anything not tie-dyed, hot pink, or blindingly printed with various combinations of the jewel tones.

"Mama, don't you have any *normal* clothes? Have you ever heard of the Gap?"

"I'm going to let that comment slide since I only just learned you hadn't been eaten by demons," Abigail said, coming up the stairs with a basketful of dogwood. She put the basket down and stepped into her closet.

"Why don't you just wear this?" she asked, pulling out a black velvet tracksuit. Aside from the leopard-print silk lining, it was in the neighborhood of decent.

"Mama! Where'd you get this? It doesn't even have a single rhinestone on it."

"It was a late-night Home Shopping Network purchase," Abigail admitted. "Sometimes I order the darndest things when I'm sleep-deprived."

Constance wiggled out of her slimed clothes and into the tracksuit. It was a little large, but it mostly fit.

"Say, are those *boxer shorts?*" Abigail was looking at Constance's discarded pile of clothes. She had been wearing the borrowed pair of Nathan's shorts. Seeing them made her face turn bright red. "You are either letting yourself go to the point where I can't even save you, or *you've bagged yourself a man.*"

"What's that about bagging?" Dead Jimmy shouted from the kitchen.

"Mama, not in front of Dead Jimmy."

"If it's that Garrett boy, then I'd say you *finally* aren't trading down," Abigail went on.

"Why would you think it's him?" Constance asked, suddenly on guard.

"Well, I wouldn't really, but given that you're so defensive, I'd say I hit a nerve."

"That Garrett boy had me arrested, for your information," Constance said, grabbing Nathan's boxers out of her mother's hands. "And Dead Jimmy sprang me, remember?"

"Yes, and I'm duly impressed," Abigail said. "I thought it would take him way longer to learn about teleporting."

"Hey—I heard that!" Dead Jimmy shouted from the kitchen.

"So, my dear, what's the battle plan?" Abigail asked.

"Well, I'm going to do what you'd do in my shoes,"

Constance said. "I'm going to consult my visions first."

Abigail beamed with pride. "That's my girl!" she said, grinning from ear to ear.

Constance took a seat on her mother's bed and willed herself to see Dante London. She told her mind to focus in on what Dante was doing right at that moment.

In an instant, she got a picture of Dante sitting in Deputy Robbie's car as the pair drove down Route 9.

"I don't see why y'all got to take me to the police station," Dante London was saying. "So some nutcase grabbed me. You'd be surprised how often that happens. Normally, I've got my bodyguards with me, but Corey insisted we go out alone."

Constance saw Frank jumping up and down frantically in the backseat. He was clearly trying to warn Dante or Robbie about something serious.

"I bet a lot of people want to grab you, for sure," Deputy Robbie said, and then blushed deep red.

"That include *you*, officer?" Dante said, sending Deputy Robbie a borderline flirty look.

Robbie was so distracted by the smile on her pouty lips and the fact that her shirt was practically transparent that he nearly ran his patrol car straight into a telephone poll. He righted the wheel and breathed out a sigh of relief.

"Will you run the siren? Pretty please."

"Yes, ma'am!" Deputy Robbie said with enthusiasm, turning on the siren and pushing his foot down on the gas. Of course, he was too busy soaking in the smile on Dante's face and the cleavage she laid out for him to see to notice there was a rather large obstruction in the middle of the road. A big, lumbering animal that looked a lot like the demon Constance had seen in the jail.

"Robbie, watch out!" Constance tried to yell, but in her visions she was, naturally, voiceless.

"Look out," Dante shouted, putting up her hands.

Robbie slammed on the brakes, but it was too late. They drove straight into a demon, which crushed the front of Robbie's car and cracked the windshield as it rolled up and over. The car skidded to a stop in a ditch on the side of the road, with Dante London shrieking. In the backseat, Frank was going crazy, jumping up and down and all around and barking up a storm.

"Did we kill it? Oh my God—is it dead?" she said. "I'm a member of PETA—they're going to have my ass on a plate!"

The demon was lying still on the road. Had Robbie killed it? Constance wondered, but then she saw it was still breathing and knew in an instant that it planned a surprise attack.

Robbie opened his door and went to investigate.

"What the hell?" Robbie said, bending over for a closer look and scratching his head as he got closer to the thing in the road and realized it wasn't a bull, or a deer, or anything *normal*.

And that's when one of the talons whipped out from the mess of feathers and fur and grabbed him by the neck. In a flash, Robbie's head popped off like a loose button and rolled off to the other side of the road.

"I'll take it from here," Asmodeus said, dropping Robbie's limp body. He picked himself up off the asphalt and smoothed a few of his ruffled feathers, heading for the police car, where Dante London, oblivious to her impending danger, was checking her makeup in the fold-down mirror.

Asmodeus would take her to the Higgins Ranch, where Constance could see the devil waiting patiently, wearing a red smoking jacket and shiny black shoes.

Constance blinked and the image was gone. When she came back to the present, her mother was sitting on the bed clapping her hands.

"You didn't even faint!" she cried, sounding proud.

"I don't have much time," Constance said, glancing out her mother's window at the setting sun. "I've got to get to the Higgins Ranch, and fast."

Thirty-Five

Nathan was not a man who did a lot of praying. He didn't feel it was right to ask something from a God he second-guessed nearly every day, but this was a special case. He wanted to get the demons who'd hurt Constance, and he needed God's help to find them.

"Don't you know something? Anything?" Nathan asked Father Daniels as the two sat in his police truck on the side of the road with the ignition on but nowhere to go. Nathan had peeled out of the police station, but soon found that Father Daniels had no idea where to lead him. In frustration, Nathan had pulled over to the side of the road, and now they'd been sitting there at least ten minutes.

"I told you. I'm not a prophet. That's the prophet's job."

"You don't have anything here that can tell you?" Nathan gestured toward the backseat of his police truck, which was full of all the weapons they'd confiscated from Father Daniels upon his arrest. Nathan had piled every last one in the back of his truck in hopes that he could use them to kill as many demons as he could.

"No," Father Daniels said, grabbing two gun belts from the backseat and slinging them over his shoulders. He holstered a semiautomatic and a few clips. "No crystal balls here. Everything here shoots something."

"You *need* to know," Nathan said, desperate. "Her mother's house? The Higgins Ranch? *Where?*" Nathan turned to Father Daniels, grabbing him by his lapels.

"Holy Mother," Father Daniels said as Nathan pushed him against the opposite car door. "You've gone and fallen in love with a prophet."

Nathan relaxed his grip a little. "What are you talking about?"

"You know what I'm talking about. You're in love with her."

Nathan released Father Daniels and shifted back to his seat. "That's none of your business."

"Maybe not, but that is a big mistake, buddy, let me tell you. Besides, she could already be gone."

"I know that. I know she probably is," Nathan said, glancing out the window toward Route 9. "So, I'm going to do everything I can to make things right with her."

"Even though she's in all likelihood dead?"

"Yes," Nathan said, setting his mouth in a firm line.

"Well, okay, then. A revenge mission, my favorite kind," Father Daniels said, rubbing his hands together. "Now, let me think. . . . Wait, I've got it. Why don't we try to find Corey Bennett? He's working with the demons. He might know something. We could shake him down for information."

"Good idea," Nathan said, grasping at the hope. Nathan grabbed the radio on his dash. "Ann," he called through the CB, "you got any word on where Corey Bennett might be? I need to find him for questioning."

"He was heading back to the set, last I heard from Robbie," Ann said. "Speaking of, he hasn't checked in lately, and he hasn't shown up here with Dante London, either."

"How long since you heard from him?"

"Half an hour, at least. Doesn't take but ten minutes to drive from where he was last. You think he's kidnapped her?"

"I don't think so," Nathan said, a feeling of dread pulling at his stomach as he exchanged a knowing glance with Father Daniels. He remembered the three-headed monster in Constance's cell. No doubt some kind of creature was after Dante, too. He felt a flash of guilt. He hoped he hadn't sent Robbie into danger. "Where was he last seen?"

"Said he was near the Crawford intersection on Route 9."

"I'm less than half a mile from there," Nathan said. "I'll look for him. Ten-four." Nathan hung up the radio and flipped on his siren. "Hang on to something," he told Father Daniels as he peeled off the side of the road, gravel flying. Then he spun his way back onto Route 9.

Nathan sped, barely slowing down at the intersection in his haste to get to the Higgins Ranch. He was so intent on getting to where he was going, he nearly didn't see the wreck in front of him, the police car with the smashed front end parked half on and half off the road.

Nathan slammed on the brakes, screeching to a halt near the wrecked police car. It had both front doors open and no one in it.

"Dammit," Nathan muttered, recognizing the license on the back as the one on the car Robbie drove. Nathan pulled himself out of the truck and walked over to survey the damage. Robbie's vehicle was clearly totaled. On the other side of the wrecked car, he saw a shoe lying in the road—Robbie's boot by the look of it. Nathan got a cold feeling down his spine, and he knew something was really, really wrong. He walked past the squad car to get a clearer view, and that was when he saw Robbie's body lying chest up near the shoulder.

It became pretty obvious that there wasn't anything to be done. He didn't see Robbie's head, but the body had his name tag on it, lying sprawled in the middle of the road.

His stomach shrank. Robbie might have been a lazy good-for-nothing, but he was *his* lazy good-for-nothing. He was a decent guy who might not have been too ambitious or hardworking, but certainly didn't deserve this.

I'm sorry, Robbie, he thought, feeling a tug of responsibility. He'd been the one to send Robbie to get Dante London, knowing full well there might be strange forces at work. But what was he supposed to do? Give Robbie a cross and some holy water? He barely even believed it himself, and yet his skepticism might very well have killed his own deputy. On some level, he knew, Robbie's death was his fault.

"Demon did this for sure," Father Daniels said, echoing Nathan's thoughts. "Wasn't too long ago, either. Blood is still fresh."

Father Daniels was right, but Nathan wondered how a priest knew that. "How can you tell?"

"Experience," Father Daniels said cryptically. "You see a lot of carnage when you're a demon fighter."

Nathan's eyes took in the scene. Robbie's death certainly hadn't resulted from an accident. The location of the body and the fact that the windshield was intact told him this happened after. He walked back to Robbie's car to inspect the passenger side. There wasn't any blood here, but there were at least four sets of footprints in the mud by the side of the road. One set looked a lot like a woman's shoe. Dante London's, probably. The other three looked like animal prints of some kind. But after about four steps, all the prints disappeared, as if they had all taken flight. They probably had, Nathan thought. It wasn't much of a stretch to imagine a demon with wings.

The guilt that was tickling his belly started to simmer and turn into anger, joining the rage he already felt about Constance. He was doubly determined to find whoever had done this and make them pay.

A scratching sound from the trunk of Robbie's wrecked car made both men jump and grab guns from their holsters: Nathan, his handgun filled with holy water bullets, and Father Daniels, the semiautomatic he kept in the back waistline of his pants. Both men pointed the guns at the trunk.

Father Daniels put his finger to his mouth. "You got a key?" he mouthed, and pantomimed. Nathan shook his head. Father Daniels silently gestured for him to pop the trunk from the inside of the car. Reluctantly, Nathan went. He kept eye contact with Father Daniels and waited until the priest had counted down to three, and then popped the trunk. Father Daniels tensed, ready to shoot, but before he could, Frank jumped out, barking.

"Jesus, Mary, and Joseph, you scared us, Frank," Father Daniels said, putting his hand to his heart.

"It was General Asmodeus!" came a clipped British accent. "He took Dante to the Higgins Ranch."

It took Nathan a moment to realize the voice had come from *the dog*.

"Hey!" Nathan cried, amazed. "I can *understand* you."

"Well, he is speaking English," Father Daniels said.

Frank raised one doggy eyebrow. "Someone had a spiritual awakening, I see."

"He's a little slow," Father Daniels said. "But he's finally on board."

"Finally!"

"You have an English accent? That's so weird," Nathan said, still looking at Frank with amazement. "I don't believe it. Constance was right."

"No duh," Frank said. "Speaking of, where is she? We have to find her."

"She's dead," Father Daniels said flatly.

"You sure?" Frank asked.

"We didn't find her body," Father Daniels said. "But Asmodeus was in her cell, and there was nothing left when he was done."

"Oh," Frank said, suddenly somber. After a moment of silence, he looked up at Nathan and Father Daniels. "It looks like it's up to us, then," he said. "You on board?" he asked Nathan.

"You bet," Nathan said, holstering his gun.

"Then let's rock and roll, fellas," Father Daniels said,

cocking his gun as he ducked inside Nathan's police truck. Frank and Nathan followed.

"Fasten your seat belts . . ." Nathan said, glancing dubiously at Frank, who was far too small for one, and added, "or just hang on." Then he flipped the siren and stomped his foot on the gas.

Thirty-six

"You ever seen the demon in chief in person?" Shadow asked Yaman, as the two hung out on the roof of the Higgins Ranch. They were waiting for the arrival of Satan.

"I saw him once," Yaman said. "Back in the 1400s. He came to earth for a brief time then, but he was across the street, and I only saw him from the back. But he's definitely shorter in person than you'd think."

"Yeah, that's what I heard. Maybe that's why he makes so few public appearances," Shadow said.

A rumble of thunder sounded in the sky, and the ground beneath the house started to shake. A few frogs fell to the ground in an odd, isolated shower.

"Ooh, I bet that's him!" Shadow said. "I wonder if he'll give me his autograph."

Yaman scowled at Shadow. "Are you serious? You will be *so* uncool if you ask for his autograph."

"What? He's our fearless leader. Why can't I ask for a hoof print?"

"For one, you'll look *really* small-time if you do," Yaman said. "That's something that an enlisted soldier would do, not a lieutenant, or should I say, soon-to-be colonel. Besides, we have to keep on the lookout for Asmodeus. Make sure that guy doesn't rat us out. I don't trust him to keep up his end of the bargain."

"Neither do I," Shadow agreed. "We should try to talk to Satan ourselves."

"We should. There's only one problem with that."

"What?"

"Satan's Demon Service. They will totally take us down if we get within ten feet of him."

"Demon Service?" Shadow asked, puzzled.

"You don't think the devil walks around without bodyguards, do you?" Below them, cracks appeared in the ground and shadows seeped out. The little shadows soon formed themselves into short, squat little shadow men with sunglasses and earpieces. "See? *Those* guys," Yaman added, pointing. The Demon Service guards quickly secured the area in and around the ranch house, with a few of them heading to the roof. One, wearing silver sunglasses, flew up to Yaman and Shadow.

"You two, back up at least twenty feet," the foot-high shadow commanded.

Shadow looked at the little thing and scoffed. "You can't be serious."

"Demon Service!" it barked, flashing a little badge. "Move *back*." It raised a tiny hand and sent a jolt of electricity into Shadow's foot, causing the big creature to jump and screech.

"Ow, that really *hurt*," Shadow complained, rubbing his foot.

"Move *back* or I will Taser you again," the little agent threatened, waving his hand. This time, Shadow and Yaman backed up, floating up over the house twenty feet.

"Those guys are real jerks," Shadow said.

"Told you," Yaman said. "We've got to find a way to get past them."

As they watched, a big crack opened up in the ground below the front door of the ranch, and a man wearing a red smoking jacket and black pants, flanked by five more Demon Service shadows, was whisked quickly into the ranch house.

"Wait—that was him?" Shadow marveled. "He *is* short!"

"Told you. And his Demon Service is supposed to make him look taller," Yaman said. "As are the lifts in his shoes."

"Hey, look, Asmodeus!" Shadow exclaimed, pointing. Yaman glanced over, and sure enough it was the general, carrying Dante London in his arms and headed to the front door of the ranch.

"Where is Ashton? 'Cause, oh my God, y'all, this is the funniest *Punk'd ever*," said Dante London.

Yaman glanced over at Shadow. "Boy, is she *dumb*," Yaman said.

"I hear that's how Satan likes them," Shadow replied.

"Hey—watch it, buddy!" Dante said, as Asmodeus's hoof rode a little higher up her skirt than it should have. Quickly, he lifted his hoof.

"Was he just trying to cop a feel?" Shadow asked.

"Well, he *is* a Lust demon. Come on, let's get a closer look." Yaman dipped down and moved to a first-story window so that he was floating outside and peered in. He motioned Shadow over. Shadow glanced around him, looking for any signs of the Demon Service, and finding none, followed Yaman.

"Wow, those CGI effects are like *soooo* cool," she said, pulling on his ram horns. "They even *feel* real."

"They *are* real," Asmodeus growled, twisting away from her grasp as he carried her up the winding staircase and into the master bedroom near the landing.

Yaman and Shadow switched windows to get a more direct view. Inside, there was a fire in the fireplace, and the devil was sitting in the oversized wingback chair, wearing his red smoking jacket and holding a snifter of brandy in one hand.

Asmodeus gently put Dante on her feet and then stood at attention, giving a three-handed salute against his three separate foreheads.

"Nicely done, Asmodeus, at ease," the devil said, in a voice rich and smooth like chocolate.

Dante paused, curious.

"She thinks he's a director or producer or something," Yaman whispered.

"No—she can't be that dumb."

"Are you, like, a producer?" Dante asked, snapping her gum and playing with a loose strand of hair.

"Told you!" Yaman whispered, nudging Shadow, who just shook his head.

"Wow, *this* is the future mother of the Antichrist? Satan would've been better off with another goat."

Yaman snickered.

"No, my dear, I'm not a producer," Satan said, and slowly shook his head.

"Then who are you?" she asked.

"Why," Satan said, flashing a gleaming white smile, "I'm your biggest fan."

"Do you smell something?" Shadow asked Yaman.

"Like what?"

Shadow made audible sniffing sounds. "Something . . . delicious."

"I don't smell anything."

"I do," Shadow said, puffing himself up. "I smell . . . dinner." Shadow's stomach rumbled so loudly that it shook the window, grabbing Satan's attention. Yaman quickly pulled Shadow out of view.

"Would you *stop* that?" hissed Yaman. "You're going to get us caught."

"I can't help it," whispered Shadow. "I'm hungry."

"Well, go find something to eat, then, before you get us both in trouble."

"Really?"

"Really!" Yaman said. "Don't come back until you're at least semifull."

"Will do," Shadow said, and then he drifted off into the night.

Thirty-seven

"Mama, it's too dangerous, you can't come," Constance said for the hundredth time, but Abigail just shook her head and refused to hand over her car keys.

"You can't tell me that the devil is loose in Dogwood and I'm going to send my only child to fight him *without me*. No way. You need me. I can draw pentagrams."

"I know, and I appreciate it, I do, but there's no way I can let you come."

"We're wasting valuable time arguing," Abigail said, tossing her a small satchel on a long cord. "It's dried dogwood blossoms soaked in holy water. I'm wearing one, and you should, too."

Constance put it around her neck.

"Will you at least let me drive?" Constance asked.

"My brand-new Beetle?" Abigail shook her head as she climbed into the driver's seat. "You may be the Chosen One, but I've got less than two hundred miles on this baby!"

Constance smiled and ducked into the passenger seat. "Fine, but let's step on it."

"I hope you don't think you're leaving without me," said Dead Jimmy, materializing in the backseat.

"Jimmy, what are you doing here?"

"Is my dead son-in-law in the back?" Abigail cried, glancing in the rearview.

"I'm going to help," he proclaimed, holding up Father Daniels's crossbow.

"Where did you get that?"

"Swiped it from the police station. Neat-o, huh?" He twirled it this way and that, and somehow in the spin it let loose an arrow, which flew forward between the two front seats and stuck in the car's felt ceiling.

"Jimmy!" shouted Abigail, furious.

"Maybe I should hold on to that," Constance said, taking the crossbow and a sack of arrows.

"Sorry," Dead Jimmy said, looking sheepish.

"He just said he was sorry," Constance told Abigail.

"Oh, I'll make that boy sorry when this is all over," Abigail said, turning the engine over. "Meantime, tell him to hold on to something. This baby has five cylinders."

Abigail's tires squealed as she peeled out of her own drive and down the street.

Less than fifteen minutes later, they were sitting outside the Higgins Ranch, the sun having dipped below the horizon, and the sky above them was somewhere between lavender and navy. Stars were starting to come out, but it wasn't too late, Constance thought. Not yet. In her vision, Satan didn't seduce Dante London until the Big Dipper was fully in view, and as of now, Constance just saw the flicker of a handle star and that was it.

"Whoo-wee, but this little car can really open up when you press her," Dead Jimmy said.

"I've never seen you drive so fast," Constance exclaimed, looking at her mother with renewed appreciation.

"Well, I've never had to save the world before," Abigail said practically. "Now what?"

"Let me see," Constance said, shutting her eyes. In an instant, she could see inside the house. Dante and the devil were up on the second floor, and he was pouring her a drink. General Asmodeus was sitting outside the room, and there were shadow guards at the bedroom door and behind the front and back doors keeping watch. Constance could also see Yaman and Shadow eavesdropping on the devil by floating outside the second-story window at the back of the house. Then, just as quickly, she saw that Shadow smelled them. In an instant, he had flown around the house and appeared behind them, grabbing Abigail straight out of the car. Constance's eyes flew wide in shock.

"Mama—you have to watch out!" said Constance, blinking back from her vision to warn her mother. But before the words were out of her mouth, Abigail was suddenly sucked out of the driver's-side window and lifted high into the air.

"The crossbow!" Dead Jimmy cried, and Constance grabbed it from the floor by her feet as she scrambled out the door.

"Ahhhhh!" Abigail screamed, as Shadow held her

upside down by one foot. The demon was the same one who'd attacked Constance at the hospital, she was sure, except this time, he had taken the shape of a half dog, half serpent, with a giant, dragonlike mouth, which at this very moment he was snapping furiously, clearly about to use it to devour her mother whole.

"Leave her alone!" Constance shouted, springing out of the car and taking aim with the crossbow. She'd never fired one on purpose before, and she had no idea how to aim. She put the butt of the handle against her shoulder, squeezed the trigger, and hoped for the best.

The arrow zipped through the air and miraculously hit the creature straight in the mouth. It wasn't so much like a shadow after all, because the arrow stuck in his jaw, causing the creature to shriek and nearly drop her mother on her head. Abigail screamed, and the monster held on, even though his jaw was now locked shut.

"Yes!" Dead Jimmy shouted. "You got him!"

But no sooner had they started to celebrate than the monster simply grew another head with another set of sharp jaws.

Constance struggled with the crossbow, trying to reload it.

"Will you quit fooling around and save me?" Abigail shouted at Constance. Abigail was dangling precariously close to one of those giant sharp teeth. She ripped off the necklace she wore and started batting Shadow with it. A few seconds later, Shadow sneezed. And then sneezed again. It was enough of a distraction that he didn't eat her.

"That's what I'm trying to do," Constance shouted, managing to get another arrow in place. She fired this one, too, but it didn't hit its target. Instead, it sailed high and nearly hit Abigail.

"Use your visions!" Abigail called out. "Don't forget your visions!"

Constance shut her eyes for the briefest of seconds, but this time directed her mind to show her where the demon would move next. She saw him inch to the right a split second before he did, and she let another arrow sail that way. This time, it struck the monster in the arm holding Abigail. The demon shrieked and dropped Abigail nearly ten feet into a puddle of mud.

"Mama!" Constance shouted, running to her, not caring that she was headed straight to Shadow, who wasn't mortally wounded, just ticked off. Constance reached Abigail, picked her up, and ran toward the closest cover she could find—a white trailer nearby. Ironically, it had a cross on the front, and there were a few holy wafers sitting on the stairs.

Briefly, Constance shut her eyes. She saw that the trailer was a props trailer used in the movie, *Devil's in the Details*, and apparently there was a dream sequence where it rained holy wafers. Inside the trailer, she also saw there was a giant replica of a hot dog. She saw herself using both. In a vision, she saw the wafers were real and had been blessed.

"Hey—ugly!" shouted Dead Jimmy from the other side of the yard. "Over here!"

Constance peeked around the trailer and saw her dead almost-ex husband luring Shadow away from them. She felt a surge of gratitude. There would be just enough time to set their plan in motion.

"Mama, help me," Constance said, as she opened the door and grabbed one end of the giant plastic hot dog. It was sitting on top of a half dozen boxes of holy wafer props.

"What are we doing with this?"

"We're going to use it to lure that Glutton demon over here," Constance said.

"We want him to eat a plastic hot dog?"

"No, we want him to eat these," Constance said, pointing to the wafers. "They may look like props, but they're real holy wafers. They've been blessed. Help me stuff them inside the hot dog."

After a few furious seconds, they'd stuffed as many of the wafers as they could into the bun of the hot dog.

"Ahhhh!" Dead Jimmy cried when Shadow got close to him. In fright, he disappeared. Shadow looked one way and then another, trying to figure out where he'd gone.

"Hey—you!" cried Constance. "I've got something for you!"

"Hmmm?" the demon mumbled, attention turning toward Constance and the trailer. When he laid eyes on the giant hot dog, sitting half in and half out of the trailer, he moved quickly.

"Come on," Constance cried, taking her mother's hand and whipping her under the trailer. In a blink, the demon had grabbed the giant hot dog and swallowed it whole. They heard it crinkle and crack as the demon crunched it to bits.

The shadow belched loudly, and then leaned down and gazed at them under the trailer.

"Run!" Constance said. "Take cover behind your car. He's going to blow!"

"Blow?" muttered Shadow, burping again. "Oooh, I don't feel so good." He moaned and rubbed his stomach, swollen like a well-fed snake's, as he lurched to one side.

Constance and Abigail skidded to the ground behind her car, and put their arms over their heads. Seconds later, the entire creature exploded like an overfilled water balloon, sending little bits and pieces of flesh in all directions, raining down on Constance and Abigail like a storm of rotten cabbage.

"Gross," Abigail said, flicking a piece of the Glutton demon off her sleeve.

"It was the only way," Constance said, getting to her feet. "Now we have to move quickly—to the kitchen window—it's open, and we can climb in without the guards seeing us, and before Shadow's partner comes to see what the commotion is all about. He'll be here in about two seconds."

"Yaman is around here?" Dead Jimmy asked, appearing by Constance's side and looking worried.

"Hopefully, we'll avoid him if we move fast," Constance said, heading toward the side of the house.

No sooner had Constance, Abigail, and Dead Jimmy ducked into the house than Yaman appeared in the back.

"Shadow?" he whispered, looking around. "What was all that noise? Shadow? Oh, Satan—that smell!" Yaman put his hand up to his nose, and then realized that the smell was his former partner in about a million pieces scattered all over the lawn. He took a look at the catering truck and the bits of wafers strewn across the ground and surmised his partner had eaten himself to death. "Gluttons," Yaman said, and shook his head.

A pair of headlights flashed down the road and then Nathan pulled up in his police truck. Yaman hid behind a nearby tree and watched.

"It's Constance's mother's car," Nathan cried, jumping out of the driver's seat. "What's she doing here?"

"I don't know," Frank said. "But we should find out."

"Let's go," Nathan said.

"Wait—we need to have a plan," Frank cautioned from the backseat window.

"Here's your *plan*," Father Daniels said, cocking a shotgun in the front seat.

Yaman watched with sharp eyes. So these guys were going to try to stop Satan. If he stopped them first, he'd get promoted for sure. He watched as they holstered a small arsenal of weapons. Still, it was just three of them, and one was a dog and the other two were merely mortals. God must have really lowered his expectations of Satan since the goat incident if he thought this lowly brigade was enough to stop them, Yaman thought. Still, Yaman knew, it would take some finesse to stop them in a way that didn't grab the attention of the Demon Service. He didn't want them taking credit for his work. Yaman considered enlisting the help of General Asmodeus, but decided against it. This promotion was going to be *all his*.

Thirty-eight

Father Daniels put on something that looked like night goggles and peered out the front windshield. "I see two demons guarding the front door, one on the landing inside, and"—he looked up—"three at the top of the stairs. And it looks like the devil is in the main room to the left of the stairs."

"Can you see anyone?" Nathan asked.

"Nope," Father Daniels said. "These babies are really only good for spotting demons. They're demon infrared. Demons don't have body heat like we do, but they do emit a certain kind of energy. These goggles pick that up."

"Demon infrared," Nathan echoed. Now he'd heard of everything.

"We should go in guns drawn," Father Daniels said, as he cocked two pistols and put them into his holsters at his hip. Then he shouldered the shotgun and adjusted the bullet belts that he wore crossed across his chest. "I'll start shooting, and you guys just keep close to my back."

"Why do you always have to go in guns blazing?" Frank asked him.

"Shock and awe—it's the only way to go," Father Daniels said.

"I'm for that," Nathan said, raring for a fight.

"Maybe we should take a calmer approach?" Frank offered. "Something quiet?"

"That's what *these* are for," Father Daniels said, screwing on a couple of silencers. "By the way, you'll need this." Father Daniels handed Nathan a shotgun.

Nathan took the gun, checking the chamber to make sure it was loaded. Father Daniels handed him more bullets.

"You see something move, you shoot it," Father Daniels said. "Hey, puppy, you need a gun, too?"

"I'll manage without," Frank said. "I should probably go around back—make sure there's nothing waiting for us there."

"Good plan," Father Daniels agreed. "Okay, ladies, we've wasted enough time," Father Daniels said, munching on half of a cigar.

"What? No pep talk?" Nathan asked him.

"Just try to keep up, Nancy Boy," Father Daniels said. "It's time to save the world." With that, he spit out the cigar and rushed to the house, with Nathan struggling to keep up. For an old man, he moved fast.

Nathan was at his back as Father Daniels took out the two guards standing watch inside the door, and then they were inside the darkened living room. Father Daniels flattened himself against the wall and signaled for Nathan to move up the stairs. Nathan had only taken two steps when he heard what he could've sworn was Constance's voice coming from the room behind him.

Was it possible? Could she still be alive?

"Wait—it's Constance," he hissed at Father Daniels, who stopped briefly to flash him a sign with his finger running across his neck. Presumably, he meant he didn't care where the prophet was. He was going after the devil.

Nathan pointed at himself and then back to the room. Father Daniels shook his head. Nathan gestured again and moved that way. Father Daniels just shrugged and headed back up the stairs. He was going to continue up without Nathan.

Nathan tightened his grip on his gun and slowly made his way to the sound of Constance's voice. He could've sworn it was coming from the kitchen, and he cautiously poked his gun through the swinging kitchen door. When he opened it, however, the room was empty.

"Con?" Nathan whispered. "You here?"

"Nathan?" came Constance's voice again, but this time Nathan couldn't tell where it was coming from. It seemed to be bouncing off the walls. "Nathan, I see you." Constance's voice suddenly changed and became deeper. Fear curled in Nathan's stomach. That wasn't Constance after all. It was a trap.

Nathan felt like there was something flicking his ear, but he was against the wall. This was impossible. He swatted at his ear, but tried to stay focused. *Don't freak out*, he told himself even as he was, quite possibly, freaking out.

"Nathan Garrett," came the eerie voice again, but this

time, two hard hands seemed to come out of the wall behind him and pushed him roughly from his hiding place. Nathan stumbled forward, trying to regain his balance and his poise, then looked up and saw Yaman standing just a few feet from him, grinning from ear to ear.

"I thought that was you," Yaman said. "What? You're not going to say hello to your old friend?"

"What are you talking about?" Nathan said, as he swung the shotgun up, aiming at Yaman's torso. But the demon flicked his hand and the gun went spinning from his grasp, whipping across the room and clattering on the floor.

Something tickled his ear again and he cringed. Now there seemed to be indistinct voices whispering all around him. Some of them were children. One of them sounded like Libby Bell. It was the same small, high voice he'd heard on the videotape of her fifth birthday party. Except now she wasn't laughing, she was crying. It sounded like she was all around the room—her ghost swirling near his ears. She was saying, "No, no, no!"

"What are you?" Nathan said, swatting at his ear again. He couldn't take the voice. Not Libby Bell's voice. The one he'd heard in countless nightmares since finding her body.

"Why, I'm a second lieutenant in the Pride Division of Satan's Army," Yaman said, giving Nathan a mock salute. "Responsible for close to seventy-five thousand deaths, including Jimmy Plyd's, one hundred thousand rapes, and one hundred eighty-seven thousand five hundred souls in hell. And counting. Oh, and ten thousand face-lifts in L.A. last year alone."

Libby Bell's voice got louder. Nathan started to feel sick to his stomach.

"Pride is a very interesting sin, you know," Yaman continued, his eyes gleaming in the dark. "It's pride that's at the root of most crimes. Take the pedophile, for instance."

Nathan shook his head. Libby Bell's cries were getting more urgent. She sounded like she was being hurt all over again.

"Sure, the lust gets him in trouble, but it's the pride that drives him to cover up that crime, and do it again and again instead of seeking help," Yaman said. "They're too proud to stop, too proud to admit they need help, and too proud to let their victims live."

Libby Bell screamed, and Nathan couldn't take it anymore. He stepped forward, pulling out his handgun from his side holster, and let loose a rain of bullets, but Yaman easily avoided the shots. He moved far too fast to be human. Before Nathan could process this, Yaman had grabbed him by the throat and shoved him against the wall, his grin only getting bigger. He leaned closer so he could whisper in Nathan's ear.

"Libby Bell is my fault," he said. "I told a man to do it, and he did, and then I killed him. He's in hell, if that's any consolation."

Nathan squirmed against Yaman's ironclad grasp. Fear had given way to rage, and all he wanted was to kill Yaman with his bare hands.

"I killed him because you were going to catch him that day in the warehouse, and I didn't want that to happen," Yaman continued. "It would've given you too much satisfaction. So I'm afraid I killed him, and then I had to kill your partner, too, because he saw me."

Nathan knew, deep down, that this was true. This was why Libby Bell's case had been so difficult. It hadn't been just human evil; there had been darker forces at work. But Nathan couldn't do anything about it now. With Yaman's hand on his throat, he couldn't breathe, and he was beginning to see stars. Pretty soon he'd be unconscious. With his last coherent thought, he told himself to be calm, and then he remembered the small cross in his pocket, Libby Bell's necklace, the one they had found on her windowsill. She'd lost it when the man had kidnapped her, and now, Nathan thought, it was time to use it.

He managed to dig it out of his pocket, and before Yaman knew what was coming, Nathan had pressed it up against his face, holding it there until he heard the sizzle as it burned a mark into his cheek. Yaman howled and dropped Nathan, who hit the floor with a thud, the cross still in his hand and smoking.

Nathan coughed, desperately filling his lungs with air, watching Yaman hold his face.

"You'll pay for that," Yaman hissed at him, and prepared to lunge.

Three shotgun blasts rang out, and Yaman was hit with buckshot in the chest and whirled backward. "This is Armani!" he shrieked, as sizzling holy water soaked through his chest and the fabric was soaked with black blood. Those were his last coherent words as he fizzled and snapped and started shrinking. He shrank so fast that his shouts and screams sounded like the voice of a chipmunk, and eventually he simply disappeared with a tiny pop.

Nathan turned and saw Father Daniels step out from the shadows.

"I hate demons who talk too much," he said, spitting. "Always the Pride ones who have to blather on. It's just plain annoying."

"Thanks," Nathan said, and meant it. "So what happened to him?" Nathan nodded to the tiny black mark that used to be Yaman.

"Exorcism," Father Daniels said matter-of-factly. "He's back in hell—for the moment."

"The moment?" Nathan echoed.

"It'll probably take a couple of decades for him to get back the strength to come back to earth," Father Daniels said. "But for now he's taken care of."

"What did I miss?" barked Frank, trotting up to Nathan's ankles.

"Only everything, Frank," Father Daniels said. "Never mind. I saved the day again. Come on, we better move fast. The other demons will know we're coming now."

As the two men and the dog moved into the living room, they came face-to-face with Constance and Abigail.

"Ahhhh!" they all shouted, pointing their weapons at each other. Realizing they were about to engage in friendly fire, they all stood down.

"Don't scare a solider like that!" Father Daniels barked.

"We heard gunshots," Constance said.

"They were for Yaman," Father Daniels said.

Constance saw Nathan at that second, and her eyes narrowed. "It's *you*," she spat, clearly not glad to see him. "Are you going to arrest us now?"

But Nathan, who was just getting over the shock of seeing her, just sputtered, "Is it *really* you? Are you alive?"

"Yes, it's me, who else would it be?" Constance snapped.

Her annoyance with him was real enough. She *was* alive, he realized in a moment of pure happiness. He ran to her and scooped her up in his arms, giving her a giant hug. "You're okay! I can't believe you're okay!" he said over and over again.

"Let me go!" Constance demanded, squirming.

Nathan let her go and she took a step backward, still angry at him.

"Constance, I'm sorry," Nathan said. "I'm sorry I didn't believe you. I believe now, I do."

Constance studied him skeptically.

"It's true," Father Daniels confirmed, nodding.

"You know we need all the help we can get," Abigail said.

"Fine," Constance told Nathan. "But you'd better not up and disappear on us."

"On my honor," Nathan said, holding up three fingers.

"You were never a Boy Scout," scoffed Constance.

"True," Nathan admitted. "But I still won't disappear on you."

"We'll see about that," Constance said. She closed her eyes for a brief spell and then opened them again. "I guess you *don't* disappear on us," she added. "At least, for now. The devil is upstairs, and Dante hasn't agreed to have sex with him yet. But there are other demons who are going to give us trouble."

"You can control your visions!" Frank exclaimed, giving an excited little hop.

"Just learned how," Constance said, nodding, a little pride in her voice.

"Better late than never," Father Daniels grumbled.

"There's just one more little thing," Constance said. "Everyone hide."

A second later, the front door opened. Corey Bennett walked through it and stalked purposefully up the stairs.

"What's he doing here?" Nathan whispered. "Should we stop him?"

"No," Constance said, shaking her head. "He's going to get what he deserves."

Thirty-nine

"Okay, like, this is *too* weird," Dante London said, snapping gum and then pulling a long strand of it between her fingers and her teeth. "You *sure* you're not a movie producer?"

The devil, who was getting a little tired of explaining himself (this was his fifth try), shook his head slowly and tried to be patient. Although patience certainly wasn't his strong suit.

Why did he go for the dumb ones? Granted, he always thought they'd be easier, but they never were. Next time, he vowed, he'd seduce a Rhodes scholar. Or at least a woman who knew the difference between Satan and satin, which Dante London didn't. That had been a fifteen-minute conversation in and of itself.

If only he didn't have to work with free will. If he were running things, he'd do away with free will, first thing. Free will and chewing gum. Dante's gum chomping was driving him insane. This was the problem with humans in general. They invented stupid things like bubble gum. Why they were God's chosen creatures was completely beyond Lucifer. In his universe, humans would rank somewhere between sloths and fungus on the interest scale. Honestly, it was why he led the revolt in heaven to begin with. The minute God announced Adam was his chosen creature—the same animal who divided the day picking his nose and scratching himself—Lucifer thought he'd lost his marbles.

Something that sounded like shotgun blasts rang out downstairs, interrupting Lucifer's thoughts.

"What was *that*?" Dante asked, perplexed.

"Damnation!" the devil shouted. He knew it was probably some of God's soldiers, come to try to thwart his plans. They were later than usual, though. Almost as if God didn't think of Satan and his Antichrist as a real threat. Hmmmm. Satan wondered if God thought he was losing his touch, since the goat incident.

"Asmodeus!" he cried.

"Yes, sir?" the general said, poking his head in the door.

"Take my Demon Service guards and find out what the hell is making all that racket," he said. "I can't concentrate in here."

"Yes, sir. Right away, sir. I'm on it."

The devil glanced at Dante and decided to try a different tack.

"If you give yourself to me, you can have anything you want. Movies, money, youth for eternity. And I can take care of all of your enemies."

"You could get rid of Lindsay Lohan?"

"It's done," the devil said, and snapped his fingers. "She's in rehab."

"Wow. You really *are* him."

The devil turned up the charm and went in for the kill, leaning over and whispering into her ear while he put his hand on her thigh. "Give yourself to me, and you'll have everything."

He touched her champagne glass and it came alive instantly with pictures of her future with him. The money and fame, a blockbuster movie career, stadiums full of people worshipping her, and never, ever being on E!'s worst-dressed list.

He started to kiss her neck, knowing that his scent was irresistible. He, like all angels, fallen or not, had the kind of pheromones women simply couldn't resist. They were working on her, the devil could feel it, and in another minute or two she'd be all his.

Then the door to the bedroom slammed open and in strode Corey Bennett.

Dante jumped up as if caught cheating. "Corey! We were just talking, I swear. He's so funny . . ."

"Are you him? Because I'm tired of dealing with your minions," Corey said, hands on his hips, ignoring Dante and addressing the devil. "I want an upgrade on my deal, and I'll only speak to the devil himself."

Two shadow guards ran in after Corey, stopping when they saw the expression on the devil's face. The devil, barely able to contain his rage, broke the champagne glass in his hands and ground his teeth together so hard they made an inhuman sound. For the sake of

Dante, though, he managed not to turn into his true self, which was what usually happened when he got angry. He got ugly. His Demon Service skidded out of the room, scared. *They should be*, thought Lucifer. He'd have their heads for letting this man by them.

"It was not wise of you to interrupt us, Corey," the devil ground out eventually, with a smile sharp as razor blades. If Corey had been a tad more perceptive, he would've been worried by the devil's tone and by his measured efforts to keep calm.

"I'm just saying that I want a new deal, okay? I helped you get what you wanted and I want what's coming to me."

"Oh, you'll get what's coming to you," the devil said, flicking his hand.

"Good, because I went through a lot of trouble to . . . hey, what's going on?"

"Corey—what's happening to your face?" Dante asked, sounding concerned.

What was happening wasn't just happening to his face, either. Corey realized in one horrible moment that the devil had decided to renege on their deal, and he was not only breaking out with the worst acne he'd ever had, but he was also gaining back all of that extra weight he'd lost when he was eighteen and then some. In minutes, he was going to be as big as a whale.

"*Noooooooooooooooo!*" he shouted, putting his hands to his face even as his butt grew five pant sizes.

"Gross!" Dante London exclaimed, watching Corey's belly fat lurch over his pants and the seams start to tear.

Even as his clothes ripped, Corey tried to press them to his body as he ran from Dante London. He couldn't have her see him like this. He couldn't have anyone see him like this. Not now, not ever.

"Now," the devil said, sending Dante one of his best seduction smiles. "Where were we?"

Forty

Constance led the group upstairs via the back staircase, giving everyone detailed instructions on just how to avoid Asmodeus, who, along with the Demon Service, was headed down the main staircase at the front of the house. At the top of the stairs, she set her mother to work drawing on the floor. In her vision, she saw her using the pentagram to keep Dante London safe, but she couldn't quite see how they would lure Dante out of the devil's bedroom.

"How are we going to get Dante over here?" Dead Jimmy whispered, as Constance sat and tried to meditate.

"I can't see that part," Constance said, blowing out a breath in frustration. "I keep trying, but I can't see it."

"That's because Dante has free will and probably hasn't decided what she's going to do yet," Frank said. "Demons are easier to predict. They usually don't change their minds at the last minute."

"Need to reload?" Father Daniels asked Nathan, handing him a clip of holy-water-filled bullets.

"Will these guns work on the devil?" Nathan asked Father Daniels.

"Hard to say," he said. "The devil's the highest-ranking person in his army, and the higher the rank, the more resistant they are to holy water. They have a higher concentration of evil in them than other demons."

"That's a long way of saying that these bullets might not work?" Nathan said.

"More like it means we'll have to use a helluva lot of them," Father Daniels said, putting two more shells in his shotgun.

Nathan glanced around and sighed. "Is it just me or did God send us to battle a little understaffed?" he asked Constance. "Is this all we got? Where are the angels with the flaming swords?"

"This was supposed to be an undercover mission," Frank explained, one tiny paw in the air. "It's all supposed to be under the radar."

Nathan just stared for a beat at the tiny dog in the pink sweater. "I still can't believe you can talk."

"Wait—you can understand him?" Constance asked, eyebrows raised. Nathan nodded.

"He's slow, our boy, but comes through in the end." Father Daniels adjusted his guns and checked for empty clips. "And, Nate, for your information, God has a thing for underdogs."

Nathan glanced at Frank and his tiny canine body and said, "Good point."

Constance closed her eyes again, hoping to see a way to get Dante out of the room. But what she saw was General Asmodeus and the Demon Service making their way up the back stairs. She only just had time to open her eyes and shout before Frank was snatched up in the air and flung over the banister and down to the first floor. She didn't have time to check on him. She threw herself on top of her mother to protect her, even as Abigail scrambled to get the very last bit of the pentagram finished. Nathan stood in front of Constance, pointing his shotgun in every direction, but clearly not knowing where to shoot.

Father Daniels laid his finger on the trigger, firing in all directions. He hit some demons, but missed most. The Demon Service shadows concentrated on him, and Asmodeus headed for the pentagram.

"I can't see where to shoot!" Nathan cried, eyes darting back and forth as he floundered, helplessly pointing his guns at nothing but blank space. "I don't see anything."

"I'll help," Constance said, peering into the dark and concentrating. Where there were just shadows, suddenly she saw the bodies of demons. Asmodeus was heading toward them, three heads bobbing in the semidark.

"He's to your left, ten o'clock," Constance said, pulling Nathan's arm to the left. Nathan aimed his gun and shot. He hit his target, but it was just a glance on the shoulder that barely stopped the demon's momentum.

"Where now? Where?" Nathan shouted.

"To the right a foot," she cried. He fired again and hit the general straight in the chest. The demon wheeled back three steps, but then righted himself and started his charge again.

"It doesn't seem to be doing anything," Constance said. "Mama—the pentagram!"

"I'm working on it!" Abigail replied, frantically trying to connect the last lines.

Next to them, there was a *flurp, flurp, flurp* sound, and Constance turned to see Dead Jimmy firing the crossbow at the creature. Only one of the arrows hit, and it landed in one of his hooved arms. Asmodeus plucked the arrow out with his beak and spat it on the ground.

Constance glanced over at Father Daniels, who was struggling to fight the small demon shadows. He ripped off his ammo vest to reveal another ammo belt underneath, this one filled with a dozen small black balloons that Constance could only guess were filled with holy water. He grabbed the balloons and started hurling them at the shadows, and where they landed, they hissed and burned.

Asmodeus had regained his footing now, and was nearly to them.

"Mama!" Constance shouted.

"I need five more seconds," she said.

"We don't have five more . . ."

"Over here, demon!" Dead Jimmy shouted, trying his best to distract Asmodeus. He fired five more arrows, sending the demon staggering backward—and down the stairs. "Yeah!" Dead Jimmy cried, pumping his fist in the air. "Take that!"

Father Daniels lobbed a grenade down the stairs, and there was a squishy-sounding explosion as holy water under pressure exploded in force, shredding what was left of Asmodeus's earthly form and sending him back to hell.

"What the hell is going on out here?" shouted Lucifer,

who came out of the bedroom wearing his red silk smoking jacket and looking every inch the angel who once waged war on God. His eyes were flashing, and his skin seemed in danger of melting straight off his bones, he was so angry. "I'm *trying* to get lucky, if anyone cares!"

He was just a few feet from the as-yet-unfinished pentagram.

"Satan!" Constance cried. She hadn't seen this part in her vision.

Nathan, not wasting a second, grabbed one of Dead Jimmy's discarded arrows from the crossbow and lunged at the devil.

"Nathan! *No!*" Constance shouted, but it was too late—he had already thrown himself on Lucifer's back. As the two struggled, he stabbed the devil in the chest with the arrow, and Satan let out an ear-piercing shriek.

"Get Dante!" Nathan shouted, as the devil, stunned, staggered backward a couple of steps, trying to figure out why the arrow had pierced his usually impervious skin.

Dante, who was standing at the doorway behind the devil looking confused, muttered, "What the hell, y'all?" just as Constance grabbed her arm and pulled her out into the hall and directly into the middle of the pentagram, which Abigail then finished with a squeaky streak of her Sharpie.

The devil pulled the arrow out of his chest and dropped it on the ground, and that's when he noticed that his lovely sacrificial virgin was standing in a protected seal along with the majorly annoying minor prophet and her mother. He also realized that the weight on his back was actually a man, and he took a moment to reflect on the fact that mankind had been like a monkey on his back since he first tricked the dimwits out of Eden.

Constance closed her eyes for just a split second, and she saw what was coming next. There was no way to warn Nathan, or even stop it, since the events unfolding were happening already. There would be no time to save him.

Nathan caught Constance's gaze then, and he seemed to already know what she'd seen. Nathan seemed resigned to his fate, calm even as he gave Constance a small smile before the devil, in a rage, sent him flying against the far wall. He landed there with a sickening crack, and then tumbled into a lifeless heap on the ground, his leg bent at an odd angle.

"Nathan!" Constance shouted, trying to run but Abigail caught her by the sleeve and held her fast inside the protection of the pentagram. The devil, panting from rage, now turned his full attention to them. Constance felt sick and hollow all at once.

"Die, Satan scum!" cried Father Daniels, who had successfully banished the Demon Service, and now turned what was left of his ammo on the devil. It didn't seem to do much serious damage, but the water balloons did do a good job of stripping the devil of his human disguise. Father Daniels leaped and rolled, and made it into the pentagram before the devil could grab him.

"You will give me my virgin," the devil hissed at them, his eyes glowing red, and the skin on his body starting to bubble with rage.

"What's going on?" Dante whimpered, watching as

her once-sexy seducer turned into some kind of hoofed animal right before her eyes. His human skin was melting away in large chunks, and underneath was red fur and brown scales.

"Do you want to boink that?" Father Daniels yelled at Dante, even as the devil sprouted giant wings.

"Hello, no!" Dante said, wrinkling her nose in disgust.

"It's just a few minutes till midnight," Father Daniels said. "We can outlast him."

"Even if we give her to you, she won't have sex with you," Constance said, finding her voice. She could feel the heat rise off Lucifer, and it felt like asphalt under a Texas July. "You've lost."

"No matter," the devil spat, his head now contorted into a half ram's, half man's, with large pointed teeth. "There are other ways."

"If you force her, you won't get your son," Father Daniels reminded him.

"At this point, I really don't care," Lucifer hissed, gnashing his large pointed teeth and curling his massive claws. "Do you know how long it's been since I got laid?"

He lunged at Constance and Dante, causing them all to scream (who wouldn't yell when Lucifer with his two tons of clawed and horned rage was coming at you?), but he hit the force field of the pentagram with a shock and was thrown backward a few steps.

He let out another shriek of frustration, one that could only come from a demon who had not gotten any for the better part of a hundred years. Just then, Frank clawed his way up the stairs, looking a little woozy from his fall but intact.

The devil saw him almost at the same time Constance did.

"Frank! Look out!" she cried, but she was a half second too late. The devil reached out and grabbed the little dog by the scruff of the neck.

"You *will* give me Dante," the devil hissed, shaking Frank hard. "Or the dog gets it."

"Let him go!" Constance shouted.

Next to her, Father Daniels tried to shoot his gun, but it clicked empty. "All out of bullets," he said forlornly.

Constance shut her eyes again, hoping for guidance. What she got was a vision that shocked her. Nathan wasn't dead after all. And he planned to save Frank. She saw it all in slow motion, Nathan picking himself up from the dust and staggering forward, barely able to stand on a badly hurt leg. He would lunge at the devil's back. But Nathan would be too slow, and the devil would crush the life out of him. There would be no doubt about his death this time. She saw herself sitting stock-still in the pentagram, watching with anguish as Nathan's limp body hit the floor.

Constance's eyes flicked open, and she saw Nathan stirring in the corner. She already knew what he planned to do before he did. But she wasn't about to let him do it. Not when she could do something. She had free will, too. And she was going to use it.

"You're not about to do something stupid, are you?" Abigail asked her.

"She does have that holy, I'm-going-to-sacrifice-myself-for-no-good-reason look on her face," Father Daniels agreed.

Constance ignored them, and stepped out of the pentagram and put her arms in the air. "Here! Lucifer!" Constance shouted. She was going to save Nathan even if he didn't know he needed saving.

"No!" Abigail shouted, too late.

Father Daniels smacked his forehead. "I knew it," he grumbled. "Prophets and saints. They just don't know what's good for them."

"Over here!" Constance continued. "Don't you want to dine on a prophet, first? God's Chosen One has to be tastier than just your average girl."

The devil stopped squeezing Frank's neck and watched her, his interest piqued. He tossed Frank aside like a stuffed animal. Frank yelped as he hit the floor, but he scrambled to his feet, relatively unharmed.

Constance took another few steps away from the pentagram to convince Lucifer she wouldn't try to lunge back in at the last second.

"You're too far!" Abigail hissed at her. "Too far!"

Constance knew she was, but she also knew that maybe she could distract the devil long enough for him not to see Nathan rising to his feet.

"Prophet," the devil hissed, locking eyes with her, and Constance suddenly felt a bone-chilling fear at the pit of her stomach that worked its way out until a cold sweat had broken out all over her body. She could feel his venom, his hate, even over the distance between them, and she knew almost instantly that her death would not be quick. And certainly not painless. It took every inch of willpower to stand still even as the devil opened his jaws and hissed. He crouched, preparing to lunge, and Constance closed her eyes quickly. She saw everything he planned to do. She also saw that it was just a minute until midnight. If she could last just one more minute, they'd all be saved.

She sidestepped his first lunge, and his second. Knowing what he planned to do in advance helped her keep one step ahead of him.

"Constance!" Nathan cried weakly.

"Stay where you are!" Constance shouted back at him, moving to the left easily as the devil hit the floor to her right.

"She's good," Father Daniels said with appreciation. "I have to tell you, she's good."

"Frank—get Nathan into the pentagram!" Constance shouted to the dog, who scampered over to Nathan, who stood on shaky feet.

It took every ounce of Constance's concentration to keep the visions straight in her head of exactly what the devil planned to do, but somehow she was making it work. She was keeping just one step ahead of him, and it was making him angrier and angrier.

"I hate prophets!" Lucifer spat, slamming a giant fist down to her right just as she skipped to the left.

Over the devil's shoulder, Constance saw Nathan and Frank moving slowly to the pentagram. Too slowly. They weren't going to make it in time, she suddenly knew.

"Maybe I'll dine on *them* first," the devil said, turning his attention to Nathan and Frank.

"Run to the seal!" Constance shouted to them as

they saw the devil turn his full attention to them. With widened eyes, Nathan tried to run, but his leg kept collapsing under his weight. Frank tried pulling with his small teeth but the dog didn't get much traction, even as Nathan limped frantically toward the pentagram. Then, out of nowhere, Dead Jimmy appeared by Nathan's side, hooking an arm under his and half lifting, half dragging him to the pentagram.

He wasn't so bad after all, that almost-ex husband of hers. Constance flicked her eyes closed and saw they would just make it, and that the devil would pause just long enough trying to decide what to do that she could make it, too. With all the strength she had left, she turned and started running. In seconds, she had skidded into the protective circle.

Lucifer howled and gnashed his teeth, turning from the prophet back to Frank and Nathan, except by now they had made it, having limped to the outer edge of the pentagram and hobbled over the seal.

The devil let out a howl so loud he sounded like a thousand toddlers who'd just dropped their ice cream cones on the pavement. Then, because things could always get worse for Lucifer, the grandfather clock in the hall chimed midnight, and he started to sink in on himself, like a giant Macy's Thanksgiving Day Parade balloon that had suddenly sprung a leak. As he shrank, Constance could've sworn he said, "Humans! Chosen Ones! My ass! You haven't seen the last of me, you glorified butt monkeys!" And then he disappeared with a tiny pop, like a Bubble Wrap bubble bursting.

A few seconds ticked by and no one said anything.

Then Abigail spoke. "Did the devil just call us butt monkeys?" she asked no one in particular. "I would've thought Lucifer could swear better than that."

"Mama! We just barely survived, and you're picking on the devil's choice of expletives?"

"I have to agree with Abigail for once in my life," Dead Jimmy said. " 'Butt monkeys' is a little lame."

"What does that even mean? It sounds like something a four-year-old would say," Abigail said. "My grand-mother curses better."

"Technically, I think he meant you're brownnos-ers who don't have minds of your own," Frank clarified, hopping up and giving his tail a wag. "In Lucifer's book, that's the worst insult there is."

Abigail seemed to take this in a moment. "Still, couldn't he throw a curse word in there? He's Lucifer. Prince of Darkness and all that. I expect something more."

"Um, guys?" Nathan said, stumbling a little. "I think my leg is broken. Could we finish this discussion in the emergency room?"

Forty-one

Nathan's leg was broken in two places, and the doctor who treated him seemed dubious of his explanation—that he'd fallen down the stairs—but they put a cast on him anyway.

"Ow! Watch it," Nathan cried to the nurse at the hospital who was handling his leg a little carelessly. She, apparently, was Lisa Hitchfield, a former girlfriend of Nathan's. She was yet another woman he'd forgotten to call back in the day, and she was taking her revenge on him one little bump at a time. Constance couldn't help but smile. She had no doubt he deserved it.

"That's karma," she said, as she and Abigail waited outside the room.

"Maybe," Abigail said. "But doesn't change the fact that you're crazy about him."

"I am not," Constance exclaimed, eyes wide.

"You are. I know for a fact." Abigail crossed her arms and nodded knowingly.

"A vision?"

"No," Abigail said, shaking her head. "I saw it with my own two eyes. You risking your life to save his."

Constance shrugged. "I would've done that for anybody."

"Mm-hmm, sure you would," Abigail said, rolling her eyes to show she didn't believe a single word. "Just for the record, it's clear he's crazy about you, too, so you shouldn't worry about keeping that guard up so high."

"He is not."

"He has to be in love with you," Abigail said. "Why else would he put up with all of this prophet stuff? Or face down the devil at the Higgins Ranch? He's a man in love."

"What about me?" Dead Jimmy asked. Constance glanced at him, then back to her mother.

"Jimmy faced down the devil, too," Constance pointed out.

"Yes, he did, and I commend him for it," Abigail said. "And not taking away from his sacrifice or anything, but he's already dead. Not much else you can do for him, you know? Nathan risked his life for you."

"Ahem," said Frank, calling their attention downward. "A word outside, Constance?"

"Don't worry. I'll make sure Nathan doesn't run off with any nurses," Abigail said.

Constance glanced to the exam room, where Lisa was moving Nathan's leg in a way that was clearly uncomfortable. "Do I get any morphine?" he was asking her, and she just gave him a tight smile. Constance didn't think he was going to get any morphine, or any chances to run off with a nurse.

Frank trotted out to the little concrete patio and walkway outside and Constance followed, taking a step out into the cool October night air. There, she saw Father Daniels smoking a cigar and Dead Jimmy sitting on the little bench.

"We dropped off the pop princess at her hotel," Father Daniels said, taking a drag of his cigar and exhaling smoke. "She still thinks it was all a practical joke."

"Not the sharpest knife in the drawer," Dead Jimmy added.

"Lucky for us," Frank said, hopping up on a little bench at the corner of the patio.

"Well, kiddo," Father Daniels said, turning to Constance and dropping his cigar into a nearby plant. "You did pretty well back there."

"Thanks," Constance said.

"What about me?" Dead Jimmy asked, annoyed. "What am I? Chopped liver?"

"You did good, too, Jimmy," Constance said, nodding at him.

"Tell that ghost he should stop whining. Well, I'm not one for a lot of touchy-feely crap. It's about time to say *adiós*." Father Daniels gave Constance a one-armed bear hug that was a lot like a head lock, and then sauntered toward his car at the other end of the parking lot.

"Good-bye to you, too, Father," Frank called. Father Daniels just held up a hand without turning back.

Frank turned to Constance. "So, do you know how many points self-sacrifice earns you in heaven?"

"There's a point system?" Constance asked, taking a seat on the little bench next to Frank.

"Yes. Sort of like an arcade game ranking," Frank said. "Naturally, Jesus is always the all-time high scorer."

"There are some things I wish I didn't know," Dead Jimmy said.

"So what do I do now?" Constance asked. "Am I still on a mission from God?"

"I don't know," Frank said. "God doesn't let people in on his plans. But you'll probably know as soon as he wants you to know. It's the nice thing about having visions. Just follow them. They'll always be true."

"Thanks, Frank. I mean it. For everything."

"No need to thank me. I should be thanking *you*. You're the one who helped me earn my wings. Next time you see me, I'll be a real angel."

Constance looked at the furry little hair ball, and felt a little warm and fuzzy, and then she felt a sneeze coming on. She sniffed it back.

"That's great. I'm really glad," she said. "And so are my nasal passages."

"Hopefully, you won't be allergic to me in my angel form."

"So that means I will see you again?"

"I think it's safe to say I'll probably see you in heaven, sometime. Unless you really make a U-turn somewhere and decide to go play for Satan's team."

"I doubt that."

"Then I will see you," Frank said, and winked.

"And so will I," Dead Jimmy piped up. Her almost-ex husband piping up reminded her that she was still wanted for murder.

"Um, Frank, one more thing," Constance asked. "I

hate to ask favors, but what about me being a suspect in Jimmy's death?"

"No need to worry," Frank said. "You aren't going to be charged with Jimmy's murder. It's all taken care of. Nathan will find some nice DNA evidence on the screwdriver that isn't yours or Jimmy's. Nathan will tell the county judge it was likely a drifter. Of course, that drifter isn't likely to be found. Nathan will keep his job and Dante London will convince the county judge that her kidnapping was all a big TV reality show prank."

"Really?"

"Really."

"Well, Jimmy, it's time to go," Frank said. "Time for us both to go to heaven."

Constance looked at the ghost of her almost-ex husband and sighed. He was a mess, true, but he'd proven himself anything but useless. His heart was in the right place, and sometimes he was, too.

"I guess my time is up," Dead Jimmy said, standing up and looking at his shoes.

"I don't really know how to thank you," Constance told her almost-ex, fighting back tears. He'd saved her more than once. Without him, she'd be dead, and so would Nathan. "For everything you did. Especially helping Nathan."

"Aw, Connie. It was nothing, really. I know you like him. I didn't want him to be eaten by the devil or anything."

"You know I like him?"

"Connie, you've *always* had a thing for him, even back when we were dating," Dead Jimmy said. "And I knew I only got you to marry me in the first place because you were trying to get over him. Only you never really did."

"No, I guess I didn't," Constance said. "You know, you're really more perceptive than people give you credit for."

"Yeah, I know. Don't go spreading it around. I've got a reputation to protect." Dead Jimmy gave her a lopsided smile.

It was finally sinking in that Constance wouldn't be seeing Jimmy anymore. And while she wasn't in love with him, she had to admit that having him in her life was better than not. She would miss him. And it was her fault he'd been killed. Frank had said people around prophets often got hurt, and he'd been right.

"Jimmy, you know, I'm sorry if my being a prophet got you killed."

"It's okay," Dead Jimmy said. "I probably wouldn't have made it into heaven any other way." Dead Jimmy looked up, and then back down. "And while we're making apologies, I want to say that I wish I'd treated you better when I was alive."

This little bit of sweetness just pushed Constance over the edge and she started to tear up.

"Aw, don't go and cry on me," Dead Jimmy said, trying to give her a hug but his arms going straight through her. "I can't hug you proper, and besides, you know you're ugly when you cry," he added with a sly, teasing smile.

Constance gave Jimmy a rueful look. "I'm going to miss you, you jerk."

"Want me to possess you one more time? You know, for old times' sake?" Jimmy asked, offering his hands. Constance held up her own in defense.

"No thanks," she said.

"Okay, then," Dead Jimmy said, stepping back. "Now, you be good while I'm gone. And remember, I can see everything you do up there in heaven, so no kinky stuff."

"That's not true, by the way," Frank said. "He can't see anything from heaven."

"I can't? Boy, that's a gyp. Not even girls' locker rooms?"

"Jimmy!"

"Nope, especially not girls' locker rooms."

"How about Budweiser? Got any of that up there?"

"We might find some for you," Frank said.

"Well, that's a plus at least," Dead Jimmy said. "Okay, boss, beam me up, Scotty, or whatever it is you do."

"Right," Frank said. "Well, good luck, Constance." He extended a little paw for a shake, but Constance scooped him up and gave him a big squeeze.

"Ach, can't breathe." Frank coughed.

"Sorry," Constance said as she loosened her grip and put the dog down gently on the asphalt, swiping at her own runny nose.

"Right, then, we're off," Frank said. "Tallyho."

And then, with a flourish, Frank literally beamed out of the little dog in a trail of bright light and stardust, simultaneously turning Dead Jimmy into sparkling light, too, and the two of them flew straight into the air and up into the starry night. The sparkling dust flew upward and onward, and Constance watched until she couldn't see it anymore.

At her feet, the dog, no longer possessed by an angel's spirit, shook his little snout, as if about to sneeze, and then started jumping up and down and making regular dog sounds, none of which Constance could understand at all, and then ran off in the direction of the road.

"Good-byes are always sad," Abigail said, walking out of the hospital and putting her arm around her daughter. Constance sniffed back a few more tears. "But only you can decide whether you need to say one more." Abigail nodded to the parking lot.

"What?" Constance asked, perplexed, and then turned and saw Nathan leaning against the front of his truck, a crutch under his left arm. She met his gaze and suddenly felt warm all over, and wondered if she would feel that way every time Nathan looked at her forevermore. She glanced at Abigail and wondered if she was right about Nathan. Did he really care about her?

She walked over to him, butterflies in her stomach.

"Aren't you afraid I'm going to arrest you?" Nathan asked her, a half smile at the corner of his mouth.

"Nope," she said. "You aren't going to. I have that on good authority."

"Hard to outsmart a prophet, I guess," Nathan said, and smiled. "So Dante isn't pressing charges?"

Constance shook her head. "She thinks it's all a prank. And she'll talk to the judge about it tomorrow. She isn't the brightest."

"Yeah, well, neither am I," Nathan said, looking at his feet. "I'm sorry I ever doubted you." His eyes were sincere. "If anything had happened to you, I would never have forgiven myself."

"Well, nothing did."

"And I'm sorry I ran out on you—twice."

"That was bad, true," Constance said. "But I think I've forgiven you."

"You have?"

"Mostly," Constance said. "Like sixty percent forgiven."

"What do I have to do to be one hundred percent forgiven?"

"Groveling might work."

"You going to let me get close enough to you to do some groveling?" Nathan asked, eyes hopeful. "Like, say, groveling on a date?"

"You could grovel on a date."

"What about groveling while holding hands?" Nathan asked, taking Constance's hand in his.

"That would be okay."

"Groveling while hugging?" Nathan asked, pulling Constance close so that they were now nose to nose.

"You might be pushing it there," she said, but she was smiling.

"But I do my best groveling when I'm kissing," Nathan told her, cocking an eyebrow, amusement dancing in his eyes. He was having fun with this, and for once, Constance didn't mind.

"Well, then," Constance said, her breath coming fast. "You'd better start kissing me, then."

And then Nathan folded her even closer, and the two kissed in a way that would make any nearby demons run screaming for the exit.

Six Months Later

Y ou sure you want to do this?" Constance asked Nathan, as the two of them stood outside St. Mary's Church. Constance was dressed in white, and Nathan had on his best suit. "You're looking a little nervous."

"Well, the last time we went to this church, you nearly shot me with a crossbow," Nathan reminded her.

"I promise I won't shoot you."

"Thanks, I think."

Constance eyed him warily. He hadn't looked this nervous since they'd driven to Dallas five months ago to return the gold cross to Libby Bell's mother. She'd had relief on her face when Nathan told her that her daughter's murderer was dead. Since then, Nathan had been almost a new person. Lighter and happier.

"We could call this whole thing off, you know," Constance said. "I could go change," she added, tugging on her white dress. "We could go get a couple of Blizzards at the Dairy Queen."

"No, I promised I'd do it, and I'm going to do it," Nathan said, determined.

"What on earth is taking so long out here?" Father Daniels said, bustling out of the church doors. "Are we going to do this baptism or not? I've got a new issue of *Guns & Ammo* to read if we're going to be here long."

"Did I mention my mom is a born-again Southern Baptist? She's going to kill me when she finds out I converted to Catholicism," Nathan said.

"Well, you heard what Father Daniels said," Constance said. "If you want to hang around me and be protected, you've got to convert so you can receive their holy sacrament and be blessed. Besides, what with being a prophet and all, I can tell you that I already know you get baptized today."

"So what was that business about the Blizzards?"

"Well, I already knew you'd say no." Constance grinned.

"It is so not fair living with a prophet," Nathan said, shaking his head. "You already know what I'm going to do in advance."

"Don't you forget it, either, mister."

"So what else should I know about?" He gave her his dimpled smile, and she felt giddy.

"Oh, well, you get baptized, and then a little while later . . ."

"Yes?"

"We just might get married." She flashed a playful grin at him.

"Just when were you going to tell me about that?" Nathan said, smiling back as he grabbed her by the arm and pulled her in close.

"Well, it was one vision I really need to see to believe."

"I don't," Nathan said.

"You see us getting married?" Constance couldn't believe her ears. "I was just kidding, you know."

"Why not get married? It'll be easier to tell Mom I eloped than I'm a Catholic." Nathan took a deep breath. "Okay, I'm ready."

"You sure?"

"Just one last thing," he said, squeezing her tight. "Can you see what I'm going to do now?"

"I have an idea," she whispered, and Nathan dipped his head and covered her lips with his.

Turn the page for a sneak peek of

Can't Teach an Old Demon New Tricks

by Cara Lockwood

Coming soon from Pocket Books

One

Would you watch your wings? They're in my face," said Gabriel Too (not *the* Gabriel, archangel, but Gabriel, lower-ranking, non-archangel—thus the "too").

"Sorry," apologized Frank the New. "I'm not used to them." Frank the New scrunched his shoulders and folded in his wings so they flapped less conspicuously as they glided toward Earth.

"It takes a while to get used to," agreed Gabriel Too, giving the new recruit a soft pat on the shoulder. "And make sure not to lose the halo. They're always slipping off. They never fit right. They should come in half sizes but they don't."

"Thanks for the advice," said Frank the New, as he adjusted his halo, which happened to be tilting a little too far to the right.

"Hang on," Gabriel Too said, holding up his hand and signaling to Frank the New that he ought to stop. "You always look both ways before crossing the jet stream."

The two paused as a 747 jet cruised by. "Okay, it's safe to go."

"Thanks for the heads-up." Frank the New kicked his feet out of the long hem of his robe. Frank was slight in build and much shorter than Gabriel. His white billowing robe swam on him and his ears were a little oversized, a combination that made him look not a little like Dopey the Dwarf. His small stature, however, didn't change the fact that if there were a fight at hand, he was going to run in, fists up. He had more courage than he did size.

"So when do we vanquish some demons?" Frank the New asked, rubbing his hands together in anticipation. He spoke in a clipped British accent, not unlike Anthony Hopkins. "I am very ready to trounce some evil."

"Whoa, whoa, *whoa* there, double-oh-seven," Gabriel Too said, holding up his hand. "Not so fast. I know you are a little tough guy, but we're just watchers. We watch."

"I'm sorry, but I am not a sidelines kind of fellow." Frank the New rolled up one of his blousy sleeves and sighed. "How are you supposed to fight evil in these robes?" he asked, sliding out a hand in a fake punch, only to have it covered by the cuff of his billowing white sleeve. He shook his hand loose and then grabbed the golden harp he'd slung under one arm. "And what's this for? Where's my flaming sword?"

"You don't get one. You don't fight evil. You just watch it."

Frank the New grimaced. "I'll have you know that I didn't stop the Antichrist by sitting around and watching." Frank the New was talking about a few months back when he was still an angel in training, and managed, with the help of a reluctant psychic, Constance Plyd, to stop the devil from impregnating a vapid pop princess, thereby preventing the conception of a half-demon who would've brought the end of the world. He also happened to do all this while in the body of a French bulldog, which he thought should've earned him extra points.

"You aren't in the Wrath Division, or even Messengers, who occasionally get to dust it up. We are *watchers*. We watch. Period."

"Well, then, the Big Guy made a mistake. I'm not a watcher. I'm a doer." Frank the New finished rolling up his sleeves and started popping his knuckles.

"The Big Guy doesn't make mistakes," Gabriel Too said. "Not even dinosaurs or the platypus. Which, by the way, is a sore subject with the Big Guy. Don't mention the platypus."

"I wasn't planning on it." As the two angels floated down from the sky, the earth came into view below, showing a truck stop and a highway, framed on both sides by long slopes of grass with cattle grazing.

"Hey, this place looks familiar," Frank the New said, nodding to the cows.

"It should," Gabriel Too replied, leading the pair across Route Nine and over to a small grassy subdivision. "This is Dogwood County—the place you saved from the Antichrist—am I right?"

Frank the New nodded.

Dogwood County, population 17,891, sat smack-dab in the middle of east Texas and was famous for award-winning chicken-fried steak, the largest pecan pie ever baked (weighing in at 35,000 pounds), and ground zero for the epic battle of good versus evil. Not that most of the Dogwood residents knew their quaint country home happened to be the place where angels and demons fought it out for the souls of all mankind. Only a select few knew about Dogwood's importance in the scheme of things, and God and the Devil hoped to keep it that way. They were waging a covert war that neither wanted on the front page of the *Dogwood County Times*.

The street below came into view, home to about five houses spread out over a little hilly patch and separated by the occasional grazing cow. Gabriel Too stopped above the house belonging to Rachel Farnsworth. Rachel was sound asleep in her bedroom, one foot sticking out of the covers and her arm thrown over her eyes. Her son, Cassidy, had come awake in his crib next door, and was eyeing a small wooden train engine on the floor. Both angels could see through the roof, one of many convenient angel powers, including the ability to be invisible and hear the voice of God without shattering into a million pieces.

"So what do we do now?" Frank the New asked, as the two settled onto a large branch of a nearby oak tree.

"We watch and report."

"But—correct me if I'm wrong—but God already knows what's going to happen. He doesn't need our little reports."

"Yes, God is omniscient. Or omnipotent? I always mix those up." Gabriel Too looked thoughtful. "Anyway, whatever it is, the short answer is, yes, God already knows everything but He has to give us something to do."

"So it's a test then?"

"Probably. Most everything is. God likes pop quizzes."

The two angels watched as Cassidy tried to stick his arm out of his crib to reach the little wooden train engine. After trying, and failing, to reach it, he stood on sure legs and started climbing up the crib's side, his dark brown curls bouncing as he went. In seconds, he'd jumped off the edge and landed in a pile of stuffed animals in the corner of his room. He pulled himself up to standing and then waddled over to the train, picking it up with a look of triumph in his bright brown eyes.

"This is a waste of time." Frank the New sank his chin into one hand. "I didn't almost die defeating the devil so I could be on babysitting duty."

"He's not, technically, a baby."

"Toddler-sitting then."

"No, no, no, I mean he's not technically human. He's half-demon. But he's definitely a toddler."

"Demon? How come I couldn't smell him out then?" Frank the New took a whiff of the air, but didn't smell the telltale sign of burnt popcorn—the trail most demons left behind.

"He's pretty good at camouflage. Must be one of his powers."

Frank the New smashed one fist into his palm. "Well, then, old sport, what are we waiting for? Let's send the demon tyke back to hell." He made as if he were going to march down there and swoop up the child.

"Hold on, buddy," Gabriel Too chided, grabbing Frank the New by the arm. "There is no vanquishing. There is no fighting. There isn't even any cussing. We don't lay a finger on that boy. We watch him. That's it. *Do you understand?*"

Frank the New crossed his arms across his chest and sighed. "Fine."

"We're supposed to sit here and wait and see if her husband shows up, and if he does, we're supposed to report back to Peter. It's the dad who's the full-blooded demon, and he's gone MIA. Everybody is looking for him, too. Heaven *and* hell."

"Why is he so important?"

Gabriel Too shrugged. "Dunno. Peter didn't tell us. We don't have the right kind of clearance."

"So we can't zap this kid?"

"Nope."

"Not even with holy water?"

"Not even with holy water."

"What if he runs out of the house and eats one of the neighbors?"

Gabriel Too looked down and saw Cassidy had made his way to the kitchen and was opening cabinet doors. His mother, who was still sleeping, hadn't heard his escape.

"We can't intervene," Gabriel Too explained. "You don't know the h-e-double-l we'd catch if we stuck our noses where they don't belong. We just watch and take notes." Gabriel Too waved around his legal notepad. "That's our job."

Below them, Cassidy was bouncing around the kitchen, half-leaping, half-flying from one counter to the next.

"I can't believe I got a desk job," said Frank the New with a sigh, as he took the notepad.

Two

Rachel Farnsworth was used to minor disasters. She was a mother.

What she wasn't used to was quiet.

It was the peace and quiet that broke Rachel's slumber the morning of her son Cassidy's first birthday. Her house was never peaceful or quiet.

She glanced at the clock and realized with a shock it was already eight-fifteen. Cassidy never slept this late, usually being up at six in the morning, having by then ripped up the bedding in his crib, dismantled the Winnie the Pooh mobile, and tried to climb over the rails at least three or four times, all while shrugging half out of his diaper and his pajamas. It was only then, normally, that he'd give a bloodcurdling scream loud enough to wake the neighbors, a sound as endearing as an ambulance siren that Rachel had come to think of as her own personal alarm clock. Her husband, Kevin, naturally slept through it, because he slept through everything. She glanced to Kevin's side of the bed and found it empty. He must've gone to work already.

Rachel threw off her covers and raced to Cassidy's room, only to come skidding to a stop halfway through the door. The crib was empty. Rachel's heart stopped. Her first thought was that he'd been kidnapped by some horrible predator, like the ones she always saw on TV being caught soliciting sex from twelve-year-old virgins. She shook the thought from her head and told herself not to panic. That was when she came to her senses and realized Cassidy must've jumped out of his crib, because there was a trail of rumpled clothes and toys along the floor. Rachel comforted herself with the knowledge that a predator wouldn't have bothered to stack up his alphabet blocks on his way out, so Cassidy had to have sprung himself. The little Houdini had done it again.

"Cass?" she called, trying not to sound mad, in case he might be about to stick his head in the oven. "Where are you?"

Cassidy could be anywhere. There wasn't a restraint made by man he couldn't get out of. Clothes, diapers, high chairs, even car seats were no match for the grubby, quick hands of Cassidy Henry Farnsworth. Even at the tender age of one, he'd mastered all but the most complex of latches. Last week, he'd even managed to open their front door and sprint out naked as a jaybird, much to the dismay of half the neighborhood. Rachel knew what the other moms said about her. That she was careless. That she didn't pay attention. But, honestly, he was simply too quick and too smart for his own good. Just last week, he'd unlatched his car seat. A flash of corduroy overalls in her rearview had clued her in to the fact that he was happily hopping up and down on a sack of groceries in the backseat. That little surprise had nearly made her veer into oncoming traffic.

Plus, he always seemed quicker than he ought to be, and smarter, too. She didn't know of other babies who took their first steps at five months, for instance. The other moms never believed her, but Rachel swore he could do things he just shouldn't be able to do.

"Ma Ma!" came a muffled shout from somewhere in the vicinity of the kitchen. This was followed by a clatter that sent Rachel sprinting. She stopped at the threshold of her kitchen and her mouth fell open.

It looked like a hurricane had blown through. Cassidy had hit the pantry and raided the snack cabinet, somehow dismantling the so-called childproof lock on it. The floor was covered with spilled Goldfish, a rumpled bag of Doritos, a half dozen apple-juice boxes, including one that was actually open and spilling out across her kitchen tile.

How on earth she'd slept through *this* little disaster, she had no idea.

"Cassidy Henry FARNSWORTH!" she cried, hands on hips, as she stared at the floor in dismay.

"Da! Mon!" he blurted, in an almost gleeful tone. "Da! Mon! Da! Mon! Da! Mon!"

She had no idea what he was saying, but she followed the sounds. But no matter where she looked, she couldn't find him.

"Cass? Cass!" He was here somewhere. She could hear him.

"Da Da Da DA!" he babbled. "Mon! Mon! Mon! Mon!"

Rachel realized, with a sinking feeling in her stomach, that the sound *wasn't* coming from the floor. Or anywhere near the floor, which was where her little one-year-old usually spent most of his time. It was coming from much, much higher.

And that's when a little cheddar-flavored Goldfish fell on her head from above like a little snowflake from Pepperidge Farm.

She looked up, dread in her throat, and saw Cassidy, naked as the day he was born, do a little jump that made the dark curls on his head bounce. He was balancing precariously on the top of her refrigerator, grubby hands full of cheddar-flavored fish crackers.

"DA! MON!" he cheered.

Rachel's whole body went cold. She flung up her arms, praying he stayed away from the edge long enough to get him down without a free fall. She didn't have time to wonder how he got there. She just wanted to get him down in one piece.

"Come to Mama," she commanded, hoping to keep the panic out of her voice. "Come now."

"No!" Cass shouted, gleefully. Standing up on the refrigerator, he raised his arms like he was preparing to do a swan dive onto her tile floor. Rachel grabbed one of his chunky legs and then the other, and soon she had him cradled safely in her arms.

"No climbing. *NO*," she said. "Why do you have to scare Mama like that?" Her heart rate was slowly returning to normal, her panic draining away. Now she had the time to wonder just how Cassidy had managed to climb up on top of the counter *and* reach the top of the refrigerator. No matter how she studied the scene of the crime, she couldn't figure it out. It was like he'd sprouted wings and flew there. She wondered, briefly, if there was an explanation she was missing. If she hadn't birthed Cassidy herself after twenty-eight hours of labor, she just might have thought he'd fallen from space in a meteor like Superman. The boy did things Rachel simply couldn't explain.